TESS GERRITSEN

Tess Gerritsen studied medicine at the University of California, and was awarded her MD in 1979. After completing her internship she practised as a doctor in Honolulu, Hawaii. While on maternity leave Gerritsen first started writing and in 1987 her first novel, *Call After Midnight*, was published. However, it was *Harvest*, Gerritsen's first medical thriller, which brought her major commercial success on its publication in 1996. It was a *New York Times* bestseller and was translated into twenty foreign languages. With later successes including *Bloodstream*, *Gravity*, *The Surgeon* and *The Apprentice*, Tess Gerritsen is now recognized as one of the forerunners in the field of gripping medical thrillers.

Tess Gerritsen lives with her family in Maine, where she writes full-time.

BY THE SAME AUTHOR

TESS GERRITSEN

Bloodstream

HARPER

HarperCollins*Publishers*
77–85 Fulham Palace Road
London, W6 8JB

The HarperCollins website address is:
www.harpercollins.co.uk

First published in the USA
by Pocket Books

This paperback re-issue edition published 2004

ISBN 978-0-00-779662-5

Typeset in Meridien by Palimpsest Book Production Limited,
Polmont, Stirlingshire
Printed and bound by Clays Ltd, St Ives plc

To Tim and Elyse

Acknowledgments

I owe many thanks to:

My husband Jacob, still my best friend after all these years.

Meg Ruley, my guardian angel and miracle worker. You walk on water.

Jane Berkey and Don Cleary for their guiding voices.

My superb editor, Emily Bestler.

The ladies of the breakfast club for delivering my weekly dose of sanity.

The memory of Rockport Police Chief Perley Sprague. Your kindness was an inspiration.

And finally, to the town of Camden, Maine, the best place on earth a writer could call home. Please rest assured this book is not about you.

Prologue

If she was still enough, quiet enough, he would not find her. He might think he knew all her hiding places, but he had never discovered her secret niche, this small hollow in the cellar wall, concealed by the shelves of her mother's canning jars. As a young child she had easily slipped into this space, and every game of hide and seek had found her curled up in her lair, giggling at his frustration as he thumped from room to room, searching for her. Sometimes the game would go on so long she'd fall asleep, and would awaken hours later to the sound of her mother's voice worriedly calling her name.

Now here she was again, in her cellar hiding place, but she was no longer a child. She was fourteen and barely able to squeeze into the niche. And this was no lighthearted game of hide and seek.

She could hear him upstairs, roaming the house,

1

searching for her. He rampaged from room to room, cursing, slamming furniture to the floor.

Please, please, please. Someone help us. Someone make him go away.

She heard him roar out her name: 'IRIS!' His footsteps creaked into the kitchen. Approached the cellar door. Her hands balled into tight fists, and her heart was a banging drum.

I am not here. I am far away, escaping, soaring into the night sky . . .

The cellar door flew open, slamming into the wall. Golden light shone down, framing him in the open doorway at the top of the stairs.

He reached up to pull on the light chain and the bare bulb came on, dimly illuminating the cavernous cellar. Cowering behind the jars of home-canned tomatoes and cucumbers, Iris heard him descend the steep stairs, each creak bringing him toward her. She pressed deeper into the hollow, flattening herself against the crumbling stone and mortar, and closed her eyes, willing herself to be invisible. Through the slamming of her own heartbeat she heard him reach the bottom of the steps.

Don't see me. Don't see me.

The footsteps moved right past the canning shelves and headed toward the far end of the cellar. She heard him kick over a box. Empty jars shattered on the stone floor. Now he was circling back, and she could hear his harsh breathing, punctuated by animal grunts. Her own breaths were coming short and fast, her hands clenched so tightly she thought her bones would shatter. The footsteps moved to the canning shelves and stopped.

Her eyes shot open, and through a chink between two jars she saw him standing right in front of her. She had slid down until her gaze was level with his belt. She cringed even lower, dropping as far below his line of sight as she could. He took a jar off the shelf and smashed it to the ground. The smell of pickles, sharp and vinegary, rose up from the stone floor. He reached for a second jar, then suddenly put it back, as though a better thought had occurred to him. He turned and walked up the cellar steps, yanking the light chain as he exited.

Once again she was in darkness.

She realized she had been crying. Her face was wet, sweat mingling with tears, but she didn't dare release even a whimper.

Upstairs the footsteps creaked toward the front of the house and then there was silence.

Had he left? Had he finally gone away?

She remained frozen, not daring to move. The minutes went by. She counted them off slowly in her head. Ten. Twenty. Her muscles were cramping, the spasms so painful she had to bite her lip to keep from crying out.

An hour.

Two hours.

Still no sound from above.

Slowly she emerged from the hiding place. She

3

stood in the darkness, waiting for the blood to recirculate in her muscles, for the feeling to come back in her legs. Listening, the whole time listening.

She heard nothing.

The cellar had no window, and she didn't know if it was still dark outside. She stepped through the broken glass on the floor and crossed to the stairs. She climbed them one at a time, pausing after each step to listen some more. When at last she reached the top, her palms were so slick she had to wipe them off on her blouse before she could open the cellar door.

The lights were on in the kitchen, and everything looked startlingly normal. She could almost believe the horror of last night was simply a bad dream. A clock ticked loudly on the wall. It was five A.M., still dark outside.

She tiptoed to the kitchen doorway and peered into the hall. One glimpse at the splintered furniture, the splashes of blood on the wallpaper, told her she had not been dreaming. Her palms were wet again.

The hallway was deserted, and the front door hung open.

She had to get out of the house. Run to the neighbors, run to the police.

She started up the hall, each step bringing her closer to escape. Terror had primed her five senses to such acuity that she registered every fragment of splintered wood on the floral carpet, every tick of the clock in the kitchen behind her. She was almost at the front door.

Then she cleared the banister and came within view of the stairs, where her mother had toppled, head down. She couldn't stop herself from staring at the body. At her mother's long hair draping the steps, like black water rippling downhill.

Nausea surging up her throat, she lurched toward the front door.

He was standing there. In his hand was an ax.

With a sob she spun around and darted up the stairs, almost slipping on her mother's blood. She heard him pounding up the steps after her. She had always been faster than he, and terror made her fly up the stairs like a panicked cat.

On the second floor landing she caught a glimpse of her father's body, lying halfway out of his bedroom doorway. There was no time to think about it, no time to absorb the horror; she was already dashing up the next flight of stairs and into the turret room.

She slammed the door and latched it just in time.

He gave a roar of rage and began pounding on the closed door.

She scurried over to the window and forced it open. Staring down at the ground far below, she knew she could not survive a fall. But there was no other way out of the room.

She yanked on a curtain, pulling it off the rod. *A rope. Have to make a rope!* She tied one end to a radiator pipe, wrenched a second curtain down, and tied the two lengths of fabric together.

A loud thud sent a splinter of wood flying at her. She glanced back and to her horror saw the tip of the ax poking through the door. Saw it pried loose again for the next swing.

He was breaking through!

She yanked down a third curtain, and with shaking hands, knotted it to the first two.

The ax came down again. The wood splintered wider, more chunks flying.

She yanked down a fourth curtain, but even as she frantically tied the last knot, she knew the rope was not long enough. She knew it was too late.

She spun around to face the door just as the ax broke through.

1

The Present

'Someone's going to get hurt out there,' said Dr Claire Elliot, looking out her kitchen window. Morning mist, thick as smoke, hung over the lake, and the trees beyond her window drifted in and out of focus. Another gunshot rang out, closer this time. Since first light, she'd heard the gunfire, and would probably hear it all day until dusk, because it was the first day of November. The start of hunting season. Somewhere in those woods, a man with a rifle was tramping around half-blind through the mist as imagined shadows of white-tailed deer danced around him.

'I don't think you should wait outside for the bus,' said Claire. 'I'll drive you to school.'

Noah, hunched at the breakfast table, said nothing. He scooped up another spoonful of Cheerios and slurped it down. Fourteen years old, and her son still ate like a two-year-old, milk splashing on the

7

table, crumbs of toast littering the floor around his chair. He ate without looking at her, as though to meet her gaze was to come face to face with Medusa. And what difference would it make if he did look at me, she thought wryly. My darling son has already turned to stone.

She said again, 'I'll drive you to school, Noah.'

'That's okay. I'm taking the bus.' He stood up and grabbed his backpack and skateboard.

'Those hunters out there can't possibly see what they're shooting at. At least wear the orange hat. So they won't think you're a deer.'

'But it looks so dorky.'

'You can take it off on the bus. Just put it on now.' She took the knit cap from the mitten shelf and held it out to him.

He looked at it, then finally, at her. He had sprouted up several inches in just one year, and they were now the same height, their gazes meeting straight on, neither one able to claim the advantage. She wondered if Noah was as acutely aware of their new physical equality as she was. Once she could hug him and a child would hug back. Now the child was gone, his softness resculpted into muscle, his face narrowed to a sharp new angularity.

'Please,' she said, still holding out the cap.

At last he sighed and jammed the cap over his dark hair. She had to suppress a smile; he did look dorky.

He had already started down the hallway when she called out: 'Good-bye kiss?'

With a look of exasperation, he turned to give her the barest peck on the cheek, and then he was out of the door.

No hugs anymore, she thought ruefully as she stood at the window and watched him trudge toward the road. It's all grunts and shrugs and awkward silences.

He stopped beneath the maple tree at the end of the driveway, pulled off the cap, and stood with his hands in his pockets, shoulders hunched against the cold. No jacket, just a thin gray sweatshirt against a thirty-seven-degree morning. It was cool to be cold. She had to resist the urge to run outside and bundle him into a coat.

Claire waited until the school bus appeared. She watched her son climb aboard without a backward glance, saw his silhouette move down the aisle and take a seat beside another student – a girl. Who is that girl? she wondered. I don't know the names of my son's friends anymore. I've shrunk to just a small corner of his universe. She knew this was supposed to happen, the pulling away, the child's struggle for independence, but she was not prepared for it. The transformation had occurred suddenly, as though a sweet boy had walked out of the house one day, and a stranger had walked back in. *You're all I have left of Peter. I'm not ready to lose you as well.*

The bus rumbled away.

Claire returned to the kitchen and sat down to her cup of lukewarm coffee. The house felt hollow and silent, a home still in mourning. She sighed and unrolled the weekly *Tranquility Gazette*. HEALTHY DEER HERD PROMISES BOUNTIFUL HARVEST, announced the front page. The hunt was on. Thirty days to bag your deer.

Outside, another gunshot echoed in the woods.

She turned the page to the police blotter. There was no mention yet of last night's Halloween disturbance, or of the seven rowdy teenagers who'd been arrested for taking their annual trick-or-treating too far. But there, buried among the reports of lost dogs and stolen firewood, was her name, under VIOLATIONS: 'Claire Elliot, age forty, operating vehicle with expired safety sticker.' She still hadn't brought the Subaru in for its safety inspection; today she'd have to drive the truck instead, just to avoid getting another citation. Irritably she flipped to the next page and was scanning the day's weather forecast – cold and windy, high in the thirties, low in the twenties – when the telephone rang.

She rose to answer it. 'Hello?'

'Dr Elliot? This is Rachel Sorkin out on Toddy Point Road. I've got something of an emergency out here. Elwyn just shot himself.'

'What?'

'You know, that idiot Elwyn Clyde. He came trespassing on my property, chasing after some poor deer. Killed it too – a beautiful doe, right in my front yard. These stupid men and their stupid guns.'

'What about Elwyn?'

'Oh, he tripped and shot his own foot. Serves him right.'

'He should go straight to the hospital.'

'Well you see, that's the problem. He doesn't want to go to the hospital, and he won't let me call an ambulance. He wants me to drive him and the deer home. Well, I'm not going to. So what should I do with him?'

'How badly is he bleeding?'

She heard Rachel call out: 'Hey, Elwyn? *Elwyn!* Are you bleeding?' Then Rachel came back on the line. 'He says he's fine. He just wants a ride home. But I'm not taking him, and I'm certainly not taking the deer.'

Claire sighed. 'I guess I can drive over and take a look. You're on Toddy Point Road?'

'About a mile past the Boulders. My name's on the mail box.'

The mist was starting to lift as Claire turned her pickup truck onto Toddy Point Road. Through stands of white pine, she caught glimpses of Locust Lake, the fog rising like steam. Already beams of sunlight were breaking through, splashing gold onto the rippling water. Across the lake, just visible through fingers of mist, was the north shore with its summer cottages, most of them boarded up for the season, their wealthy owners gone home to Boston or New York. On the south shore, where Claire now drove, were the more modest homes, some of them little more than two-room shacks tucked in among the trees.

She drove past the Boulders, an outcropping of granite stones where the local teenagers gathered to swim in the summertime, and spotted the mailbox with the name *Sorkin*.

A bumpy dirt road brought her to the house. It was a strange and whimsical structure, rooms added haphazardly, corners jutting out in unexpected places. Rising above it all, like the tip of a crystal breaking through the roof, was a glassed-in belfry. An eccentric woman would have an eccentric house, and Rachel Sorkin was one of Tranquility's odd birds, a striking, black-haired woman who strode once a week into town, swathed in a purple hooded cape. This looked like a house in which a caped woman might reside.

By the front steps, next to a neatly tended herb garden, lay the dead deer.

Claire climbed out of her truck. At once two dogs bounded out of the woods and barred her way, barking and growling. Guarding the kill, she realized.

Rachel came out of the house and yelled at the dogs: 'Get out of here, you bloody animals! Go home!' She grabbed a broom from the porch and came tearing down the steps, long black hair flying, the broom thrust forward like a lance.

The dogs backed away.

'Ha! Cowards,' said Rachel, lunging at them with the broom. They retreated toward the woods.

'Hey, you leave my dogs alone!' shouted Elwyn Clyde, who had limped out onto the porch. Elwyn was a prime example of an evolutionary dead end: a fifty-year-old lump bundled in flannel, and doomed to eternal bachelorhood. 'They're not hurtin' nothin'. They're just watchin' after my deer.'

'Elwyn, I got news for you. You killed this poor creature on my property. So she's mine.'

'What you gonna do with a deer? Blasted vegetarian!'

Claire cut in: 'How's the foot, Elwyn?'

He looked at Claire and blinked, as though surprised to see her. 'I tripped,' he said. 'No big deal.'

'A bullet wound is always a big deal. May I take a look at it?'

'Can't pay you . . .' He paused, one scraggly eyebrow lifting as a sly thought occurred. ''Less you want some venison.'

'I just want to make sure you're not bleeding to death. We can settle up some other time. Can I look at your foot?'

'If you really want to,' he said, and limped back into the house.

'This should be a treat,' said Rachel.

It was warm inside the kitchen. Rachel threw a birch log into the wood stove, and sweet smoke puffed out as she dropped the cast iron lid back in place.

'Let's see the foot,' said Claire.

Elwyn hobbled over to a chair, leaving smears of blood on the floor. He had his sock on, and there was a jagged hole at the top, near the big toe, as though a rat had chewed through the wool. 'Hardly bothering me,' he said. 'Not worth all this fuss, if you ask me.'

Claire knelt down and peeled off the sock. It came away slowly, the wool matted to his foot not by blood but by sweat and dead skin.

'Oh God,' said Rachel, cupping her hand over her nose. 'Don't you ever change your socks, Elwyn?'

The bullet had passed through the fleshy web between the first and second toe. Claire found the exit wound underneath the foot. There was only a little blood oozing out now. Trying not to gag on the smell, she tested movement of all the toes, and determined that no nerves had been damaged.

'You'll have to clean it and change the bandages every day,' she said. 'And you need a tetanus shot, Elwyn.'

'Oh, I got one of them already.'

'When?'

'Last year, from ol' Doc Pomeroy. After I shot myself.'

'Is this an annual event?'

'That one went through my other foot. 'Tweren't a big deal.'

Dr Pomeroy had died back in January, and Claire had acquired all his old medical records when she'd bought the practice from his estate eight months ago. She could check Elwyn's file and confirm the date of his last tetanus shot.

'I guess it's up to me to clean that foot,' said Rachel.

Claire took out a small bottle of Betadine from her medical bag and handed it to her. 'Add that to a warm bucket of water. Let him soak in it for a while.'

'Oh, I can do that myself,' said Elwyn, and got up.

'Then we might as well just amputate right now!' snapped Rachel. 'Sit *down*, Elwyn.'

'Gee,' he said, and sat down.

Claire left a few packets of bandages and gauze wrappings on the table. 'Elwyn, you come into my office next week, so I can check the wound.'

'But I got too much to do –'

'If you don't come in, I'll have to hunt you down like a dog.'

He blinked at her in surprise. 'Yes, ma'am,' he said meekly.

Suppressing a smile, Claire picked up her medical bag and walked out of the house.

The two dogs were in the front yard again, fighting over a filthy bone. As Claire came down the steps, they both spun around to stare at her.

The black one trotted forward and growled.

'Shoo,' Claire said, but the dog refused to back down. It took another few steps forward, teeth bared.

The tan dog, spotting opportunity, snatched the

15

bone in its teeth and began dragging away the prize. It got halfway across the yard before the black dog suddenly noticed the thief and streaked back into the fight. Yelping and growling, they thrashed around the yard in a tangle of black and tan. The bone lay, forgotten, beside Claire's pickup truck.

She opened the door and was just sliding in behind the steering wheel when the image registered in her brain. She looked down at the ground, at the bone.

It was less than a foot long, and stained a rusty brown with dirt. One end had broken off, leaving jagged splinters. The other end was intact, the bony landmarks recognizable.

It was a femur. And it was human.

Ten miles out of town, Tranquility Police Chief Lincoln Kelly finally caught up with his wife.

She was doing about fifty in a stolen Chevy, weaving left and right, the loose tailpipe kicking up sparks every time she hit a dip in the road.

'Man oh man,' said Floyd Spear, sitting beside Lincoln in the cruiser. 'Doreen got her snookerful today.'

'I've been on the road all morning,' said Lincoln. 'Didn't get a chance to check up on her.' He turned on the siren, hoping that would induce Doreen to slow down. She sped up.

'Now what?' asked Floyd. 'Want me to call for backup?'

16

Backup meant Hank Dorr, the only other officer on patrol duty that morning.

'No,' said Lincoln. 'Let's see if we can't talk her into pulling over.'

'At sixty miles an hour?'

'Get on the bullhorn.'

Floyd picked up the mike and his voice boomed out over the speaker: 'Hey, Doreen, pull over! C'mon, Sweetheart, you're gonna hurt someone!'

The Chevy just kept dipping and weaving.

'We could wait till she runs out of gas,' Floyd suggested.

'Keep talking to her.'

Floyd tried the mike again. 'Doreen, Lincoln's here! C'mon, Sweetheart, pull over! He wants ta 'pologize!'

'I want to *what*?'

'Pull over, Doreen, and he'll tell you himself!'

'What in hell are you talking about?' said Lincoln.

'Women always expect a man to apologize.'

'But I didn't do anything!'

Up ahead, the Chevy's brake lights suddenly lit up.

'See?' said Floyd as the Chevy rolled to a stop at the side of the road.

Lincoln pulled up behind it and climbed out of the cruiser.

Doreen sat hunched behind the steering wheel, her red hair wild and tangled, her hands shaking. Lincoln opened the door, reached over his wife's lap, and removed the car keys. 'Doreen,' he said wearily, 'you gotta come back to the station.'

'When are you coming home, Lincoln?' she asked.

'We'll talk about that later. Come on, Honey, let's get in the cruiser.' He reached for her elbow but she shook him off and slapped his hand for good measure.

'I just want to know when you're coming home,' she said.

'We've talked about this and talked about this.'

'You're still married to me. You're still my husband.'

'And there's just no point in talking about it any more.' Again he took her elbow. He already had her out of the Chevy when she hauled off and slugged him in the jaw. He staggered back a few steps, his whole head ringing.

'Hey!' said Floyd, grabbing Doreen's arms. 'Hey now, you don't wanna go doing that!'

'Lemme go!' screeched Doreen. She broke out of Floyd's grasp and took another swing at her husband.

This time Lincoln ducked, which only made his wife madder. She got in one more swing before Lincoln and Floyd managed to get her arms secured.

'I hate to do this,' said Lincoln. 'But you're just not being reasonable today.' He snapped the handcuffs on her wrists. She spat at him. He wiped his sleeve across his face, then patiently guided his wife into the backseat of the cruiser.

'Oh man,' said Floyd. 'You know we're gonna have to book her.'

'I know.' Lincoln sighed and slid in behind the wheel.

'You can't divorce me, Lincoln Kelly!' said Doreen. 'You promised to love and cherish!'

'I didn't know about the bottle,' said Lincoln, and he turned the car around.

They drove at a leisurely speed toward town, Doreen cussing a purple streak the whole time. It was the drinking that did it; it seemed to pop the cork off her bottle of demons.

Two years ago, Lincoln had moved out of their house. He figured he'd given the marriage his best effort and ten years of his life. He wasn't by nature a quitter, but the despair had finally gotten to him. That and the sense that, at forty-five, his life was racing by, joyless and unfruitful. He wished he could do right by Doreen, wished that he could recapture some of that old affection he'd felt for her early on in their marriage, when she'd been bright and sober, not bubbling over with anger as she was now. Sometimes he'd search his own heart for whatever trace of love might still linger, some small spark among the ashes, but there was nothing left. The ashes were cold. And he was tired.

He had tried to stand by her, but Doreen couldn't even see clear to help herself. Every few months, when her rage boiled up, she'd spend the day drinking. Then she'd 'borrow' someone's car and go for one of her famous high-speed drives. People in town knew to stay off the roads when Doreen Kelly got behind the wheel.

Back at the Tranquility police station, Lincoln let Floyd do the booking and locking up. Through the two closed doors leading to the cell, he could hear Doreen yelling for a lawyer. He supposed he should call one for her, though no one in Tranquility wanted to take her on. Even down south as far as Bangor, she'd worn out her welcomes. He sat at his desk, flipping through the Rolodex, trolling for a lawyer's name. Someone he hadn't called in a while. Someone who didn't mind being cussed out by a client.

It was all too much, too early in the morning. He shoved away the Rolodex and ran his hand through his hair. Doreen was still yelling in the back room. This would all be reported in that nosy *Gazette*, and then the Bangor and Portland papers would pick it up because the whole damn state of Maine thought it was funny and so very quaint. *Tranquility police chief arrests own wife. Again.*

He reached for the telephone and was dialing the number for Tom Wiley, attorney at law, when he heard a knock at his door. Glancing up, he saw Claire Elliot walk into his office, and he hung up.

'Hey, Claire,' he said. 'Got your safety sticker yet?'

'I'm still working on it. But I'm not here about

20

my car. I want to show you something.' She set a dirty bone down on his desk.

'What's this?'

'It's a femur, Lincoln.'

'What?'

'A thigh bone. I think it's human.'

He stared at the dirt-encrusted bone. One end was splintered off, and the shaft showed the gnawings of animal teeth. 'Where did you find this?'

'Rachel Sorkin's place.'

'How did Rachel get it?'

'Elwyn Clyde's dogs dragged it into her yard. She doesn't know where it came from. I was over there this morning, after Elwyn shot himself in the foot.'

'Again?' He rolled his eyes and they both laughed. If every village had an idiot, then Tranquility's would be Elwyn.

'He's okay,' she said. 'But I guess a gunshot wound should be reported.'

'Consider it done. I already have a folder for Elwyn and his gunshot wounds.' He gestured to a chair. 'Now tell me about this bone. Are you sure it's human?'

She sat down. Though they were looking directly at each other, he felt a barrier of reserve between them that was almost physical. He had sensed it the first time they'd met, soon after she'd moved to town, when she had attended to a prisoner suffering from abdominal pain in Tranquility's three-cell jail. Lincoln had been curious about her from the

21

start. Where was her husband? Why was she alone raising her son? But he had not felt comfortable asking her personal questions, and she did not seem to invite such intrusion. Pleasant but intensely private, she seemed reluctant to let anyone get too close to her, which was a shame. She was a pretty woman, short but sturdy, with luminous dark eyes and a mass of curly brown hair just starting to show the first strands of silver.

She leaned forward, her hands resting on his desk. 'I'm not an expert or anything,' she said, 'but I don't know what other animal this bone could come from. Judging by the size, it looks like a child's.'

'Did you see any other bones around?'

'Rachel and I searched the yard, but we didn't find any. The dogs could've picked this up anywhere in the woods. You'll have to search the whole area.'

'Could be from an old Indian burial.'

'Possibly. But doesn't it still have to go to the medical examiner?' Suddenly she turned, her head cocked. 'What's all that commotion?'

Lincoln flushed. Doreen was shouting in her cell again, letting fly a fresh torrent of abuse. 'Damn you, Lincoln! You jerk! You liar! Damn you to hell!'

'It sounds like somebody doesn't like you very much,' said Claire.

He sighed and pressed his hand to his forehead. 'My wife.'

Claire's gaze softened to a look of sympathy. It was apparent she knew about his problems. Everyone in town did.

'I'm sorry,' she said.

'Hey, loser!' Doreen yelled. 'You got no right to treat me like this!'

With deliberate effort, he redirected his attention to the thigh bone. 'How old was the victim, do you think?'

She picked up the femur and turned it over in her hands. For a moment she held it with quiet reverence, fully aware that this broken length of bone had once supported a laughing, running child. 'Young,' she murmured. 'I would guess under ten years old.' She lay it on the desk and stared down in silence.

'We haven't had any missing children reported recently,' he said. 'The area's been settled for hundreds of years, and old bones are always turning up. A century ago, it wasn't all that unusual to die young.'

She was frowning. 'I don't think this child died from natural causes,' she said softly.

'Why do you say that?'

She reached over to turn on his desk lamp, and held the bone close to the light. 'There,' she said. 'It's so crusted over, you can barely see it through the dirt.'

He reached in his pocket for his glasses – another reminder of the years' passage, of his youth slipping away. Bending closer, he tried to see what she was pointing at. Only when she'd scraped away a clot of dirt with her fingernail did he see the wedge-shaped gash.

It was the mark of a hatchet.

2

When Warren Emerson finally regained consciousness, he found he was lying next to the woodpile
and the sun was shining in his eyes. His last
memory was of shade, of silvery frost on the grass
and bulging pockets of soil, heaved up from the
cold. He'd been splitting firewood, swinging the
ax and enjoying the sharp ring it made in the crisp
air. The sun had not yet cleared the pine tree in
his front yard.

Now it was well above the tree, which meant
he had been lying here for some time, perhaps an
hour, judging by its position in the sky.

Slowly Warren sat up, his head aching as it
always did afterwards. His hands and face were
numb from the cold; both of his gloves had fallen
off. He saw the ax lying beside him, its blade buried
deep in one end of a maple log. A day's worth of
firewood, already split, lay scattered around him.
It took him a painfully long time to register these
observations, and to consider the significance of

each in turn. The thoughts came to him with effort, as though dragged from a great distance, arriving tattered and in disarray. He was patient with himself; eventually it would all make sense.

He had come out soon after sunrise to split his wood for the day. The result of his labor now lay all around him. He had almost completed the morning chore, had just swung his ax into that last log, when the darkness came over him. He had fallen onto the woodpile; that would explain why some of the logs had rolled off the top. His underwear was soaked; he must have wet himself, as he often did during a fit. Looking down at his clothes, he saw that his jeans were saturated.

There was blood on his shirt.

He staggered to his feet and walked slowly back into the old farmhouse.

The kitchen was hot and stuffy from the wood-stove; it made him feel a little dizzy, and his vision had started to fade around the edges by the time he reached the bathroom. He sat down on the chipped toilet lid, clutching his head, waiting for the clouds to lift from his brain. The cat came in and rubbed against his calf, meowing for attention. He reached down to her and drew comfort from the softness of her fur.

His face was no longer numb from the cold, and he was now aware of pain throbbing insistently in his temple. Clutching the sink for support, he rose to his feet and looked in the mirror. Just over his left ear, the gray hair was stiff and matted with blood. A streak of it had dried across his cheek, like war paint. He stared at his own reflection, at a face deeply etched by sixty-six years of hard winters and honest work and loneliness. His only companion was the cat, now meowing at his feet, not from affection but hunger. He loved the cat, and someday he would mourn her passing with tears and a solemn burial and nights of longing for the sound of her purring, but he was under no illusion that she loved him.

He removed his clothes, the frayed and blood-stained shirt, the urine-soaked jeans. He undressed with the same care he devoted to every other task in his life, leaving his clothes in a tidy heap on the toilet lid. He turned on the shower and stepped in without waiting for the water to warm up; the discomfort was only momentary, scarcely worth a shiver in the context of his cold and uncomfortable life. He washed the blood out of his hair, the laceration stinging from the soap. He must have sliced his scalp open when he fell on the woodpile. It would heal, as all his other cuts had. Warren Emerson was a walking testament to the durability of scar tissue.

The cat renewed her meowing as soon as he stepped out of the shower. It was a pitiful sound, despairing, and he could not listen to it without feeling guilty. Still naked, he walked to the kitchen, opened a can of Little Friskies chicken bits, and spooned it into Mona's cat bowl.

She gave a soft growl of pleasure and began to

eat, no longer caring whether he came or went. Except for his skill with a can opener, he was extraneous to her existence.

He went to the bedroom to dress.

Once it had been his parents' room, and it still contained all their possessions. The spindle bed, the bureau with the brass knobs, the photographs hanging up in their tin picture frames. As he buttoned his shirt, his gaze lingered on one photo in particular, of a dark-haired girl with smiling eyes. What was Iris doing at this moment? he wondered, as he did every day of his life. Did she ever think of him? His gaze moved on to another photo. It was the last one taken of his family, his mother plump and smiling, his father ill at ease in a suit and tie. And wedged between them, with his hair slicked to one side, was little Warren.

He reached out, fingers touching the photo of his own twelve-year-old face. He could not remember that boy. Up in the attic were the toy trains and the adventure books and the brittle crayons that once belonged to the child in that photo, but that was a different Warren who'd played in this house, who had stood smiling between his parents for a Sunday photograph. Not the Warren he saw when he looked in the mirror.

Suddenly he felt a terrible longing to touch that child's toys again.

He climbed the steps to the attic and dragged the old blanket chest under the light. With the bare bulb swinging overhead, he lifted the chest lid.

Inside were treasures. He took them out one by one and set them on the dusty floor. The cookie tin with all the Matchbox cars. The Lincoln Logs. The leather pouch of marbles. At last he found what he'd been looking for: the set of checkers.

He lay out the board and set up the checkers, red on his side, black on the opposite.

Mona came padding up to the attic and sat beside him, her breath smelling of chicken. For a moment she regarded the board with feline disdain. Then she tiptoed over to it and sniffed at one of the black pieces.

'Is that your first move then?' said Warren. It was not a very smart move, but then, what did one expect from a cat? He moved the black piece for her, and she seemed satisfied.

Outside the wind blew, rattling loose shutters. He could hear the branches of the lilac tree scratch against the clapboards.

Warren advanced a red checker and he smiled at his companion. 'Your move, Mona.'

At six-thirty, as she did every weekday morning, five-year-old Isabel Morrison crept into her older sister's bedroom and climbed under the covers with Mary Rose. There she wriggled like a happy worm in the warm sheets and hummed to herself as she waited for Mary Rose to wake up. There would always be a great deal of sighing and moaning, and Mary Rose would turn from one side to another, her long brown hair tickling

Isabel's face. Isabel thought Mary Rose was the most beautiful girl on earth. She looked like the sleeping Princess Aurora, waiting for her prince to kiss her. Sometimes Isabel would pretend *she* was Prince Charming, and even though she knew girls weren't supposed to kiss each other, she would plant her lips on her sister's mouth and announce: 'Now you have to wake up!'

One time, Mary Rose had been awake all along, and had sprung up like a giggling monster and tickled Isabel so mercilessly that both girls had fallen off the bed in a duet of happy squeals.

If only Mary Rose would tickle her now. If only Mary Rose would be her normal self.

Isabel leaned close to her sister's ear and whispered, 'Aren't you going to wake up?'

Mary Rose pulled the covers over her head. 'Go away, pest.'

'Mommy says it's time for school. You have to wake up.'

'Get out of my room!'

'But it's time for –'

Mary Rose gave a growl and lashed out with an angry kick.

Isabel slithered to the far side of the bed, where she lay in troubled silence, rubbing her sore shin and trying to understand what had just happened. Mary Rose had never kicked her before. Mary Rose always woke up with a smile and called her Dizzy Izzy and braided her hair before school.

She decided to try again. She crawled on hands

and knees to her sister's pillow, peeled back the sheets, and whispered into Mary Rose's ear: 'I know what Mommy and Daddy are getting you for Christmas. You wanna hear?'

Mary Rose's eyes shot open. She turned to look at Isabel.

With a whimper of fear, Isabel scrambled off the bed and stared at a face she scarcely recognized. A face that frightened her. 'Mary Rose?' she whispered.

Then she ran out of the room.

Her mother was downstairs in the kitchen, stirring a pot of oatmeal and trying to hear the radio over the screeches of their parakeet, Rocky. As Isabel came tearing into the kitchen, her mother turned and said, 'It's seven o'clock. Isn't your sister getting up?'

'Mommy,' Isabel wailed in despair. 'That's not Mary Rose!'

Noah Elliot did a 360 kick-flip, popping the skateboard off the curb, into the air, and landing it neatly on the blacktop. *All right! Nailed it!* Baggy clothes flapping in the wind, he rode the board all the way down to the teachers' parking lot, ollied the curb, and came around again, a sweet ride all the way.

It was the only time he felt in control of his life, when he was riding his board, when for once, he determined his own fate, his own course. These days it seemed too many things were decided by other people, that he was being dragged, kicking and screaming, into a future he'd never asked for. But when he was riding his board, with the wind in his face and the pavement streaking by, he owned the moment. He could forget he was trapped in this nowhere town. He could even forget, for one brief and exhilarating ride, that his dad was dead and that nothing could ever be right again.

He felt the freshmen girls watching him. They were standing in a tight group behind the trailer classrooms, glossy heads bent close together as they made giggly girl sounds. All their faces moved in unison as their eyes tracked Noah on his board. He rarely talked to them, and they rarely talked to him, but every lunch period, there they'd be, watching him as he worked through his repertoire.

Noah wasn't the only skateboarder at Knox High School, but he was definitely the best, and the girls kept their focus on him, ignoring the other boys whizzing around on the blacktop. Those boys were just posers anyway, dudes pretending to be skaters, all dressed up in gear straight out of the CCS catalogue. They had the uniform down right – Birdhouse shirts and Kevlar shoes and pants so big the cuffs dragged on the ground – but they were still posers in a hick town. They hadn't skated with the big boys in Baltimore.

As Noah circled around to make his return run, he noticed the gleam of blond hair at the edge of the track field. Amelia Reid was watching him.

She stood off by herself, cradling a book as usual. Amelia was one of those girls who seemed dipped in honey, she was so perfect, so golden. Nothing at all like her two jerky brothers, who were always hassling him in the cafeteria. Noah had never noticed her watching him before, and the realization that her attention was at this very moment focused on *him* made his knees go a little wobbly.

He ollied the board and almost lost it on the landing. *Focus, dude! Don't bite it.* He zipped down to the faculty parking lot, spun around, and came rumbling up the concrete ramp. There was a handrail on one side, slanted downward. He spun around, and popped up onto the railing. It would've been a sweet slide all the way down.

Except for the fact Taylor Darnell chose just that moment to walk in front of him.

Noah yelled, 'Outta the way!' but Taylor didn't react in time.

At the last possible instant, Noah rolled off his board and tumbled to the pavement. The skateboard, its momentum established, slid all the way down the rail and smacked into Taylor's back.

Taylor whirled, yelling: 'What the hell, man? Who threw that?'

'Didn't throw it, dude,' said Noah, picking himself up from the ground. His palms were both scraped, and his knee was throbbing. 'It was an accident. You just got in the way.' Noah bent down to pick up the skateboard, which had landed wheels up. Taylor was an okay kid, one of the first who'd come up to say hello when Noah first arrived in town eight months ago. Sometimes, they even hung out together in the afternoons, showing each other new skateboard tricks. So Noah was shocked when Taylor suddenly shoved him, hard. 'Hey! Hey, what's your problem?' said Noah.

'You threw it at me!'

'No I didn't.'

'Everyone saw it!' Taylor looked around at the bystanders. 'Didn't you see it?'

No one said anything.

'I told you, it was an accident,' said Noah. 'I'm really sorry, man.'

There was laughter over by the trailer classrooms. Taylor glanced at the girls and realized they were watching the exchange, and his face turned a furious red. 'Shut up!' he yelled at them. 'Idiot girls!'

'Geez, Taylor,' said Noah. 'What's your problem?'

The other skaters had popped up their boards and were now standing around, watching. One of them joked,

'Hey, why did Taylor cross the road?'

'Why?'

'Cause he got his dick stuck in the chicken!'

All the skaters laughed, including Noah. He couldn't help it.

He was unprepared for the blow. It seemed to come out of nowhere, a sucker punch to the jaw. His head snapped up and he stumbled backwards and fell, his butt hitting the blacktop. There he sat for a moment, ears roaring and vision blurred as his shock gave way to hurt rage. *He was my friend, and he hit me!*

Noah staggered back to his feet and lunged at Taylor, tackling him head on. They both sprawled to the ground, Noah on top. They rolled over and over, both boys flailing, neither one able to get in a decisive blow. Noah finally pinned him, but it was like holding down a spitting cat.

'Noah Elliot!'

He froze, his hands still trapping Taylor's wrists. Slowly he turned his head and saw the principal, Miss Cornwallis, standing over them. The other kids had all backed away and were watching from a safe distance.

'Get up!' said Miss Cornwallis. 'Both of you!'

At once Noah released Taylor and rose to his feet. Taylor, his face by now almost purple with rage, screamed: 'He shoved me! He shoved me and I tried to defend myself!'

'That's not true! He hit me first!'

'He threw his skateboard!'

'I didn't throw anything. It was an accident!'

'Accident? You liar!'

'Both of you, be quiet!' yelled Miss Cornwallis.

There was shocked silence in the schoolyard as everyone stared at the principal. They'd never heard her yell before. She was a prim but handsome woman who wore suits and low heels to school and kept her blond hair neatly tucked into a

French twist. To see her shouting was a revelation to them all.

Miss C. took a deep breath, swiftly recovering her dignity. 'Give me the skateboard, Noah.'

'It was an accident. I didn't hit him.'

'You were pinning him on the ground. I saw it.'

'But I didn't hit him!'

She held out her hand. 'Give it to me.'

'But –'

'Now.'

Noah walked over to his board, lying a few feet away. It was well-worn, one chipped edge crisscrossed with electrician's tape. The board had been a birthday gift when he turned thirteen. He'd added the decals underneath it – a green dragon with red fire shooting out of its mouth – and had broken in the wheels riding the streets of Baltimore where he used to live. He loved this board, because it reminded him of everything he'd left behind. Everything he still missed. He held it for a moment, then, wordlessly, handed it to Miss C.

She took it with a look of distaste. Turning to address the other students she said, 'There'll be no more skating on school grounds. I want all the skateboards brought home today. And if I see any boards tomorrow, I'll confiscate them. Is that clear?'

There was a silent nodding of heads.

Miss C. turned to Noah. 'You're in detention until three-thirty this afternoon.'

'But I didn't do anything!'

'You come to my office now. You're going to sit and think about what you did do.'

Noah started to argue, then swallowed his words. Everyone was looking at him. He glimpsed Amelia Reid standing by the track field, and his face flushed with humiliation. In silence, head down, he followed Miss C. toward the building.

The other skaters sullenly parted to let them through. Only as Noah was walking away from them did he hear one of the boys mutter:

'Thanks, Elliot. You screwed it up for the rest of us.'

If one wished to take the pulse of the town of Tranquility, the place to go was Monaghan's Diner. This was where the Dinosaur Club met every day at noon. It was not really a club, but a coffee klatch, six or seven retirees who, for want of a job to go to, hung around Nadine's counter, admiring the pies under the plastic bells. Claire had no idea how the club got its name. Her guess was that one of the men's wives, in a fit of pique over her husband's daily absence, one day blurted out something like: 'Oh, you and that bunch of old dinosaurs!' And the name stuck, as good names do. They were all men, all well past sixty. Nadine was only in her fifties, but she was an unofficial Dinosaur because she worked behind the counter and had the good humor to tolerate their bad jokes and cigarette smoke.

Four hours after the thigh bone was found,

Claire stopped in at Monaghan's for lunch. The Dinosaurs, seven of them today, all wearing blaze orange over flannel shirts, sat in their usual place, the far left barstools near the milkshake machine.

Ned Tibbetts turned and nodded as Claire came in the door. Not a warm greeting, but gruffly respectful. 'Mornin', Doc.'

'Morning, Mr Tibbetts.'

'Gonna be a mean wind blowing in today.'

'It's already freezing outside.'

'Coming out of the northwest. Could have snow tonight.'

'Cup of coffee, Doc?' asked Nadine.

'Thank you.'

Ned turned back to the other Dinosaurs, who'd variously acknowledged her entrance, and were now back in conversation. She knew only two of them by name; the others were merely familiar faces. Claire sat alone at her end of the counter, as befitted her outsider status. Oh, people were cordial enough to her. They smiled, they were polite. But to these natives, her eight months in Tranquility was but a temporary sojourn, a city girl's fling with the simple life. Winter, they all seemed to agree, would be the test. Four months of snowstorms and black ice would drive her back to the city, as it had driven off the last two doctors from away.

Nadine slid a steaming cup of coffee in front of Claire. 'Guess you know all about it, don't you?' she said.

'All about what?'

'That bone.' Nadine stood watching her, patiently waiting for her contribution to the community pool of knowledge. Like most Maine women, Nadine did a lot of listening. It was the men who seemed to do all the talking. Claire heard them when she walked through the local hardware store or the five-and-dime or the post office. They stood around and gabbed while their wives waited, silent and watchful.

'I hear it's a kid's bone,' said Joe Bartlett, swiveling on the stool to look at Claire. 'A thigh bone.'

'That right, Doc?' another one asked.

The other Dinosaurs turned and looked at Claire.

She said, with a smile, 'You already seem to know everything about it.'

'Heard it was whacked up good. Maybe a knife. Maybe an ax. Then the animals got at it.'

'You boys sure are cheerful today,' snorted Nadine.

'Three days in those woods, raccoons and coyotes clean your bones straight off. Then Elwyn's dogs come along. Hardly ever feeds 'em, y'know. Bone like that's a tasty snack. Maybe his dogs've been chewing on it for weeks. Elwyn, he wouldn't think to give it a second look.'

Joe laughed. 'That Elwyn, he just plain doesn't think.'

'Maybe he shot the kid himself. Mistook it for a deer.'

Claire said, 'It looked like a very old bone.'

39

Joe Bartlett waved at Nadine. 'I made up my mind. I'll have the Monte Cristo sandwich.'

'Whooee! Joe's goin' fancy on us today!' said Ned Tibbetts.

'What about you, Doc?' asked Nadine.

'A tuna sandwich and a bowl of mushroom soup, please.'

As Claire ate her lunch, she listened to the men talk about whom the bone might belong to. It was impossible not to listen in; three of them wore hearing aids. Most of them could remember as far back as sixty years ago, and they batted the possibilities around like a birdie in play. Maybe it was that young girl who'd fallen off Bald Rock Cliff. No, they'd found her body, remember? Maybe it was the Jewett girl – hadn't she run off when she was sixteen? Ned said no, he'd heard from his mother that she was living in Hartford; the girl'd have to be in her sixties now, probably a grandmother. Fred Moody said his wife Florida said the dead girl had to be from away – one of the summer people. Tranquility kept track of its own, and wouldn't someone remember if a local kid had vanished?

Nadine refilled Claire's cup of coffee. 'Don't they just go on and on?' she said. 'You'd think they was planning world peace.'

'How do they know so much about it, anyway?'

'Joe's second cousin to Floyd Spear, over at the police department.' Nadine began to wipe down the counter, long, brisk strokes that left behind a faintly chlorinated smell. 'They say some bone expert's driving up from Bangor today. Way I figure, it's gotta be one of those summer people.'

That, of course, was the obvious answer – one of the summer people. Whether it was an unsolved crime or an unidentified body, the all-purpose answer served. Every June, Tranquility's population quadrupled when wealthy families from Boston and New York began arriving for their lakeside vacations. Here, in this peaceful summertime colony, they would linger on the porches of their shorefront cottages while their children splashed in the water. In the shops of Tranquility, cash registers would ring merrily as the summer folk pumped dollars into the local economy. Someone had to clean their cottages, repair their fancy cars, bag their groceries. The business from those few short months was enough to keep the local population fed through the winter.

It was the money that made the visitors tolerable. That and the fact that every September, with the falling of the leaves, they would once again vanish, leaving the town to the people who belonged here.

Claire finished her lunch and walked back to her office.

Tranquility's main street followed the curve of the lake. At the top of Elm Street was Joe Bartlett's gas and garage, which he'd run for forty-two years until he retired; now his daughter's two girls pumped gas and changed oil. A sign above the garage proudly proclaimed: Owned and Operated by Joe Bartlett and Granddaughters. Claire had always liked that sign; she thought it said a lot for Joe Bartlett.

At the post office, Elm Street curved north. Already that northwest wind was starting to blow in across the lake. It blasted through the narrow alleys between buildings, and walking along the sidewalk was like passing through a series of icy wind tunnels. In the window above the five-and-dime, a black cat gazed down at her, as though pondering the stupidity of creatures out in such weather.

Next to the five-and-dime was the yellow Victorian where Claire had her medical practice.

The building had once served as Dr Pomeroy's business and residence. The door still had the old frosted glass with the lettering: MEDICAL OFFICE. Although the name *James Pomeroy, M.D.*, had been replaced by *Claire Elliot, M.D., Family Practice*, she sometimes imagined she could see the shadow of the old name lingering like a ghost in the pebbled glass, refusing to yield to the new occupant.

Inside, her receptionist, Vera, was yakking on the phone, her bracelets clattering as she flipped through the appointment book. Vera's hairstyle was like her personality: wild and woolly and a little frazzled. She cupped her hand over the receiver and said to Claire, 'Mairead Temple's in the exam room. Sore throat.'

'How's the rest of the afternoon look?'

'Two more coming in, and that's it.'

Which added up to only six patients all day, worried Claire. Since the summer tourists departed, Claire's practice had contracted. She was the only doctor with an office right in Tranquility, yet most of the locals drove the twenty miles to Two Hills for medical care. She knew why; not many in town believed she'd last through one hard winter, and they saw no point getting attached to a doctor who'd be gone by the following autumn.

Mairead Temple was one of the few patients Claire had managed to attract, but it was only because Mairead owned no car. She'd walked a mile into town, and now she sat on the exam table, still wheezing slightly from the cold weather. Mairead was eighty-one and she had no teeth or tonsils. Nor did she have much deference for authority.

Examining Mairead's throat, Claire said, 'It does look pretty red.'

'I coulda told you that myself,' Mairead answered.

'But you don't have a fever. And your lymph nodes aren't swollen.'

'Hurts wicked bad. Can't hardly swallow.'

'I'll take a throat culture. By tomorrow we'll know if it's strep. But I think it's just a virus.'

Mairead, her eyes small and suspicious, watched Claire peel open a throat swab. 'Dr Pomeroy always gave me penicillin.'

'Antibiotics don't work on a virus, Mrs Temple.'

'Always made me feel better, that penicillin.'

'Say "ah."'

Mairead gagged as Claire swabbed her throat. She looked like a tortoise, leathery neck extended, toothless mouth snapping at the air. Eyes watering, she said: 'Pomeroy was in practice a long time. Always knew what he was doing. All you young doctors, you coulda learned a thing or two from him.'

Claire sighed. Would she always be compared to Dr Pomeroy? His gravestone sat in a place of honor in the Mountain Street Cemetery. Claire saw his cryptic notes in the old medical charts, and sometimes she sensed his ghost dogging her on her rounds. Certainly it was Pomeroy's ghost that now came between her and Mairead. Dead though he was, he would always be remembered as the town doctor.

'Let's listen to your lungs,' said Claire.

Mairead grunted and tugged at her clothes. It was cold outside, and she had dressed for it. A sweater, a cotton shirt, thermal underwear, and a bra all had to be pulled free before Claire could set her stethoscope on her chest.

Through the thump-thump of Mairead's heart, Claire heard a distant tapping and she looked up.

Vera stuck her head in the room. 'Call on line two.'

'Can you take a message?'

'It's your son. He won't talk to me.'

'Excuse me, Mrs Temple,' Claire said, and went into her office to take the call. 'Noah?'

'You have to pick me up. I'm gonna miss the bus.'

'But it's only two-fifteen. The bus hasn't left yet.'

'I'm in detention. I can't leave until three-thirty.'

'Why? What happened?'

'I don't wanna talk about it now.'

'I'm going to find out anyway, honey.'

'Not *now*, Mom.' She heard him sniffle, heard the tears break through his voice. 'Please. Please, can you just come and get me?'

The phone went dead. Haunted by the image of her son, crying and in trouble, Claire quickly dialed the school back. But by the time she reached the secretary, Noah had already left the office, and Miss Cornwallis was not available to speak to her.

Claire had an hour to finish with Mairead Temple, see two new patients, and drive to the school.

Feeling pressured now, and distracted by Noah's crisis, she stepped back into the exam room and was dismayed to see that Mairead already had put her clothes back on.

'I'm not quite finished examining you,' said Claire.

'Yeah, y'are,' grunted Mairead.

'But Mrs Temple –'

'Came for penicillin. Didn't come to get no Q-Tip shoved down my throat.'

'Please, won't you just sit down? I know I do

45

things a little differently from Dr Pomeroy, but there's a reason for it. Antibiotics don't stop a virus, and they can cause side effects.'

'Never caused me no side effects.'

'It only takes a day to get back the culture results. If it's strep, I'll give you the medicine then.'

'Gotta walk all the way into town. Takes up half my day.'

Suddenly Claire understood what the real issue was. Every lab test, every new prescription, meant a mile-long walk into town for Mairead, and then another mile walk home.

With a sigh, she pulled out a prescription pad. And for the first time that visit, she saw Mairead's smile. Satisfied. Triumphant.

Isabel sat quietly on the couch, afraid to move, afraid to say a word.

Mary Rose was very, very mad. Their mother was not home yet, so Isabel was all alone with her sister. She had never seen Mary Rose behave this way, pacing back and forth like a tiger in the zoo, screaming at her. At her, Isabel! Mary Rose was so angry, it turned her face wrinkled and ugly, not like Princess Aurora anymore, but more like an evil queen. This was not her sister. This was a bad person inside her sister's body.

Isabel huddled deeper into the cushions, watching furtively as the bad person in Mary Rose's body stalked through the living room, muttering. *Never get to go anywhere or do anything because of you! Stuck at home all the time. A baby-sitter slave! I wish you were dead. I wish you were dead.*

But I'm your sister! Isabel wanted to wail, though she didn't dare make a peep. She began to cry, silent tears plopping onto the cushions, making big wet stains. Oh no. Mary Rose would be mad about that, too.

Isabel waited until her sister's back was turned, then she quietly slipped off the couch and darted into the kitchen. She would hide in here, out of Mary Rose's way, until their mother came home. She ducked around the corner of a kitchen cabinet and sat down on the cold tiles, hugging her knees to her chest. If she just stayed quiet, Mary Rose wouldn't find her. She could see the clock on the wall, and she knew that when the little hand was on the five, their mother would come home. She needed to pee, now, but she would just have to wait because she was safe here.

Then Rocky the parakeet began to screech. His cage was a few feet away, by the window. She looked up at him, silently imploring him to be quiet, but Rocky was not very smart and he kept screeching at her. Their mother had said it many times: 'Rocky is just a birdbrain,' and he was proving it now by all the noise he made.

Be quiet! Oh please be quiet or she'll find me!

Too late. Footsteps creaked into the kitchen. A drawer was yanked open and silverware clanged to the floor. Mary Rose was flinging around forks and spoons. Isabel wrapped herself into a ball and squeezed more tightly against the cabinet.

Rocky the traitor stared at her as he squawked, as though to shout out: 'There she is! There she is!'

Now Mary Rose paced into view, but she wasn't looking at Isabel. She was staring at Rocky. She went to the cage and stood looking at the parakeet, who continued to screech. She opened the door and thrust in her hand. Rocky's wings flapped in panicked whooshes of flying feathers and birdseed. She captured the struggling bird, a squirming puff of powder blue, and took him out of the cage. With one quick twist, she snapped the bird's neck.

Rocky went limp.

She flung the body against the wall. It plopped to the floor in a sad little heap of feathers.

A silent scream boiled up in Isabel's throat. She choked it back and buried her face against her knees, waiting in terror for her sister to break her neck as well.

But Mary Rose walked right out of the kitchen. Right out of the house.

3

Noah was sitting on the front steps of the high school when Claire arrived at four o'clock. She had rushed through her last two appointments, and had driven straight to the school five miles away, but she was a half hour late, and she could see he was angry about it. He didn't say a word, just climbed into the truck, and slammed the door shut.

'Seat belt, honey,' she said.

He yanked on the shoulder strap and rammed the buckle in. They drove for a moment in silence.

'I've been sitting around forever. What took you so long?' he said.

'I had patients to see, Noah. Why were you in detention?'

'It wasn't my fault.'

'Whose fault was it, then?'

'Taylor. He's turning into such a jerk. I don't know what's wrong with him.' Sighing, he slumped into his seat. 'And I used to think we were friends. Now it's like he hates me.'

She glanced at him. 'Is this Taylor Darnell you're talking about?'

'Yeah.'

'What happened?'

'It was an accident. My skateboard ran into him. Next thing I know, he's shoving me around. So I shoved him back, and he fell.'

'Why didn't you call a teacher?'

'There weren't any around. Then Miss Cornwallis comes out and suddenly Taylor starts yelling that it's *my* fault.' He turned away from her, but not before she'd glimpsed the embarrassed swipe of his hand across his eyes. He tries so hard to be grown up, she thought with a twinge of pity, but he's really still a child.

'She took my skateboard, Mom,' he said softly. 'Can you get it back for me?'

'I'll call Miss Cornwallis tomorrow. But I want you to call Taylor and apologize.'

'He turned on me! He's the one who should apologize!'

'Taylor's not having an easy time of it, Noah. His parents just got divorced.'

He looked at her. 'How do you know? Is he your patient?'

'Yes.'

'What did you see him for?'

'You know I can't talk about that.'

'Like you ever talk to me about anything,' he muttered, and turned once again to stare out the window.

50

She knew better than to rise to the bait, so she said nothing, preferring silence to the argument that would surely erupt between them if she allowed him to provoke her.

When he spoke again, it was so quietly she almost didn't hear him. 'I want to go home, Mom.'

'That's where I'm taking you.'

'No, I mean *home*. To Baltimore. I don't want to stay here anymore. There's nothing here but trees and a bunch of old guys driving around in their pickup trucks. We don't belong here.'

'This is our home now.'

'Not mine.'

'You haven't tried very hard to like it here.'

'Like I had a choice? Like you asked *me* if we should move?'

'We'll both learn to like it. I'm still adjusting, too.'

'So why did we have to move?'

Gripping the steering wheel, she stared straight ahead. 'You know why.' They both knew what she was talking about. They'd left Baltimore because of *him*, because she'd taken a hard look at her son's future and was frightened by what she saw. An enlarging circle of troubled friends. Repeated calls from the police. More courtrooms and lawyers and therapists. She had seen their future in Baltimore, and she'd grabbed her son and run like hell.

'I'm not going to turn into some perfect preppie just because you drag me up to the woods,' he said.

'I can mess things up just as good right here. So we might as well go back.'

She pulled into their driveway and turned to face him. 'Messing up is not going to get you back to Baltimore. Either you get your life together or you don't. It's your choice.'

'When is anything my choice?'

'You have lots of choices. And from now on, I want you to make the right ones.'

'You mean the ones *you* want.' He jumped out of the truck.

'Noah. Noah!'

'Just leave me *alone*!' he yelled. He slammed the door shut and stalked off to the house.

She didn't follow him. She just sat clutching the steering wheel, too tired and upset at that moment to deal with him. Abruptly she shifted into reverse and backed out of the driveway. They both needed time to cool down, to get their emotions under control. She turned onto Toddy Point Road and headed along the shore of Locust Lake. Driving as therapy.

How easy it had all seemed when Peter was alive, when one of his cross-eyed looks was all that was needed to make their son laugh. The days when they were still happy, still whole.

We haven't been happy since you died, Peter. I miss you. I miss you every day, every hour. Every minute of my life.

The lights from lakeside cottages shimmered through her tears as she drove. She rounded the curve, drove past the Boulders, and suddenly the lights were no longer white but blue, and they seemed to be dancing among the trees.

It was a police cruiser, and it was parked on Rachel Sorkin's property.

She pulled to a stop in the driveway. Three vehicles were in the front yard, two police cruisers and a white van. A Maine state trooper was talking to Rachel on the porch. Beneath the trees, flashlight beams zigzagged across the ground.

Claire spotted Lincoln Kelly emerging from the woods. It was his silhouette she recognized as he passed before one of the searchlights. Though not a tall man, Lincoln was straight and solid and he moved with a quiet assuredness that made him seem larger than he was. He stopped to speak to the state trooper, then he noticed Claire and crossed the yard to her truck.

She rolled down the window. 'Have you found any more bones?' she asked.

He leaned in, bringing with him the scent of the forest. Pine trees and earth and wood smoke. 'Yep. The dogs led us over to the streambed,' he said. 'That bank eroded pretty badly this spring, after all those floods. That's what uncovered the bones. But I'm afraid wild animals have already scattered most of them in the woods.'

'Does the ME think it's a homicide?'

'It's no longer an ME's case. The bones are too old. There's a forensic anthropologist in charge now, if you'd like to talk to her. Name's Dr Overlock.'

He opened the truck door and Claire climbed out. Together they walked into the gloom of the woods. Dusk had rapidly thickened to night. The ground was uneven, layered with dead leaves, and she found herself stumbling in the underbrush. Lincoln reached out to steady her. He seemed to have no trouble navigating in the darkness, his heavy boots connecting solidly with the ground.

Lights were shining among the trees, and Claire heard voices and the sound of trickling water. She and Lincoln emerged from the woods, onto the stream bank. A section of the eroded bank had been cordoned off by police tape strung between stakes, and on a tarp lay the mud-encrusted bones that had already been unearthed. Claire recognized a tibia and what looked like fragments of a pelvis. Two men wearing waders and headlamps stood knee-deep in the stream, gingerly excavating the side of the bank.

Lucy Overlock was standing among the trees talking on a cell phone. She was like a tree herself, tall and strapping, dressed in a woodsman's wardrobe of jeans and work boots. Her hair, almost entirely gray, was tied back in a tight, no-nonsense ponytail. She saw Lincoln, gave a harassed wave, and continued with her phone conversation.

'. . . no artifacts yet, just the skeletal remains. But I assure you, this burial doesn't fall under NAGPRA. The skull looks Caucasoid to me, not Indian. What do you mean, how can I tell? It's obvious! The brain-case is too narrow, and the facial breadth just isn't wide enough. No, of course it's not absolute. But the site is on Locust Lake, and there's never been a Penobscot settlement here. The tribe wouldn't even fish in this lake, it's such a taboo place.' She looked up at the sky and shook her head. 'Certainly, you can examine the bones for yourself. But we have to excavate this site now, before the animals do any more damage, or we'll lose the whole thing.' She hung up and looked at Lincoln in frustration. 'Custody battle.'

'Over bones?'

'It's that NAGPRA law. Indian graves protection. Every time we find remains, the tribes demand one hundred percent confirmation it's not one of theirs. Ninety-five percent isn't good enough for them.' Her gaze turned to Claire, who'd stepped forward to introduce herself.

'Lucy Overlock,' said Lincoln. 'And this is Claire Elliot. The doctor who found the thigh bone.'

The two women shook hands, the no-nonsense greeting of two medical professionals meeting over a grim business.

'We're lucky you're the one who spotted the bone,' said Lucy. 'Anyone else might not have realized it was human.'

'To be honest, I wasn't entirely sure,' said Claire. 'I'm glad I didn't drag everyone out here for a cow bone.'

'It's definitely not a cow.'

One of the diggers called out from the streambed: 'We found something else.'

Lucy dropped knee-deep into the stream and aimed a flashlight at the exposed bank.

'There,' said the digger, gently prodding the soil with a trowel. 'Looks like it might be another skull.'

Lucy snapped on gloves. 'Okay, let's ease it out.'

He slid the tip of his trowel deeper into the bank and gingerly pried away caked mud. The object dropped into Lucy's gloved hands. She scrambled out of the water and up onto the bank. Kneeling down, she surveyed her treasure over the tarp.

It was indeed a second skull. Under the floodlight, Lucy carefully turned it over and examined the teeth.

'Another juvenile. No wisdom teeth,' Lucy noted. 'I see decayed molars here and here, but no fillings.'

'Meaning no dental work,' said Claire.

'Yes, these are old bones. A good thing for you, Lincoln. Otherwise, this would be an active homicide case.'

'Why do you say that?'

She rotated the skull, and the light fell on the crown, where fracture lines radiated out from a central depression, the way a soft-boiled egg cracks when it is struck with the back of a spoon.

'I don't think there's any doubt,' she said. 'This child died a violent death.'

The chirp of a beeper cut through the silence,

startling them all. In the stillness of those woods, that electronic sound was strangely foreign. Disconcerting. Both Claire and Lincoln automatically reached for their respective pagers.

'It's mine,' said Lincoln, glancing at his readout. Without another word, he took off through the woods toward his cruiser. Seconds later, Claire saw the dome light flashing through the trees as his vehicle streaked away.

'Must be an emergency,' said Lucy.

Officer Pete Sparks was already at the scene, trying to talk old Vern Fuller into putting down his shotgun. Night had fallen, and Lincoln's first glimpse of the situation was of two wildly gesturing silhouettes intermittently backlit by the flashing dome light of Pete's cruiser. Lincoln pulled to a stop in Vern's driveway and cautiously stepped out of his vehicle. He heard bleating sheep, the restless clucking of chickens. The sounds of a working farm.

'You don't need the gun,' Pete was saying. 'Just go back in the house, Vern, and we'll look into this.'

'Like you looked into it the last time?'

'I didn't find anything the last time.'

'That's because you take so damn long gettin' here!'

'What's the problem?' said Lincoln.

Vern turned to him. 'That you, Chief Kelly? Then you tell this – this boy here that I'm not about to hand over my only protection.'

57

'I'm not asking you to hand it over,' said a weary-sounding Pete. 'I just want you to stop waving it around. Go inside and put the gun away, so nobody gets hurt.'

'I think that's a good idea,' said Lincoln. 'We don't know what we're dealing with, so you go in and lock the door, Vern. Stay close to the phone, just in case we need you to call for backup.'

'Backup?' Vern gave a grunt. 'Yeah. Okay, I'll do that.'

The two cops waited for the old man to stomp into the house and shut the door.

Then Pete said, 'He's blind as a bat. Wish we could get that shotgun away from him. Every time I come out here, I half expect to get my head blown off.'

'What's the problem, anyway?'

'Aw, it's the third time he's called nine-one-one. I'm so busy runnin' my tail off with all these other calls, it takes me a while to get here. He always has the same complaint about some wild animal stalking his sheep. Probably just seeing his own shadow, that's what.'

'Why does he call us?'

''Cause Fish and Game takes even longer to respond. I been here twice this week, didn't find anything. Not even a coyote print. Today's the first time I seen Vern this riled up. Thought I'd better get you out, just in case he decided to shoot *me* 'stead of some wild animal.'

Lincoln glanced at the house, and saw the old

man's face silhouetted in the window. 'He's watching. Might as well check the property, just to keep him happy.'

'Says he saw the animal over by the barn.'

Pete turned on his flashlight, and they started across the yard, toward the sound of bleating sheep. Lincoln felt the old man's gaze every step of the way. Let's just humor him, he thought. Even if it is a waste of our time.

He was startled when Pete suddenly halted, his flashlight beam trained on the barn door.

It hung open.

Something wasn't right. It was after dark, and the door should have been latched to protect the animals.

He turned on his flashlight as well. They approached more slowly now, their jerky beams guiding the way. At the entrance to the barn they paused. Even through the earthy melange of farmyard odors, they could smell it: the scent of blood.

They stepped into the barn. At once the bleating intensified, the sound as disturbing as the cries of panicked children. Pete swung his flashlight in a wide arc, and they caught glimpses of pitchforks and fluttering chickens and sheep fearfully bunched together in a pen.

Lying on the sawdust floor was the source of that foul odor.

Pete stumbled out of the building first, and retched into the weeds, one hand propped up against the barn wall. 'Jesus. Jesus.'

'It's just a dead sheep,' said Lincoln.

'I never seen a coyote do that. Lay out the offal . . .'

Lincoln aimed his beam at the ground, quickly scanning the area around the barn door. All he saw was a jumble of boot prints, his and Pete's and Vern Fuller's. No tracks. How could an animal leave no tracks?

A twig snapped behind him, and he whirled around to see Vern, still clutching the shotgun.

'It's a bear,' said the old man. 'That's what I seen, a bear.'

'A bear wouldn't do this.'

'I know what I saw. Whyn't you believe me?'

Because everyone knows you're half blind.

'It went that way, into the woods,' said Vern, pointing to the forested edge of his property. 'I followed it over there, just before dark. Then I lost it.'

Lincoln saw that the boot tracks did indeed head toward the forest, but Vern had retraced his steps several times, obscuring any animal footprints.

He followed the trail over to the woods. There he stood for a moment, peering into the blackness. The trees were so thick they seemed to form an impenetrable wall that even his flashlight beam could not pierce.

By now Pete had recovered, and was standing by his side. 'We should wait till daylight,' Pete whispered. 'Don't know what we're dealing with.'

'I know it's not a bear.'

'Yeah, well, I'm not scared of bears. But if it's something else . . .' Pete drew his weapon. 'Rumor has it a cougar was spotted up at Jordan Falls last week.'

Now Lincoln drew his weapon as well as he moved slowly into the woods. He took half a dozen steps, the crack of breaking twigs under his boot as loud as gunfire. All at once he froze, staring at that wall of trees. The forest seemed to close in. The hairs on the back of his neck were standing up.

There's something out there. It's watching us.

Every instinct screamed at him to retreat. He backed away, his heart racing, his boots setting off explosions of noise. Only when he and Pete had emerged completely from the woods did that feeling of imminent danger fade away.

They stood once again in front of Vern Fuller's barn, and the sheep were still bleating. He looked down at the boot prints. Suddenly his head came up.

'What lies beyond those woods?' he asked.

'Goes back a ways,' said Vern. 'Other side's Barnstown Road. Bunch of houses.'

Houses, thought Lincoln.

Families.

Noah was watching TV when Claire got home. As she hung up her coat in the hallway, she recognized the theme music from *The Simpsons* cartoon playing in the other room, and she heard Homer Simpson's loud burp and Lisa Simpson's mutter of disgust. Then she heard her son laugh, and she thought: *I'm so glad my son still laughs at cartoons.*

She went into the front parlor and saw Noah flopped back against the couch cushions, his face briefly lit up with laughter. He looked at her, but didn't say anything.

She sat down beside him and propped her feet up on the coffee table, next to his. Big feet, little feet, she thought with quiet amusement. Noah's feet had grown so huge, they almost looked like a clown's beside hers.

On the TV, an enormously fat Homer was bouncing around in a flowery muumuu, and shoveling food into his mouth.

Noah laughed again, and so did Claire. This was exactly the way she wanted to spend the rest of the evening. They would watch TV together, and eat popcorn for dinner. She leaned toward him, and they affectionately bumped heads together.

'I'm sorry, Mom,' he said.

'It's okay, Honey. I'm sorry I was late picking you up.'

'Grandma Elliot called. A little while ago.'

'Oh? Does she want me to call her back?'

'I guess.' He watched the TV for a while, his silence stretching through the string of commercials. Then he said, 'Grandma wanted to make sure we were okay tonight.'

Claire gave him a puzzled look. 'Why?'

'It's Dad's birthday.'

On the TV, Homer Simpson in his flowered

muumuu had hijacked an ice cream truck and was driving it at breakneck speed, gobbling ice cream the whole way. Claire watched in stunned silence. *Today was your birthday*, she thought. *You've been dead only two years, and already we're losing bits and pieces of your memory.*

'Oh god, Noah,' she whispered. 'I can't believe it. I completely forgot.'

She felt his head droop heavily against her shoulder. And he said, with quiet shame, 'So did I.'

Sitting in her bedroom, Claire returned Margaret Elliot's call. Claire had always liked her mother-in-law, and through the years, their affection had grown to the point that she felt far closer to Margaret than she ever had to her own coldly aloof parents. Sometimes it seemed to Claire that everything she knew about love, about passion, had been taught to her by the Elliot family.

'Hi, Mom. It's me,' said Claire.

'Sixty-two degrees and sunny in Baltimore today,' Margaret replied, and Claire had to laugh. Ever since she'd moved to Tranquility, this had been the running joke between them, their comparison of weather reports. Margaret had not wanted her to leave Baltimore. 'You have no idea what real cold is,' she'd told Claire, 'and I'm going to keep reminding you of what you've left behind.'

'Thirty-five degrees here,' Claire dutifully reported. She looked out her window. 'It's getting colder. Darker.'

'Did Noah tell you I called earlier?'

'Yes. And we're doing fine. We really are.'

'Are you?'

Claire said nothing. Margaret had the uncanny talent for reading emotions from just the simple inflection of one's voice, and already she had sensed something amiss.

'Noah told me he wants to come back here,' said Margaret.

'We just moved.'

'You can always change your mind.'

'Not now. I've made too many commitments here. To this new practice, the house.'

'Those are commitments to *things*, Claire.'

'No, they're really commitments to Noah. I need to stay here, for him.' She paused, suddenly aware that, as much as she loved Margaret, she was feeling a little irritated. She was also weary of the gentle but repeated hints that she should return to Baltimore. 'It's always hard for a kid to make a fresh start, but he'll adjust. He's too young to know what he wants.'

'That's true, I suppose. What about you? Do you still want to be there?'

'Why are you asking, Mom?'

'Because I know it would be hard for me, moving to a new place. Leaving behind my friends.'

Claire stared at the dresser mirror, at her own tired face. At the reflection of her bedroom, which still had few pictures on the wall. It was merely a collection of furniture, a place to sleep, not yet part of a real home.

'A widow needs her friends, Claire,' said Margaret.

'Maybe that was one of the reasons I had to leave.'

'What do you mean?'

'That's what I was to everyone – the widow. I'd walk into my clinic, and people would give me those sad and sympathetic looks. They were all afraid to laugh or tell jokes when I was around. And no one, no one ever dared to talk about Peter. It's as if they thought I'd break down in sobs if they just mentioned his name.'

There was silence on the line, and Claire suddenly regretted having spoken so frankly.

'It doesn't mean I ever stop missing him, Mom,' she said softly. 'I see him every time I look at Noah's face. The resemblance is so amazing. It's like watching Peter grow up.'

'In more ways than one,' Margaret said, and Claire was relieved to hear the warmth had not left her mother-in-law's voice. 'Peter wasn't the easiest child to raise. I don't think I ever told you about all the trouble he got into when he was Noah's age. That's where Noah gets his streak of mischief, you know. From Peter.'

Claire had to laugh. *He certainly didn't get it from me, his boringly scrupulous mother, whose most serious crime was neglecting to get that safety sticker.*

'Noah's got a good heart, but he's still only fourteen,' said Margaret with a friendly note of warning. 'Don't be too terribly shocked if there's more mischief on the way.'

Later, as Claire headed back downstairs, she smelled the odor of burning matches, and she thought: Well, here it comes, then. More mischief. He's sneaking another cigarette. She followed the scent to the kitchen and came to a halt in the doorway.

Noah was holding a lit match. He glanced at her, and quickly shook it out. 'It's all the candles I could find,' he said.

In silence she approached the kitchen table. Her vision suddenly blurred with tears as she gazed at the Sara Lee layer cake he had taken out of the freezer. Flames danced atop eleven candles.

Noah struck another match and lit the twelfth flame on the cake. 'Happy birthday, Dad,' he said softly.

Happy birthday, Peter, she thought, and blinked away her tears.

And she and her son blew out the candles.

4

Mrs Horatio was going to pith a frog.

'It doesn't hurt them a bit, once you've penetrated their brain stem,' she explained. 'The needle goes in at the base of the skull, and you wiggle it around a little to destroy all the sensory tracts running up to the brain. This paralyzes them, stops any conscious movement, but it keeps their spinal reflexes intact for study.' She reached into the jar and picked up a squirming frog in one hand. With her other hand, she reached for the pithing needle. It was humongous.

Though a ripple of nausea stirred in his stomach, Noah sat perfectly still at his desk in the third row. He was careful to keep his legs casually thrown out in front of him, his expression bored.

He could hear the other students squirm in their chairs, the girls mostly. To his right, a horrified Amelia Reid covered her mouth with her hand.

He let his gaze slide around the room and he silently pronounced judgment as he looked at each student in turn. *Nerd. Jock. Kiss-ass preppie.* Except for Amelia Reid, none of them were kids he cared to hang out with. None of them were interested in hanging out with *him*, either, but that was okay. His mom might like it in this town, but he didn't plan on staying forever.

Graduate, and then I'm outta here, outta here, outta here.

'Taylor, stop fidgeting and pay attention,' said Mrs Horatio.

Noah glanced sideways, and saw that Taylor Darnell was gripping his desk with both hands and staring at the exam paper he'd just gotten back that morning. Mrs Horatio had scrawled a giant D plus in red marker. The test paper was covered with Taylor's angry slashes in black ink. Next to the humiliating grade, he'd written: 'Die, Mrs Whoratio.'

'Noah, are you paying attention?'

Noah flushed and turned his gaze back to the front of the class. Mrs Horatio was holding up the frog for all to see. She actually looked like she was enjoying herself as she placed the tip of the pithing needle against the back of the frog's head. Her eyes were bright, her mouth puckered and eager as she jammed the needle into the brainstem. The frog's hind legs thrashed, its webbed feet slapping in pain.

Amelia gave a whimper and dropped her head down, her blond hair cascading over the desk. Chairs were squeaking all over the room now.

68

Someone called out with a note of desperation: 'Mrs Horatio, can I be excused?'

'. . . have to move the needle back and forth with a certain amount of force. Don't worry about the feet flapping around like this. It's purely reflex action. Just the spine shooting off impulses.'

'Mrs Horatio, I *have* to use the bathroom . . .'

'In a minute. First, you have to see how I do this.' She twisted the needle and there was a soft *crack*.

Noah thought he was going to puke. Struggling to maintain that look of utterly cool nonchalance, he turned away, his hands clenched under his desk. *Don't puke, don't puke, don't puke.* He focused on Amelia's blond hair, which he'd often admired. Rapunzel hair. He stared at it, thinking how much he'd like to stroke it. He'd never even dared talk to Amelia. She was like a girl in a golden bubble, beyond the reach of any mere mortal.

'There now,' said Mrs Horatio. 'That's all there is to it. You see, class? Total paralysis.'

Noah forced his gaze back to the frog. It lay on the teacher's desk, a limp, flappy carcass. Still alive, if you believed old Horatio, but showing no signs of it. He felt a sudden and overwhelming pity for that frog, imagined himself sprawled across that desk, eyes open and aware, body unresponsive. Darts of panic going nowhere, just exploding like firecrackers in your brain. He himself felt paralyzed and numb.

'Now each of you pair up with a lab partner,' said Mrs Horatio. 'And scoot your desks together.'

Noah swallowed and looked sideways at Amelia. She gave a helpless nod.

He moved his desk next to hers. They didn't speak to each other; it was a partnership based purely on proximity, but hey, whatever it took to get up close. Amelia's lips were trembling. He wanted very much to comfort her, but he didn't know how to, so he just sat there, his face assuming, by default, its usual bored expression. *Say something nice to her, moron. Something to impress her. You may never get another chance!*

'Frog sure looks dead,' he said.

She shuddered.

Mrs Horatio came walking down the aisle carrying the jar of frogs. She stopped beside Noah and Amelia.

'Take one. Each team works on a frog.'

The blood drained from Amelia's face. It was up to Noah.

He shoved his hand in the jar and grabbed a wriggling frog. Mrs Horatio slapped a pithing needle down on his desk. 'Get started, you two,' she said, and moved on to the next team.

Noah looked down at the frog he was holding. It stared back at him, bug-eyed. He picked up the pithing needle, then he looked at the frog again. Those eyes were begging him, *Let me live, let me live!* He put down the needle, his nausea back full force, and looked hopefully at Amelia. 'You wanna do the honors?'

'I can't,' she whispered. 'Don't make me, *please*.'

One of the girls screamed. Noah glanced sideways and saw Lydia Lipman leap out of her chair and scramble away from her lab partner, Taylor Darnell. There was a wooden *thud, thud, thud*, as Taylor stabbed his pithing needle into the frog. Blood spattered on his desk.

'Taylor! Taylor, stop it!' said Mrs Horatio.

He kept stabbing. *Thud, thud*. The frog looked like green hamburger. 'D plus,' he muttered. 'I studied all week for that test. You can't give me a D plus!'

'Taylor, go to the principal's office.'

He stabbed the frog harder. 'You can't give me a lousy D plus!'

She grabbed his wrist and tried to take the needle away from him. 'Go see Miss Cornwallis *now*!'

Taylor yanked away, knocking the dead frog off his desk. It tumbled into Amelia's lap. With a shriek, she jumped to her feet and the small corpse splatted to the floor.

'Taylor!' Mrs Horatio yelled. Again she grabbed his wrist, this time forcing him to drop the pithing needle. 'Leave this room immediately!'

'Fuck you!'

'What did you say?'

He stood up and shoved his chair to the floor. 'Fuck you!'

'You are suspended as of right now! You've been sullen and disrespectful all week. This is it, buddy. You're out of here!'

He kicked the chair. It bounced up the aisle and

71

crashed into a desk. Grabbing his shirt, she tried to march him toward the door, but he twisted free and shoved her backwards. She fell against a desk, toppling the jar. It shattered, and frogs leaped free, scattering away in a writhing carpet of green.

Slowly Mrs Horatio rose to her feet, fury blazing in her eyes. 'I'm going to have you expelled!'

Taylor reached into his backpack.

Mrs Horatio's gaze froze on the gun in his hand. 'Put it down,' she said. 'Taylor, put it down!'

The explosion seemed to punch her in the abdomen. She staggered backwards, clutching her belly, and dropped to the floor with a look of disbelief. Time seemed to halt, frozen for one interminable moment as Noah stared down in horror at the bright river of blood streaming toward his sneakers. Then a girl's terrified shriek pierced the silence. In the next instant, chaos exploded all around him. He heard chairs slam to the floor, saw a fleeing girl stumble and fall to her knees in the broken glass. The air itself seemed misted with blood and panic.

Another gunshot exploded.

Noah's gaze swept around in a slow-motion pan of fleeing bodies, and he saw Vernon Hobbs tumble forward and crash into a desk. The room was a blur of flying hair and churning legs. But Noah himself could not seem to move. His feet were mired in a waking nightmare, his body refusing to obey his brain's commands of *Run! Run!*

His gaze panned back across the chaos to Taylor

72

Darnell, and to his horror he saw that the gun was now pointed at Amelia's head.

No, he thought. *No!*

Taylor fired.

A streak of blood magically appeared on Amelia's temple and the rivulet slowly dripped down her cheek, yet she remained standing, her eyes wide and focused like a condemned animal's on the gun barrel. 'Please, Taylor,' she whispered. 'Please, don't . . .'

Taylor raised the gun again.

All at once, Noah's legs broke free of their nightmare paralysis, his body moving of its own accord. His brain registered a multitude of details at once. He saw Taylor's head come up, face rotating toward Noah. He saw the gun slowly sweep around in an arc. He saw the look of surprise in Taylor's eyes as Noah came flying at him.

Another bullet exploded out of the barrel.

'I've just noticed my patient was admitted. Why didn't anyone call me?'

The ward clerk looked up from her desk and seemed to shrink when she saw it was Claire asking the question. 'Uh . . . which patient, Dr Elliot?'

'Katie Youmans. I saw her name posted on one of the doors, but she's not in the room. I can't find her chart in the rack.'

'She was admitted just a few hours ago, through the ER. She's in X-ray right now.'

'No one notified me.'

The clerk's gaze dropped like a stone to her desk. 'Dr DelRay's taken over as attending physician.'

Claire absorbed this dismaying news in silence. It was not uncommon for patients to switch physicians, sometimes for the most trivial of reasons. Two of Adam DelRay's patients had transferred to Claire's practice as well. But she was surprised that this particular patient would choose to leave her care.

Sixteen years old, and mildly retarded, Katie Youmans had been living with her father when she was brought in to see Claire for a bladder infection. Claire had noticed at once the circumferential bruises on the girl's wrists. Forty-five minutes of gentle questioning and a pelvic examination had confirmed Claire's suspicions. Katie was removed from her father's abusive household and placed in foster care.

Since then, the girl had thrived. Her bruises, both physical and emotional, finally faded. Claire had counted Katie as one of her triumphs. Why would the girl switch doctors?

She found Katie in X-ray. Through the small viewing window, Claire saw the girl lying on the table, her lower leg positioned beneath the X-ray tube.

'Can I ask what the admitting diagnosis is?' Claire asked the tech.

'They told me cellulitis of the right foot. Her chart's over there, if you want to look at it.'

Claire picked up the medical record and flipped to the admission note. It had been dictated by Adam DelRay at seven A.M. that morning.

Sixteen-year-old white female who stepped on a tack two days ago. This morning she awakened with fever, chills, and swollen foot . . .

Claire skimmed the history and physical, then turned the page and read the therapeutic plan.

Quickly she picked up the phone to page Adam DelRay.

A moment later, he walked into X-ray, looking crisply starched as usual in his long white coat. Though he had always been cordial toward her, he had never displayed any real warmth, and she suspected that under his Yankee reserve burned a masculine sense of competition, perhaps even resentment, that Claire had lured away two of his patients.

Now he had laid claim to one of hers, and she had to suppress her own feelings of competitiveness. Only the well-being of Katie Youmans should concern her now.

'I've been following Katie as an outpatient,' she said. 'I know her pretty well, and –'

'Claire, it's just one of those things.' He lay a reassuring hand on her shoulder. 'I hope you don't take it personally.'

'That's not why I paged you.'

'It was just more convenient for me to admit her. I was in the ER when she came in. And her guardian felt Katie needed an internist.'

'I'm perfectly capable of treating cellulitis, Adam.'

'What if it turns into osteomyelitis? It could get complicated.'

'Are you saying a family physician isn't qualified to take care of this patient?'

'The girl's guardian made the decision. I just happened to be available.'

By now Claire was too angry to respond. Turning, she stared through the window at her patient. At her ex-patient. Suddenly she focused on the girl's IV, and she noticed the handwritten label affixed to the bag of dextrose and water. 'Is she already getting antibiotics?'

'They just hung it,' said the X-ray tech.

'But she's allergic to penicillin! That's why I paged you, Adam!'

'The girl never said anything about allergies.'

Claire ran into the next room, snagged the IV line, and closed off the infusion. Glancing down at Katie, she was alarmed to see the girl's face was flushed. 'I need epinephrine!' Claire called out to the X-ray tech. 'And IV Benadryl!'

Katie was moving restlessly on the table. 'I feel funny, Dr Elliot,' she murmured. 'I'm so hot.' Wheals had swollen on her neck in bright blotches of red.

The tech took one look at the girl, muttered 'Oh, shit,' and yanked open the drawer for the anaphylaxis kit.

'She didn't tell me she was allergic,' said DelRay, defensively.

'Here's the epi,' said the tech, handing Claire the syringe.

'I can't breathe!'

'It's okay, Katie,' soothed Claire, uncapping the needle. 'You'll feel better in just a few seconds . . .' She pierced the girl's skin and injected a tenth of a cc of epinephrine.

'I – can't – *breathe*!'

'Benadryl, twenty-five milligrams IV!' Claire snapped. 'Adam, give her the Benadryl!'

DelRay stared down with stunned eyes at the syringe the X-ray tech had just slapped in his hand. In a daze, he injected the drug into the line.

Claire whipped out her stethoscope. Listening to the girl's lungs, she heard tight wheezes on both sides. 'What's the blood pressure?' she asked the tech.

'I'm getting eighty over fifty. Pulse one-forty.'

'Let's move her to ER, STAT.'

Three pairs of hands reached out to slide the girl onto the gurney.

'Can't breathe – can't breathe –'

'Jesus, she's really swelling up!'

'Just keep moving!' said Claire.

Together they propelled the gurney out of X-ray and ran it down the hallway. They careened around the corner and banged through double doors into the ER. Dr McNally and two nurses looked up, startled, as Claire announced:

'She's going into anaphylactic shock!'

The response was immediate. The ER staff swung

the gurney into a treatment room. An oxygen mask was pressed to the girl's face and EKG leads clapped to her chest. Within minutes a hefty dose of cortisone was dripping into her IV.

Her own heart was still pounding when Claire finally left the room to let McNally and his staff take over. She saw Adam DelRay standing at the nurses' desk, furiously scribbling in Katie's hospital record. As she approached, he quickly shut the chart.

'She never told me she was allergic,' he said.

'The girl is borderline retarded.'

'Then she should be wearing a MedAlert bracelet. Why isn't she?'

'She refuses to.'

'Well, I can't guess these things!'

'Adam, all you had to do was call me when she came in. You knew she was my patient, and that I'm familiar with her history. All you had to do was ask.'

'The guardian should have told me. I can't believe it never even occurred to that woman to –'

He was interrupted by the loud squeal of the ER radio. They both looked up as the transmission came crackling through.

'Knox Hospital, this is unit seventeen, unit seventeen. We have gunshot victim en route, ETA five minutes. Do you copy?'

One of the nurses darted out of the treatment room and snatched up the microphone. 'This is Knox ER. What's that about a gunshot wound?'

'Multiple victims en route. This one's critical – more on the way.'

'How many? Repeat, *how many?*'

'Uncertain. At least three –'

Another voice cut into the frequency. 'Knox Hospital, this is unit nine. En route with gunshot wound to the shoulder. Do you copy?'

In panic, the nurse grabbed the telephone and hit O. 'Disaster code! Call a disaster code! This is not a drill!'

Five doctors. That was all they could round up in the building during the frantic moments before the first ambulance arrived: Claire, DelRay, McNally from the ER, a general surgeon, and one terrified pediatrician. No one knew any details yet, not the location of the shooting, nor the number of victims. All they knew was that something terrible had happened, and that this tiny rural hospital was not prepared to deal with the aftermath. The ER turned into a maelstrom of noise and activity as personnel scrambled to prepare for the injured. Katie, now stabilized, was whisked out and shoved into the hallway to free up the treatment room. Cabinets clanged open, bright lights flared on. Claire pitched in to hang IV bags, lay out instrument trays, and rip open packets of gauze and sutures.

The approaching wail of the first ambulance brought a split second's hush to the ER. Then everyone surged out the double doors to meet the first victim. Standing among that crowd of personnel, Claire heard no one speak; they were all focused on the swelling scream of the siren as it drew near.

Abruptly the siren was cut off and the flashing red light swerved into view.

Claire pushed forward as the ambulance backed up to the entrance. The vehicle's rear door swung open, and the stretcher rolled out with the first victim. It was a woman, already intubated. The surgical tape used to secure the ET tube obscured the lower half of her face. The bandage on her abdomen was soaked with blood.

They rolled her straight into the trauma room and slid her onto the table. A confusing chorus of voices was shouting simultaneously as the woman's clothes were cut away, the EKG leads and oxygen lines connected, a BP cuff wrapped around one arm. A rapid sinus rhythm raced across the cardiac monitor.

'Systolic's seventy!' a nurse called out.

'Drawing the type and cross!' said Claire. She grabbed a sixteen-gauge IV catheter off the tray and snapped a tourniquet around the patient's arm. The vein barely plumped up; the patient was in shock. She stabbed the vein with the IV needle and slid the plastic catheter into place. With a syringe, she withdrew several tubes of blood, then attached the IV tubing to the catheter. 'Another lactated Ringer's going in, wide open!' she called out.

'Systolic's sixty, barely palpable!'

The surgeon said, 'Belly's distended. I think it's full of blood. Open that surgical tray, and get suction ready!' He looked at McNally. 'You're first assist.'

'But she needs to be in the OR –'

'No time. We have to find out where the blood's coming from.'

'I've lost her BP!' a nurse yelled.

The first incision was swift and brutal, one long slash down the center of the abdomen, parting the skin. With a deeper incision, the surgeon cut through the yellow layer of subcutaneous fat, and slit into the peritoneum.

Blood spilled out, streaming onto the floor.

'I can't see where it's coming from!'

The suction wasn't clearing the blood fast enough. In desperation, McNally stuffed two sterile towels into the abdomen and pulled them out again, soaking red and dripping.

'Okay, I think I see it. Bullet nicked the aorta –'

'Jesus, it's gushing!'

A ward clerk yelled through the doorway, 'Two more have arrived! They're wheeling them in now!'

McNally glanced across the table at Claire, and she saw panic in his eyes. 'You're *it*,' he snapped. 'Go, Claire.'

With her heart in her throat, she pushed out of the trauma room and saw the first stretcher being wheeled into one of the treatment rooms.

The patient was a sobbing red-haired boy, shirt cut away, blood soaking through the bandage on his shoulder. Now a second stretcher whisked in the door – a blond teenage girl, half her face covered with blood.

Children, she thought. *These are only children. My god, what has happened?*

She went first to the girl, who was crying but able to move all her extremities. At that first glimpse of blood on the girl's face, Claire nearly panicked, thinking: gunshot wound to the head. She forced herself to pause and take the girl's hand, to calmly ask her name, even while her own heart was thundering. It took only a few questions to confirm that Amelia Reid was fully oriented, and her mental status was clear. The wound was just a superficial graze of the temple, which Claire quickly cleaned and dressed.

Turning her attention to the red-haired boy, she saw that he was already being attended to by the pediatrician.

'Are there any others on the way?' she asked the ward clerk.

'None en route. There may be more at the scene . . .'

A second surgeon arrived, trotting in through the ER doors and announcing: 'I'm here! Who needs me?'

'Trauma room!' said Claire. 'Dr McNally needs to be relieved.'

He was just about to push through the door

when a nurse popped out, almost slamming into him.

'Do we have that O-neg blood for Horatio yet?' she yelled to the ward clerk.

Horatio? Claire hadn't recognized the patient under all that surgical tape, but she knew the name, Dorothy Horatio.

My son's biology teacher. She looked at the clock and saw it was eleven-thirty. Period three. Noah would be in biology – in Mrs Horatio's class.

Another doctor arrived, another pair of hands – the obstetrician from Two Hills. She took one last glance around the room, and saw that the situation was under control.

She made the only decision a panicked mother could make.

She ran outside to her car.

The twenty-mile drive passed in a blur of autumn fields, the mist rising in wisps, stands of pine trees. Here and there farmhouses with tumbling porches. She had driven this country road every day for eight months, but never at this speed, never with her hands shaking and her heart sick with fear. She took the last rise with the accelerator floored and her Subaru leaped past the familiar sign:

You Are Now Leaving Two Hills. Come Back Soon!

And then, a hundred yards beyond that, a second sign, smaller, paint chipping.

She swerved onto School Road and saw the flashing lights of half a dozen emergency vehicles. Police cruisers were parked in a jumble near the high school's red brick front entrance, along with two fire trucks – a full-scale disaster response.

Claire abandoned her car and ran toward the school's front lawn, where dozens of stunned-looking students and teachers had gathered behind a tangle of police tape. Scanning the faces, she didn't see Noah.

A Two Hills policeman stopped her at the front door. 'No one's allowed inside.'

'But I have to go in!'

'Only emergency personnel.'

She took a quick breath. 'I'm Dr Elliot,' she said, her voice steadier. 'I'm a physician from Tranquility.'

He let her pass.

She pushed through the front door into the high school. The building was nearly a century old, and inside hung the musty odors of teenage sweat and dust stirred up by thousands of feet trudging up and down the staircase. She ran up the steps to the second floor.

The doorway to the biology classroom was criss-crossed by strands of police tape. Beyond the tape were overturned chairs, broken glass, and scattered papers. Frogs hopped through the debris.

There was blood – pools of it congealing in gelatinous lakes on the floor.

'Mom?'

Her heart leaped at the voice. She whirled to see her son standing at the far end of the hall. In the dim light of that long corridor, he seemed frighteningly small to her, his blood-streaked face pale and thin.

She ran to him and threw her arms around his rigid body, pulling him, forcing him, into an embrace. She felt his shoulders melt first, then his head drooped against her and he was crying. No sound came out; there was just the shuddering of his chest and warm tears sliding onto her neck. At last she felt his arms come around her, circle her waist. His shoulders might be as broad as a man's, but it was a child who clung to her now, a child's grief that spilled out in tears.

'Are you hurt?' she asked. 'Noah, you're bleeding. Are you *hurt*?'

'He's fine, Claire. The blood isn't his. It's the teacher's.'

She looked up and saw Lincoln Kelly standing in the hall, his grim expression reflecting the day's terrible events. 'Noah and I just finished going over what happened. I was about to call you, Claire.'

'I was at the hospital. I heard there was a shooting.'

'Your son grabbed the gun away from the boy,' said Lincoln. 'It was a crazy thing to do. A brave thing to do. He probably saved a few lives.' Lincoln's gaze dropped to Noah, and he added softly: 'You should be proud of him.'

'I wasn't brave,' blurted out Noah. He pulled away from Claire, ashamedly wiping his eyes. 'I was scared. I don't know why I did it. I didn't know what I was doing . . .'

'But you did it, Noah.' Lincoln lay a hand on the boy's shoulder. It was a man's blessing, brusque and matter-of-fact. Noah seemed to draw sustenance from that simple touch. A mother, thought Claire, cannot knight her own son. It must be done by another man.

Slowly Noah straightened, his tears at last under control. 'Is Amelia okay?' he asked her. 'They took her in the ambulance.'

'She's fine. Just a scratch on her face. I think the boy will be fine as well.'

'And . . . Mrs Horatio?'

She shook her head. And said, gently, 'I don't know.'

He took a deep breath and wiped an unsteady hand across his eyes. 'I – I have to go wash my face . . .'

'You do that,' said Lincoln gently. 'Take your time, Noah. Your mom will be waiting for you.'

Claire watched her son walk away down the hall. As he passed the biology classroom he slowed down, his gaze drawn, against his will, to the open doorway. For a few seconds he stood hypnotized by the terrible view beyond that police tape. Then, abruptly, he pushed into the boys' restroom.

'Who was it?' said Claire, turning to Lincoln. 'Who brought the gun to school?'

'It was Taylor Darnell.'

She stared at him. 'Oh god. He's my patient.'

'That's what his father told us. Paul Darnell says the boy can't be held responsible. That he has attention deficit disorder and can't control his impulses. Is that true?'

'ADD doesn't cause violent behavior. And Taylor doesn't have it, anyway. But I can't comment on this case, Lincoln. I'm betraying confidentiality.'

'Well, *something's* wrong with the kid. If you're his doctor, maybe you should take a look at him before he's moved to the Youth Center.'

'Where is he now?'

'We're holding him in the principal's office.' Lincoln paused. 'Just a word of warning, Claire. Don't get too close.'

5

Taylor Darnell sat handcuffed to a chair, swinging his foot, *bam, bam, bam!* against the principal's desk. He didn't look up when Claire and Lincoln walked into the room, didn't even seem to notice they were there. Two Maine state cops were in the room with him. They looked at Lincoln and shook their heads, their thoughts transparent: *This one is totally bonkers.*

'We just got a call from the hospital,' one of the state cops said to Lincoln. 'The teacher's dead.'

No one spoke for a moment; both Claire and Lincoln absorbed the terrible news in silence.

Then Claire asked, softly: 'Where is Taylor's mother?'

'She's still on her way back from Portland. She drove down there on business.'

'And Mr Darnell?'

'I think he's rounding up a lawyer. They're going to need one.'

Taylor was kicking his foot against the desk again in a ceaseless, accelerating beat.

Claire set her medical bag down on a chair and approached the boy. 'You remember me, Taylor, don't you? I'm Dr Elliot.' He didn't answer, just kept up that angry banging. Something was very wrong. This was more than adolescent rage she was looking at. It appeared to be some sort of drug-induced psychosis.

Without warning, Taylor's gaze rose and locked on hers, focusing with predatory intensity. His pupils dilated, irises darkening to ebony pools. His lips curled up, canines gleaming, and from his throat escaped an animal sound, half hiss, half growl.

It happened so fast she had no time to react. He sprang to his feet, dragging the chair up with him, and lunged at her.

The impact of his body slamming into hers sent her toppling backwards to the floor. His teeth sank into her jacket, ripping the fabric, sending goose down and feathers flying in a white cloud. She caught a glimpse of three frantic faces as the cops struggled to separate them. They wrenched Taylor away, dragging him backwards even as he continued to thrash.

Lincoln grasped her arm and lifted her back to her feet. 'Claire – Jesus –'

'I'm okay,' she said, coughing on goose down. 'Really, I'm fine.'

One of the state cops yelped. 'He just bit me! Look, I'm bleeding!'

Even cuffed to the chair, the boy was fighting, bucking against his restraints. 'Let me go!'

he shrieked. 'I'll kill you all if you don't let me *go*!'

'He should be locked up in a freaking kennel!'

'No. No, there's something seriously wrong here,' said Claire. 'It looks like a drug psychosis to me. PCP or amphetamines.' She turned to Lincoln. 'I want this boy moved to the hospital. Now.'

'Too much movement,' said Dr Chapman, the radiologist. 'We're not going to get very clear definition here.'

Claire leaned forward, watching intently as the first cross-section of Taylor Darnell's brain appeared on the computer screen. Each image was a compilation of pixels formed by thousands of tiny X-ray beams. Aimed at different angles along one plane, the beams distinguished between fluid and solid and air, and the various densities were reproduced in the image on the screen.

'See that fuzziness there?' said Chapman, pointing to the movement artifact.

'We can't make him hold still unless we put him under anesthesia.'

'Well, that's an option.'

Claire shook her head. 'His mentation's cloudy enough. I don't want to risk anesthesia right now. I'm just trying to rule out any mass shifts before I do the lumbar puncture.'

'You really think encephalitis could explain these symptoms?' Chapman looked at her, and she saw skepticism in his eyes. In Baltimore, she'd been a respected family practitioner. But here she still had to prove herself. How long would it take before her new colleagues stopped questioning her judgment and learned to trust her?

'At this point, I have no choice,' she said. 'The initial screen for both methamphetamine and PCP came back negative. But Dr Forrest thinks this is clearly an organic psychosis, not psychiatric.'

Chapman was obviously unimpressed by Dr Forrest's clinical skills. 'Psychiatry is hardly an exact science.'

'But I agree with him. The boy's shown alarming personality changes in just the last few days. We have to rule out infection.'

'What's the white cell count?'

'Thirteen thousand.'

'A little high, but not all that impressive. What about the differential?'

'His eosinophil count is high. Way off the scale, in fact, at thirty percent.'

'But he has a history of asthma, right? That could account for it. It's some sort of allergic response.'

Claire had to agree. Eosinophils were a type of white blood cell that proliferated most commonly in response to allergic reactions or asthma. High eosinophil counts could also be caused by a variety of other illnesses such as cancer, parasitic infections, and autoimmune diseases. In some patients, no discernible cause was ever found.

'So what happens now?' asked the Maine state trooper, who'd been watching the procedure with a look of growing impatience. 'Can we move him to the Youth Center or not?'

'We have more tests to run,' said Claire. 'The boy could be seriously ill.'

'Or he could be faking it. That's what it looks like to me.'

'And if he's sick, you could find him dead in his cell. I wouldn't want to make that mistake, would you?'

Without comment, the trooper turned and stared through the CT viewing window at his prisoner.

Taylor was lying on his back, wrists and ankles restrained. His head was hidden inside the CT cradle, but they could see the movement of his feet, twisting against the restraints. *Now comes the hard part*, she thought. *How do we hold him in position long enough for the lumbar puncture?*

'I can't afford to miss a CNS infection,' said Claire. 'With an elevated white blood count and changes in mental status, I have no choice but to do the spinal tap.'

Chapman at last seemed to agree. 'From what I see here on the scan, it looks safe enough to proceed.'

They wheeled Taylor out of X-ray and into a private room. It took two nurses and a male orderly to transfer the struggling boy to the bed.

'Turn him on his side,' said Claire. 'Fetal position.'

'He's not going to lie still for this.'

'Then you'll have to sit on him. We need this spinal tap.'

Together they rolled the boy on his side, his back to Claire. The orderly flexed Taylor's hips, forcibly pushing the knees toward the chest. One nurse pulled the shoulders forward. Taylor snapped at her hand, almost catching her finger in his jaws.

'Watch his teeth!'

'I'm trying to!'

Claire had to work fast; they couldn't keep the boy immobilized much longer. She lifted the hospital gown, exposing his back. With his body curled into a fetal position, the vertebral spines poked out clearly under the skin. In rapid order she identified the space between the fourth and fifth spinous processes in the lower back, and swabbed the skin with Betadine, then alcohol. She snapped on sterile gloves and picked up the syringe with local anesthetic.

'I'm putting in the Xylocaine now. He's not going to like this.'

Claire pricked the skin with the twenty-five-gauge needle and gently injected the local anesthetic. At the first sting of the drug, Taylor shrieked with rage. Claire saw one of the nurses glance up, fear in her eyes. None of them had ever dealt with anything like this, and the violence coursing through this boy's body was frightening them all.

Claire reached for the spinal needle. It was three inches long, twenty-two-gauge gleaming steel, the hub end open to allow cerebrospinal fluid to drip out.

'Steady him. I'm doing the tap now.'

She pierced the skin. The Xylocaine had numbed the area, so he didn't feel any pain – not yet. She kept pushing the needle deeper, aiming the tip between the spinous processes, toward the dura mater of the spinal cord. She felt a slight resistance, then a distinct pop as the needle penetrated the protective dura.

Taylor screamed again and began to thrash.

'Hold him! You have to hold him!'

'We're trying! Can you hurry it up?'

'I'm already in. It'll just be another minute now.' She held a test tube under the open hub of the needle and caught the first drop of CSF as it slid out. To her surprise, the fluid was crystal clear with no blood, no telltale cloudiness of infection. This was not an obvious case of meningitis. *So what am I dealing with?* she wondered as she carefully collected CSF in three different test tubes. The fluid would be sent immediately to the lab, where it would be analyzed for cell count and bacteria, glucose and protein. Just by looking at the fluid in the tubes, she knew that the results would be normal.

She withdrew the needle and applied a bandage to the puncture site. Everyone in the room seemed to give a simultaneous sigh of relief; the procedure was over.

But the answer was no closer.

* * *

Later that evening, she found Taylor's mother downstairs in the tiny hospital chapel, gazing numbly at the altar. They had spoken earlier, when Claire had requested the mother's consent for the lumbar puncture. At the time, Wanda Darnell had been a bundle of nerves, all jittery hands and trembling lips. She had been on the road all day, first the two-hundred mile drive to Portland to visit her divorce attorney, and then the harrowing drive back, after the police had contacted her with the terrible news.

Now Wanda seemed exhausted, all her adrenaline depleted. She was a small woman, dressed in an ill-fitting skirt suit that made her look like a child playing grown-up in her mother's clothes. She looked up as Claire came into the chapel and barely managed a nod of greeting.

Claire sat down and gently placed her hand on Wanda's. 'The lab results have come back on the spinal tap, and they're completely normal. Taylor doesn't have meningitis.'

Wanda Darnell released a deep sigh, her shoulders slumping forward in the oversize suit jacket. 'That's good, then?'

'Yes. And judging by the CT scan, he has no tumors or signs of hemorrhage in his brain. So that's good, too.'

'Then what's wrong with him? Why did he do it?'

'I don't know, Wanda. Do you?'

She sat very still, as though struggling to come

up with an answer. 'He hasn't been . . . right. For almost a week.'

'What do you mean?'

'He's been out of control, angry at everyone. Cursing and slamming doors. I thought it was because of the divorce. He's had such a hard time of it . . .'

Claire was reluctant to bring up the next subject, but it had to be addressed. 'What about drugs, Wanda? That could change a child's personality. Do you think he's been experimenting with anything?'

Wanda hesitated. 'No.'

'You don't sound sure.'

'It's just that . . .' She swallowed, tears flashing in her eyes. 'I feel like I hardly know him anymore. He's my son, and I don't even recognize him.'

'Have you seen any warning signs?'

'He's always been a little difficult. That's why Dr Pomeroy thought he might have attention deficit disorder. Lately, it seems he's gotten worse. Especially since he started hanging out with those awful boys.'

'Which boys?'

'They live up the road from us. J.D. and Eddie Reid. And then there's that Scotty Braxton. All four of them got into trouble with the police back in March. Last week, I told Taylor he had to stay away from the Reid brothers. That's when we got into our first really big fight. That's when he slapped me.'

'*Taylor* did?'

Wanda's head drooped, the victim ashamed she'd been abused. 'We've hardly spoken to each other since then. And when we do talk, it's so obvious that . . .' Her voice slid to a whisper. 'That we hate each other.'

Gently Claire touched Wanda's arm. 'Believe it or not, disliking your own teenager isn't all that abnormal.'

'But I'm also afraid of him! That's what makes it even worse. I dislike him *and* I'm scared of him. When he hit me, it was like having his father back in the house.' She touched her fingers to her mouth, as though remembering some long-faded bruise. 'Paul and I are still in a custody fight. Two of us battling over a boy who doesn't like either of us.'

Claire's beeper went off. She glanced at the digital readout and saw the lab was paging her. 'Excuse me,' she said, and left the chapel to make the call from the hospital lobby.

Anthony, the lab supervisor, answered the phone. 'The Bangor lab just called with more of Taylor's results, Dr Elliot.'

'Did anything turn up positive on the specific screens?'

'I'm afraid not. There's no alcohol, cannabis, opioids, or amphetamines in his blood. That's a negative for every drug you wanted screened.'

'I was so sure,' she said in bewilderment. 'I don't know what else could cause this behavior.

There must be some drug I've forgotten to test for.'

'There *may* be something. I ran his blood through our hospital gas chromatography machine, and an abnormal peak showed up at one minute, ten seconds' retention time.'

'What does that mean?'

'It doesn't pinpoint any particular drug. But there is a peak, which indicates something out of the ordinary is circulating in his blood. It could be completely innocuous – an herbal supplement, for instance.'

'How do we find out what it is?'

'We'd need more extensive analysis. The Bangor lab isn't equipped to do that. We have to draw more blood and send it to our reference lab in Boston. They can simultaneously screen for hundreds of different drugs.'

'Then let's do it.'

'Well, here's the problem. It's the other reason I paged you. I just got an order to cancel any and all remaining drug tests. It's signed by Dr DelRay.'

'What?' She shook her head in disbelief. '*I'm* Taylor's doctor.'

'But DelRay's writing orders, and his are contradictory to yours. So I'm not sure what to do.'

'Look, let me talk to the mother and I'll clear this up right now.' She hung up and returned to the chapel.

Even before she opened the door, she could hear a man's voice, raised in anger.

'. . . never exerted any control! Completely useless, that's what you are. No wonder he's so screwed up!'

Claire pushed into the chapel. 'Is there a problem here, Wanda?'

The man turned to her. 'I'm Taylor's father.'

Personal crises bring out the worst in people, but Paul Darnell was probably not likable even at his best. A partner in the largest accounting firm in Two Hills, he was far more stylishly garbed than his wife, who seemed to shrink to inconsequential size in her ill-fitting suit. The brief interaction Claire had witnessed between these two ex-spouses told her what this marriage must have been like: Paul the aggressor, full of demands and complaints. Wanda always appeasing, retreating.

'What is this about my son taking illegal drugs?' he asked.

'I'm trying to find a reason for what happened today, Mr Darnell. I was just asking your wife –'

'Taylor hasn't been taking any drugs. Not since you stopped the Ritalin.' He paused. 'And he was fine on the Ritalin. I never understood why you took him off it.'

'It's been two months since I discontinued it. This personality change is more recent.'

'Two months ago, he was fine.'

'No he wasn't. He was tired and listless. And that diagnosis of ADD was never really established. It's not the same as diagnosing hypertension, where there are definite parameters to go by.'

'Dr Pomeroy was certain of the diagnosis.'

'ADD has turned into a catchall for all childhood misbehavior. When a student's failing in class, or he gets into mischief, parents want to find a reason. I didn't agree with Pomeroy's diagnosis. When in doubt, I prefer not to push pills on children.'

'And look what's happened. He's out of control. He's been out of control for weeks.'

'How would you know, Paul?' said Wanda. 'How long has it been since you actually spent time with your own son?'

Paul turned to his ex-wife with such a look of hatred, Wanda shrank back. 'You're the one who's supposed to be in charge,' he said. 'I knew you couldn't handle him. You screwed it up as usual, and now our son's going to end up in jail!'

'At least I didn't provide him with the gun,' she said softly.

'What?'

'It was your gun he brought to school. Did you ever notice it was missing?'

He stared at her. 'The little *shit*! How did he get –'

'This isn't helping!' Claire cut in. 'We need to focus on Taylor. On how to explain his behavior.'

Paul turned to his wife. 'I've asked Adam DelRay to take over. He's upstairs looking at Taylor now.'

Paul's blunt announcement left Claire speechless. So this was why DelRay had written orders;

he was the new attending. She'd just been fired from the case.

'But Dr Elliot's his doctor!' Wanda protested.

'I know Adam, and I trust his judgment.'

Meaning he doesn't trust mine?

'I don't even like Adam DelRay,' said Wanda. 'He's your friend, not mine.'

'You don't have to like him.'

'If he's taking care of my son, I do.'

Paul's laughter was grating. 'Is that how you choose a doctor, Wanda? Pick whoever gives you the most warm fuzzies?'

'I'm doing what's best for Taylor!'

'And that's exactly why he ended up *here*.'

Claire's temper at last burst through. 'Mr Darnell,' she said, 'this is *not* the time to be attacking your wife!'

He turned to Claire, and his contempt was clearly meant for her as well. '*Ex*-wife,' he corrected. And he turned and walked out of the chapel.

She found Adam DelRay sitting at the nurses' station, writing in Taylor's chart. Although it was late in the evening, his white coat was starched and fresh, and Claire felt rumpled by comparison. Whatever embarrassment he'd suffered earlier that day during the crisis with Katie Youmans had been conveniently forgotten, and he regarded Claire with his usual irritating self-confidence.

'I was about to page you,' he said. 'Paul Darnell just decided –'

'I've already spoken to him.'

'Oh. So you know.' He gave an apologetic shrug. 'I hope you don't take it personally.'

'It's the parents' decision. They have a right to make it,' she acknowledged grudgingly. 'But since you're taking over, I thought you should know the boy has an abnormal peak on gas chromatography. I suggest you order a comprehensive drug screen.'

'I don't think that's necessary.' He set the chart down and stood up. 'The most likely drugs have been ruled out.'

'That peak needs to be identified.'

'Paul doesn't want any more drug tests.'

She shook her head, puzzled. 'I don't understand his objections.'

'I believe he reached that decision after speaking with his attorney.'

She waited for him to walk away before picking up the chart. She flipped to the progress notes and with growing dismay read DelRay's entry.

History and physical dictated.
Assessment:
1. Acute psychosis secondary to abrupt Ritalin withdrawal.
2. Attention Deficit Disorder.

Claire dropped into the nearest chair, her legs suddenly unsteady, her stomach queasy. So this was their criminal defense strategy. That the boy

102

was not responsible for his actions. That Claire should be blamed, because she took him off the Ritalin, triggering a psychotic break. That she was the one who should be blamed. *I'm going to end up in court.*

This was why Paul didn't want to find any drug in the boy's bloodstream. It would shift the blame away from Claire.

Agitated, she flipped to the front of the chart and read DelRay's orders.

Cancel comprehensive drug/tox screen.
Refer all future questions and lab reports to me.
Dr Elliot is no longer the attending physician.

She slapped the chart shut and felt her nausea intensify. Now it was no longer just Taylor's life on the line; it was her practice, and her reputation as well.

She thought of the first rule of defensive medicine: cover your ass. You can't get sued if you can prove you didn't make a mistake. If you can back up your diagnosis with lab tests.

She had to get a sample of Taylor's blood. This was her last chance to draw the specimen; by tomorrow, any drug would be cleared from his system, and there'd be nothing left to detect.

She crossed the nurses' station to the supply room, pulled open a drawer, and collected a Vacutainer syringe, alcohol swabs, and three red-top blood tubes. Her heart was racing as she walked up the hall to Taylor's room. The boy was no longer her patient, and she had no right to be doing this, but she needed to know what drug, if any, was circulating in his bloodstream.

The state trooper gave her a nod of greeting as she approached.

'I need to draw blood,' she said. 'Would you mind holding down his arm for me?'

He didn't look happy about it, but he followed her into the room.

Draw it quick and get out of here. With shaking hands she snapped on the tourniquet and twisted off the needle cap. *Get out of here before someone finds out what you're doing.* She swabbed Taylor's arm with alcohol and he gave a shout of rage, twisting against the trooper's restraining grip. Claire's pulse accelerated as she pierced the skin and felt that subtle and satisfying pop as the needle penetrated the vein. *Hurry. Hurry.* She filled one tube, slipped it into her lab coat pocket, then squeezed another into the Vacutainer. Dark blood streamed out.

'I can't hold him still,' said the trooper, wrestling for control as the boy bucked and cursed.

'I'm almost done.'

'He's trying to bite me!'

'Just keep him still!' she snapped, her ears ringing with the boy's shrieks. She slipped the third tube into place and watched as a fresh stream of blood shot out. *Just one more. Come on, come on.*

'What the hell is going on in here?'

Claire looked up, so startled she let the needle

slip out of the vein. Blood dribbled from the puncture wound and dripped onto the sheets. Quickly she snapped off the tourniquet and applied gauze to the boy's arm. Cheeks burning with shame, she turned to face Paul Darnell and Adam DelRay, who were staring at her incredulously from the doorway. Two nurses peered over their shoulders.

The trooper said, 'She was just drawing some blood. The boy got a little noisy.'

'Dr Elliot isn't supposed to be in here,' said Paul. 'Didn't you hear about the new orders?'

'What orders?'

'I'm the boy's physician now,' snapped DelRay. 'Dr Elliot has no authority. She shouldn't even be in here.'

The trooper stared at Claire, and his anger was unmistakable. *You used me.*

Paul thrust out his hand. 'Give me the blood tubes, Dr Elliot.'

She shook her head. 'I'm following up an abnormal test. It could affect your son's treatment.'

'You're no longer his doctor! Give me the tubes.'

She swallowed hard. 'I'm sorry, Mr Darnell. But I can't.'

'This is assault!' Paul turned to the others in the room, and his face was florid with outrage. 'That's what this is, you know! She assaulted my son with that needle, and she knows she has no authority!' He looked at Claire. 'You'll be hearing from my attorney.'

'Paul,' interjected DelRay, playing the role of

diplomat to the hilt. 'I'm sure Dr Elliot doesn't want this kind of complication in her life.' He turned to her and spoke with the smug voice of reason. 'Come on, Claire. This is turning into a circus. Just give me the tubes.'

She looked down at the two tubes she was holding, weighing their value against a charge of assault. Against the probable loss of her hospital privileges. She felt the gaze of everyone in the room watching, even enjoying, her humiliation.

In silence she handed over the blood tubes.

DelRay took them with a look of triumph. Then he turned to the Maine state trooper. 'The boy is my patient. Is that clear?'

'Perfectly clear, Dr DelRay.'

No one said a word to Claire as she walked out of the ward, but she knew they were staring at her. She kept her gaze focused straight ahead as she turned the corner and punched the down button. Only when she'd stepped into the elevator and the door slid shut did she finally allow her hand to slip into her coat pocket.

The third blood tube was still there.

She rode the elevator to the basement lab and found Anthony sitting at his lab bench, surrounded by racks of test tubes.

'I've got a sample of the boy's blood,' she told him.

'For the drug screen?'

'Yes. I'll fill out the requisition myself.'

'The forms are on that shelf over there.'

She took one off the stack and frowned at the letterhead, Anson Biologicals. 'Are we using a new reference lab? I've never seen one of these forms before.'

He glanced up from a whirring centrifuge. 'We just switched over to Anson a few weeks ago. The hospital signed a new contract with them for our complex chem and radioimmunoassay work.'

'Why?'

'I think it was a cost issue.'

She scanned the form, then checked off the box for *gas chromatography/mass spectrometry; comprehensive drug and tox screen*. In the space for comments at the bottom of the page, she wrote: 'Fourteen-year-old boy with apparent drug-induced psychosis and aggression. This lab test is for my personal research only. Report results directly to me.' And she signed her name.

Noah answered the knock on his front door and found Amelia standing outside in the dark. She was wearing a bandage, a bright slash of white across her temple, and he could tell it hurt her to smile. In her discomfort, the best she could muster was a crooked lifting of one side of her mouth.

He was so surprised by her unexpected visit, he couldn't think of a single intelligent thing to say, so he just gaped at her, as dazzled as a peasant who suddenly finds himself in the presence of royalty.

'This is for you,' she said, and she held out a

small brown package. 'I'm sorry I couldn't find anything nice to wrap it in.'

He took the package, but his gaze remained on her face. 'Are you all right?'

'I'm okay. I guess you heard that Mrs Horatio . . .' She paused, swallowing back tears.

He nodded. 'My mom told me.'

Amelia touched the bandage on her face. Again he saw a flash of tears in her eyes. 'I met your mom. In the emergency room. She was really nice to me . . .' She turned and glanced over her shoulder at the darkness, as though expecting to see someone watching her. 'I've got to go now –'

'Did someone drive you here?'

'I walked.'

'You walked? In the dark?'

'It's not so far. I live just the other side of the lake, right past the boat ramp.' She backed away from the door, blond hair swaying. 'I'll see you in school.'

'Wait. Amelia!' He held up the gift. 'What's this for?'

'To thank you. For what you did today.' She took another retreating step, and was almost swallowed up in darkness.

'Amelia!'

'Yes?'

Noah paused, not knowing what to say. The silence was broken only by the rustle of dead leaves scattering across the lawn. Amelia stood on the farthest edge of the light spilling from the open doorway, her face a pale oval eclipsing into night.

'You want to come inside?' he asked.

To his surprise she seemed to consider the invitation. For a moment she lingered between darkness and light, advance and retreat. She looked over her shoulder again, as though seeking permission. Then she nodded.

Noah found himself panicking over the disorder in the front parlor. His mom had been home for only a few hours that afternoon, to comfort him and cook dinner. Then she'd driven back to the hospital to see Taylor. No one had tidied up the parlor, and everything was still lying where Noah had dropped it that afternoon – backpack on the couch, sweatshirt on the coffee table, dirty tennis shoes in front of the fireplace. He decided to bypass the parlor and led Amelia into the kitchen instead.

They sat down, not looking at each other, two foreign species struggling to find a common language.

She glanced up as the phone rang. 'Aren't you going to answer that?'

'Naw. It's another one of those reporters. They've been calling all afternoon, ever since I got home.'

The answering machine picked up, and as he'd predicted, a woman's voice came on: 'This is Damaris Horne of the *Weekly Informer*. I'd really, really like to talk to Noah Elliot, if I could, about that amazing act of heroism today in the classroom.

The whole country wants to hear about it, Noah. I'll be staying at the Lakeside B and B, and I could offer some financial compensation for your time, if that would make it more worth your while . . .'

'She's offering to pay you just to talk?' asked Amelia.

'Crazy, isn't it? My mom says it's a sure sign I *shouldn't* talk to that lady.'

'But people do want to hear about it. About what you did.'

What I did.

He gave a shrug, feeling unworthy of all the praise, of Amelia's praise, most of all. He sat listening as the call ended. The silence returned, interrupted only by the soft beep of the message reminder.

'You can open it now. If you want,' said Amelia.

He looked down at the gift. Though the wrapping was plain brown paper, he took great effort not to tear it, because it seemed uncouth to go ripping it open in front of her. Gingerly he peeled off the tape and folded back the wrapping.

The pocket knife was neither large nor impressive. He saw scratches on the handle, and realized it was not even new. She'd given him a used knife.

'Wow,' he managed to say with some measure of enthusiasm. 'This is a nice one.'

'It belonged to my dad.' She added, quietly: 'My real dad.'

He looked up as the implication of those words sank in.

110

'Jack is my stepfather.' She uttered that last word as though it were an object of disgust.

'Then J.D. and Eddie . . .'

'They're not my real brothers. They're Jack's boys.'

'I guess I wondered about it. They don't look like you.'

'Thank god.'

Noah laughed. 'Yeah, that's not a family resemblance I'd want to have, either.'

'I'm not even allowed to talk about my real dad, because it makes Jack mad. He hates to be reminded there was someone else before him. But I want people to know. I want them to know Jack has nothing to do with who I am.'

Gently he placed the knife back in her hand. 'I can't take this, Amelia.'

'I want you to.'

'But it's got to mean a lot to you, if it belonged to him.'

'That's why I want you to have it.' She touched the bandage on her temple, as though pointing to the evidence of her debt to him. 'You were the only one who did anything. The only one who didn't run.'

He didn't confess the humiliating truth: *I wanted to run, but I was so terrified I couldn't move my legs*.

She looked up at the kitchen clock. With a start of panic, she abruptly stood up. 'I didn't know it was so late.'

He followed her to the front door. Amelia had

just stepped out when headlights suddenly cut through the trees. She spun around to face them, and then seemed to freeze as the pickup truck roared up the driveway.

The door swung open and Jack Reid stepped out, whippet thin and scowling. 'Get in the truck, Amelia,' he said.

'Jack, how did you –'

'Eddie told me you'd be here.'

'I was just about to walk home.'

'Get in the truck *now*.'

Instantly she clammed up and obediently slid into the passenger seat.

Her stepfather was about to climb back behind the wheel when he met Noah's gaze.

'She doesn't hang out with boys,' he said. 'I want you to know that.'

'She only came by to say hello,' said Noah angrily. 'What's the big deal?'

'The deal, boy, is that my daughter's off limits.' He climbed in and slammed the door.

'She's not even your daughter!' Noah yelled, but he knew the man couldn't hear him over the revving engine.

As the truck swung around in the driveway, Noah caught one last glimpse of Amelia's profile, framed by the passenger window, her terrified gaze focused straight ahead.

6

The first snowflakes spiraled down through the bare branches and gently dusted the excavation site. Lucy Overlock glanced up at the sky and said, 'This snow's going to stop, isn't it? It has to stop, or it'll obscure everything.'

'It's already melting,' said Lincoln. He sniffed the air and knew, by some instinct developed during a lifetime in these woods, that the snow would not last long. These flakes were merely a whispered warning, deceptively gentle, of the wintry months to come. He did not mind the snow, did not even resent all the inconveniences that came with it, the shoveling, the plowing out, the nights without power when the lines went down from the weight of it. It was the darkness he disliked. Darkness fell so early these days. Already daylight was fading, and the trees were featureless black slashes against the sky.

'Well, we might as well pack it up for the day,' said Lucy. 'And hope it's not buried under a foot of snow by tomorrow.'

Now that the bones were no longer of interest to the police, Lucy and her grad students had assumed the responsibility of protecting the dig. The two students pulled a tarp over the excavation site and staked it in place. It was a futile precaution; a marauding raccoon could rip it away with one slash of its claws.

'When will you finish here?' asked Lincoln.

'I'd like to take several weeks,' said Lucy. 'But with the weather turning bad, we'll have to rush. One hard freeze, and that's it for the season.'

Headlights flickered through the trees. Lincoln saw that another vehicle had pulled into Rachel Sorkin's driveway.

He tramped back through the woods, toward the house. In the last few days, the front yard had become a parking lot. Next to Lincoln's vehicle was Lucy Overlock's Jeep and a beat-up Honda, which he assumed belonged to her grad student.

At the far end of the driveway, parked under the trees, was yet another vehicle – a dark blue Volvo. He recognized it, and he crossed the yard to the driver's side.

The window hummed open an inch. 'Lincoln,' the woman said.

'Evening, Judge Keating.'

'You have time to talk?' He heard the locks click open.

Lincoln circled to the passenger side and slid in, shutting the door. They sat for a moment, cocooned in silence.

114

'Have they found anything else?' she asked. She didn't look at him but gazed straight ahead, her eyes focused somewhere among the trees. In the car's gloom, she seemed younger than her sixty-six years, the lines in her face fading to uniform smoothness. Younger and not so formidable.

'There were only the two skeletons,' said Lincoln.

'Both were children?'

'Yes. Dr Overlock estimates their ages at around nine or ten years old.'

'Not a natural death?'

'No. Both deaths were violent.'

There was a long pause. 'And when did this happen?'

'That's not so easy to determine. All they have to go on are some artifacts found with the remains. They've dug up some buttons, a coffin handle. Dr Overlock thinks it's probably part of a family cemetery.'

She took her time absorbing this information. Her next question came out softly tentative: 'So the remains are quite old?'

'A hundred years, more or less.'

She released a deep breath. Was it Lincoln's imagination or did the tension suddenly melt from her silhouette? She seemed to fall almost limp with relief, her head tilting back against the neck rest. 'A hundred years,' she said. 'Then it's nothing to worry about. It's not from –'

'No. It's unrelated.'

She gazed ahead, at the congealing darkness.

'Still, it's such a strange coincidence, isn't it? That very same part of the lake . . .' She paused. 'I wonder if it happened in the fall.'

'People die every day, Judge Keating. A century's worth of skeletons – they all have to be buried somewhere.'

'I heard there was a hatchet mark on one of the thigh bones.'

'That's true.'

'It will have people wondering. Remembering.'

Lincoln heard the woman's fear, and he wanted to reassure her, but could not bring himself to make physical contact. Iris Keating was not a touchable woman. Her emotional barrier was so thick, it would not have surprised him to reach out and feel a shell.

He said, 'It was a long time ago. No one remembers.'

'This town remembers.'

'Only a few. The older ones. And they don't want to talk about it any more than you do.'

'Still, it's a matter of public record. And now all those reporters are in town. They'll be asking questions.'

'What happened half a century ago isn't relevant.'

'Isn't it?' She looked at him. 'This is how it began last time. The killings. It started in the fall.'

'You can't interpret every violent act as history repeating itself.'

'But history *is* violence.' Once again, she faced

116

forward, her gaze directed toward the lake. Night had fallen and through the bare trees, the water was only a faint glimmer. 'Don't you feel it, Lincoln?' she asked softly. 'There's something wrong about this place. I don't know what it is, but I've felt it since I was small. I didn't like living here, even then. And now . . .' She reached for the ignition and started the engine.

Lincoln stepped out of the car. 'It's a slippery road tonight. Drive carefully.'

'I will. Oh, and Lincoln?'

'Yes?'

'I'm told there's a new opening in that alcohol rehab program in Augusta. It might be the place for Doreen. If you can talk her into it.'

'I'll try. I just keep hoping that one of these days it'll take.'

He thought he saw pity in her eyes. 'I wish you luck. You deserve a lot better, Lincoln.'

'I'm managing all right.'

'Of course you are.' He realized, then, that it wasn't pity, but admiration he heard in her voice. 'You're one of the few men in this world who would.'

A photo of Mrs Horatio was propped up on the coffin, a picture of her as a young woman of eighteen, smiling, almost pretty. Noah had never thought of his biology teacher as pretty, nor had he imagined her as ever having been young. In his mind, Dorothy Horatio had sprung up on this

117

earth already middle-aged, and now, in death, she would remain eternally so.

Moving with the long line of students, he shuffled dutifully toward the coffin, past the photo of Mrs Horatio in her past incarnation as an actual human female. It was a shock to confront that eerily familiar image of Mrs Horatio before the extra pounds and wrinkles and gray hair. To realize that the photo had been taken when she was not much older than Noah. What happens when we get old? he wondered. Where does the kid part of us go?

He stopped before the coffin. It was closed, which was a mercy; he didn't think he could handle seeing his dead teacher's face. It was terrible enough just to imagine how she must look, hidden beneath that mahogany lid. He had not particularly liked Dorothy Horatio. Not at all, in fact. But today he had met her husband and adult daughter, had seen them both sobbing, their arms flung around each other, and had come to realize a startling truth: that even the Mrs Horatios of this world have people who love them.

In the coffin's polished surface, he could see his own face, bland and composed. Emotions hidden beneath an expressionless mask.

He had not been so composed at the last funeral he'd attended.

Two years ago, he and his mother had stood holding hands as they gazed at his father's coffin. The lid had been left open, so people could gaze down at his gaunt face as they said their good-byes. When the time had come to leave, Noah had refused to go. His mother had tried to lead him away, but he had sobbed: *You can't leave Daddy in there! Go back, go back!*

He blinked and touched his hand to Mrs Horatio's coffin. It was smooth and glossy. Like fine furniture.

Where does the kid part of us go?

He realized that the line ahead of him had vanished, that people behind him were waiting for him to move forward. He continued past the coffin, walked up the aisle, and fled out the mortuary doors.

Outside it was lightly snowing, the cold kiss of flakes soothing to his face. He was relieved none of the reporters had followed him out. All afternoon, they'd chased him around with their tape recorders, wanting just a sentence from the boy who'd courageously wrestled the gun away from the killer. The hero of Knox High School.

What a joke.

He stood across the street from the mortuary, shivering in the gloom as he watched people walk out of the building. They each performed the identical into-the-cold ritual: the appraising glance at the sky, the shudder, the hugging close of one's coat. Just about everyone in town had come to pay their last respects, but he scarcely recognized some of them, so transformed were they by their suits and ties and mourning dresses. No one wearing the usual flannels and jeans. Even Chief Kelly was wearing a suit and tie.

Noah watched as Amelia Reid stepped out the mortuary doors. She was breathing quickly, deeply, and she sagged against the building as though she'd been pursued and was desperately trying to catch her breath.

A car drove by, its tires crunching across the crystalline snow as it passed between them.

Noah called out to her: 'Amelia?'

She looked up, startled, and saw him. She hesitated, glancing up and down the street, as though to assure herself it was safe to proceed. He felt his heart beat faster as she crossed the street to join him.

'Pretty grim in there,' he said.

She nodded. 'I couldn't listen to it anymore. I didn't want to start crying in front of everyone.'

Neither did I, he thought, but would never admit it.

They stood together in the gloom, not looking at each other, both of them moving their feet to stay warm. Both of them searching for some thread of conversation. He took a deep breath and said, suddenly, 'I hate funerals. They remind me of . . .' He stopped.

'They remind me of my dad's funeral, too,' she said softly. And she looked up as snowflakes spiraled down from the darkening sky.

*   *   *

Warren Emerson walked on the side of the road, his boots crunching the frost-stiffened grass. He wore a blaze-orange vest and an orange cap, yet he couldn't help flinching every time another gun went off in the woods. Bullets, after all, were colorblind. It was cold this morning, far colder than yesterday, and his fingers ached in their thin woolen gloves. He shoved his hands into his pockets and kept trudging, not worried about the cold, knowing that in another mile he would cease to notice it.

He had walked this road over a thousand times, in every season of the year, and could trace his progress by the landmarks he passed. The toppled stone wall was four hundred paces from his front yard. The Murrays' tumbledown barn was nine hundred fifty paces. At two thousand paces, the turnoff to Toddy Point Road, he reached the halfway mark. The landmarks became more frequent as he approached the outskirts of town. So did the traffic, every so often a car or truck rattling by, tires spitting up dirt.

Local drivers seldom stopped to offer Warren a ride into town. In the summertime he caught plenty of rides, from tourists who considered Warren Emerson, shuffling along in his boots and baggy trousers, an example of living, breathing local color. They'd pull over and invite him to climb in for a lift. During the drive they'd ply him with an endless stream of questions, always the same ones: 'What do you folks do in the winter?' 'You lived here all your life?' 'You ever met Stephen

121

King?' Warren's answers never went beyond a simple yes or no, an economy of words which the tourists invariably found amusing. They'd pull into town, let him off at the general store, and wave so sincerely you'd think they were saying good-bye to their best friend. Wicked friendly people, those tourists; every autumn, he was sorry to see them go, because it meant another nine months of walking down this road, with not a single driver who'd stop for him.

The townspeople were all afraid.

Were he licensed to drive, he often thought, he would not be so unsympathetic to an old man. But Warren could not drive. He had a perfectly fine old Ford gathering dust in the barn – his father's car, a 1945, scarcely driven – yet Warren could not use it. A danger to himself and to others. That's what the doctors had said about his driving.

So the Ford stayed in the barn, over fifty years now, and it was as shiny as the day his father had parked it there. Time was kinder to chrome than it was to a man's face. To a man's heart. *I am a danger to myself and to others.*

His hands at last were starting to feel warm.

He pulled them from his pockets and swung his arms as he walked, heart pumping faster, sweat gathering under his cap. Even on the most frigid of days, if he walked fast enough, far enough, the cold would cease to matter.

By the time he reached town, he'd unbuttoned his coat and removed the cap. When he walked into Cobb and Morong's General Store, he found it almost unbearably hot inside.

As soon as the door swung shut behind him, the store seemed to fall silent. The clerk looked up, then looked away. Two women standing by the vegetable bin ceased their chatter. Though no one was staring, he could feel their attention focused on him as he picked up a shopping basket and walked up the aisle, toward the canned goods. He filled his basket with the same items he bought every week. Cat food. Chili with beef. Tuna. Corn. He went down the next row for the dried beans and oatmeal, then to the vegetable bin for a sack of onions.

He carried the basket, now heavy, to the checkout counter.

The cashier avoided looking at him as she tallied up the items. He stood before the register, his blaze orange vest screaming out to the world, *Look at me, look at me*. Yet no one did. No one met his gaze.

In silence he paid the cashier, picked up the plastic grocery sacks, and turned to leave, steeling himself for the long walk home. At the door, he stopped.

On the newsstand was this week's issue of the *Tranquility Gazette*. There was one copy left. He stared at the headline and suddenly the grocery sacks slipped out of his grasp and thudded to the floor. With shaking hands he reached for the newspaper.

HIGH SCHOOL SHOOTING LEAVES TEACHER DEAD, TWO

STUDENTS WOUNDED: 14-YEAR-OLD BOY ARRESTED.

'Hey! You gonna pay for that paper?' the clerk called out.

Warren didn't answer. He just stood by the door, his eyes fixed in horror on a second headline, almost lost in the bottom right corner: YOUTH BEATS PUPPY TO DEATH: CITED FOR CRUELTY.

And he thought: *It's happening again.*

Damaris Horne was stuck in purgatory, and all she could think about was how to get back to Boston. So this is how my editor punishes me, she thought. We get into a tiff, and he assigns me to the story no one else wants. Welcome to Hicksville-by-the-Lake, otherwise known as Tranquility, Maine. Good name. The place was so tranquil, they should issue it a death certificate. She drove up Main Street, thinking that this was the perfect model for how a town would look after a neutron bomb hit it: no people, no signs of life, just standing buildings and deserted sidewalks. Nine hundred ten residents supposedly lived in this town, so where were they all? In the woods, gnawing lichen off the trees?

She drove past Monaghan's Diner, and through the front window she caught a glimpse of a plaid shirt. Yes! A sighting of the local natives in their ceremonial dress. (What was the mystical significance of plaid, anyway?) Further up the street, she had another sighting: a shabbily dressed old geezer came out of Cobb and Morong's, clutching his grocery sacks. She stopped to let him cross the street, and he shuffled past, head bent in a look of permanent weariness. She watched him walk along the lakeshore, a slow-moving silhouette laboring across a bleak backdrop of bare trees and gray water.

She drove on, to the Lakeside Bed and Breakfast, her home for the indefinite future. It was the only local inn still open this late in the year, and although she sneeringly referred to it as the Bates Motel, she knew she was lucky to have found any room at all, what with the other regional reporters arriving in town.

She walked into the dining room and saw that most of her competition were still stuffing themselves at the breakfast buffet. Damaris always skipped breakfast, which put her ahead of the game this morning. It was eight A.M., and she'd already been up for two and a half hours. At six, she'd been at the hospital to observe the boy being transferred out to his new home, the Maine Youth Center. At seven-fifteen, she'd driven over to the high school. There she'd sat in her parked car and watched the kids in their baggy clothes gather in front of the building, waiting for first bell, looking like teenagers everywhere.

Damaris crossed to the coffee pot and poured herself a cup. Sipping it black, she glanced around the room at the other reporters until her gaze settled on the freelancer, Mitchell Groome. Though he couldn't be much older than forty-five, Groome's face was all sad droops, like a hound in mourning. Still, he seemed fit enough – perhaps even athletic. Best of all, he had noticed her gaze, and was looking back at her, albeit with puzzlement.

She set down her empty cup and strolled out of the dining room, knowing, without even a backward glance, that Groome was watching her.

Hicksville had just gotten a little more interesting.

Up in her room, she took a few minutes to review her notes from the interviews she'd conducted over the last few days. Now came the hard part – putting it all together in an article that would make her editor happy and catch the eyes of bored New England housewives cruising past the tabloid stands.

She sat at her desk and stared out the window, wondering how to turn this tragic but nonetheless commonplace tale into something a little more titillating. What made this case special? What new angle would entice a reader to reach for a copy of the *Weekly Informer?*

She suddenly realized she was staring straight at it.

Across the street was a rundown old building, the windows boarded up. The faded sign said Kimball's Furniture.

The address was 666.

The sign of the Beast.

As her laptop computer powered up, she quickly shuffled through her notes, searching for the quote she remembered from yesterday. Something a woman had said in the local grocery store.

She found it. 'I know the explanation for what happened at the school,' the woman had said. 'Everyone knows it, but no one wants to admit it. They don't want to sound superstitious or uneducated. But I'll tell you what it is: it's this new Godlessness. People have pushed the Lord out of their lives. They've replaced Him with something else. Something no one dares speak of.'

Yes! thought Damaris, and she was grinning as she began to type.

'Last week, Satan arrived in the bucolic town of Tranquility, Maine . . .'

Sitting in her wheelchair before the living room window, Faye Braxton watched her thirteen-year-old son step off the school bus and begin to hike up the long dirt driveway to the house. It was a daily event she usually looked forward to, seeing Scotty's slight figure at last emerge through the bus doors, his shoulders weighed down by the heavy backpack, his head craned forward with the effort to lug his burden of books up the weedy and sloping front yard.

He was still so small. It pained her to see how little he had grown in the last year. While many of his classmates had shot past him in both height and bulk, there was her Scotty, left behind in pale adolescence, and so anxious to grow up he had nicked his chin last week while trying to shave his nonexistent beard. He was her firstborn, her best friend. She wouldn't have minded at all if time suddenly stood still, and she could keep him as he'd always been, a sweet and loving child. But she knew the child would soon be gone.

The transformation had already begun.

She'd seen the first hint of it a few days ago, when he had stepped off the bus as usual. She'd been at the window, watching him walk toward the house, when she saw something happen that was both inexplicable and frightening. In the front yard, he had suddenly halted and gazed up at a tree in which three gray squirrels perched. She'd thought he was merely curious. That like his younger sister Kitty, he would try to coax them down to be petted. So she was startled when he bent down, picked up a rock, and flung it at the tree.

The squirrels scampered to higher branches.

As she'd watched in dismay, Scotty had hurled another rock, and another, his thin body winding up like a tautly coiled spring of fury, the stones flying into the branches. When at last he stopped, he was breathing hard and exhausted. Then he'd turned to the house.

The look on his face had made her jerk back from the window. For one horrifying moment she'd thought: *That is not my son.*

Now, as she watched him approach the house, she wondered which boy would step through the door. Her son, her *real* son, sweet and smiling, or the ugly stranger who looked like Scotty? In the past, she would have dealt firmly with him for throwing rocks at animals.

In the past, she was never afraid of her own child.

Faye heard Scotty's footsteps on the porch. Heart pounding, she swiveled her wheelchair around to face him as he came in the door.

7

Anyone could see that fourteen-year-old Barry Knowlton was his mother's child. The resemblance was startling enough to take in with a single glance. Barry and Louise were like a pair of cheerful dumplings, both of them red-haired and apple-cheeked, both with pliant pink mouths. Their smiles of greeting promised to dispel even Claire's gloom.

Since the classroom shooting nearly a week ago, Claire had awakened each morning to the awful realization that her move to Tranquility had been a mistake. Only eight months ago, she had arrived here full of confidence, had used most of her savings to buy a medical practice she was certain would succeed. And why wouldn't it? She'd had a thriving practice in Baltimore. But one very public lawsuit would destroy everything.

Every day at work, when she saw the mailman stride up the front walk, she braced herself for the delivery of a letter she dreaded receiving.

Paul Darnell had said she'd be hearing from his attorney, and she had no doubt he'd follow up on his threat.

Is it too late to leave? That was the question she asked herself every day now. *Is it too late to move back to Baltimore?*

She forced herself to smile as she stepped into the exam room to see Barry and his mother. Here, at least, was a bright spot in her day.

They both looked genuinely pleased to see her. Barry had already pulled off his boots and was standing on the scale, watching expectantly as the counterweight arm bobbed up and down.

'Hey, I think I lost another pound!' he announced.

Claire checked the chart, then glanced at the reading. 'Down to two hundred forty-seven pounds. That's two pounds you've lost. Good for you!'

Barry stepped off the scale, which sent the counterweight tilting up with a loud clap. 'I think my belt feels looser already!'

'Let me listen to your heart,' said Claire.

Barry waddled over to the exam table, carefully climbed up onto the footstool, and plopped onto the table. He peeled off his shirt, baring folds of pale and sagging flesh. As Claire listened to his heart and lungs and took his blood pressure, she felt his gaze, curious and engaged, following her every move. The first time they'd met, Barry had told her he wanted to be a doctor, and he seemed to relish these bimonthly visits as field trips into his future profession. The occasional blood test, an ordeal for most patients, was a fascinating procedure for Barry, an opportunity to ask in sometimes endless detail about needle gauges and syringe volumes and the purpose of each different colored blood tube.

If only Barry would pay as much attention to what he put in his mouth.

She finished her exam, then stood back and regarded him for a moment. 'You're doing a good job, Barry. How is the diet coming?'

He gave a shrug. 'Okay, I guess. I'm trying real hard.'

'Oh, he loves to eat! That's the problem,' said Louise. 'I try my best cooking low-fat meals. But then his daddy comes home with a box of doughnuts and, well . . . it's so hard to resist. It just about breaks my heart to see the way Barry looks at us, with those big hungry eyes of his.'

'Could you discourage your husband from bringing home doughnuts?'

'Oh, no. Mel, he's got this . . .' She leaned forward and said, confidentially: 'Overeating problem.'

'Is that so?'

'I gave up on Mel long ago. But Barry, he's still so young. It's not good for a boy his age to carry around all that weight. And the other kids, they can be so mean about it.'

Claire looked sympathetically at Barry. 'You're having problems at school?'

A light seemed to dim in the boy's eyes. He

looked down, all cheerfulness gone. 'I don't much like school anymore.'

'The other kids tease you?'

'They don't ever *stop* with the fat boy jokes.'

Claire glanced at Louise, who shook her head sadly. 'He has an IQ of a hundred thirty-five, and he doesn't want to go to school. I don't know what to do about it.'

'I'll tell you what, Barry,' said Claire. 'We're going to show everyone how determined you are. You're too intelligent to let those other kids defeat you.'

'Well, they aren't all that bright,' he agreed hopefully.

'You have to outsmart your own body as well. That's the part that takes effort. And Mom and Dad have to work with you, not against you.' She looked at Louise. 'Mrs Knowlton, you have a smart and wonderful boy here, but he can't do this alone. This takes the whole family.'

Louise sighed, already preparing for the daunting task ahead. 'I know,' she said. 'I'll talk to Mel. No more doughnuts.'

After the Knowltons left, Claire walked into Vera's office. 'Don't we have a patient at three o'clock?'

'We did,' said Vera, looking puzzled as she hung up the phone. 'That was Mrs Monaghan. It's the second cancellation we've had today.'

Claire glimpsed movement in the waiting room. Through the sliding business window, she saw a man sitting on the couch. Large, homely, his sad-clown face emphasized by an unflattering crewcut, he looked as if he'd rather be anywhere else than in a doctor's office. 'Well, who's that?'

'Oh, he's just some magazine reporter who wants to talk to you. His name's Mitchell Groome.'

'I hope you told him I'm not available.'

'I gave him your standard "no comment" line. But this guy insists on waiting around for you.'

'Well, he can wait all he wants. I'm not talking to any more reporters. Is there anyone left on the schedule?'

'Elwyn Clyde. Wound check on his foot.'

Elwyn. Claire pressed her hand to her head, already anticipating a headache. 'Do we have air freshener on hand?'

Vera laughed and clapped a can of Glade on the desk. 'We're all ready for Elwyn. After him, you're free for the day. Which works out well, because you have a meeting with Dr Sarnicki this afternoon. He just called a little while ago.'

Dr Sarnicki was chief of staff at the hospital. This was the first Claire had heard about any meeting.

'Did he say what it's about?'

'Something about a letter he just received. He said it was urgent.' Vera's gaze suddenly shot to the front window and she jumped to her feet. 'Damn it, there they are again!' she said, and dashed out the side door.

Claire looked out the window to see Vera, all flashing bangles and earrings, shaking her fist at two boys with skateboards. One of the boys was yelling back at her now, his voice cracking in adolescent outrage.

'We didn't do anything to your stupid car!'

'Then who left that giant scratch on the door, huh? Who?' demanded Vera.

'Why're you always blaming us? Like kids are always the ones who get dumped on!'

'I see you here again, I'm calling the police!'

'This is a public sidewalk! We gotta right to skate here!'

A tapping on glass drew Claire's attention. Mitchell Groome's hang-dog face was gazing at her through the receptionist's window.

She slid the window open. 'Mr Groome, I'm not talking to any reporters.'

'I just wanted to tell you something.'

'If it's about Taylor Darnell, you can talk to Dr Adam DelRay. He's the boy's physician now.'

'No, it's about your receptionist's car. The one that got scratched. Those boys out there didn't do it.'

'How do you know?'

'I saw it happen yesterday. Some old woman scraped past it with her car. I assumed she was going to leave a note on the windshield. Obviously she didn't, and I think your receptionist has already reached her own conclusions.' He glanced out the window, at the argument raging outside, and he shook his head. 'Why do we always treat kids like the enemy?'

'Because they so often behave like an alien species?'

He gave her a sympathetic smile. 'Spoken like someone who has an alien living in the house.'

'Fourteen years old. You can probably tell by all the gray hairs on my head.' They regarded each other for a moment through the window.

'Are you sure you won't talk to me?' he asked. 'It would just be for a few minutes.'

'I can't discuss my patients. It's a confidentiality issue.'

'No, I'm not going to ask about Taylor Darnell specifically. I'm after more general information, about the other kids in town. You're the only doctor in Tranquility, and I assume you have a good idea of what's going on around here.'

'I've only been in town eight months.'

'But you'd be aware of drug abuse among the local kids, wouldn't you? It could explain the boy's behavior.'

'I hardly think one incident, tragic as it was, means that this town has a drug problem.' Her gaze suddenly focused on the view through the front window. The boys with the skateboards were gone. The mail carrier had arrived, and was chatting with Vera on the sidewalk. He handed Vera an armful of mail. Was there a letter from Paul Darnell's attorney in that stack?

Groome said something, and she realized he had moved closer, and was practically leaning through the open business window.

'Let me tell you a story, Dr Elliot. It's about a perfect little town called Flanders, Iowa. Population four thousand. A clean, decent place where everyone knows everyone else. The sort of people who go to church and join the PTA. Four murders later – all of them committed by teenagers – the shell-shocked residents of Flanders finally got around to facing up to reality.'

'Which was?'

'Methamphetamine. An epidemic of abuse in the local schools. It turned that town into the dark side of America.'

'But what does that have to do with Tranquility?'

'Haven't you been reading your own newspaper? Look around at what's happening to your neighbors. First, there was that street brawl on Halloween night. Then a boy beats his dog to death, and fistfights are breaking out in the school. Finally, there's the shooting.'

She was focused on the front sidewalk again, where the mailman was still shooting the breeze with Vera. *For heaven's sakes, bring in the mail!*

'I followed the Flanders story for months,' said Groome. 'I watched that town implode on itself. Parents blaming the schools. Kids turning on their teachers, on their own families. When I heard about the problems in your town, methamphetamine was the first thing I thought of. I know you must have run a drug screen on that Darnell boy. Could you just tell me one thing: Did methamphetamine turn up in his system?'

Still distracted, she answered: 'No, it didn't.'

'Did anything else?'

She didn't answer. In truth, she didn't know, because she hadn't heard back from the lab in Boston.

'Then there *was* something,' he said, picking up on her silence.

'I'm not the boy's physician. You have to ask Dr DelRay.'

Groome gave a dismissive snort. 'DelRay says it's Ritalin withdrawal psychosis. Something so rare, there's only a few anecdotal reports that it even exists.'

'You don't accept his diagnosis?'

He looked her straight in the eye. 'Don't tell me you do?'

She was beginning to like Mitchell Groome.

The front door opened and Vera stomped in, carrying the mail. Unceremoniously she dumped the whole pile on her desk. Claire eyed the stack of business-size envelopes, and her throat went dry.

'Excuse me,' she said to Groome. 'I have work to do.'

'Flanders, Iowa. Just keep it in mind,' he said, and with a wave, walked out of the building.

Claire picked up the mail, headed straight to her office, and shut the door.

Sitting at her desk, she swiftly shuffled through the envelopes, then sank back with a sigh of relief. Another day's reprieve; no attorney's name was on any of the return addresses. Maybe Paul Darnell had been bluffing; maybe there would be no repercussions after all.

For a moment she sat with her head tilted back, her tension melting. Then she reached for the first envelope and tore it open. Seconds later she was sitting up, rigid, in her chair.

Inside was a short note from Rachel Sorkin, the woman who'd reported Elwyn Clyde's gunshot wound.

Dr Elliot,
   This letter came in my mail today. I thought you should know about it.

Rachel.
   P.S. I don't believe a word of it.

Attached to it was a typewritten letter:

To whom it may concern,
   I am writing to inform you of a disturbing incident. On November third, Dr Claire Elliot assaulted a hospital patient. Although there were a number of witnesses, this event has not been made public. If Dr Elliot is your physician, you may wish to reconsider your options. Patients have a right to know.

A concerned health care professional

There were three men waiting for her in the medical staff office. She knew Dr Sarnicki only slightly, but her impressions of him had been favorable. A comfortably rumpled man with a gentle voice, he was known to be a caring physician as well as a skillful diplomat who had helped ease tensions during the hospital's recent contract negotiations with the nurses. The second man was Roger Hayes, the hospital administrator, whom she scarcely knew at all except as a bland and smiling man.

The third man she knew only too well. It was Adam DelRay.

They greeted her with polite nods as she sat down at the conference table. She was already strung so tight she felt close to snapping in two. On the table in front of Sarnicki was a copy of the same anonymous letter that Rachel had forwarded to her.

'You've seen this already?' he said.

She gave a grim nod. 'One of my patients sent me a copy. I've called around, and so far I've confirmed that at least six others have received it.'

'Mine arrived in the departmental mail this morning.'

'This has been blown completely out of proportion,' said Claire. 'I certainly did not assault the patient. The letter's designed to do only one thing, and that's to damage my reputation.' She looked directly at Adam DelRay. He returned her gaze without flinching, without even a flicker of guilt in his eyes.

'What exactly happened on November third?' asked Hayes.

She answered evenly: 'I drew blood from Taylor Darnell, to send off for a comprehensive drug and tox screen. I've already told Dr Sarnicki who else was in the room. Who witnessed it. I didn't abuse the patient. It was just a blood draw.'

'Tell them the rest,' said DelRay. 'Or are you going to leave out the most important detail? Which is, you had no authority to draw his blood.'

'So why did you?' asked Hayes.

'The boy had a drug-induced psychosis. I wanted that drug identified.'

'There is no drug,' said DelRay.

'You don't know that,' she said. 'You never ran the test.'

'There is no drug.' He slapped a sheet of paper on the table. She stared in dismay at the letterhead: Anson Biologicals.

'I have the results right here. Apparently, Dr Elliot managed to get a blood tube out to the reference lab without the father's knowledge. Or permission. Anson faxed the report to the hospital this morning.' He added, with a note of smugness, 'It's negative. No drugs, no toxins.'

Why had the lab disregarded her instructions? Why had they sent the report to the hospital?

She said, 'Our own lab found an unidentified peak on gas chromatography. There *was* something in his blood.'

DelRay laughed. 'Have you seen our lab's gas

chromatography machine? It's an antique. A hand-me-down from Eastern Maine Medical Center. You can't trust our results.'

'But it did need a followup test.' She looked at Sarnicki. 'That's why I drew the blood. Because Adam refused to.'

'She made an unauthorized blood draw,' said DelRay.

Hayes sighed. 'It's a mountain out of a molehill, Adam. The boy wasn't harmed, and he's doing fine at the Youth Center.'

'She ignored the father's wishes.'

'But one blood draw does not make a lawsuit.'

Claire's chin snapped up in alarm. 'Is Paul Darnell talking about legal action?'

'No, not at all,' said Hayes. 'I spoke to him this morning, and he reassured me he wasn't suing anyone.'

'I'll tell you why he's not suing,' said DelRay. 'It's because that ex-wife of his threatened to sabotage any lawsuit. It's an automatic reflex for bitter ex-wives. Whatever the husband wants, the wife blindly opposes.'

Thank you, Wanda, thought Claire.

'Then this whole incident is now a nonissue,' said Sarnicki, looking relieved. 'As far as I can see, no action is necessary.'

'What about the letter?' said Claire. 'Someone is trying to ruin my practice.'

'I'm not sure what we can do about an anonymous letter.'

'It's signed "A health care professional."' She looked pointedly at DelRay.

'Now wait a *minute*,' he snapped. 'I had nothing to do with it.'

'Paul Darnell, then,' she said.

'There were a couple of nurses who were there too, remember? In fact, this sort of sneaky letter is more a woman's style.'

'What the hell does that mean?' she shot back in outrage. '"A woman's style?"'

'I'm just calling it as I see it. Men are upfront about these things.'

Sarnicki warned, 'Adam, this isn't helping.'

'I think it is helping,' said Claire. 'It shows us exactly what he thinks about women. Are you implying, Adam, that we're all liars?'

'Now this really isn't helping,' said Sarnicki.

'She's putting words in my mouth! I didn't send those letters, and neither did Paul! Why should we? Everyone in town's already heard the gossip!'

'I'm cutting off this meeting *now*,' said Sarnicki, banging on the table for silence.

That's when they all heard the announcement over the hospital address system. It was barely audible through the closed doors of the meeting room.

'Code blue, ICU. Code blue, ICU.'

Instantly Claire shot to her feet. She had a stroke patient in the ICU.

She bolted out of the meeting room and ran for

the stairwell. Two flights up, she stepped into the intensive care unit and was relieved to see that her patient was not the one being coded. The crisis was in cubicle six, where a crowd of personnel had massed around the doorway.

They parted to let Claire enter.

The first thing she noticed was the smell. It was the odor of smoke and singed hair, and it came from the massive, soot-streaked man lying in the bed. McNally from the ER was crouched behind the patient's head, trying without success to insert an endotracheal tube. Claire looked up at the heart monitor.

The rhythm was sinus bradycardia. The patient's heart was beating, but slowly.

'Does he have a blood pressure?' she asked.

'I think I'm getting a systolic of ninety,' said a nurse. 'He's so big, I'm having trouble hearing it.'

'I can't get him intubated!' said McNally. 'Go ahead, bag him again.'

The respiratory tech clapped an oxygen mask on the patient's face and squeezed the reservoir bag, forcing oxygen into the lungs.

'His neck's so short and fat I can't even see the vocal cords,' said McNally.

'Anesthesia's coming in from home,' a nurse said. 'Should I also call a surgeon?'

'Yeah, call him. This one's gonna need an emergency tracheotomy.' He looked at Claire. 'Unless you think you can intubate him.'

She doubted she could, but she was willing to try.

Heart pounding, she circled around to the patient's head and was about to insert the laryngoscope into his mouth when she noticed the man's eyelids were flickering.

She straightened in surprise. 'He's conscious.'

'What?'

'I think he's awake!'

'Then why isn't he breathing?'

'Bag him again!' said Claire, stepping aside to let the respiratory tech back in. As the mask was replaced, as more oxygen was forced into the man's lungs, Claire swiftly reviewed the situation. The man's eyelids were indeed twitching, as though he was struggling to open them. Yet he was not breathing, and his limbs remained flaccid.

'What's the history?' she asked.

'Came in through the ER this afternoon,' said McNally. 'He's a volunteer fireman who collapsed at the scene. We don't know if it was smoke inhalation or a cardiac event – they had to drag him out of the building. We admitted him for superficial burns and a possible MI.'

'He's been doing fine up here,' an ICU nurse said. 'In fact, he was talking to me just a little while ago. I gave him his dose of gentamicin and he suddenly went bradycardic. That's when I realized he'd stopped breathing.'

'Why's he getting gentamicin?' asked Claire.

'The burns. One of the wounds got pretty contaminated.'

'Look, we can't keep bagging him all night,' said McNally. 'Did you call the surgeon?'

'Done,' a nurse answered.

'Then let's get him prepped for the tracheotomy.'

Claire said, 'He may not need one, Gordon.'

McNally looked skeptical. 'I couldn't get that ET tube in. Can you?'

'Let's try something else first.' Claire turned to the nurse. 'Give him an amp of calcium chloride, IV.'

The nurse glanced questioningly at McNally, who shook his head in puzzlement.

'Why on earth are you giving calcium?' he asked.

'Just before he stopped breathing,' said Claire, 'he got the antibiotic, right?'

'Yeah, for the open burn wound.'

'Then he had the respiratory arrest. But he *hasn't lost consciousness*. I think he's still awake. What does that mean?'

Suddenly McNally understood. 'Neuromuscular paralysis. From the gentamicin?'

She nodded. 'I've never seen it happen, but it's been reported. And it's reversed by calcium.'

'I'm giving the calcium chloride now,' said the nurse.

Everyone watched. The prolonged silence was broken only by the intermittent whoosh of oxygen being bagged through the mask. The patient's eyelids responded first. Slowly they fluttered open, and he looked up, struggling to focus on Claire's face.

'He's moving air!' said the respiratory tech.

Seconds later, the patient coughed, took a noisy breath, and coughed again. He reached up and tried to push away the mask.

'I think he wants to talk,' said Claire. 'Let him speak.'

The patient responded with a look of profound relief as the mask was removed from his face.

'Sir, did you want to say something?' Claire asked.

The man nodded. Everyone leaned forward, eager to hear his first words.

'Please,' he whispered.

'Yes?' prompted Claire.

'Let's not . . . do that . . . again.'

As laughter broke out all around her, Claire patted the man on the shoulder. Then she looked at the nurses. 'I think we can cancel the tracheotomy.'

'I'm glad someone around here still has a sense of humor,' McNally said as he and Claire walked out of the cubicle a few minutes later. 'It's been pretty grim recently.' He paused in the nurses' station and looked at the bank of monitors. 'I don't know where we're going to put anyone else.'

Claire was startled to see eight cardiac rhythms tracing across the screens. She swung around, her gaze sweeping the ICU in disbelief.

147

Every bed was filled.

'What on earth has been going on?' said Claire. 'When I made rounds this morning, there was only my one patient in here.'

'It started on my shift. First a little girl with a skull fracture. Then a wreck up on Barnstown Road. Then some nutty kid sets his house on fire.' McNally shook his head. 'It's been going nonstop in the ER all day, and the patients still keep coming in.'

Over the hospital address system, they heard the page: 'Dr McNally to the ER. Dr McNally to the ER.'

He sighed and turned to leave. 'It must be the full moon.'

Noah shed his jacket and lay it across the boulder. The granite felt warm, a day's worth of sunshine radiating back from the stone. Turning, he squinted across the lake. The afternoon was windless, the water a glassy, brilliant mirror reflecting sky and leafless trees.

'I wish it was summer again,' said Amelia.

He looked up at her. She was perched on the highest rock, chin resting on her blue-jeaned knees. Her blond hair was tucked behind one ear, revealing the streak of healing flesh on her temple. He wondered if she'd have a scar, and almost wished there would be one – just a small scar, so she would never forget him. Every morning, looking in her mirror, she'd see that faint

trace of the bullet and would remember Noah
Elliot.

Amelia tilted her face toward the sun. 'I wish
we could skip winter. Just one winter.'

He clambered up onto her rock and sat down
beside her. Not too close, not too far. Almost, but
not quite, touching. 'I don't know, I'm kind of
looking forward to it.'

'You haven't seen what it's like here.'

'So what is it like?'

She stared across the lake with what was almost
an expression of dread. 'In a few weeks, it'll start
to freeze over. First there'll be patches of ice along
the shore. By December, it'll be frozen all the way
across, thick enough to walk on. That's when it
starts to make these sounds at night.'

'What sounds?'

'Like someone moaning. Like someone in pain.'

He started to laugh, but then she looked at him,
and he fell silent.

'You don't believe me, do you?' she said. 'Sometimes I wake up at night and I think I'm having
a nightmare. But it's just the lake. Making those
horrible sounds.'

'How can it?'

'Mrs Horatio says . . .' She stopped, remembering that Mrs Horatio was dead. She looked back
at the water. 'It's because of the ice. The water
freezes and expands. It's always pushing, pushing
against the banks, trying to escape, but it can't
because it's trapped. That's when you hear the

moaning. It's the pressure building up, building until it can't take any more. Until it finally crushes itself.' She murmured: 'No wonder it makes such terrible sounds.'

He tried to imagine what the lake would look like in January. The snow drifting against the banks, the water turned to a glaring sheet of ice. But today the sun was bright in his eyes, and with the warmth radiating off the stone, the only images that came to mind were of summer.

'Where do the frogs go?' he asked.

She turned to him. 'What?'

'The frogs. And the fish and things. I mean, the ducks all migrate, they get away from here. But what do the frogs do? Do you think they just freeze up like green Popsicles?'

He'd meant to make her laugh, and he was glad to see a smile appear on her face. 'No, they don't become Popsicles, silly. They bury themselves in the mud, way at the bottom.' She picked up a pebble and tossed it into the water. 'We used to have lots and lots of frogs around here. I remember catching bucketfuls of them when I was little.'

'Used to?'

'There aren't so many now. Mrs Horatio says . . .' Again, that pause of remembered loss. Again, that sad sigh before she continued. 'She said that it could be acid rain.'

'But I heard plenty of frogs this summer. I used to sit here and listen to them.'

'I wish I'd known about you then,' she said wistfully.

'I knew about you.'

She looked at him in puzzlement. Reddening, he averted his gaze. 'I used to watch you in school,' he said. 'Every lunchtime in the cafeteria, I'd be looking at you. I guess you didn't notice.'

He felt his face flush hotter, and he stood up, his gaze on the water, avoiding hers. 'You ever go swimming? I used to come here every day.'

'This is where all the kids hang out.'

'So where were you last summer?'

She gave a shrug. 'Ear infection. The doctor wouldn't let me swim.'

'Bummer.'

There was a silence. 'Noah?' she said.

'Yeah?'

'Do you ever feel like . . . not going home?'

'You mean like running away?'

'No, it's more like *staying* away.'

'Staying away from what?'

She didn't answer his question. When he turned to look at her, she had already risen to her feet and was hugging her arms to her chest. 'It's getting cold.'

Suddenly he too noticed the chill. Only the rock retained any warmth, and he could feel it quickly dissipating as the sun dropped behind the trees.

The surface of the water rippled, then flattened to black glass. The lake seemed alive at that moment, a single fluid organism. He wondered if everything she'd said about the lake was true, if it really did moan on winter nights. He supposed it could happen. Water expands as it freezes – a scientific fact. The ice would solidify at the surface first, a fine crust that slowly thickens through the dark months of winter, layer building upon layer. And far below, deep in the bottom mud, the frogs would burrow with nowhere else to go. They would be trapped beneath the ice. Entombed.

Sweat filmed Claire's face as she strained at the oars. She felt them drag evenly through the water, felt the satisfying lurch of the rowboat as it cut across the surface of the lake. Over the months her rowing had grown smoothly efficient. Back in May, when she'd first dipped oars into water, it had been a humbling experience. One or both oars would whip wildly across the water, throwing up spray, or she'd favor one oar over the other and would end up rowing in circles. Control was the key. Power, perfectly balanced. Fluid movements, gliding, not splashing.

She had it down, now.

She rowed to the center of the lake. There she raised the oars, lay them in the boat, and sat back to drift. The sun had just dropped behind the trees, and she knew the sweat would soon feel like rime against her skin, but for these few moments, while she was still flushed from exertion, she enjoyed dusk without noticing its chill. The water rippled, black as oil. On the opposite shore, she saw the lights of houses where suppers were being prepared, where families came together in warm and complete universes. *The way we three used to be when you were alive, Peter. Not shattered, but whole.*

She stared across at the glow of those houses, her longing for Peter suddenly so overwhelming it hurt her to breathe. On summer days, when they had gone rowing in their neighborhood pond, Peter had always been the one to wield the oars. Claire would perch in the bow and admire his graceful rhythm, the way his muscles stood out and his smiling face glowed with perspiration. She'd been the pampered passenger, magically ferried across the water by her lover.

She listened to the ripples slap the hull, and could almost imagine Peter was sitting across from her now, his gaze focused sadly on hers. *You have to learn to row alone, Claire. You must be the one to guide the boat.*

How can I, Peter? I'm already foundering. Someone's trying to drive me from this place. And Noah, our darling Noah, has grown so distant.

She felt tears chilling on her face. Felt his presence so clearly, she thought if she could just reach out, he'd be there. Warm and alive, flesh and blood.

But he wasn't there, and she was alone in the boat.

She continued to drift, nudged toward land by the wind. Overhead the stars grew brilliant. Now the boat slowly rotated and she saw, in the distance, the northern shoreline, where seasonal cottages stood dark and boarded up for the winter.

A sudden splash made her sit up in surprise. Turning, she stared at the nearby shore, and made out a man's silhouette. He was standing on the bank, his thin frame slightly bent, as though peering down at the water. He jerked and lunged sideways. There was another loud splash, and his silhouette dropped from sight. It could be only one person.

Quickly Claire wiped the tears from her face and called out: 'Dr Tutwiler? Are you all right?'

The man's head popped back up into view. 'Who's there?'

'Claire Elliot. I thought you'd fallen in the water.'

He finally seemed to locate her in the gloom and he gave a wave. She had met the wetlands biologist only a few weeks before, soon after he'd moved into the Alford cottage, which he was renting for the month. They'd both been rowing on the lake that morning, and as their boats drifted past each other through the mist, they had waved in greeting. Ever since, whenever she rowed past his cottage, they would say hello. Sometimes he'd bring out jars with the latest addition to his amphibian collection. *The frog dweeb*, Noah called him.

Her boat drifted closer to shore, and she saw Max's glass jars lined up on the bank. 'How is your frog collection coming?' she asked.

'It's getting too cold now. They're all heading for deep water.'

'Have you found any more six-legged specimens?'

'One this week. It really makes me worry about this lake.'

Now her rowboat had reached the shore and bumped up against the mud. Max stood above her, a spindly silhouette, moonlight reflecting off his glasses.

'It's happening in all these northern lakes,' he said. 'Amphibian deformities. A massive die-off.'

'How did the lake samples turn out? The ones you collected last week?'

'I'm still waiting for the results. It can take months.' He paused, glancing around at the sudden sound of chirping. 'What's that?'

Claire sighed. 'My beeper.' She'd almost forgotten it was still clipped to her belt. She saw a local exchange on the luminous readout.

'It's a long row back to your house,' he said. 'Why don't you use my telephone?'

She made the call from his kitchen, the whole time staring at the glass jars sitting on his countertop. These were not cucumbers floating in brine. She picked up a jar and saw an eye staring back at her. The frog was strangely pale, the color of human flesh, mottled with purplish blotches. Both hind legs branched into two, forming four separate flippers. She looked at the label: 'Locust Lake. November 10.' Shuddering, she put down the jar.

On the phone, a woman answered, her voice slurred, obviously drunk. 'Hello? Who's this calling?'

'This is Dr Elliot. Did you page me?' Claire winced as the receiver was slammed down. She heard footsteps, then recognized Lincoln Kelly's voice, speaking to the woman.

'Doreen, can I have my phone?'

'Who are all these women calling you?'

'Give me the phone.'

'You're not sick. Why's the doctor calling?'

'Is that Claire Elliot?'

'Oh, it's *Claire* now. First names!'

'Doreen, I'm going to drive you home in a minute. Now let me speak to her.'

At last he came on the line, sounding embarrassed. 'Claire, are you still there?'

'I'm here.'

'Look, I'm sorry about what just happened.'

'Don't worry about it,' she said, and thought: *You have enough things in your life to worry about.*

'Lucy Overlock suggested I give you a call. She's finished the dig.'

'Any interesting conclusions?'

'I think you've already heard most of it. The burial's at least a hundred years old. The remains were of two children. Both of them had obvious signs of trauma.'

'So it was an old homicide.'

'Apparently. She's presenting the details tomorrow, to her undergraduate class. It may be more than you care to hear, but she thought I should invite you. Since you're the one who found the first bone.'

'Where's the class held?'

'In the museum lab, at Orono. I'm driving there, if you'd care to ride with me. I'll leave around noon.'

In the background, Doreen whined, 'But tomorrow's Saturday! Since when do you work on Saturday?'

'Doreen, let me finish this call.'

'That's how it always is! You're always too busy. Never here for me –'

'Put on your coat, and get in the car. I'll take you home.'

'Hell, I can drive myself.' A door slammed shut.

'Doreen!' said Lincoln. 'Give me back those car keys! Doreen!' His voice came back on the line, hurried. Frantic. 'I have to go. Will I see you tomorrow?'

'Noon. I'll be waiting.'

8

'Doreen tries,' said Lincoln, his gaze fixed on the road. 'She really does. But it's not easy for her.'

'Or for you either, I imagine,' said Claire.

'No, it's been hard all around. It has been for years.'

It had been raining when they left Tranquility. Now the rain was thickening to sleet, and they heard it tick-ticking against the windshield. The road had turned treacherous as the temperature dropped to that dangerous transition between freeze and thaw, the blacktop collecting a frosting of watery ice. She was glad Lincoln was behind the wheel, not her. A man who has lived forty-five winters in this climate knows enough to respect its perils.

He reached down to turn up the defroster and streaks of condensation began to clear from the glass.

'We've been separated two years,' he said. 'The

problem is, she just can't let go. And I don't have the heart to force it.'

They both tensed as the car ahead suddenly braked and began to fishtail, sliding from one side of the road to the other. It barely pulled out of its skid in time to avoid an oncoming truck.

Claire sat back, her heart pounding. 'Jesus.'

'Everyone's driving too damn fast.'

'Do you think we should turn around and go home?'

'We're more than halfway there. Might as well keep going. Or do you want to call it off?'

She swallowed. 'I'm okay with this if you are.'

'We'll just take our time. It means we'll probably be home late.' He glanced at her. 'What about Noah?'

'He's pretty self-sufficient these days. I'm sure he'll be fine.'

Lincoln nodded. 'He seems like a great kid.'

'Yes he is,' she said. And amended her answer with a rueful smile. 'Most of the time.'

'Guess it's not as easy as it looks,' said Lincoln. 'I hear that all the time from parents. That raising a kid is the hardest job in the world.'

'And it's a hundred times harder when you're doing it alone.'

'So where's Noah's dad?'

Claire paused. The answer to that question almost had to be forced out. 'He died. Two years ago.' She barely registered his murmured response of, 'I'm sorry.' For a moment, the only sound was the windshield wiper scraping sleet from the glass. Two years, and she still had trouble talking about it. She still couldn't bring herself to use the word *widow*. Women should not be made widows at the age of thirty-eight.

And laughing, loving, thirty-nine-year-old men should not die of lymphoma.

Through the freezing mist, she saw emergency lights flashing ahead. An accident. Yet she felt strangely safe riding in this man's car. Protected and insulated from harm. They inched past a string of emergency vehicles: two police cruisers, a tow truck, and an ambulance. A Ford Bronco had slid off the road and now lay on its side, glistening with rime. They drove past it in silence, both of them sobered by that stark reminder of how quickly life can be altered. Ended. It was one more gloomy note to an already depressing day.

Lucy Overlock arrived late to her own class. Fifteen minutes after her two graduate and ten undergraduate students stood assembled in the university museum's basement lab, Lucy herself strode in, her slicker dripping. 'With this weather, I probably should have canceled,' she said. 'I'm glad you all made it anyway.' She hung up her rain gear, under which she wore her usual jeans and flannel shirt, practical attire considering their surroundings. The museum basement was both dank and dusty, a cluttered cavern that smelled like the artifacts it contained. Along both walls were shelves lined with hundreds of

160

wooden boxes, contents labeled in faded type-script: 'Stonington #11: shell implements, arrow-heads, miscellaneous.' 'Pittsfield #32: partial skel-etal remains, adult male.'

At the center of the room, on a broad work table draped with a plastic tarpaulin, lay the new additions to this neatly catalogued charnel house.

Lucy flicked on a wall switch. Fluorescent lamps hummed on, their unnatural glare illuminating the table. Claire and Lincoln joined the circle of students. The lights were unforgiving, casting the faces around the table in harsh relief.

Lucy removed the tarp.

The skeletal remains of the two children had been laid out side by side, the bones placed in their approximate anatomical positions. One skeleton was missing its rib cage, one lower leg, and the right upper extremity. The other skeleton appeared to be largely intact except for the missing small bones of the hands.

Lucy took her position at the head of the table, near the skulls. 'What we have here is a sampled assemblage of human remains from dig number seventy-two at the southern end of Locust Lake. The dig was completed yesterday. For reference purposes, I've tacked the site map over there, on the wall. As you can see, the site is located right on the edge of the Meegawki Stream. That area had heavy rains and flooding this past spring, which is probably the reason this gravesite became exposed.' She looked down at the table. 'So, let's begin. First, I want all of you to examine the remains. Feel free to pick them up, look them over carefully. Ask any questions you have about the site. Then let's hear your conclusions as to age, race, and length of burial. Those of you who took part in the dig – please hold your tongues. Let's see what the others can deduce on their own.'

One of the students reached for a skull.

Lucy stepped back and quietly circled the table, sometimes glancing over her students' shoulders to watch them work. This assembly made Claire think of some grotesque dining ritual: the remains laid out like a feast on the table, all those eager hands reaching for the bones, turning them under the light, passing them to other hands. At first there was no conversation, the silence broken only by the occasional whisk of a tape measure being extended, retracted.

One of the skulls, missing its mandible, was handed to Claire.

The last time she'd held a human skull was in medical school. She rotated it beneath the light. Once she could name every foramen, every pro-tuberance, but like so many other facts crammed into her memory during four years of training, those anatomical names had been forgotten, dis-placed by more practical data like billing codes and hospital phone numbers. She turned the skull upside down and saw that the upper teeth were still in place. The third molars had not yet erupted. *A child's mouth*.

Gently she set down the skull, shaken by the reality of what she'd just cradled in her hands. She thought of Noah at age nine, his hair a whorl of dark curls, his face silky smooth against hers, and she stared at that skull of a child whose flesh had long since rotted away.

She was suddenly aware of Lincoln's hand, resting on her shoulder. 'You all right?' he asked, and she nodded. His gaze was sad, almost mournful under the harsh lights. Are we the only ones haunted by this child's life? she wondered. The only ones who see more than an empty shell of calcium and phosphate?

One of the female students, a younger, slimmer version of Lucy, asked the first question. 'Was this a coffin burial? And was the terrain field or woods?'

'The terrain was moderately wooded, all new growth,' answered Lucy. 'We did find iron nails and fragments of the coffin, but the wood was mostly rotted away.'

'And the soil?' a male student asked.

'Clay, moderately saturated. Why do you ask?'

'A high clay content helps preserve remains.'

'Correct. What other factors affect the preservation of remains?' Lucy glanced around the table. Her students responded with an eagerness that struck Claire as almost unseemly. They were so focused on mineralized remains, they had forgotten

163

what these bones represented. Living, laughing children.

'Soil compaction – moisture –'

'Ambient temperature.'

'Carnivores.'

'Depth of burial. Whether it's exposed to sunlight.'

'The age at time of death.'

Lucy's gaze shot to the student who'd spoken. It was the young Lucy clone, also dressed in jeans and a plaid shirt. 'How does the deceased's age affect the bony remains?'

'The skulls of young adults remain intact longer than skulls of elderly people, perhaps because of heavier mineralization.'

'That doesn't tell me how long these particular skeletons have been lying in the ground. When did these individuals die?'

There was silence.

Lucy did not seem disappointed by their lack of response. 'The correct answer,' she said, 'is: We can't tell. After a hundred years, some skeletons may crumble to dust, while others will show almost no weathering. But we can still draw a number of conclusions.' She reached across the table and picked up a tibia. 'Note the flaking and peeling in some of the long bones, where circumferential lamellar bone has natural cleavage lines. What does this indicate to you?'

'Changing wet and dry periods,' said the Lucy clone.

'Right. These remains were temporarily protected by the coffin. But then the coffin rotted, and the bones were exposed to water, especially near that streambed.' She glanced at a young man Claire recognized as one of the grad students who'd helped excavate the site. With his long blond hair tied back in a ponytail, and three gold earrings in one ear, he could easily have passed for a rogue sailor in an earlier century. The one incongruous note to his appearance was his scholarly wire-rim spectacles. 'Vince,' said Lucy, 'tell us about the flood data for that area.'

'I've searched back as far as the records go, to the 1920s,' said Vince. 'There were two episodes of catastrophic flooding: in the spring of 1946, and then again, this past spring, when the Locust River overflowed its banks. I assume that's how this burial site became exposed. Erosion of the Meegawki streambed due to heavy rain.'

'So we have two recorded periods of site saturation, followed by drier years, which have caused this flaking and peeling of cortical bone.' Lucy set down the tibia and picked up the femur. 'And now for the most interesting finding of all. I'm referring to this gash here, on the back of the femoral shaft. It looks like a cut mark, but the bone is so badly weathered, the gash has lost its definition. So we can't tell if there's been a green bone response.' She noticed Lincoln's questioning look. 'A green bone response is what happens when living bone bends or twists while being stabbed. It tells you whether the bone was cut postmortem or antemortem.'

'And you can't tell from this bone?'

'No. It's been exposed too long to the elements.'

'So how can you determine if this was a homicide?'

'We have to turn our attention to the other bones. And here we'll find your answer.' She reached for a small paper bag. Tipping it sideways, she emptied the contents on the table.

Small bones clattered out like gray dice.

'The carpals,' she said. 'These are from the right hand. Carpals are quite dense – they don't disintegrate as quickly as other bones. These were found buried deep and packed in a dense clump of clay, which further preserved them.' She began to shuffle through the carpals like a seamstress searching for just the right button. 'Here,' she said, choosing one pebble and holding it up to the light.

The gash was immediately apparent, and so deep it had nearly cleaved the bone in two.

'This is a defense injury,' said Lucy. 'This child – let's call her a girl – raised her arms to defend herself against her attacker. The blade stabbed her in the hand – deeply enough to almost split the carpal bone. The girl is only eight or nine and rather small in stature, so she can hardly fight back. And whoever plunged that knife in is quite strong – strong enough to stab right through her hand.

166

'The girl turns. Maybe the blade is still lodged in her flesh, or maybe the attacker has pulled it out and is preparing to stab again. The girl would try to run away, but she is pursued. Then she stumbles, or he brings her down, and she falls to the ground, prone. I assume it's prone, because there are cut marks on the thoracic vertebrae, a broad blade, possibly a hatchet, sinking in from behind. There is also the cut mark in the femur – a blow to the back of the thigh, which means she's lying on the ground now. None of these injuries are necessarily fatal. If she is still alive, she's bleeding heavily. What happens next, we don't know, because the bones don't tell us. What we do know is that she is lying face down on the ground and she can't run, she can't defend herself. And someone has just sunk a hatchet or an ax into her thigh.' Gently she placed the carpal bone on the table. It was only the size of a pebble, the broken remnant of a terrible death. 'That's what these bones tell me.'

For a moment no one spoke. Then Claire said, softly: 'What happened to the other child?'

Lucy seemed to rouse herself from a trance, and she looked at the second skull. 'This was a child of similar age. Many of its bones are missing, and those we do have are severely weathered, but I can tell you this much: he – or she – suffered a crushing and probably fatal blow to the skull. These two children were buried together, in the same coffin. I suspect they died during the same attack.'

'There must be records of it,' said Lincoln. 'Some old news account of who these children were.'

'As a matter of fact, we do know their names.' It was Vince talking, the ponytailed grad student. 'Because of the date on a coin found in the same soil stratum, we knew their deaths occurred sometime after 1885. I searched the county deed records and learned that a family by the name of Gow owned that entire tract of land extending along the southern curve of Locust Lake. These bones are the mortal remains of Joseph and Jennie Gow, siblings, ages eight and ten.' Vince gave a sheepish grin. 'It seems that what we've dug up here, folks, is the Gow family cemetery.'

This revelation did not strike Claire as a particularly humorous revelation, and she was disturbed by the fact several of the students laughed.

'Because it was a coffin burial,' explained Lucy, 'we suspected this might be a family cemetery. I'm afraid we've disturbed their final resting place.'

'Then you know how these children died?' asked Claire.

'News accounts are hard to come by, because that particular area was sparsely populated at the time,' said Vince. 'What we do have available are the county death records. The Gow children's deaths were both recorded on the same day: November fifteenth, 1887. Along with the deaths of three other members of their family.'

There was a moment of horrified silence.

'Are you saying all five people died on the *same* day?' asked Claire.

Vince nodded. 'It appears this family was massacred.'

9

Carrot sticks and boiled potatoes and a microscopic sliver of chicken breast.

Louise Knowlton gazed down at the barren plate she'd just set before her son and she ached with maternal guilt. She was starving her own child. She saw it in his face, in those hungry eyes, the weak slump of his shoulders. Sixteen hundred calories a day! How could anyone survive on that! Barry had indeed lost weight, but at what price? He was but a shadow of his formerly robust 265-pound self, and even though she knew he needed to lose weight, it was clear to her, the one person in the world who knew him best, that her darling child was suffering.

She sat down at her own plate, on which she'd piled fried chicken and buttered biscuits. A solid, healthy meal for a cold night. Looking across the table, she met her husband's gaze. Mel was silently shaking his head. He couldn't stand it either, watching their son go hungry.

'Barry, sweetie, why don't you have just one biscuit?' offered Louise.

'No, Mom.'

'It's not so many calories. You can scrape off the gravy.'

'I don't want any.'

'Look how flaky they are! It's that recipe from Barbara Perry's mom. It's the bacon fat that makes them so good. One little bite, Barry. Just try one bite!' She held out a steaming biscuit to his lips. She could not stop herself, could not suppress the impulse, reinforced by fourteen years of motherhood, to feed that pink and needy mouth. This was more than food; this was love, in the shape of a crusty biscuit dripping butter onto her fingers. She waited for him to accept the offering.

'I told you, I don't want any!' he yelled.

It was as shocking as a slap in the face. Louise sat back, stunned. The biscuit tumbled from her fingers and plopped into the lake of gravy glistening on her plate.

'Barry,' said his father.

'She's always shoving food at me! No wonder I look like this! Look at both of you!'

'Your mother loves you. Look how you've hurt her feelings.'

Louise sat with trembling lips, trying not to cry. She gazed down at the bountiful dinner she had set on the table. It represented two hours of work in the kitchen, a labor of love, and oh how she loved her son! Now she saw the meal for what it

171

was: the wasted efforts of a fat and stupid mother. She began to cry, her tears dribbling into the cream cheese mashed potatoes.

'Mom.' Barry groaned. 'Ah geez. I'm sorry.'

'Never mind.' She held up a hand to ward off his pity. 'I understand, Barry. I understand, and I won't do it again. I swear I won't.' She blotted away the tears with the napkin and for a few seconds managed to regain her dignity. 'But I try so hard and – and—' She buried her face in the napkin, her whole body quaking with the effort not to cry. It took a moment for her to realize Barry was talking to her.

'Mom. Mom?'

She gulped in a breath and forced herself to look at him.

'Can I have a biscuit?'

Wordlessly she held out the platter. She watched him take a biscuit, split it open, and slather it with butter. She held her breath as he took the first bite, as the look of bliss rippled across his face. He had craved it all along, but had denied himself the pleasure. Now he gave himself up to it, eating a second. And a third. She watched him take every bite, and she felt a mother's satisfaction, deep and primal.

Noah leaned against the side of the school building, smoking a cigarette. It had been months since he'd last lit up, and it made him cough, his lungs rebelling against the smoke. He imagined all those poisons swirling into his chest, the ones his mom was always lecturing him about, but in the general scheme of his life in this dreary town, he figured a little poison was hardly worth worrying about. He took another drag and coughed some more, not really enjoying the experience. But there wasn't much else to do between classes, not since the skateboards were banned. At least out here, standing alone by the Dumpster, no one would hassle him.

He heard the soft growl of an engine, and he glanced toward the street. A dark green car was creeping by, so slowly it barely seemed to move. The windows were too darkly tinted to see through, and Noah couldn't tell if it was a man or woman behind the wheel.

The car stopped right across the street. Somehow Noah knew the driver was staring at him, just as surely as Noah was staring back.

He dropped the cigarette and quickly crushed it under his shoe. No sense getting caught; the last thing he needed was another detention. The evidence now obliterated, he turned and brazenly faced the unseen driver. He felt a sense of victory when the car drove away.

Noah looked down at the crushed cigarette, only half smoked. What a waste. He was weighing the chances of salvaging what remained when he heard the school bell ring, signaling the end of break.

Then he heard the shouting. It came from the front of the school.

He rounded the corner of the building and saw a crowd of kids milling on the lawn, chanting: 'Cat fight! Cat fight!'

This should be something to see.

He pushed forward, trying to get a peek at the action before the teachers broke it up, and the two battling girls practically flew right into him. Noah stumbled backwards to a safer distance, shocked by the viciousness of the fight. This was worse than any brawl between two boys; this really *was* a cat fight, the girls clawing at each other's faces, yanking at hair. The shouts of the crowd rang in his ears. He looked around at the circle of spectators, and saw their frenzied faces, smelled the blood lust, strong as musk.

A strange excitement coiled inside him. He felt his hand close into a fist, felt heat rush to his face. Both the girls were bloodied now, and the sight of it enthralled him. Provoked him. He pushed forward, jostling with the crowd for a better view, and was angry when he could not get closer.

'Cat fight! Cat fight!'

He began to chant too, his excitement building with every glimpse of a bloodied face.

Then his gaze froze on Amelia, standing at the far edge of the lawn, and instantly he fell silent. She was staring at the crowd in disbelief and horror.

Shamefaced, he turned before she could see him, and he fled into the building.

In the boys' restroom, he stared at himself in

the mirror. *What happened to everyone out there?* he thought. *What happened to me?*

He splashed icy water on his face, and scarcely felt its sting.

'They were fighting over a boy,' said Fern. 'At least, that's the story I got. It started off with a few insults, and the next thing you know, they were clawing each other's faces.' She shook her head. 'After Mrs Horatio's funeral, I was hoping the kids would support each other. Stand by each other. But this is the fourth fight we've had in two days, Lincoln. I can't control them. I need a policeman to stand watch in this school.'

'Well, it seems like overkill,' he responded doubtfully, 'but I can have Floyd Spear drop in a few times during the school day, if you want.'

'No, you don't understand. We need someone here all day. I don't know what else is going to work.'

Lincoln sighed and ran his hand through his hair. It seemed to Fern that he was getting grayer every day, just as she was. This morning, she had noticed the telltale hairs sprouting among her blond ones, had realized that the face she saw in the mirror was that of a middle-aged woman. Seeing the changes in Lincoln's face, though, was somehow more painful than confronting her own aging image, because she carried such vivid memories of the man he'd been at twenty-five: dark-haired, dark-eyed, already a face of strength and character. The days before Doreen caught his eye. She regarded the deepening lines in his face and thought, as she so often did: *I could have made you so much happier than Doreen has.*

Together they walked to her office. Fourth period classes had started, and their footsteps echoed in the empty hallway. A banner sagged overhead: Harvest Dance November 20! From Mr Rubio's classroom came the sound of bored voices raised in unison: *Me llamo Pablo. Te llamas Pablo. Se llama Pablo* . . .

Her office was her private territory, and it reflected the way she lived her life, everything neat and in its place. Books lined up, spines out, no stray papers on the desk. Controlled. Children thrived on order, and Fern believed that only through absolute order could a school function properly.

'I know it's asking for a manpower commitment,' she said, 'but I want you to consider assigning a full-time officer to this school.'

'It means pulling a man off patrol, Fern, and I'm not convinced it's necessary.'

'And what are you patrolling out there? Empty roads! The trouble in this town is right here, in this building. This is where we need a policeman.'

At last he nodded. 'I'll do what I can,' he said, and stood up. His shoulders seemed to sag with the burdens they carried. All day he wrestles with the problems of this town, she thought guiltily, and he gets no praise, only demands and criticism. Then he has no one to go home to, no one to comfort him. A man who makes the mistake of marrying the wrong woman should not have to suffer for the rest of his life. Not a man as decent as Lincoln.

She walked him to the door. They were close enough to touch each other, and the temptation to reach out, to throw her arms around him, was so overwhelming she had to close her hands into fists to resist it.

'I look at what's happening,' she said, 'and I can't help but wonder what I'm doing wrong.'

'You haven't done anything wrong.'

'Six years as principal, and suddenly I'm fighting to keep order in my school. Fighting to keep my job.'

'Fern, I really think it's just a temporary reaction to the shooting. The kids need time to recover.' He gave her shoulder a reassuring pat and he turned to the door. 'It'll pass.'

Once again Claire was staring into Mairead Temple's mouth. It seemed like familiar territory to her now, the furry tongue, the tonsillar pillars, the uvula hanging down in a quivering flap of pink flesh. And that smell, like an old ashtray, the same smell that permeated Mairead's kitchen, where they were now sitting. It was Tuesday, the day Claire made house calls, and Mairead was the next to last patient on her schedule. When one's medical practice is failing, when patients are switching to other doctors, desperate measures are called for. A home visit to Mairead Temple's smoky kitchen qualified as a desperate measure. Anything to keep a patient happy.

Claire turned off her pen light. 'Your throat looks about the same to me. It's just a little red.'

'Still hurts wicked bad.'

'The culture came back negative.'

'You mean I don't get any more penicillin?'

'I'm sorry, but I can't justify it.'

Mairead clacked her dentures together and glared at Claire with pale eyes. 'What kinda treatment is that?'

'Well, I'll tell you, Mairead, the best treatment is prevention.'

'So?'

'So . . .' Claire eyed the pack of menthol cigarettes lying on the kitchen table. In the advertisements, it was a brand usually associated with slim sophisti-cates, women in slinky gowns trailing furs and men. 'I think it's time for you to quit smoking.'

'What's wrong with penicillin?'

Claire ignored the question, turning her atten-tion instead to the wood-burning stove in the center of the overheated kitchen. 'That's not good for your throat, either. It dries out the air and fills it with smoke and irritants. You do have an oil furnace, don't you?'

'Wood's cheaper.'

'You'd feel better.'

'I get the wood free, from my nephew.'

'All right,' sighed Claire. 'So how about just quitting the cigarettes?'

178

'How about the penicillin?'

They looked at each other, budding enemies over a handful of three-buck pills.

In the end, Claire surrendered. She didn't have the stamina for an argument this late in the afternoon, not with someone as mulish as Mairead Temple. *Just this once* was what she told herself as she rummaged for the appropriate antibiotic samples.

Mairead crossed to the woodstove and threw in another log. Smoke puffed out, adding to the general haze hanging over the room.

Even Claire's throat was beginning to feel sore.

Mairead picked up a pair of tongs and poked at the logs on the fire. 'I heard more talk about those bones,' she said.

Claire was still counting out sample tablets. Only when she looked up did she see Mairead was studying her, eyes strangely alert. Feral.

Mairead turned and slapped the stove's cast-iron door shut. 'Old bones, that's what I heard.'

'Yes, they are.'

'How old?' The pale eyes were once again locked on hers.

'A hundred years, maybe more.'

'They sure about that?'

'I believe they're quite sure. Why?'

The unsettling gaze slid away from hers again. 'You never know what goes on around these parts. No big surprise they found the bones on her property. You know what she is, don't you? She's not the only one around here, either. Last Halloween, they lit themselves a big bonfire, over in Warren Emerson's cornfield. That Emerson, he's another one.'

'Another what?'

'What do you call 'em when they're men? A warlock.'

Claire burst out laughing. It was the wrong thing to do.

'You go ask around town,' insisted Mairead, now angry. 'They'll all tell you there was a bonfire up in Emerson's field that night. And right afterwards, those kids caused all that trouble in town.'

'It happens everywhere. Kids always get rowdy on Halloween.'

'It's their holy night. Their black Christmas.'

Looking into the other woman's eyes, Claire realized she didn't like Mairead Temple. 'Everyone is entitled to their beliefs. As long as no one gets hurt.'

'Well, that's the question, isn't it? We just don't know. Look what's happened around here since then.'

Abruptly Claire shut her medical bag and stood up. 'Rachel Sorkin minds her own business, Mairead. I think everyone else in this town should do likewise.'

The bones again, thought Claire as she drove to her last house call of the day. Everyone wants to know about the bones. Whom they belonged to, when they were buried. And today a new question, one that had taken her by surprise: why were they found in Rachel Sorkin's yard.

It's their holy night, their black Christmas.

In Mairead's kitchen, Claire had laughed. Now, driving through the deepening gloom, she found nothing humorous about the conversation. Rachel Sorkin was the outsider, the black-haired woman from away who lived alone by the lake. That's how it had always been through the ages; the young woman alone was an object of suspicion, the subject of gossip. In a small town she is the anomaly that requires explanation. She is the town siren, the irresistible temptation for otherwise virtuous husbands. Or she is the shrew no man wants to marry, or the twisted female with unnatural desires. And if one is also attractive, like Rachel, or exotic, or peculiar of taste and whim, then suspicion is mixed with fascination. Fascination which could turn to obsession for someone like Mairead Temple, who brooded all day in her grim kitchen, smoking cigarettes that promised glamor but delivered bronchitis and yellow teeth. Rachel did not have yellow teeth. Rachel was beautiful and unencumbered and a little eccentric.

Rachel must therefore be a witch.

Since Warren Emerson had lit a bonfire in his cornfield on Halloween night, he must be a witch as well.

Though dusk had not yet fallen, Claire turned on her headlights and drew some measure of reassurance from the glow of her dashboard. This time of year, she thought, brings out irrational fears in all of us. And the season hasn't yet reached its darkest point. As the nights grow longer and the first heavy snows begin to fall, cutting off all access to the outside world, this bleak and lonely landscape becomes our universe. And it's an unforgiving one, where a patch of black ice, and a night's bitter cold, can act as both judge and executioner.

She arrived at a rural mailbox labeled 'Braxton' and turned onto the dirt road. Her patient's house stood surrounded by neglected fields. The clap-boards were stripped bare, the wood weathered to silver. On the front porch, half a cord of firewood was stacked up precariously against the crooked railing. It would all come tumbling down one of these days – the railing, the porch, the house itself. Divorced, forty-one-year-old Faye Braxton, who lived here with her two children, was as structurally unsound as her dwelling. Both her hips had been destroyed by rheumatoid arthritis, and she could not even step out of this dismal home without assistance.

Carrying her medical bag, Claire climbed the steps to the front porch. Only then did she realize something was not right.

It was thirty-five degrees outside, and the front door was open.

She poked her head inside the house and called into the gloom: 'Mrs Braxton?' She heard a shutter banging in the wind. And she heard something else – the faint patter of footsteps, running in an upstairs room. One of the children?

Claire stepped into the house and closed the door against the cold. No lamps were on, and the fading daylight glowed dimly through thin living room curtains. She felt her way down the hall, searching for the light switch. At last she found it and flicked it on.

At her feet, a naked Barbie doll lay on the threadbare runner. Claire reached down for it. 'Mrs Braxton? It's Dr Elliot.'

Her announcement was met with silence.

She looked down at the Barbie doll and saw that half of its blond hair had been cut away. When she had last visited this house, three weeks ago, she had seen Faye Braxton's seven-year-old daughter Kitty clutching a Barbie doll like this one. It had been dressed in a pink prom gown and the long blond hair had been tied back with a scrap of green rickrack.

A chill slithered up her spine.

She heard it again: the rapid *thump-thump-thump* of footsteps moving across the ceiling. She looked up toward the stairs, toward the second floor. Someone was home, yet the heat was off, the house was freezing, and none of the lights were on.

Slowly she backed away, then turned and fled the house.

Sitting in her car, she used her cell phone to call the police.

Officer Mark Dolan answered.

'This is Dr Elliot. I'm at the Braxton residence. Something's wrong here.'

'What do you mean, Dr Elliot?'

'I found the front door open, and there's no heat on, no lights. But I heard someone moving around upstairs.'

'Is the family home? Have you checked?'

'I'd rather not go upstairs.'

'All you'd have to do is take a look. We're already swamped with calls, and I don't know when I can get a man over there.'

'Look, could you just send someone? I'm telling you, it doesn't feel right.'

Officer Dolan gave a loud sigh. She could almost see him at his desk, rolling his eyes in derision. Now that she had actually voiced her fears, they did not seem significant. Perhaps she hadn't heard footsteps at all, but merely that loose shutter swinging in the wind. Perhaps the family was away. The police will arrive and find nothing, she thought, and tomorrow the whole town will be laughing at the cowardly doctor. Her reputation had already suffered enough blows this week.

'Lincoln's somewhere over that way,' Dolan finally said. 'I'll ask him to swing by when he gets the chance.'

She hung up, already regretting the call. Stepping out of the car again, she looked up at the house. Dusk had thickened to night. I'll cancel the dispatch and save myself the embarrassment, she thought. She went back into the house.

Standing at the foot of the stairs, she gazed up toward the second-floor landing, but heard no sound from above. She grasped the banister. It was oak, solid and reassuring. She began to climb, driven upward by pride, by grim determination not to be the butt of the latest town joke.

On the second floor, she turned on the light switch and confronted a narrow hallway, the walls dingy from little hands trailing smudges. She poked her head into the first room on the right.

It was Kitty's bedroom. Ballerinas danced across the curtains. Scattered on the bed were girl things: plastic barrettes, a red sweater embroidered with snowflakes, a child's backpack in pink and purple. On the floor was Kitty's beloved Barbie doll collection. But these were not pampered recipients of a young girl's love. These dolls had been viciously abused, their clothes ripped to shreds, their limbs splayed out as though in horror. A single doll's head, torn from its body, stared up at her with bright blue eyes.

The chill was back in her spine.

She backed into the hall, and her gaze suddenly shifted to another doorway, to the unlit room beyond. Something shimmered in the darkness, a strange luminescence, like the green glow of a watch face. She stepped into the room and turned on the light. The green glow vanished. She was in a boy's room, untidy, with books and dirty socks scattered on the bed and floor. A rubbish can overflowed with crumpled papers and Coke cans. It was the typical disarray left by a thirteen-year-old. She turned off the light.

And saw it again – the green glow. It came from the bed.

She stared down at the pillow, splashed with a bright luminescence, and touched the linen; it was cool, but not damp. Now she noticed the faint streaks of luminescence on the wall as well, just above the bed, and one brilliant emerald splash on the sheet.

Thump, thump, thump. Her gaze shot upward, and she heard a whimper, a child's soft cry.

The attic. The children were in the attic.

She left the boy's room, stumbling over a tennis shoe as she reemerged in the hallway. The attic stairs were steep and narrow; she had to grasp the flimsy handrail as she climbed. When she reached the top, she was standing in impenetrable darkness.

She took a step forward, and brushed past a hanging light chain. One tug, and the bare lightbulb came on, its dim glow illuminating only a small circle of the attic. In the shadowy periphery she could make out a jumble of old furniture and cardboard boxes. A coat rack, its prongs wide as elk's antlers, cast a threatening shadow across the floor.

Next to one of the boxes, something moved.

Quickly she shoved aside the box. Behind it,

curled up on a bundle of old coats, was seven-year-old Kitty. The girl's skin felt icy, but she was still alive, her throat issuing soft little moans with every breath. Claire reached down to pick her up, and realized the girl's clothes were saturated. In horror she lifted her glistening hand to the light.

Blood.

The only warning she had was the creak of the floorboard. *Someone is standing behind me.*

Claire turned just as the shadow exploded toward her. The impact slammed hard against her chest and she flew backwards, pinned under the weight of her attacker. Claws grappled at her throat. She tried to tear them away, frantically thrashing left, then right, a dozen shadowy images swirling before her eyes. The coat rack slammed to the floor. Under the swaying light, she caught sight of her attacker's face.

The boy.

He tightened his grip around her throat, and as her vision began to blacken, she saw his lips curl back, his eyes narrow to angry slits.

She clawed at his eye. Shrieking, the boy released her, stumbling away. She scrambled to her feet just as the boy lunged at her again. She dodged sideways and he flew past her and landed among the cardboard boxes, scattering books and tools across the floor.

They both spotted the screwdriver at the same time.

Simultaneously they sprang toward it, but he

was closer. He snatched it up and brought it high over his head. As it came stabbing down, she raised both hands to catch the boy's wrist. His strength shocked her. She was forced down to her knees. The blade of the screwdriver wavered closer, even as she fought to keep it at bay.

Then, through the roar of her own pulse, she heard a voice calling her name. She screamed out: 'Help me!'

Footsteps thudded up the stairs. Suddenly the weapon was no longer stabbing toward her. The boy pivoted, his weapon redirected as Lincoln flew toward him. She saw the boy fall backwards, sprawling to the floor. Saw the boy and Lincoln rolling over and over in a blur of thrashing limbs, furniture and boxes scattering around them. The screwdriver skittered off into the shadows. Lincoln pinned the boy facedown on the floorboards and Claire heard the metallic click of handcuffs snapping shut. Even then, the boy continued to struggle, kicking out blindly. Lincoln dragged him over to an attic support post and tightly lashed him there with his belt.

When at last he turned to Claire, he was breathing hard, and a bruise was swelling up on one cheek. For the first time he noticed the girl, lying among the boxes.

'She's bleeding!' said Claire. 'Help me get her downstairs, where there's light!'

He scooped the girl into his arms.

By the time he lay her on the kitchen table, she

had stopped breathing. Claire gave her three quick breaths, then felt for a carotid pulse, but could not detect one. 'Get an ambulance here now!' she said to Lincoln. Positioning her hands over the girl's sternum, Claire began chest compressions. The blouse was soaked, and her hands kept slipping as she pumped. Fresh blood seeped through the fabric. *She is only seven years old. How much blood can a child lose? How much longer can I keep her brain cells alive?*

'Ambulance is on the way!' said Lincoln.

'Okay, I need you to cut off her blouse. We have to see where she's bleeding.' Claire paused to give the girl three more breaths. She heard fabric ripping and saw that Lincoln had already bared the girl's chest.

'Jesus,' he murmured.

Blood dribbled from half a dozen stab wounds.

She placed her hands back on the sternum and resumed cardiac compressions, but with every pump, more blood spilled out of the girl's body.

A siren wailed closer, and through the kitchen window they saw strobelike flashes of light as the ambulance pulled into the front yard. Two EMTs swept into the house, took one look at the child on the table, and threw open their emergency kit. Claire continued pumping on the chest as the EMTs intubated, inserted an IV, slapped on EKG leads.

'Have we got a rhythm?' Claire asked, holding compressions.

'Rapid sinus tach.'

'BP?'

She heard the *whiff, whiff* of the blood pressure cuff, then the answer. 'Barely palpable at fifty. Ringer's lacate going wide open in this IV. Having trouble getting this second line started . . .'

Another siren screamed into the yard, and more footsteps banged into the house. Officers Mark Dolan and Pete Sparks crowded into the kitchen. Dolan met Claire's gaze, and he quickly looked away, sensing her reproach. *I told you something was wrong!*

'There's a boy upstairs in the attic,' said Lincoln. 'I've already got him cuffed. Now we have to find the mother.'

'I'll check the barn,' said Dolan.

Claire protested, 'Faye's in a wheelchair! She couldn't get out to the barn. She's got to be somewhere in this house.'

Ignoring her, Dolan turned and headed straight out the door.

She focused her attention back on the girl. Now that they were getting a pulse, she could stop pumping on the chest, and she was acutely aware that her hands were sticky with blood. She heard Lincoln and Pete running from room to room in search of Faye, heard the EMT's radio crackle with questions from the Knox Hospital ER.

'How much blood loss?' It was McNally's voice on the radio.

'Her clothes are saturated,' answered the EMT.

'At least six stab wounds to the chest. We've got sinus tach at one-sixty, BP palpable at fifty. One IV in. We can't get a second line started.'

'Breathing?'

'No. She's tubed and we're bagging her. Dr Elliot's here with us.'

'Gordon,' Claire called out. 'She needs immediate thoracotomy! Get a surgeon there, and let's just *move* her!'

'We'll be waiting for you.'

Though it took only seconds to transfer the girl into the ambulance, Claire felt as if everything were moving in excruciatingly slow motion. She saw it all through a cloud of panic: the heartbreakingly small body being strapped into the stretcher, the tangle of EKG wires and IV line, the tense faces of the EMTs as they ran the girl down the porch steps and slid her into the ambulance.

Claire and one of the EMTs climbed in beside the girl and the door slammed shut. She knelt beside the stretcher, bagging the lungs and fighting to keep her balance as they bumped down the Braxton driveway, then swung onto the main road.

On the cardiac monitor, the girl's heart rhythm stumbled. Two premature ventricular beats. Then three more.

'PVCs,' said the EMT.

'Go ahead with the lidocaine.'

The EMT had just started to inject the drug when the ambulance hit a pothole. He sprawled backwards, his arm snagging the IV line. The catheter slid out of the girl's vein, sending a spray of Ringer's lactate into Claire's face.

'Shit, I've lost the line!' he said.

An alarm beeped on the monitor. Claire glanced up to see a string of PVCs skipping across the screen. At once she began cardiac compressions. 'Hurry with that second line!'

Already he was ripping open a package, pulling out a fresh catheter. He tied a tourniquet on Kitty's arm and slapped the flesh a few times, trying to get a vein to plump up. 'I can't find one! She's lost too much blood.'

The girl was in shock. Her veins had collapsed.

The alarm squealed. Ventricular tachycardia was racing across the screen.

In panic, Claire gave Kitty's chest a sharp thump. Nothing changed.

She heard the whine of the defibrillator. The EMT had already punched the charge button and was slapping contact pads on Kitty's chest. Claire pulled away as he positioned the paddles and discharged the current.

On the monitor, the tracing shot up, then slid back to a rapid sinus tachycardia. Both Claire and the EMT released loud sighs of relief.

'That rhythm's not going to hold,' said Claire. 'We need the IV.'

Fighting to keep his balance in the swaying ambulance, he wound the tourniquet around the opposite arm and again searched for a vein. 'I can't find one.'

'Not even the antecubital?'

'It's already blown. We lost it trying to get the IV started earlier.'

She glanced up at the monitor. PVCs were beginning to march across the screen again. They were still miles away from the ER, and the girl's rhythm was deteriorating. They had to get an IV in her now.

'Take over CPR,' she said. 'I'll start a subclavian line.'

They scrambled to switch positions.

Claire's heart was hammering as she crouched beside Kitty's chest and stared down at the collarbone. It had been years since she'd inserted a child's central venous line. She would have to insert a needle under the clavicle, angling the tip toward the large subclavian vein, while running the danger of puncturing the lung. Her hands were already trembling; in the swaying ambulance, they would be even less steady.

The girl is in shock, and dying. I have no choice.

She opened the central venous line kit, swabbed the skin with Betadine, and snapped on sterile gloves. Then she took a shaky breath. 'Hold compressions,' she said. She placed the tip of the needle beneath the collarbone and pierced the skin. With steady pressure she advanced the needle, the whole time gently applying suction to the attached syringe.

Dark blood suddenly flashed back.

'I'm in the vein.'

The alarm squealed. 'Hurry! She's in V. tach!' said the EMT.

Lord, don't send us over a pothole. Not now.

Holding the needle absolutely still, she removed the syringe and threaded the J wire through the hollow needle, into the subclavian vein. Her guide wire was in position; the most delicate part of the procedure was over. Moving swiftly now, she slid the catheter into place, withdrew the wire, and connected the IV tubing.

'Good show, doc!'

'Lidocaine's going in. Ringer's at wide open.' Claire glanced at the monitor.

Still in V. tach. She reached for the paddles, and was just placing them on Kitty's chest when the EMT said, 'Wait.'

She looked at the monitor. The lidocaine was taking effect; the V. tach had stopped.

The abrupt lurch of the braking ambulance alerted them to their arrival. Claire braced herself as the vehicle swung around and backed up into the ER bay.

The door swung open and suddenly McNally and his staff were there, half a dozen pairs of hands reaching to pull the stretcher out of the vehicle.

They had only a bare-bones surgical team waiting in the trauma room, but it was the best McNally could round up on such short notice: an anesthetist, two obstetrical nurses, and Dr Byrne, a general surgeon.

At once Byrne moved into action. With a scalpel, he slashed the skin above Kitty's rib and with almost savage force shoved in a plastic chest tube. Blood gushed through the tube and poured into the glass reservoir. He took one look at the rapidly accumulating blood and said, 'We have to crack the chest.'

They had no time for the ritual hand scrub. While McNally performed a cutdown on the girl's arm for another IV line, and a unit of O-neg blood pumped in, Claire slipped into a surgical gown, thrust her hands into sterile gloves, and took her place across from Byrne. She could see from his white face that he was scared. He was not a thoracic surgeon, and clearly he knew he was in over his head. But Kitty was dying, and there was no one else to turn to.

'Hail Mary, full of grace,' he muttered, and started up the sternal saw.

Wincing at the whine of the saw, Claire squinted against the spray of bone dust, into the widening gap of Kitty's chest cavity. All she could see was blood, glistening like red satin under the lights. A massive hemothorax. As Byrne positioned the retractors, widening the gap, Claire suctioned, temporarily clearing the cavity.

'Where's it coming from?' muttered Byrne. 'The heart looks undamaged.'

And so small, thought Claire with sudden anguish. *This child is so very small* . . .

'We've got to clear away this blood.'

As Claire suctioned deeper, a tiny spurt suddenly appeared from the lacerated lung, pumping out an arc of blood.

'I see it,' he said, and snapped on a clamp.

Another spurt appeared, fresh blood swirling bright red into the darker pool.

'That's two,' he said with a tense note of triumph, clamping off the second bleeder.

'I'm hearing a BP!' said a nurse. 'Systolic's seventy!'

'Hanging the second unit of O-neg.'

'There,' said Claire, and Byrne clamped off the third telltale spurt.

Claire suctioned again. For a moment they watched the open chest, waiting in dread for the blood to reaccumulate. Everyone in the room fell silent. The seconds ticked by.

Then Byrne glanced across at her. 'You know that Hail Mary I just said?'

'Yes?'

'It seems to be working.'

Pete Sparks was waiting for her when Claire finally emerged from the trauma room. Her clothes were splattered with blood, but he didn't seem to notice it; they had seen so much violence that night, perhaps they could no longer be shocked by the sight of gore.

'How's the girl?' he asked.

'She made it through surgery. As soon as her blood pressure's stabilized, they'll be transferring her to Bangor.' Claire gave him a tired smile. 'I think she'll be fine, Pete.'

'We brought the boy here,' he said.

'Scotty?'

He nodded. 'The nurses put him in that exam room over there. Lincoln thought you'd better take a look at him. There's something wrong.'

With growing apprehension, she crossed the ER and came to an abrupt halt in the exam room doorway. There she stood staring into the room, saying nothing, a chill rising up her spine.

She almost jumped when Pete said, quietly, 'You see what I mean?'

'What about his mother?' she asked. 'Did you find Faye?'

'Yes, we found her.'

'Where?'

'In the cellar. She was still in her wheelchair.' Pete looked into the exam room, and as if repelled by what he saw, he took a fearful step backwards. 'Her neck was broken. He pushed her down the stairs.'

10

From the other side of the X-ray viewing window, Claire and the CT technician watched Scotty Braxton's head disappear into the mouth of the scanner. His limbs and chest were firmly strapped to the table, but his hands continued to twist against the leather restraints and his wrists had already been chafed raw, streaking the leather with blood.

'We're not going to get any decent shots,' said the tech. 'Still too much movement. Maybe you can give him some more Valium?'

'He's already got five milligrams on board. I hate to obscure his neuro status,' said Claire.

'It's either that or no CT.'

She had no choice. She filled the syringe and entered the scan room. Through the window, she saw the state trooper watching her. She approached the table and reached for the IV port. Without warning the boy's hand shot open. She jerked away just as his fingers clamped down like a trap.

The cop stepped into the room. 'Dr Elliot?'

'I'm okay,' she said, heart pounding. 'He just startled me.'

'I'm right here. Go ahead and give him the medicine.'

Quickly she snatched up the IV line, plunged the needle in the rubber dam, and injected the full two milligrams.

The boy's hand finally fell still.

From behind the window, she watched as the scanner began to whir and click, bombarding his head with a shifting sequence of X-ray beams. The first slice, from the top of the cranium, appeared on the computer screen.

'Looks normal so far,' said the tech. 'What are you expecting to see?'

'Any anatomical abnormality that might explain his behavior. A mass, a tumor. There has to be a reason for this. He's the second boy I've seen with uncontrollable aggression.'

They all turned as Lincoln came into the CT room. The tragedy had taken its toll on him; she could see it in his face, in the shadows under his eyes and the sadness of his gaze. For him, the death of Faye Braxton had been only the start of an endless night of press conferences and meetings with state police investigators. He shut the door and seemed to breathe a sigh of relief that he had at last found a quiet, albeit temporary, retreat.

He crossed to the window and gazed at the boy lying on the table. 'What have you found so far?'

'The preliminary drug screens were just called back from Bangor. His blood's negative for amphetamines, phencyclidine, and cocaine. The usual drugs associated with violence. Now we have to rule out other causes for his behavior.' She looked through the glass at her patient. 'It's just like Taylor Darnell. And this boy has never been on Ritalin.'

'Are you sure?'

'I'm their family doctor. I have all Scotty's records from Dr Pomeroy's files.'

They both stood with shoulders propped wearily against the window, conserving energy for the hours that lay ahead. It was the only time they ever seemed to interact, she realized. When they were both tired or scared or distracted by crisis. Neither one of them looking his best. They held no illusions about each other, because they had been through the worst together. *And I've only learned to admire him more*, she thought with surprise.

The tech said, 'Here come the final cuts.'

Both Claire and Lincoln stirred from their exhausted daze and crossed to the computer terminal. She sat down to watch as the cross sections of brain appeared on the screen. Lincoln moved behind her, his hands resting on the back of her chair, his breath warming her hair.

'So what do you see?' asked Lincoln.

'No midline shift,' she said. 'No masses. No bleeding.'

'How can you tell what you're looking at?'

'The whiter it is, the denser it is. Bone is white,

air is black. As you cut lower in the cranium, you'll begin to see parts of the sphenoid bone appearing, at the base of the brain. What I'm looking for is symmetry. Since most pathology affects only one side of the brain, I check for differences between the two sides.'

A new cut appeared. Lincoln said, 'That view doesn't look symmetrical to me.'

'You're right, it isn't. But I don't worry about that particular asymmetry because it doesn't involve the brain. It's in one of the bony sinuses.'

'What are you looking at?' asked the tech.

'The right maxillary sinus. You see? It's not completely lucent. There seems to be something clouding it.'

'A mucoid cyst, I'd guess,' said the tech. 'We see that sometimes in patients with chronic allergies.'

'It certainly wouldn't explain his behavior,' said Claire.

The phone rang. It was Anthony, calling from the lab.

'You might want to come down and look at this, Dr Elliot,' he said. 'It's the gas chromatogram on your patient.'

'Has something shown up in his blood?'

'I'm not sure.'

'Explain this test to me,' said Lincoln. 'What are you measuring here?'

Anthony patted the boxlike gas chromatograph and grinned like a proud father. The tabletop instrument was a recent acquisition, a valuable hand-me-down from Eastern Maine Medical Center in Bangor, and he hovered over it protectively. 'What this piece of equipment does,' he explained, 'is separate mixtures into their individual components. It does this by making use of each molecule's known equilibrium between the liquid phase and the gas phase. You remember high school chemistry?'

'It wasn't my favorite subject,' Lincoln admitted.

'Well, every substance can exist either as a liquid or a gas. For instance, if you heat water, you make steam – which is the gas phase of H-two-oh.'

'Okay, I'm following you.'

'Coiled inside this machine is a capillary column – a very long, very thin tube that, if you laid it out straight, would stretch about half the length of a football field. It's filled with an inert gas that won't react with anything. Now, what I do is inject the sample to be tested into this port here. It gets heated and vaporized to gas, and the different types of molecules travel along that tube at different rates of speed, depending on their mass. That separates them. As they come out the other end of the tube, they pass through a detector and it's recorded on a strip-chart. The time it takes for each substance to emerge is called "retention time." We already know the retention times for hundreds of different drugs and toxins. This test clues us in to the presence of a particular substance in a patient's blood.' He picked up a syringe and screwed it into the port. 'Watch the screen. See what happens when I inject the patient's sample.' Anthony squeezed down on the syringe.

On the computer screen, an uneven line appeared. They watched the tracing for a moment, but it only looked like 'noise' to Claire – minor, nonspecific readings indicating the biochemical soup that makes up human plasma.

'Just be patient,' said Anthony. 'It shows up at about one minute, ten seconds.'

'What does?' asked Claire.

He pointed to the screen. 'That.'

Claire stared as the line suddenly shot up to a peak and promptly dropped back down again to the uneven baseline. 'What *was* that?' she asked.

Anthony went to the printer, where a hard copy was being simultaneously recorded on paper. He tore off the sheet and spread it out on the lab counter for Claire and Lincoln to see.

'That peak,' he said, 'is something I can't identify. The retention time places it in the steroid class, but you can also see a similar peak for certain vitamins and endogenous testosterone. It'd take a more sophisticated lab to identify exactly what this is.'

'You mentioned endogenous testosterones,' said Claire. 'Could this be an anabolic steroid? Something a teenage boy might abuse?' She looked at Lincoln. 'It would explain the symptoms. Body builders sometimes use steroids to bulk up their muscle mass. Unfortunately it has side effects, one of them being uncontrollable aggression. They call it *'roid rage.'*

'It's something to consider,' said Anthony. 'Some sort of anabolic steroid. Now look at this.' He went to his desk and retrieved another sheet of graph paper.

'What is it?'

'It's Taylor Darnell's gas chromatogram, taken the day he was admitted.' He lay the second sheet next to Scotty Braxton's tracing.

The pattern was identical. A single, well-defined peak at one minute, ten seconds.

'Whatever this substance is,' said Anthony, 'it's in the blood of both boys.'

'The comprehensive drug screen on Taylor's blood was reported negative.'

'Yeah, I called the reference lab about that. They questioned *our* results. As if I'm imagining this peak or something. I admit, this is an older machine, but these results are reproducible every time.'

'Who did you talk to?'

'A biochemist at Anson Biologicals.'

Claire looked down at the two graphs, the papers laid out one over the other, the tracings practically superimposed. Two boys with the same bizarre behavior. The same unidentifiable substance in their bloodstreams. 'Send them Scotty Braxton's blood,' she said. 'I want to know what this peak is.'

Anthony nodded. 'I've got the requisition right here for you to sign.'

By two A.M., Claire had reviewed every X-ray, every blood test, and was no closer to an answer. In exhaustion she lingered beside the boy's bed, silently studying her patient. She tried to think of what she might have missed. The lumbar puncture was normal, as were the blood chemistries and EEG. The CT scan had shown only the mucoid cyst in the right maxillary sinus – probably a result of chronic allergies. Allergies would also explain the one abnormality in his white blood cell count: a high percentage of eosinophils. *Like Taylor Darnell*, she suddenly recalled.

Scotty stirred from his Valium-induced sleep and opened his eyes. A few blinks, and his gaze fixed on Claire.

She turned off the light to leave. Even in the darkness, she could see the gleam of his eyes focused on her.

Then she realized it was not his eyes she saw glowing.

Slowly she crossed back to the bed. She could make out the white linen beneath his head, the darker shape of his head against the pillow. On his upper lip shimmered a brilliant patch of phosphorescent green.

'Sit down, Noah,' said Fern Cornwallis. 'There's something we need to discuss.'

Noah hesitated in the doorway, reluctant to step into the principal's office. Enemy territory. He didn't know why he'd been pulled out of class to see her, but judging by the expression on Miss C.'s face, he suspected it couldn't be anything good.

The other kids had eyed him with speculative looks when the message had crackled over the intercom in band class: *Noah Elliot, Miss Cornwallis wants to see you in her office. Now.* Acutely aware of everyone's gaze, he had set down his saxophone and made his way through the maze of chairs and music stands to the door. He knew his classmates were wondering what he'd done wrong.

He had no idea.

'Noah?' said Miss C., pointing to the chair.

He sat down. He didn't look at her, but at her desk, which was neat beyond belief. No human had a desk like that.

'I received something in the mail today,' she said. 'I need to ask you about it. I don't know who sent it. But I'm glad they did, because I need to know when one of my students requires extra guidance.'

'I don't know what you're talking about, Miss C.'

In answer, she slid a photocopied news clipping across the desk. He took one glance and felt his face blanch. It was from *The Baltimore Sun*:

ONE YOUTH IN CRITICAL CONDITION
AFTER CRASH OF STOLEN CAR: FOUR
YOUTHS IN CUSTODY.

Who knew about it? he thought. And, more important: *Why are they doing this to me?*

Miss Cornwallis said, 'You moved here from Baltimore. Didn't you?'

Noah swallowed. 'Yes, ma'am,' he whispered.

'There are no names mentioned in this article. But there was a note attached, suggesting I talk to you about this.' She looked straight at him. 'This is about you, isn't it?'

'Who sent it?'

'That's not important right now.'

'It's one of those reporters.' His chin suddenly jutted up in anger. 'They've been following me around, asking questions. Now they're trying to get back at me!'

'For what?'

'For not talking to them.'

She sighed. 'Noah, three teachers had their cars broken into yesterday. Do you know anything about it?'

'You're looking for someone to blame. Aren't you?'

'I'm just asking if you know anything about the cars.'

He stared her straight in the eye. 'No,' he said, and stood up. 'Now can I go?'

She didn't believe him; he could see it in her face. But there was nothing more she could say.

She nodded. 'Go back to class.'

He walked out of her office, past the snoopy

school secretary, and stormed into the hallway. Instead of returning to band class, he fled outside and sat down, shaking, on the front steps. He wasn't wearing a jacket, but he scarcely noticed the cold; he was fighting too hard not to cry.

I can't live here any more, either, he thought. *I can't live anywhere. No matter where I go, someone will find out about me. About what I did.* He hugged his knees and rocked back and forth, wanting desperately to go home, now, but it was too far to walk, and his mom couldn't come and get him.

He heard the gym door slam shut, and he turned to see a woman with wild blond hair walk out of the building. He recognized her; it was that reporter, Damaris Horne. She crossed the street and climbed into a car. A dark green car.

She's the one.

He ran across the street. 'Hey!' he yelled, and slapped her door in fury. 'You stay the hell away from me!'

She rolled down her window and looked at him with almost predatory interest. 'Hello, Noah. You want to talk about something?'

'I just want you to stop trying to ruin my life!'

'How am I ruining your life?'

'Following me around! Telling people about Baltimore!'

'What does Baltimore have to do with any-thing?'

He stared at her, suddenly realizing she had no

idea what he was talking about. He backed away. 'Forget about it.'

'Noah, I haven't been following you around.'

'Yes you have. I've seen your car. You drove past my house yesterday. And the day before.'

'No, I didn't.'

'You were tailing my mom and me in town!'

'Okay, that time I just happened to be behind you. So what? Do you know how many reporters are in town right now? How many green cars are cruising around?'

He backed away some more. 'Just stay away from me.'

'Why don't we talk? You can tell me what's really going on in the school. What all the fights are about. Noah? Noah!'

He turned and fled into the building.

Two pit bulls growled and barked at Claire's car, their claws scraping at her door. She stayed safely shut inside and stared across the front yard, at the ramshackle farmhouse. In the front yard, years of junk had accumulated. She saw a trailer propped up on bricks and three broken-down cars, in various states of being cannibalized. A cat peered fearfully through the open door of a rusting clothes dryer. In the land of Yankee thrift, it was not unusual to find front yards like this. Families who have known poverty hoard their junk like treasure.

She honked, then rolled down her window a

few inches and called out through the crack: 'Hello? Is anyone home?'

A tattered curtain flicked aside in the window, and a moment later, the door opened and a blond man of about forty stepped out. He crossed the yard and regarded her with unsmiling eyes as the dogs barked and jumped at his feet. Everything about him seemed thin – his face, his receding hair, his pencil-sketch mustache. Thin and resentful.

'I'm Dr Elliot,' she said. 'Are you Mr Reid?'

'Yeah.'

'I'd like to talk to your sons, if I may. It's about Scotty Braxton.'

'What about him?'

'He's in the hospital. I'm hoping your sons can tell me what's wrong with him.'

'You're the doctor. Don't you know?'

'I believe it's a drug psychosis, Mr Reid. I think he and Taylor Darnell both took the same drug. Mrs Darnell said Scotty and Taylor spent a lot of time with your sons. If I can talk to them –'

'They can't help you,' said Jack Reid, and he stepped away from her car.

'They may all have been experimenting with the same drug.'

'My boys know better than that.' He turned back to the house, his contempt for her apparent in the angry set of his shoulders.

'I don't want to get your sons in trouble, Mr Reid!' she called out. 'I'm just trying to get information!'

A woman stepped out onto the porch. She cast a worried look at Claire, then said something to Reid. In reply, he shoved her back into the house. The dogs trotted away from Claire now, and were watching the porch, attracted by the promise of new conflict.

Claire rolled down her window and stuck her head out. 'If I can't talk to your sons, I'll call the police to do it for me. Would you prefer to speak to Chief Kelly?'

He turned to look at her, his face tight with anger. Now the woman cautiously poked her head out and stared at Claire as well.

'This will be strictly confidential,' said Claire. 'Let me talk to them, and I'll keep the police out of it.'

The woman said something to Reid – a plea, by the look of her body language. He gave a snort of disgust and stomped into the house.

The woman crossed to Claire's car. Like Reid she was blond, her face washed-out and colorless, but there was no hostility in her eyes. Rather, there was a disturbing lack of any emotion, as though she had long ago buried her feelings in some deep, safe place.

'The boys just got home from school,' the woman said.

'Are you Mrs Reid?'

'Yes, ma'am. I'm Grace.' She looked at the house. 'Those boys've been in enough trouble. Chief Kelly said if it happened again . . .'

'He doesn't have to know about this. I'm here only because of my patient, Scotty. I need to know what drug he's taken, and I think your boys can tell me.'

'They're Jack's boys, not mine.' She turned to face Claire, as though it was very important that this fact be understood. 'I can't force them to talk to you. But you can come inside. First let me tie up these dogs.'

She grabbed both pit bulls by their collars and pulled them over to the maple tree, where she restrained them. They shot to the ends of their chains, barking wildly as Claire stepped out of the car and followed the woman up to the porch.

Stepping into the house was like entering a warren of caves, low-ceilinged and cluttered.

'I'll get them,' said Grace, and she disappeared up a narrow stairway, leaving Claire alone in the living room. The TV was on, tuned to the shopper's channel. On the coffee table, someone had written on a notepad: 'Chanel #5, 4 oz., $14.99.' She breathed in the air of that house, with its odors of mildew and cigarettes, and wondered if perfume alone could mask this smell of poverty.

Heavy footsteps thudded on the stairs, and two teenage boys slouched into the room. Matching buzz cuts made their blond heads seem unnaturally small. They said nothing, but stood looking at her with incurious blue eyes. The blandness of teenagers.

'This is Eddie and J.D.,' said Grace.

'I'm Dr Elliot,' said Claire. She looked at Grace, who understood the meaning of that glance, and quietly left the room.

The boys plopped down on the couch, their gazes automatically shifting to the TV. Even when Claire reached for the remote and turned it off, their gazes remained fixed on the blank screen, as though by habit.

'Your friend Scotty Braxton's in the hospital,' she said. 'Did you know that?'

There was a long silence. Then Eddie, the younger boy, perhaps fourteen, said: 'We heard he went crazy last night.'

'That's right. I'm his doctor, Eddie, and I'm trying to find out why. Whatever you tell me, it's just between us. I need to know what drug he's taken.'

The boys exchanged a look that Claire didn't understand.

'I know he took something,' she said. 'So did Taylor Darnell. It showed up in both their blood tests.'

'So why're you asking us?' It was J.D. talking now, his voice deeper than Eddie's, and vibrating with contempt. 'Sounds like you already know.'

'I don't know what the drug is.'

'Is it a pill?' asked Eddie.

'Not necessarily. I believe it's some kind of hormone. It could be a pill, a shot, or even a plant of some kind. Hormones are chemicals made by living things. Plants and animals, insects.

They affect our bodies in a lot of different ways. This particular hormone makes people violent. It makes them kill. Do you know how he got it?'

Eddie's gaze dropped, as though he was suddenly afraid to look at her.

In frustration she said, 'I just saw Scotty this morning, at the hospital, and he's tied down like an animal. Oh, it's bad for him now, but it's going to be a lot worse when the drug wears off. When he wakes up and remembers what he did to his mother. To his sister.' She paused, hoping her words were penetrating their thick skulls. 'His mother is dead. His sister is still recovering from her wounds. For the rest of her life, Kitty will remember her brother as the boy who tried to kill her. This drug has ruined Scotty's life. And Taylor's. You have to tell me where they got it.'

Both boys stared down at the coffee table, and she saw only the bristly tops of their heads. In boredom, J.D. picked up the remote and turned on the TV. The shopping channel blared out a sales pitch for a genuine man-made emerald pendant on a fourteen-carat gold chain. High-fashion elegance for only seventy-nine ninety-nine.

Claire snatched the remote from J.D.'s hand and angrily shut off the TV. 'Since you two don't have anything to say to me, I guess you'll have to talk to Chief Kelly.'

Eddie started to speak, then glanced at his older

brother and clammed up again. Only then did Claire notice the essential difference between the two. Eddie was afraid of J.D.

She set her business card down on the coffee table. 'If you change your minds, that's where you can reach me,' she said, her gaze directed at Eddie. Then she walked out of the house.

As she stepped off the porch, the two pit bulls came charging at her, only to be yanked to a stop by their chains. Jack Reid was chopping kindling in the front yard, his ax ringing out against a tree stump. He made no effort to quiet his animals; maybe he enjoyed the spectacle of watching them terrify this unwanted visitor. Claire continued across the yard, past the rusting clothes dryer and a car gutted of engine parts. As she walked past Reid, he stopped swinging his ax and looked at her. Sweat beaded his brow and dampened the pale mustache. He leaned against the ax handle, the blade at rest on the stump, and there was mean satisfaction in his eyes.

'Had nothing to say to you, did they?'

'I think they have plenty to say. It will all come out eventually.'

The dogs were barking with renewed agitation, their chains scraping against the maple tree. She cast a glance their way, then looked back at Reid, whose hands had tightened around the ax handle.

'If you're hunting for trouble,' he said, 'best check under your own roof.'

'What?'

He gave her an ugly smile, then raised his ax and brought it down, hard, on a log of firewood.

Claire was in her office later that afternoon when the call came. She heard the phone ringing in the outer office, and then Vera appeared in the doorway.

'She wants to talk to you. She says you were over at her house today.'

'Who's calling?'

'Amelia Reid.'

At once Claire picked up her extension. 'This is Dr Elliot.'

Amelia's voice was muffled. 'My brother Eddie – he asked me to call you. He's afraid to do it himself.'

'And what does Eddie want to tell me?'

'He wants you to know—' There was a pause, as though the girl had stopped to listen. Then her voice came back on, so soft it was almost inaudible. 'He said to tell you about the mush-rooms.'

'What mushrooms?'

'They were all eating them. Taylor and Scotty and my brothers. The little blue mushrooms, in the woods.'

Lincoln Kelly stepped out of his truck and his boot landed on a twig, the snap of dead wood echoing like gunshot across the still lake. It was late afternoon, the sky leaden with rain clouds, the water flat as black glass. 'A little late in the year to go hunting for mushrooms, Claire,' he said dryly.

'But a-hunting we will go.' She reached into the back of her pickup and grabbed two leaf rakes, one of which she handed to Lincoln. He took it with obvious reluctance. 'They're supposed to be a hundred yards upstream from the Boulders,' she said. 'They're growing under some oak trees. Little blue mushrooms with narrow stalks.'

She turned to face the woods. They were not at all inviting, the trees bare and absolutely still, the gloom thickening beneath them. She had not wanted to come out here this late in the day, but a storm was predicted. Already a half inch of rain had fallen, and with the temperature expected to plummet tonight, by tomorrow everything would be covered with snow. This was their last chance to comb bare ground.

'This could be the common factor, Lincoln. A natural toxin from plants growing right in these woods.'

'And the kids were eating these mushrooms?'

'They made it some sort of ritual. Eat a mushroom, prove you're a man.'

They walked along the riverbed, hiking through ankle-deep leaves and thickets of wild raspberry canes. Twigs littered the forest floor, and every step made a sharp explosion of sound. A walk in the woods in late fall is not a silent experience.

The forest opened to a small clearing, where the oak trees had grown to towering heights.

'I think this is the place,' she said.

They began to rake aside the leaves. They worked with quiet urgency as sleet fell, stinging pellets of it mixed with rain, coating everything with a glaze of ice. They uncovered toadstools and white fairy rings and brilliant orange fungi.

It was Lincoln who found the blue one. He spotted the tiny nubbin poking up from a crevice formed by two tree roots. He brushed away the oak leaves and uncovered the cap. Darkness was already falling, and the mushroom's color was apparent only under the direct beam of his flashlight. They crouched side by side, battered by rain and sleet, both of them too chilled and miserable to feel much sense of triumph as Claire slipped the specimen into a Ziploc bag.

'There's a wetlands biologist up the road,' she said. 'Maybe he'll know what it is.'

In silence they sloshed back through the mud and emerged from the woods. On the bank of Locust Lake, they both halted in surprise. Half the shoreline was almost completely dark. Where the lights of houses should have glowed, there was only the occasional glimmer of candlelight through a window.

'It's a bad night to lose power,' said Lincoln. 'Temperature's going to drop into the twenties.'

'Looks like my end of the lake still has electricity,' she noted with relief.

'Well, keep the firewood handy. There's probably ice building up on the lines. You could lose yours next.'

She threw the rakes in the back of her truck, and was circling around to the door when something in the lake caught her eye. It was only a faint glimmer, and she might have missed it had it not been for the contrasting blackness of the Boulders jutting into the water.

'Lincoln,' she said. *'Lincoln!'*

He turned from his cruiser. 'What?'

'Look at the lake.' Slowly she walked toward the small tongue of water lapping at the mud.

He followed her.

At first he couldn't seem to comprehend what he was seeing. It was only a vague shimmer, like moonlight dancing on the surface. But there was no moon out tonight, and the streak of light wavering on the water was a phosphorescent green. They climbed onto one of the rocks and looked across the water. In wonder, they watched the streak undulate like a snake on the surface, its coils a swirl of bright emerald. Not a purposeful movement, but a lazy drifting, its form contracting, then expanding.

Suddenly the clatter of sleet intensified, and needles of ice stippled the lake.

The phosphorescent coils shattered into a thousand bright fragments and disintegrated.

For a long time, neither Claire nor Lincoln spoke. Then he whispered, 'What the hell was that?'

'You've never seen it before?'

'I've lived here all my life, Claire. I've never seen anything like it.'

The water was dark, now. Invisible. 'I have,' she said.

11

'I'm not an expert on mushrooms,' said Max Tutwiler. 'But I might recognize a toxic variety if I saw one.'

Claire took the mushroom out of the Ziploc bag and handed it to him. 'Can you tell us what this is?'

He slipped on his spectacles, and by the light of a kerosene lamp, studied the specimen. He turned it over, examining every detail of the delicate stalk, the blue-green cap.

Sleet *tick-ticked* against the cottage windows and wind moaned in the chimney. The power had gone out an hour before, and Max's cottage was getting colder by the minute. The rising storm seemed to make Lincoln restless. Claire could hear him moving around the room, fussing with the cold woodstove, tightening the window latches. The ingrained habits of a man who has known hard winters. He lit newspapers and kindling in the stove and threw in a log, but the wood was green, and produced more smoke than heat.

Max did not look well. He sat clutching a blanket, a box of Kleenex by his chair. A shivering testament to the miseries of a winter flu and a cottage without heat.

At last he looked up with rheumy eyes. 'Where did you find this mushroom?'

'Upstream from the Boulders.'

'Which boulders?'

'That's the name for the place – the Boulders. It's a hangout for the local kids. They found dozens of those mushrooms this summer. It's the first year they've noticed them. But then, it's been a strange year.'

'How so?' asked Max.

'We had all those floods last spring. And then the hottest summer on record.'

Max nodded soberly. 'Global warming. The signs are everywhere.'

Lincoln glanced at the window, where needles of sleet tapped at the glass, and laughed. 'Not tonight.'

'You have to look at the big picture,' said Max. 'Weather patterns changing all over the world. Catastrophic droughts in Africa. Floods in the Midwest. Unusual growing conditions lead to unusual things growing.'

'Like blue mushrooms,' said Claire.

'Or eight-legged amphibians.' He pointed to the bookshelf, where his specimen jars were displayed. There were eight jars now, each containing a freak of nature.

Lincoln picked up one of the jars and stared at a two-headed salamander. 'Jesus. You found this in our lake?'

'In one of the vernal ponds.'

'And you think this is because of global warming?'

'I don't know what's causing it. Or which species will be affected next.' Max refocused his bleary eyes on the mushroom. 'It's not surprising that plant life would be affected.' He turned the mushroom over and gave it a sniff. 'This damn cold has blocked up my nose. But I think I can smell it.'

'What?'

'The scent of anise.' He held it out to her.

'I smell it too. What does it mean?'

He rose and pulled down *An Illustrated Textbook of Mycology* from the bookshelf. 'This species grows in both hardwood and coniferous forests, from midsummer through fall.' He opened the book to a color plate. '*Clitocybe odora*. The anise funnel cap. It contains a small amount of muscarine, that's all.'

'Is that our toxin, then?' asked Lincoln.

Claire sank back in her chair and gave a sigh of disappointment. 'No, it's not. Muscarine causes mostly gastrointestinal or cardiac symptoms. Not violent behavior.'

Max returned the mushroom to the Ziploc bag. 'Sometimes,' he said, 'there is no explanation for violence. And that's the frightening thing about it. How unexpected it can be. How often it happens without rhyme or reason.'

Wind rattled the door. Outside, the sleet had turned to snow, and it tumbled past the window in a thick whirl of white. The wood stove gave off only the barest suggestion of heat. Lincoln crouched down to check the fire.

It had gone out.

'Lincoln and I saw something tonight. On the lake,' said Claire. 'It was almost like an hallucination.'

She and Max sat facing the hearth in Claire's parlor, their backs turned against the shadows. She had coaxed him out of his unheated cottage, had offered him a bed in her guest room, and now that dinner was over, they sat before the fire and took turns pouring from a bottle of brandy. Flames hissed brightly around a log, but for all that light, all that combustion, precious little heat seemed to penetrate the room's chill. Outside, snowflakes skittered against the window and stray branches of forsythia, bone bare, clawed at the glass.

'What did you see in the lake?' he asked.

'It was floating on the surface of the water, near the Boulders. This swirl of green light, just drifting by. Not solid, but liquid. Changing shape, like a slick of oil.' She took a sip of brandy and stared at the fire. 'Then the sleet began to fall, churning the water. And the green light, it just disintegrated.' She looked at him. 'It sounds crazy, doesn't it?'

'It could be a chemical spill. Fluorescent paint in the lake, for instance. Or it could be a biological phenomenon.'

'Biological?'

He pressed his hand to his forehead, as though to ease a headache beginning to build there. 'There are bioluminescent strains of algae. And certain bacteria glow in the dark. There's one species that forms a symbiotic relationship with luminescent squid. The squid attracts mates by flashing a light organ powered by glowing bacteria.'

Bacteria, she thought. A floating mass of them.

'Scotty Braxton's pillow was stained with a luminescent substance,' she said. 'At first I thought he'd been using some sort of hobby paint. Now I wonder if it was bacterial.'

'Have you cultured it?'

'I cultured his nasal discharge. I asked the lab to identify every organism that grows out, so it will take time to get the results. What have you found in the lake water?'

'None of the cultures are back yet, but maybe I should take a few more samples before I pack up and leave.'

'When are you leaving?'

'I rented the cottage through the end of this month. But with the weather turning so cold, I might as well cut it short and go back to Boston. To central heating. I have enough data already. Samples from a dozen different Maine lakes.' He looked at the window, at the snow falling outside, thick as a curtain. 'I leave this place to hardier souls like you.'

The flames were dying. She stood up, took a

birch log from the pile, and threw it onto the fire. The papery bark caught instantly, snapping and sparkling. She watched it for a moment, savoring the heat, feeling it flush her cheeks. 'I'm not such a hardy soul,' she said softly. 'I'm not sure I belong here, either.'

He poured more brandy into his glass. 'There's a lot about this place that takes getting used to. The isolation. The people. They're not easy to get to know. In the month I've been here, you're the only one who's invited me to dinner.'

She sat down and regarded him with a new measure of sympathy. She recalled her own introduction to Tranquility. After eight months, how many people here did she really know? She'd been warned it would be this way, that the locals were wary of outsiders. People from away drift to Maine like loose bits of fluff, linger for a season or two, and then scatter to the four winds. They have no roots here, no memories. No permanence. Mainers know this, and they greet each new resident with suspicion. They wonder what has driven this stranger into their midst, what secrets lie hidden in some past life. They wonder if the stranger has somehow carried with him the very contagion he is trying to escape. Lives that fall apart in one city often fall apart yet again in another.

Mainers can see the progression. First the new house, enthusiastically purchased, the garden with freshly tamped-down daffodil beds, the snow boots and L.L. Bean jackets. A winter or two goes by.

The daffodils bloom, fade, bloom untended. The heating bill astounds. The storm windows linger months past thaw. The stranger begins to shuffle pale-faced around town, to talk longingly of Florida, to recall beaches he has lolled upon, and to dream of towns that have neither mud season nor snowplows. And the house, so lovingly restored, soon collects one more decoration: a For Sale sign.

People from away have no permanence. Even she was not sure she would stay here.

'Why did you want to move here, then?' he asked.

She settled back in her chair and watched the flames engulf the birch log. 'I didn't move here because of me. It was because of Noah.' She looked up toward the second floor, toward her son's bedroom. It was silent upstairs, just as Noah had been silent all evening. At dinner he had scarcely said a word to their guest. And afterwards, he had gone straight to his room and shut the door.

'He's a handsome boy,' said Max.

'His father was very good-looking.'

'And his mother isn't?' Max's glass of brandy was almost empty, and he seemed flushed in the firelight. 'Because you are.'

She smiled. 'I think you're drunk.'

'No, what I'm feeling right now is . . . comfortable.' He set his glass on the table. 'It was Noah who wanted to move?'

'Oh, no. He had to be dragged, kicking and

screaming. He didn't want to leave his old school or his friends. But that's exactly why we *had* to leave.'

'The wrong crowd?'

She nodded. 'He got into trouble. The whole group of them did. I was taken completely by surprise when it happened. I couldn't control him, couldn't discipline him. Sometimes . . .' She sighed. 'Sometimes I think I've lost him entirely.'

The birch log slid, sizzling into the embers. Sparks leaped up and drifted gently down into the ashes.

'I had to take some sort of drastic action,' she said. 'It was my last chance to exert control. In another year or two, he would have been too old. Too strong.'

'Did it work?'

'You mean, did all our troubles go away? Of course not. Instead, I've taken on a whole new slew of troubles. This creaky old house. A medical practice that I seem to be slowly killing.'

'Don't they need a doctor here?'

'They had a town doctor. Old Dr Pomeroy, who died last winter. They can't seem to accept me as even a pale substitute.'

'It takes time, Claire.'

'It's been eight months, and I can't even turn a profit. Someone with a grudge has been sending anonymous letters to my patients. Warning them off.' She looked at the bottle of brandy, thought: *What the hell*, and poured herself another glass. 'Out of the frying pan, into the fire.'

'Then why do you stay?'

'Because I keep hoping it'll get better. That winter will pass, it'll be summer again, and we'll both be happy. That's the dream, anyway. It's the dreams that keep us going.' She sipped her brandy, noticing that the flames were now pleasantly out of focus.

'And what is your dream?'

'That my son will love me the way he used to.'

'You sound as if you have doubts.'

She sighed, and raised the glass to her lips. 'Parenthood,' she said, 'is nothing but doubts.'

Lying in bed, Amelia could hear the sound of slapping in her mother's room, could hear the stifled sobs and whimpers and the angry grunts that punctuated each blow.

Dumb bitch. Don't you ever go against me. You hear? You hear?

Amelia thought of all the things she could do about it – all the things she'd already done in the past. None of them had worked. Twice she'd called the police; twice they'd taken Jack away to jail, but within days he'd returned, welcomed back by her mother. It was no use. Grace was weak. Grace was afraid of being alone.

I will never, ever, let a man hurt me and get away with it.

She covered her ears and buried her head under the sheets.

*   *   *

J.D. listened to the sound of blows and could feel himself getting excited. Yeah, that's the way to treat 'em, Dad. It's what you always told me. A firm hand keeps 'em in line. He rolled up close to the wall, placing his ear against the plaster. His dad's bed was right on the other side. As he had on so many other nights, J.D. would press up close, listening to the rhythmic squeak of his father's bed, knowing exactly what was going on in the next room. His dad was something else, a man like no other, and although J.D. was a little afraid of him, he also admired him. He admired the way ol' Jack took control of his household and never let the females get high and mighty. It's the way the Good Book meant it to be, Jack always said, the man as master and protector of his house. It made sense. The man was larger, stronger, of course he was meant to be in charge.

The slapping had stopped, and now it was just the bed squeaking up and down. That's how it always ended. A little discipline and then some good old-fashioned making up. J.D. was getting more and more excited, and the ache down there got to be unbearable.

He got up and felt his way past Eddie's bed, toward the door. Eddie was sound asleep, the dumb cluck. It was embarrassing to have such a weak wuss for a brother. He went into the hall and headed toward the bathroom.

Halfway there, he paused outside his stepsister's closed door. He pressed his ear to it, wondering if Amelia was awake, if she too was listening to the squeaking of their parents' bed. Juicy little Amelia, the untouchable. Right under the same roof. So close he could almost hear the sound of her breathing, could smell her girl-scent wafting out from under the door. He tried the knob and found it was locked. She always kept it locked, ever since that night he'd sneaked into her room to watch her sleep, and she'd awakened to find him unbuttoning her pajama top. The little tease had screamed, and his dad had come tearing into the room with a loaded shotgun, eager to blow away some intruder.

When all the female caterwauling had died down, and J.D. had slunk back to his own room, he'd heard his dad say, 'The boy's always been a sleepwalker. Didn't know what he was doing.' J.D. had thought he was off the hook. Then his dad had come into J.D.'s room and whacked him so hard across the face, he'd seen exploding lights.

Amelia got a lock put in her door the next day.

J.D. closed his eyes and felt sweat dampen his upper lip as he pictured his luscious stepsister lying in her bed, slender arms flung out. He thought of her legs as he'd seen them this summer, long and tan in her white shorts, just the softest hint of golden down on her thighs. Sweat was breaking out on his forehead now, and on his palms. He felt his heart beat hard. His senses had sharpened to such acuteness, he could hear the night humming

231

around him, fields of energy looping and swirling in electric flashes.

He had never felt so powerful.

Again he gripped the doorknob, and its resistance suddenly enraged him. *She* enraged him, with her superior ways and her disapproval. He reached down and touched himself, but really, he was touching *her*, taking command of *her*. Making her do what he wanted. And even though sex was what his body craved, when he finally released himself, the image that came unbidden into his mind was of his own fingers, like thick ropes, wrapped around Amelia's slender neck.

12

Noah shoved two slices of bread in the toaster and jammed down the lever. 'He stayed all night, didn't he?'

'It was too cold for him to sleep in the cottage. He'll be going back today.'

'So are we taking in every strange guy who doesn't know how to keep his woodstove lit?'

'Please keep your voice down. He's still sleeping.'

'It's my home too! Why should I have to whisper?'

Claire sat at the breakfast table, staring at her son's back. Noah refused to look at her and stood hulking by the kitchen counter, as though the toaster required all his concentration.

'You're mad because I had a houseguest? Is that it?'

'You don't even know him, and you invite some strange guy to spend the night.'

'He's not a strange guy, Noah. He's a scientist.'

'Like scientists aren't strange?'

'Your father was a scientist.'

'Is that supposed to make me like this guy?'

The toast popped up. Noah threw the slices onto a plate and sat down at the table. She watched in puzzlement as he picked up a knife and began to slash the toast into smaller and smaller squares. It was bizarre, and she'd never seen him do this before. He's transferring his rage, she thought. Taking it out on the bread.

'I guess my mother isn't so perfect after all,' he said, and she flushed, stung by the cruel comment. 'You're always telling me to keep *my* nose clean. I'm not the one having sleepovers.'

'He's just a friend, Noah. I have a right to have friends, don't I?' She added, recklessly, 'I even have a right to boyfriends.'

'Go ahead!'

'In four years, you'll be in college. You'll have your own life. Why can't I have mine?'

Noah crossed back to the sink. 'You think I have a life?' He laughed. 'I'm on permanent probation. Being watched all the time. By *everyone*.'

'What do you mean?'

'My teachers all look at me like I'm some kind of criminal. Like it's just a matter of time before I screw up.'

'Did you do something to draw their attention?'

In fury he whirled around to face her. 'Yeah, it's my fault! It's always my fault!'

'Noah, is there something you aren't telling me?'

With an angry sweep of his hand, he knocked two coffee cups off the counter and into the dishwater. 'You already think I'm a screw-up! You're never happy with me. No matter how perfect I try to be.'

'Don't whine to me about having to be perfect. I'm not allowed to screw up either. Not as a mother, not as a doctor, and I'm getting pretty sick of it. Especially when no matter how hard I try, you always blame me for *something*.'

'What I blame you for,' he shot back, 'is dragging me to this dump of a town.' He stalked out of the house, and the slam of the front door seemed to echo forever.

She reached for her coffee, which by now was lukewarm, and sipped it fiercely, hands shaking around the cup. What had just happened? Where did all that rage come from? They'd argued in the past, but never had he tried so hard to hurt her. Never had he cut so close to the bone.

She heard the rumble of the school bus as it drove away.

She looked down at his plate, at the uneaten toast. It had been slashed to crumbs.

'This isn't the right place for him, Dr Elliot,' said the nursing supervisor. Eileen Culkin was short but powerfully built for a woman, and with her booming voice and background as an army nurse, she commanded instant respect. When Eileen spoke, the doctors listened.

Though Claire was in the middle of reviewing Scotty Braxton's chart, she set it aside and turned to face Eileen. 'I haven't seen Scotty yet this morning,' she said. 'Have there been more problems?'

'Even after you ordered that extra sedation at midnight, he didn't sleep. He's quiet now, but last night, he was awake the entire shift, screaming at the guard to unlock his handcuffs. Disturbing all the other patients. Dr Elliot, that boy needs to be in juvenile lockup, or a psychiatric unit. Not a medical ward.'

'I haven't finished the evaluation. There are labs still pending.'

'If he's stable, couldn't you move him? The nurses are afraid to go in the room. They can't even change his sheets without three people restraining him. We'd like him moved, the sooner the better.'

Time to make a decision, thought Claire as she walked down the hall to Scotty's room. Unless she could diagnose a life-threatening illness, she couldn't keep him in the hospital any longer.

The state trooper stationed outside Scotty Braxton's hospital room gave Claire a nod of greeting. 'Morning, doc.'

'Good morning. I understand he's been quite a handful.'

'He's been better the last hour. Not a peep out of him.'

'I need to examine him again. Could you stand by, just in case?'

236

'Sure thing.' He pushed open the door and managed to take one step into the room before he froze. '*Jesus Christ.*'

At first all Claire registered was the horror in his voice. Then she pushed past him, into the room. She felt the rush of cold air coming through the open window, and saw the blood. It was spattered across the empty bed, a shocking spray of it staining the pillow and the sheets, thickly smearing the empty handcuff dangling from the side rail. On the floor just below the handcuff, a pool of red had gathered. The human tissue lying at the edge of that pool would have been unrecognizable, save for the fingernail and the white nubbin of bone protruding from one end of the torn flesh. It was the boy's thumb; he had chewed it off.

Groaning, the trooper sank to the floor and dropped his head into his lap. 'Jesus,' he kept murmuring. 'Jesus . . .'

Claire saw the prints of bare feet tracking across the room. She ran to the open window and stared down at the ground one story below.

There was blood mixed with the churned-up snow. Footprints, and more blood, trailed away from the building, toward the forested perimeter of the hospital grounds.

'He's gone into the woods!' she said, and ran out of the room to the stairwell.

She dashed down to the first floor, and pushed out through the fire exit, sinking at once into ankle-deep wet snow. By the time she'd circled around the building to Scotty's window, icy water had seeped into her shoes. She picked up the trail of Scotty's blood and followed it across the wide expanse of snow.

At the edge of the woods she halted, trying to see what lay in the shadow of the evergreens. She could make out the boy's footprints, trailing into the underbrush, and here and there a bright splash of blood.

Heart thudding, she eased into the woods. The most dangerous animal is the one in pain.

Her ungloved hands were numb from cold, from fear, as she moved aside a branch and peered deeper into the woods. Behind her, a twig snapped sharply. She spun around and almost cried out with relief when she saw it was the trooper, who'd followed her out of the building.

'Did you see him?' he asked.

'No. His footprints lead into the woods.'

He waded toward her through the snow. 'Security's on the way. So's the emergency room staff.'

She turned to face the trees. 'Do you hear that?'

'What?'

'Water. I hear water.' She began to run, ducking under low branches, stumbling through underbrush. The boy's footprints were weaving back and forth now, as though he had been staggering. Here was churned-up snow, where he'd fallen. Too much blood loss, she thought. He's stumbling and on the verge of collapse.

The sound of rushing water grew louder.

She broke through a tangle of evergreens and emerged on the bank of a creek. Rain and melting snow had swollen it to a torrent. Frantically she scanned the snow for the boy's prints and spotted them moving parallel to the creek for several yards.

Then, at the water's edge, the footprints abruptly vanished.

'You see him?' the guard yelled.

'He's gone into the water!' She splashed knee-deep into the creek. Reaching underwater, she blindly grabbed whatever her hands encountered. She came up with branches, beer bottles. An old boot. She waded in deeper, up to her thighs, but the water was moving too fast and she felt the torrent pulling her downstream.

Stubbornly she braced her foot against a rock. Once again, she plunged her arms deep into the icy water.

And found an arm.

At her scream, the trooper came splashing to her side. The boy's hospital gown had snagged on a branch; they had to rip the fabric free. Together they lifted him from the creek and dragged him up the bank, onto the snow. His face was blue. He was not breathing, nor did he have a pulse.

She began CPR. Three breaths, filling his lungs, then cardiac compressions. One-one-thousand, two-one-thousand, the sequence automatic and well rehearsed. As she pumped on his chest, blood gushed from his nostril and spilled to the snow. Reestablish circulation, and blood flows to the brain, to the vital organs, but it also means the body bleeds again. She saw a fresh stream of dark red trickle from his torn hand.

Voices drew near, and then footsteps were running toward them. Claire stepped back, wet and shivering, as the ER personnel lifted Scotty onto a stretcher.

She followed them back to the building, and into a trauma room exploding with noise and chaos. On the monitor, the cardiac tracing showed a pattern of ventricular fibrillation.

A nurse hit the defibrillator charge button and slapped paddles on the boy's chest. Scotty jerked as the electrical current shot through his body.

'Still in V. fib,' said Dr McNally. 'Resume compressions. Did you get the bretylium in?'

'Going in now,' a nurse said.

'Everyone back!' Another shock to the heart.

'Still in V. fib,' said McNally. He glanced at Claire. 'How long was he underwater?'

'I don't know. Possibly up to an hour. But he's young, and that water's close to freezing.' Even an apparently dead child could sometimes be revived after cold-water immersion. They couldn't give up yet.

'Core body temp's up to thirty-two degrees centigrade,' a nurse said.

'Maintain CPR and get him warmed up. We might have a chance.'

'What's all this blood from the nose?' a nurse asked. 'Did he hit his head?'

A trickle of bright red slid down the boy's cheek and splattered to the floor.

'He was bleeding when we pulled him out,' said Claire. 'He could have fallen on the rocks.'

'There's no scalp or facial trauma.'

McNally reached for the paddles. 'Stand back. Let's shock him again.'

Lincoln found her in the doctors' lounge. She had changed into hospital scrubs, and was huddled on the couch, numbly sipping coffee, when she heard the door swing shut. He moved so quietly she did not realize it was him until he sat down beside her and said, 'You should go home, Claire. There's no reason for you to stay. Please, go home.'

She blinked and dropped her head in her hands, fighting not to cry. To weep in public over a patient's death was to show loss of control. A breach of professional facade. Her body went rigid with the struggle to hold back tears.

'I have to warn you,' he said. 'When you leave the building, you'll find a mob scene downstairs. The TV crews have parked their vans right outside the exit. You can't walk to the parking lot without running their gauntlet.'

'I have nothing to say to them.'

'Then don't say anything. I'll help you get through it, if you want me to.' She felt Lincoln's hand settle on her arm. A gentle reminder that it was time to leave.

'I called Scotty's next of kin,' she said, wiping a

241

hand across her eyes. 'There's only his mother's cousin. She just came up from Florida, to be with Kitty while she recovers. I told her Scotty was dead, and you know what she said? She said, "It's a blessing."' She looked at Lincoln and saw disbelief in his eyes. 'That's what she called it, *a blessing*. Divine punishment.'

He slipped his arm around her, and she pressed her face to his shoulder. He was silently granting her permission to cry, but she didn't allow herself that luxury. There was still that gauntlet of reporters to confront, and she would not show them a face swollen with tears.

He was right beside her as they walked out of the hospital. As soon as the cold air hit them, so did the barrage of questions.

'Dr Elliot! Is it true Scotty Braxton was abusing drugs?'

'—rumors of a teenage murder ring?'

'Did he really chew off his own thumb?'

Dazed by the assault of shouts, Claire waded blindly into the gathering, not seeing any of the faces as she pushed through. A cassette recorder was thrust into her face, and she found herself staring at a woman with a lion's mane of blond hair.

'Isn't it true this town has a history of murder going back hundreds of years?'

'What?'

'Those old bones they found by the lake. It was a mass murder. And a century before that –'

Swiftly Lincoln stepped between them. 'Get out of here, Damaris.'

The woman gave a sheepish laugh. 'Hey, I'm just doing my job, Chief.'

'Then go write about alien babies! Leave her alone.'

A new voice called out: 'Dr Elliot?'

Claire turned to focus on the man's face, and she recognized Mitchell Groome. The reporter stepped toward her, his gaze searching hers. 'Flanders, Iowa,' he said quietly. 'Is it happening here?'

She shook her head. And said, softly: 'I don't know.'

13

Warren Emerson's lungs hurt from the cold. His outdoor thermometer had registered nine degrees this morning, so he had dressed warmly. He was wearing two shirts and a sweater under his jacket, had pulled on a hat and mittens and wound a scarf around and around his neck, but you could not protect against the cold air you breathed in. It seared his throat and made his chest ache, his lungs spasm. He sounded like a locomotive chugging down the road. *Wheeze-cough, wheeze-cough.* Not even winter yet, he thought, and already the world has turned to ice. The bare trees were encased in it, their branches glittering and crystalline. He had to walk with care on the slick road, deliberately planting each footstep on the speckled ice, where the county trucks had left their spray of sand. It took twice the effort just to stay on his feet, and by the time he reached the edge of town, the muscles in his legs were trembling.

The check-out lady at Cobb and Morong's General Store raised her head as Warren walked into the store. He smiled at her, as he did each week, always in hope that she would return the greeting. He saw her lips start to tilt up in an automatic welcome, then her eyes focused on Warren's face and her smile froze, not quite formed. She looked away.

In silent defeat, Warren turned and reached for a shopping cart.

He followed the same tired routine he always did, his boots shuffling across the creaky floorboards. He stopped in the aisle of canned vegetables and stared at the array of creamed corn and green beans and beets, at the labels with their bright illustrations of summer succulence. Labels lie, he thought. There is no comparison between that can of orange cubes and a carrot pulled fresh and sweet from warm soil. He stood there without reaching for a single item, his thoughts drifting instead to the summer vegetables he had grown and now missed so much. He counted the months until spring, added on the months needed for a new crop to mature. His whole life, it seemed, was spent waiting for winter to pass, or preparing for winter to come. He thought: *Enough is enough. I've lived too many winters already. I cannot bear to live through another one.*

He left his cart where it was standing, and he walked past the eternally unsmiling cashier and out the door.

He stood on the sidewalk outside Cobb and Morong's and gazed across the road, at the newly frozen lake. Its surface was as bright as a polished mirror, flawlessly silvered, unmarred by even a wisp of snow. Skating ice, he thought, remembering the winters of his childhood, his feet gliding, the delicious scrape, scrape of his blades. Soon there would be children skating out there with their hockey sticks and their bright winter jackets, like confetti blowing across the ice.

But I have had enough of winter. I want no more of it.

He breathed in and felt, deep in his lungs, the sting of cold air. Sharp. Punishing.

The cat was back in the window of the five-and-dime on Elm Street. He was cleaning himself, his fur glossy and raven-black in the sunshine. As Claire walked past, he paused from his self-administered bath and stared at her in disdain.

She glanced up at the sky. It was a hard blue, the kind of sky that precedes a wretchedly cold night. Since Scotty Braxton's death four days ago, winter had asserted itself with cruel finality. A dull sheen of ice now covered the entire lake, and in the newspaper obituaries this morning, the announcements of funeral arrangements had all concluded with the same phrase: 'Burial will be in the spring.' When the ground has thawed. When the earth reawakens.

Will I still be here in the spring?

She turned into Tannery Alley. Over a doorway hung a sign, swaying like a tavern placard in the wind:

Police, Town of Tranquility

She walked straight into Lincoln's office, and placed the latest issue of the *Weekly Informer* on his desk.

He looked over his glasses at her. 'Problem, Claire?'

'I just came from Monaghan's Diner, where everyone was talking about *that*. Damaris Horne's latest piece of trash.'

He glanced down at the headline: SMALL TOWN GRIPPED BY EVIL. 'It's just a Boston tabloid,' he said. 'No one takes that stuff seriously.'

'Have you read it?'

'No.'

'Everyone at Monaghan's has. And they're so scared, they're talking about keeping loaded guns handy, just in case some devil-possessed teenager tries to steal their precious truck or something.'

Lincoln groaned and pulled off his glasses. 'Oh, hell. This is the last thing I need.'

'I sewed up three patients with lacerations yesterday. One of them was a *nine*-year-old who punched his fist through a window. We're having enough trouble with the kids in this town. Now the adults have gone crazy, too.' She planted both hands on his desk. 'Lincoln, you can't wait until the town meeting to talk to these people. You have to head off the hysteria now. Those Dinosaurs have declared open season on children.'

'Even imbeciles have a right to free speech.'

'Then at least gag your own men! Who's this cop Damaris quotes from your department?' She pointed to the tabloid. 'Read it.'

He looked down at the section she'd indicated.

What is behind this small town's epidemic of violence?

Many here think they know the reason for it, but their explanations are so disturbing to local authorities that few will speak on the record. One local policeman (who wishes to remain unidentified) privately confirmed the harrowing claims made by local citizens: that Satanists have taken hold of Tranquility.

'We're well aware there are witches living here,' he said. 'Sure, they call themselves "wiccans" and claim they're innocently worshiping earth spirits or some such. But witchcraft has been linked to devil worship through the ages, and you can't help but wonder what these so-called earth worshipers are really doing out there in the woods at night.' When asked to elaborate, he said, 'We've had a number of complaints from citizens who've heard drumming in the woods. Some people have seen lights flickering up on Beech Hill, which is uninhabited forest.'

Late-night drumming and weird lights in the woods aren't the only alarming signs that something is amiss in this isolated village. Rumors of Satanic rituals have long been part of local lore. One woman recalls hearing whispered stories from her childhood of secret ceremonies and infants vanishing soon after birth. Others in town recount horrifying childhood tales of ceremonies in which small animals or even children have been offered up in the name of Satan . . .

'Which one of your officers is talking to this reporter?' Claire demanded.

His face suddenly dark with anger, Lincoln shot to his feet and stalked to the doorway. 'Floyd! Floyd! Who the hell talked to that Damaris Horne woman?'

Floyd's response was slightly tremulous. 'Uh . . . you did, Lincoln. Last week.'

'Someone else in this department has too. Who was it?'

'It wasn't me.' Floyd paused, and added confidentially, 'She kinda scares me, that Damaris lady. Gives you the impression she'd like to eat y'up alive.'

Lincoln returned to his desk and sat down, his anger still evident. 'We've got six men in this department,' he said to Claire. 'I'll do my best to track it down. But anonymous leaks are next to impossible to trace.'

'Could she have made up the quotes?'

'She might. Knowing Damaris.'

'How well *do* you know her?'

'Better than I care to.'

'What does that mean?'

'Well, we're not running off to Rio together,' he snapped back. 'She's a goddamn persistent woman, and she seems to get whatever she goes after.'

'Including the local police.'

She saw fresh anger flare up in his eyes. Their gazes held for a moment, and she felt an unexpected spark of attraction. It surprised her, coming as it did at that instant. This morning he was not looking his best. His hair was ruffled, as though he'd been running his hands through it in frustration, and he was more rumpled than usual, his shirt wrinkled, his eyes bleary from lack of sleep. All the stress of his job, of his personal life, was written right there on his face.

In the next room, the phone rang. Floyd reappeared in Lincoln's doorway. 'The cashier from Cobb and Morong's just called. Dr Elliot, you might want to head over there.'

'Why?' asked Claire. 'What happened?'

'Oh, it's that old Warren Emerson again. He's having another seizure.'

A crowd of bystanders had gathered on the sidewalk. At their center lay an old man dressed in frayed clothes, his limbs jerking in a grand mal seizure. A scalp wound was oozing blood, and in the bitter wind, an alarming splash of red had flash-frozen on the sidewalk. None of the bystanders had attempted to help the man; instead they were all standing back, as though afraid to touch him, afraid even to approach him.

Claire knelt down, and her first concern was to prevent him from injuring himself or aspirating secretions into his lungs. She rolled the man onto his side, loosened his scarf, and wedged it under his cheek to protect it from the icy sidewalk. His skin was florid from the cold, not cyanotic; his pulse was rapid but strong.

'How long has he been seizing?' she called out.

Her question was met with silence. She glanced up at the bystanders and saw that they had backed away even farther, that their gazes were focused not on her, but on the man. The only sound was the wind, blowing in from the lake, whipping at coats and scarves.

'How long?' she repeated, her voice now sharp with impatience.

'Five, maybe ten minutes,' someone finally answered.

'Has an ambulance been called?'

There was a shaking of heads, a collective shrug of shoulders.

'It's just old Warren,' said a woman whom Claire recognized as the cashier from the general store. 'He never needed an ambulance before.'

'Well, he needs one now!' snapped Claire. 'Call one!'

'Seizures are slowing down,' said the cashier. 'It'll be over in a minute.'

The man's limbs were jerking only intermittently now, his brain firing off the final bursts of its electrical storm. At last he lay flaccid. Claire again checked his pulse and found it still strong, still steady.

'See, he's okay,' said the cashier. 'Always comes out of it fine.'

'He needs stitches. And he needs neurological evaluation,' said Claire. 'Who's his doctor?'

'It used to be Pomeroy.'

'Well, someone must be prescribing seizure meds for him now. What's his medical history? Does anyone know?'

'Why don't you ask Warren? He's waking up.'

She looked down and saw Warren Emerson's eyes slowly open. Though he was surrounded by people, he gazed straight up at the sky, as though seeing it for the first time.

'Mr Emerson,' she said. 'Can you look at me?'

For a moment he didn't respond; he seemed lost in wonder, his eyes following the slow drift of a cloud overhead.

'Warren?'

At last he focused on her, his brow wrinkling as though he was struggling to understand why this strange woman was talking to him.

'I had another one,' he murmured. 'Didn't I?'

'I'm Dr Elliot. The ambulance is on its way, and we'll be taking you to the hospital.'

'I want to go home . . .'

'You've split open your scalp and you need stitches.'

'But my cat – my cat's at home.'

'Your cat will be fine. Who's your doctor, Warren?'

He seemed to be struggling to remember. 'Dr Pomeroy.'

'Dr Pomeroy has passed away. Who is your doctor now?'

He shook his head and closed his eyes. 'Doesn't matter. It doesn't matter anymore.'

Claire heard the wail of the approaching ambulance. It pulled to a stop at the curb and two EMTs stepped out.

'Oh, it's just Warren Emerson,' one of them said, as though he ran into the same patient every day. 'He have another seizure?'

'And a pretty deep scalp wound.'

'Okay, Warren, ol' buddy,' said the EMT. 'Looks like you're going for a ride.'

By the time the ambulance drove away, Claire's fury was boiling over. She looked down at the blood, solidified on the ice. 'I can't believe you people,' she said. 'Did anyone try to help him? Does anyone give a damn?'

'They're just scared,' said the cashier.

Claire turned to look at the woman. 'At the very least you could have protected his head. A seizure's nothing to be afraid of.'

'We're not afraid of that. It's *him*.'

She shook her head in disbelief. 'You're afraid of an old man? What possible threat could he be?'

Her question was met with silence. Claire looked around at the other faces, but no one returned her gaze.

No one said a thing.

By the time Claire arrived at the hospital, the ER physician had already sutured Warren Emerson's lacerated scalp and was scribbling notes on a clipboard. 'Needed eight stitches,' said McNally. 'Plus he had some minor frostbite of the nose and ears. Must've been lying in the cold for a while.'

'At least twenty minutes,' said Claire. 'You think he needs admission?'

'Well, the seizures are a chronic problem, and he seems to be neurologically intact. But he did hit his head. I can't tell if the loss of consciousness was due to the seizure or the head bonk.'

'Does he have a primary care physician?'

'Not currently. According to our records, his last hospitalization was back in '89, when Dr Pomeroy admitted him.' McNally signed off on the ER sheet and looked at Claire. 'You want to take him?'

'I was about to suggest it,' she said.

McNally handed her Emerson's old hospital chart. 'Happy reading.'

The file contained the record for Emerson's 1989 hospitalization as well as the summaries from numerous ER visits over the years. She turned first to the 1989 admission history and physical and recognized Dr Pomeroy's spidery handwriting. It was a skimpy entry, recording only the essential facts:

History: 57-year-old white male, accidentally struck left foot with ax while chopping kindling five days ago. Wound has turned swollen and painful and patient now unable to bear weight.

Physical: Temperature 99 degrees. Left foot has two-inch laceration, skin edges closed. Surrounding skin is warm, red, tender. Enlarged groin nodes on left.

Diagnosis: Cellulitis.

Rx: Intravenous antibiotics.

There was no past medical history, no social history, nothing to indicate that a living, breathing human was attached to that infected foot.

She flipped to the ER records. There were twenty-five sheets for twenty-five visits going back thirty years, all the visits for the same reasons: *'Chronic epileptic with seizure ...' 'Seizure, scalp wound ...' 'Seizure, lacerated cheek ...'* Seizure, seizure, seizure. In every case, Dr Pomeroy had simply released him without further investigation. Nowhere did she find a record of any diagnostic workup.

Pomeroy may have been beloved by his patients, but in this case, he had clearly been negligent.

She stepped into the exam room.

Warren Emerson was lying on his back on the

treatment table. Surrounded by all that gleaming equipment, his clothes seemed even more frayed, more shabby. A large patch of his hair had been shaved, and the newly sutured scalp laceration was now dressed with gauze. He heard Claire enter the room and slowly turned to look at her. He seemed to recognize her; a faint smile formed on his lips.

'Mr Emerson,' she said. 'I'm Dr Elliot.'

'You were there.'

'Yes, when you had the seizure.'

'I wanted to thank you.'

'For what?'

'I don't like waking up alone. I don't like it when . . .' He fell silent and stared at the ceiling. 'Can I go home now?'

'That's what we have to talk about. Since Dr Pomeroy died, no one's been following you. Would you like me to be your doctor?'

'Don't much need a doctor anymore. Nothing anyone can do for me.'

Smiling, she squeezed his shoulder. He seemed buried, mummified beneath all those musty layers of clothes. 'I think I can help you. The first thing we have to do is get your seizures controlled. How often do you have them?'

'I don't know. Sometimes I wake up on the floor, and I figure that's what happened.'

'There's no one else at home? You live alone?'

'Yes, ma'am.' He gave her a sad wisp of a smile. 'I mean, except for my cat, Mona.'

'How often do you *think* you've had seizures?'

He hesitated. 'A few times a month.'

'And what medicines do you take?'

'I gave them up years ago. Weren't doing me any good, all those pills.'

She gave an exasperated sigh. 'Mr Emerson, you can't just stop taking medications.'

'But I don't need them anymore. I'm ready to die now.' He said it quietly, without fear, without the faintest note of self-pity. It was merely a statement of fact. *I am going to die soon, and there's nothing to be done about it.*

She had heard other patients make such predictions. They would enter the hospital in far-from-terminal condition, yet they'd say to Claire, with quiet conviction, 'I am not going home this time.' She would try to reassure them, but would already be feeling that premonitory chill of death. Patients always seem to know. When they say they are going to die, they do.

Looking into Warren Emerson's calm eyes, she felt that chill. She shook it off, and proceeded to do the physical exam.

'I have to look in your eyes,' she said, reaching for the ophthalmoscope.

He sighed in resignation and allowed her to examine his retinas.

'Have you ever seen a neurologist about your seizures? A brain specialist?'

'I saw one way back. When I was seventeen.'

She straightened in surprise and flipped off the

ophthalmoscope light. 'That's almost fifty years ago.'

'He said I had epilepsy. That I'd have it for the rest of my life.'

'Have you seen a neurologist since then?'

'No, ma'am. Dr Pomeroy, he took care of me after I moved back to Tranquility.'

She continued her exam, finding no neurologic abnormalities. His heart and lungs were normal, his abdomen without masses.

'Did Dr Pomeroy ever do a brain scan on you?'

'He did an X-ray, few years ago, after I fell down and hit my head. He thought maybe I'd cracked my skull, but I didn't. Got too hard a head, I guess.'

'Have you been to any other hospital?'

'No, Ma'am. Been in Tranquility most all my life. Never had call to go anywhere else.' He sounded regretful. 'Now it's too late.'

'Too late for what, Mr Emerson?'

'God doesn't give us a second chance.'

She had found nothing abnormal. Still, she felt uneasy about letting him go home to an empty house.

Also, what he'd said still bothered her: *I'm ready to die now.*

'Mr Emerson,' she said, 'I want to keep you in the hospital overnight and run a few tests. Just to make sure there's nothing new causing these seizures.'

'I been having them most of my life.'

'But you haven't been checked out in years. I want to start you on medication again, and get some pictures of your brain. If everything looks fine, I'll let you go home tomorrow.'

'Mona doesn't like to go hungry.'

'Your cat will be fine. Right now you have to think about yourself. Your own health.'

'Haven't fed her since last night. She'll be yowling –'

'I'll make sure your cat's fed, if that'll keep you here. How about it?'

He studied her for a moment, trying to decide whether he could entrust the welfare of his best, perhaps only, friend to a woman he scarcely knew.

'The tuna,' he said finally. 'Today, she'll expect the tuna.'

Claire nodded. 'The tuna it is.'

Back in the nurses' station, the first call she made was to the X-ray department. 'I'm admitting a patient named Warren Emerson, and I want to order a CT scan of his head.'

'Diagnosis?'

'Seizures. Rule out brain tumor.'

She was writing Warren's history and physical when Adam DelRay strolled into the ER, shaking his head. 'I just saw them wheel Warren Emerson out of the elevator,' he said to one of the nurses. 'Who on earth admitted him?'

Claire looked up, her feelings of dislike for him

259

stronger than ever. 'I did,' she said coolly. 'He had a seizure today.'

He snorted. 'Emerson's had seizures for years. He's a lifelong epileptic.'

'One can always grow a new brain tumor.'

'Hey, if you want to take him on, you get the halo. Pomeroy complained about him for years.'

'Why?'

'Never took his meds. That's why he keeps seizing. Plus he's on Medicaid, so good luck getting paid. But I guess there are worse ways to spend our tax dollars than serving old Emerson breakfast in bed.' He laughed and walked away.

She signed her name so hard the tip of her pen almost sliced through the paper. All these tests she'd ordered, plus a night's stay in the hospital, added up to an expensive hunch on her part. Perhaps Emerson's memory was faulty; perhaps Dr Pomeroy had performed a recent diagnostic workup, though she doubted it. From what she'd seen of his charts, Pomeroy had been a lackadaisical clinician, more likely to write a prescription for some new pill than to painstakingly investigate the reasons for a patient's symptoms.

She left the hospital and drove back to Tranquility. By the time she reached her office, she was focused on only one thing: reviewing Emerson's outpatient chart and proving to herself that her decision to admit him was justified.

Vera was on the telephone when Claire walked

in. Waving the phone, Vera said, 'You've got a call from a Max Tutwiler.'

'I'll take it in my office. Could you get Warren Emerson's file for me?'

'Warren *Emerson*?'

'Yes, I've just admitted him for seizures.'

'Why?'

Claire halted in her office doorway and turned to glare at Vera. 'Why does everyone in this town question my judgment?'

'Well, I was just *wondering*,' said Vera.

Claire shut the door and sank behind her desk. Now she'd have to apologize to Vera. Add it to her ever-growing list of mea culpas. She was in no mood to talk to anyone right now; reluctantly she picked up the telephone.

'Hello, Max?'

'Good time to call?'

'Don't even ask.'

'Oh. I'll keep it short, then. I thought you'd want to know they've confirmed the identity of that blue mushroom. I sent it to a mycologist, and he agreed it's *Clitocybe odora*, the anise funnel cap.'

'How toxic is it?'

'Only mildly so. The small amounts of muscarine wouldn't cause much beyond some mild gastrointestinal upset.'

She sighed. 'So that's a dead end.'

'It would appear so.'

'What about those lake water samples? Are the results back?'

'Yes, I have some of the preliminary findings here. Let me get the printout . . .'

Vera knocked on the door and came in with Warren Emerson's chart. She didn't say a word, just dropped the folder on the desk and walked out again. While waiting for Max to come back on the line, Claire opened the chart and glanced at the first page. It was dated 1932, the year of Emerson's birth. It described the uncomplicated labor and delivery of a healthy boy to a Mrs Agnes Emerson. The doctor's name was Higgins. The next few pages were devoted to well-baby checks and routine childhood visits.

She turned to a new page in the chart and frowned at the date: 1956. There had been a ten-year gap between the previous entry and this one. For the first time, Dr Pomeroy's signature appeared in the chart. She started to read Pomeroy's entry, but was interrupted by Max's voice on the line.

'Bacterial cultures are still pending,' he said. 'So far I see that dioxin, lead, and mercury levels are all within safe limits . . .'

Claire's attention was suddenly riveted on the chart. On what Pomeroy had written in the last paragraph: '*Has committed no other violent acts since his arrest in 1946.*'

'. . . by next week, we should know more,' Max said. 'But so far, the water quality seems pretty good. No evidence of any chemical contamination.'

'I've got to go,' she cut in. 'I'll call you later.'

She hung up and reread Pomeroy's entry from beginning to end. It was written in the year Warren Emerson had turned twenty-five years old.

The year he'd been released from the State Mental Hospital in Augusta.

Nineteen forty-six. In which month had Warren Emerson committed violence?

Claire stood in the basement archives room of the *Tranquility Gazette*, staring at a wooden cabinet that took up an entire wall. Each drawer was labeled by year. She opened the drawer for 1946, July to December.

Inside lay six issues of the *Gazette*. In 1946, it had been a monthly newspaper. The pages were brittle and yellow, the ads adorned with wasp-waisted women in bouffant skirts and smart little hats. Gingerly she leafed through the July issue, scanning the headlines: RECORD HEAT MAKES UP FOR RAINY SPRING ... BIGGEST SUMMER VISITOR COUNT EVER ... MOSQUITO ALERT ... BOYS CAUGHT WITH ILLEGAL FIREWORKS ... JULY 4TH PARADE DRAWS RECORD CROWDS. The same headlines that seem to appear every July, she thought. Summer has always been the season for parades and biting bugs, and these headlines brought back memories of her first summer in Maine. The crunch of sweet corn on the cob and snap peas, the tang of citronella on her skin. It had been a good summer, as it had been in 1946.

She turned to the August and September issues, where she read more of the same, news of fish fries and church dances and swim races in the lake. There was unpleasant news as well: a three-car accident had sent two visitors to the hospital and a house had burned down due to a cooking mishap. Shoplifters had taken their toll on area stores. Life was not perfect in Vacationland.

She turned to the October issue and found herself staring at a headline in bold print:

15-YEAR-OLD BOY SLAYS PARENTS, THEN FALLS TO HIS DEATH; YOUNGER SISTER'S ACTIONS 'CLEARLY SELF-DEFENSE.'

The juvenile was not named, but there were photographs of the murdered parents, a handsome, dark-haired couple smiling in their Sunday best. She focused on the caption beneath the photo, identifying the murdered couple: Martha and Frank Keating. Their last name was familiar; she knew of a local judge named Iris Keating. Were they related?

Her gaze dropped to another headline below it: FISTFIGHT BREAKS OUT IN HIGH SCHOOL CAFETERIA.

Then another: BOSTON VISITOR MISSING; GIRL LAST SEEN WITH AREA YOUTHS.

The basement was unheated, and her hands felt like ice. But the chill came from within.

She reached for the November issue and stared at the front page. At the headline screaming up at her.

14-YEAR-OLD ARRESTED FOR MURDER OF

PARENTS: FRIENDS AND NEIGHBORS STUNNED BY
CRIMES OF 'SENSITIVE CHILD.'
The chill had spread all the way up her spine.
She thought: *It's happening all over again.*

14

'Why didn't you tell me? Why did you keep it a secret?'

Lincoln crossed the room to shut his office door. Then he turned to face Claire. 'It was a long time ago. I didn't see the point of dredging up old history.'

'But it's the history of this town! Considering what's happened in the last month, it strikes me as relevant.'

She placed the photocopied articles from the *Tranquility Gazette* on his desk. 'Look at this. In 1946, seven people were murdered and one girl from Boston was never found. Obviously violence is nothing new to this town.' She tapped the stack of papers. 'Read the articles, Lincoln. Or do you already know the details?'

Slowly he sat down, staring at the pages. 'Yes, I know most of the details,' he said softly. 'I've heard the stories.'

'Who told you?'

'Jeff Willard. He was chief of police when I was first hired twenty-two years ago.'

'You hadn't heard about it before then?'

'No. And I grew up here. I knew nothing about it until Chief Willard told me. People just don't talk about it.'

'They'd rather pretend it never happened.'

'There's also our reputation to consider.' He looked up, at last meeting her gaze. 'This is a resort town, Claire. People come here to escape the big city, escape crime. We're not eager to reveal to the world that we've had our own problems. Our own murder epidemic.'

She sat down, her gaze now level with his. 'Who knows about this?'

'The people who were here then. The older ones, now in their sixties and seventies. But not their children. Not my generation.'

She shook her head in amazement. 'They kept it a secret all these years?'

'You understand why, don't you? It's not just the town they're protecting. It's their families. The kids who committed those crimes were all local. Their families still live here, and maybe they're still ashamed. Still suffering the aftermath.'

'Like Warren Emerson.'

'Exactly. Look at the life he's had. He lives alone, and has no friends. He's never committed another crime, yet he's shunned by everyone. Even by the kids, who have no idea why they're supposed to steer clear of him. They just know from their grandparents that Emerson is a man to be avoided.' He looked down at the photocopied article. 'So that's the background on your patient. Warren Emerson is a murderer. But he wasn't the only one.'

'You must have seen the parallels, Lincoln.'

'Okay, I admit there are some.'

'Too many to list.' She reached for the photocopied articles and flipped to the October issue. 'In 1946, it started off with fights in the schools. Two kids were expelled. Then there were windows smashed in town, homes vandalized – again, adolescents were blamed. Finally, the last week of October, a fifteen-year-old boy hacks his parents to death. His younger sister pushes him out the window in self-defense.' She looked up at him. 'It only gets worse from there. How do you explain it?'

'When violence occurs, Claire, it's only human nature to ask why. But the truth is, we don't always know why people kill each other.'

'Look at the sequence of events. Last time it started off with a quiet town. Then here and there, kids start to misbehave. Hurt each other. In a matter of weeks, they're killing people. The town's in an uproar, everyone demanding that something be done. And suddenly – magically – it all just *stops*. And the town goes back to sleep again.' She fell silent, her gaze dropping to the headline. 'Lincoln, there's something else that's strange about it. In the city, the most dangerous time of year is the summer, when the heat makes everyone's temper flare. Crime always takes a nosedive when it gets cold. But in this town, it's different. The violence starts in October, and peaks in November.' She looked up at him. 'Both times, the killing started in the fall.'

The beeping of her pocket pager startled her. She glanced at the number on the display, and reached for Lincoln's phone.

A CT technician answered her call. 'We just finished the brain scan on your patient, Warren Emerson. Dr Chapman's on his way over to read it now.'

'You see anything?' asked Claire.

'It's definitely abnormal.'

Dr Chapman clipped the CT films to the X-ray viewing box and flipped on the switch. The light flickered on, illuminating the transverse cuts of Warren Emerson's brain. 'This is what I'm talking about,' he said. 'Right here, extending into the left frontal lobe. You see it?'

Claire stepped closer. What he'd pointed out was a small, spherelike density located at the front of the brain, just behind the eyebrow. It appeared to be solid, not cystic. She glanced at the other cuts on view, but saw no other masses. If this was a tumor, then it appeared to be localized. 'What do you think?' she asked. 'A meningioma?'

He nodded. 'Most likely. See how smooth the edges are? Of course you'll need tissue diagnosis to confirm it's benign. It's about two centimeters in diameter, and it seems to be thickly encapsulated. Walled off by fibrous tissue. I suspect it can be removed without any residual tumor left behind.'

'Could this be the cause of his seizures?'

'How long has he had them?'

'Since his late teens. Which would make it close to fifty years.'

Chapman glanced at her in surprise. 'And this mass was never picked up?'

'No. Since he's had the seizures most of his life, I think Pomeroy assumed it wasn't worth pursuing.'

Chapman shook his head. 'That makes me rethink my diagnosis. First of all, you rarely see meningiomas in young adults. Also, a meningioma would continue to grow. So either this isn't the cause of his seizures, or this is not a meningioma.'

'What else could it be?'

'A glioma. A metastasis from some other primary.' He shrugged. 'It could even be an old walled-off cyst.'

'This mass looks solid.'

'If this was from TB, for instance, or a parasite, the body would launch an inflammatory reaction. Surround it or bind it up with scar tissue. Have you checked his TB status?'

'He was PPD-negative ten years ago.'

'Well, in the end, it's still a pathologic diagnosis. This patient needs a craniotomy and excision.'

'I guess this means we have to transfer him to Bangor.'

'We don't do craniotomies in this hospital. Our docs usually refer neurosurgery cases to Clarence Rothstein, out at Eastern Maine Medical Center.'

'You'd recommend him?'

Chapman nodded and flicked off the light box. 'He's got very good hands.'

Steamed broccoli and rice and a pathetic little dab of cod.

Louise Knowlton didn't know if she could bear it any longer, watching her son slowly starve. He had lost two more pounds, and the strain showed in his grim expression, his flashes of irritability. He was no longer her cheerful Barry.

Louise looked across the table at her husband and read the same thought in Mel's eyes: *It's the diet. He's behaving this way because of the diet.*

Louise pointed to the platter of french fries that she and Mel had been sharing. 'Barry, sweetie, you look so hungry! A few of those won't matter.'

Barry ignored her, and kept scraping his plate with the fork, eliciting teeth-shattering squeals against the china.

'Barry, stop that!'

He looked up. Not just a glance, but the coldest, flattest stare she had ever seen.

With trembling hands, Louise extended the platter of french fries. 'Oh please, Barry,' she murmured. 'Eat one. Eat them all. It will make you feel so much better if you just eat something.'

She gave a startled gasp as Barry shoved his chair

back and abruptly stood up. Without a word he walked away and slammed his bedroom door shut. A moment later they heard the incessant gunfire of the video game as their son blasted away hordes of virtual enemies.

'Did something happen in school today?' asked Mel. 'Those kids picking on him again?'

Louise sighed. 'I don't know. I don't know anything anymore.'

They sat listening to the accelerating blast of gunfire. To the cries and moans of virtual victims as they lay dying in some Super Nintendo hell.

Louise looked down at the pile of limp and soggy french fries and she shuddered. For the first time in her life, she pushed her dinner away, unfinished.

Noah's stereo was playing full blast when Claire arrived home. The headache that had been building all afternoon seemed to tighten around her cranium, digging its claws into her forehead. She hung up her coat and stood at the bottom of the steps, listening to the relentless pounding of drums, the chanting of lyrics. She couldn't understand a single word. How am I supposed to monitor my child's music when I don't even know what the songs are saying?

This could not go on. She couldn't deal with the noise, not tonight. She called up the stairs: 'Noah, turn it down!'

The music played on, unabating. Unbearable.

She climbed the steps, her irritation swelling to anger. Reaching his room, she found the door locked. She pounded on it and yelled: 'Noah!'

It took a moment before the door swung open. The music rushed at her, engulfing her in a tidal wave of noise. Noah hulked in the doorway, his shirt and trousers so baggy they hung like tattered ceremonial robes.

'Turn it down!' she yelled.

He flipped the amplifier switch and the music abruptly went dead. Her ears were still ringing in the silence.

'What are you trying to do, make yourself deaf? And drive me totally nuts in the process?'

'You weren't home.'

'I *was* home. I've been yelling, but you couldn't hear me.'

'I'm hearing you now, okay?'

'In ten years you're not going to hear a thing if you keep playing your music that loud. You're not the only one who lives under this roof.'

'How can I forget when you keep reminding me?' He dropped like a stone into a chair and swiveled around to face his desk. Turning his back on her.

She stood watching him. Even though he was flipping the pages of a magazine, she knew by the muscles tensed in his shoulders that he wasn't really reading. He was too aware of *her*, of her anger toward him.

She came into his room and wearily sat down

on the bed. After a moment she said, 'I'm sorry I yelled at you.'

'You do it all the time now.'

'Do I?'

'Yeah.' He flipped a page.

'I don't mean to, Noah. I have so many things going wrong at once, I can't seem to deal with them all.'

'Everything's all screwed up since we moved here, Mom. *Everything*.' He slapped the magazine shut and dropped his head in his hands. His voice was barely a whisper. 'I wish Dad was here.'

For a moment they were both silent. She heard his tears fall on the page of the magazine, heard his sharp intake of breath as he struggled for control.

She stood up and placed her hands on his shoulders. They were tense, all his muscles knotted with the effort not to cry. We are so much alike, she realized, both of us constantly fighting to rein in our emotions, to stay in control. Peter had been the exuberant member of the family, the one who screamed with delight on roller coasters and roared with laughter in movie theaters. The one who sang in the shower and set off smoke alarms with his cooking. The one who had never hesitated to say 'I love you.'

How sad you would be to see us now, Peter. Afraid to reach out to each other. Still mourning, still crippled by your death.

'I miss him too,' she whispered. She let her arms slip around her son and she rested her cheek in his hair, inhaling the boy-smell she loved so much. 'I miss him too.'

Downstairs, the doorbell rang.

Not now. Not now.

She held on, ignoring the sound, shutting out everything but the warmth of her son in her arms.

'Mom,' said Noah, shrugging her off. 'Mom, someone's at the door.'

Reluctantly she released her hold on him and straightened. The moment, the opportunity, had passed, and she was staring once again at his rigid shoulders.

She went downstairs, angry at this new intrusion, at yet another demand tugging her away from her son. She opened the front door to find Lincoln standing in the bitterly cold wind, his gloved hand poised to ring the bell again. He had never stopped in at her house before, and she was both surprised and puzzled by his visit.

'I have to talk to you,' he said. 'Can I come in?'

She had not yet lit a fire in the front parlor, and the room was cold and depressingly dark. Quickly she turned on all the lamps, but light was poor compensation for the chill.

'After you left my office,' he said, 'I got to thinking about what you'd said. That there's a pattern to the violence in this town. That there's some sort of connection between 1946 and this year.' He reached in his jacket and took out the sheaf of photocopied news articles she'd left him. 'Guess what? The answer was staring right at us.'

'What answer?'

'Look at the first page. The October issue, 1946.'

'I've already read that article.'

'No, not the story about the murder. The article at the bottom. You probably didn't notice it.'

She smoothed the page on her lap. The article he'd referred to was partly cut off; only the top half had been included in the photocopy. The headline read: REPAIRS ON LOCUST RIVER BRIDGE COMPLETED.

'I don't know what you're getting at,' she said.

'We had to repair that same bridge this year. Remember?'

'Yes.'

'So *why* did we have to repair it?'

'Because it was broken?'

He ran his hand through his hair in frustration. 'Geez, Claire. Think about it! Why'd the bridge need repairs? Because it got washed away. We had record rainfall this past spring, and it flooded the Locust River, washed out two homes, tore out a whole series of footbridges. I called the U.S. Geological Survey to confirm it. This year was the heaviest rainfall we've had *in fifty-two years*.'

She looked up, suddenly registering what he was trying to tell her. 'Then the last time the rainfall was this heavy . . .'

'Was the spring of 1946.'

She sat back, stunned by the coincidence. 'Rainfall,' she murmured. 'Moist soil. Bacteria. Fungi . . .'

'Mushrooms are fungi. What about those blue ones?'

She shook her head. 'Max had their identity confirmed. They're not very toxic. But heavy rains would encourage the growth of other fungi. In fact, it's a fungus that caused mass occurrences of St Vitus' dance.'

'Is that a seizure?'

'The medical term for St Vitus' dance is *chorea*. It's a writhing, dancelike movement of the limbs. Occasionally, there'll be reports of mass occurrences. It may even have inspired the witchcraft accusations in Salem.'

'A medical condition?'

'Yes. After a cold, wet spring, rye crops can be infected by this fungus. People eat the rye, and they develop chorea.'

'Could we be dealing with a form of St Vitus' dance?'

'No, I'm just saying there are examples throughout history of human diseases linked to climate. Everything in nature is intimately bound together. We may *think* we control our environment, but we're affected by so many organisms we can't see.' She paused, thinking about Scotty Braxton's negative cultures. So far nothing had grown out from either his blood or spinal fluid. Could there be a locus of infection she had missed? An organism so unusual, so unexpected, the lab would have discounted it as error?

'There must be a common factor among these children,' she said. 'Exposure to the same contaminated food, for instance. All we have is this apparent association between rainfall and violence. It could be just coincidence.'

He sat in silence for a moment. She had often studied his face, admiring the strength she saw there, the calm self-confidence. Today she saw the intelligence in his eyes. He had taken two completely disparate bits of information and had recognized a pattern that she had not even noticed.

'Then what we need to find,' he said, 'is the common factor.'

She nodded. 'Could you get me into the Maine Youth Center? So I can talk to Taylor?'

'That could be a problem. You know Paul Darnell still blames you.'

'But Taylor's not the only child affected. Paul can't blame me for everything else that's gone wrong in this town.'

'Not now, he can't.' Lincoln rose to his feet. 'We need answers before the town meeting. I'll get you in to see the boy, Claire. One way or another.'

Standing at the parlor window, she watched him walk down the icy driveway to his truck. He moved with the balanced stride of a man who'd grown up in this unforgiving climate, each step planted squarely, the boot sole stamped down to catch the ice. He reached the truck, opened the door, and for some reason glanced back at her house.

Just for an instant, their gazes met.

And she thought, with a strange sense of wonder, *How long have I been attracted to him? When did it start? I can't remember.* Now it was one more complication in her life.

As he drove away, she remained at the window, staring at a landscape bled of all color. Snow and ice and bare trees, all of it fading to black.

Upstairs, Noah's music had started again.

She turned from the window and flicked off the parlor lamp. That's when she suddenly remembered the promise she'd made to Warren Emerson, and she groaned.

The cat.

Night had fallen by the time she drove up the lower slope of Beech Hill and pulled into Emerson's front yard. She parked next to the woodpile, a perfectly circular tower of stacked logs. She thought of the many hours it must have taken him to arrange his wood with such precision, each log placed with the same care one usually gave to constructing a stone wall. And then to pull it down again, bit by bit, as winter consumed his annual work of art.

She turned off her engine and looked up at the old farmhouse. No lights were on inside. She used a flashlight to guide herself up the icy front steps to the porch. Everything seemed to sag and she had the strange illusion that she was tilting sideways, sliding toward the edge, toward oblivion. Warren had told her the door would be unlocked, and it was. She stepped inside and turned on the lights.

The kitchen sprang into view with its worn linoleum and chipped appliances. A small gray cat stared up at her from the floor. They had startled each other, she and the cat, and for a few seconds they both froze.

Then the cat shot out of the room and vanished somewhere into the house.

'Here, kitty, kitty! You want your dinner, don't you? Mona?'

She had planned to take Mona to a kennel for boarding. Warren Emerson had already been transferred to Eastern Maine Medical Center for his craniotomy, and would remain hospitalized for at least a week. Claire didn't relish the thought of driving here every day just to feed a cat. But it appeared the cat had different ideas.

Her frustration mounted as she went from room to room in search of the uncooperative Mona, turning on lights as she went. Like so many other farmhouses of its era, this one had been built to house a large family, and it consisted of many small rooms, made even more claustrophobic by the clutter. She saw piles of old newspapers and magazines, bundled grocery sacks, crates filled with empty bottles. In the hallway she had to turn sideways to navigate a narrow tunnel between stacked books. Such hoarding was usually a sign of mental illness, but Warren had organized his clutter in a logical fashion, the books segregated from the magazines, the brown paper bags all folded and bound together with twine. Perhaps this was merely Yankee frugality carried to an extreme.

It provided plenty of cover for a fugitive cat.

She'd made a complete circuit of the downstairs without spotting Mona. The cat must be hiding in one of the upstairs rooms.

She started up the steps, then halted, her hands suddenly sweating. *Deja vu*, she thought. I have lived this before. A strange house, a strange staircase. Something terrible waiting for me in the attic . . .

But this was not Scotty Braxton's house, and the only thing lurking upstairs was a frightened animal.

She forced herself to continue climbing as she called out, 'Here, kitty!' if only to prop up her faltering courage. There were four doors on the second floor, but only one was open. If the cat had fled upstairs, she had to be in that room.

Claire stepped through the doorway and turned on the light.

Her gaze was drawn at once to the black and white photographs – dozens of them hanging on the wall or propped up on the dresser and nightstand. A gallery of Warren Emerson's memories. She crossed the room and stared at three faces smiling back at her from one of the photos, a middle-aged couple with a young boy. The woman was round-faced and plain, her hat tilted at a comically drunken pitch. The man beside her seemed to be sharing in the joke; his eyes were bright with laughter. They each rested one hand on the shoulders of the boy standing between them, physically claiming him as their own, their shared possession.

And the boy with the cowlick and the missing front teeth – this must be young Warren, basking in the glow of his parents' attention.

Her gaze moved to the other photographs and she saw the same faces again and again, different seasons, different places. Here a shot of the mother proudly holding up a pie. There a shot of father and son on a riverbank with their fishing poles. Finally, a school photo of a young girl, apparently Warren's sweetheart, for at the bottom someone had drawn in a heart containing the words *Warren and Iris forever*. Through tears, Claire stared at the nightstand, at a glass of water resting there, half full. At the bed, where gray hairs had been shed on the pillow. Warren's bed.

Every morning he would wake up alone in this room, to the sight of his parents' photos. And every night, the last image he'd register was of their faces, smiling at him.

She was crying now, for the child he once was. A lonely little boy trapped in an old man's body.

She went back downstairs to the kitchen.

There was no sense chasing after a cat that didn't want to be captured. She would simply leave food in the dish, and come back another time. Opening the pantry door, she found herself staring at dozens of çans of cat food stacked on the shelves. There was scarcely anything in the kitchen for a man to eat, but pampered Mona was certainly well-supplied.

Today she'll be expecting tuna.

Tuna it would be. She emptied the can into the cat dish and placed it on the floor next to the bowl of water. She filled another bowl with dried cat food, enough to last several days. She cleaned out the litterbox. Then she turned off the lights and walked out.

Sitting in her car, she glanced one last time at the house. For most of his life, Warren Emerson had lived within those walls, without human companionship, without love. He would probably die in that house alone, with only a cat to witness his exit.

She wiped the tears from her eyes. Then she turned the car around and drove down the dark road for home.

That night Lincoln called her.

'I spoke to Wanda Darnell,' he said. 'I told her there may be a biological reason for her son's actions. That other children in town have been affected, and we're trying to track down the cause.'

'How did she react?'

'I think she's relieved. It means there's something external to blame. Not the family. Not her.'

'I understand that perfectly.'

'She's given permission for you to interview her son.'

'When?'

'Tomorrow. At the Maine Youth Center.'

A long row of beds lined the wall of the silent dormitory room. The morning sun shone in through windows above, one bright square of light spilling down on the boy's thin shoulders. He sat on the bed with his legs tucked up against his chest. His head was bowed. This was not the same boy she had seen four weeks ago, cursing and thrashing. This was a child who'd been beaten down, hopes and dreams trampled, only his physical shell remaining.

He did not look up as Claire approached, her footsteps echoing on the worn planks. She stopped beside his bed. 'Hello, Taylor. Do you feel like talking to me?'

The boy lifted one shoulder, barely a shrug, but at least it was the semblance of an invitation.

She reached for a chair, her gaze falling briefly on the small pine desk next to his bed. It was a badly abused piece of furniture, its surface gouged with four-letter words and the initials of countless young residents. She wondered if Taylor had already carved his mark into this permanent record of despair.

She slid the chair to his bed and sat down. 'Whatever we talk about today, Taylor, is just between us, okay?' He gave a shrug, as if it hardly mattered. 'Tell me about what happened, that day in school. Why did you do it?'

He turned his cheek against his knees, as though suddenly too exhausted to hold up his head. 'I don't know why.'

'Do you remember that day?'

'Uh-huh.'

'Everything?'

He swallowed hard, but didn't say anything. His face suddenly rippled with anguish and he closed his eyes, squeezing them so tight his whole face seemed to collapse on itself. He took a deep breath and what should have been a howl of pain came out only as a high, thin keening.

'I don't know. I don't know why I did it.'

'You brought a gun to school that day.'

'To prove I had one. They didn't believe me. They said I was making it up.'

'Who didn't believe you?'

'J.D. and Eddie. They're always bragging that their dad lets them shoot his guns.'

Jack Reid's sons again. Wanda Darnell had said they were a bad influence, and she'd been right.

'So you brought the gun to school,' said Claire. 'Did you plan to use it?'

He shook his head. 'I just had it in my backpack. But then I got a D on my test. And Mrs Horatio – she started yelling at me about that stupid frog.' He began to rock, hugging his knees, every breath catching in a sob. 'I wanted to kill them all. It was

285

like I couldn't stop myself. I wanted to make them all pay.' He stopped rocking and went very still, his eyes unfocused, gazing at nothing. 'I'm not mad at them anymore. But now it's too late.'

'It may not be your fault, Taylor.'

'Everyone knows I did it.'

'But you just told me you weren't in control.'

'It's still my fault . . .'

'Taylor, look at me. I don't know if anyone's told you about your friend, Scotty Braxton.'

Slowly the boy's gaze lifted to hers.

'The same thing happened to him. And now his mother is dead.'

She saw, by his look of shock, that he had not been told the news.

'No one can explain why he snapped. Why he attacked her. You're not the only one it's happened to.'

'My dad says it's because you took away my medicine.'

'Scotty wasn't taking any medicine.' She paused, searching his eyes. 'Or was he?'

'No.'

'This is very important. You have to tell me the truth, Taylor. Did either of you boys take any drugs?'

'I *am* telling the truth.'

He looked at her, his gaze unflinching. And she believed him.

'What about Scotty?' he asked. 'Is Scotty coming here?'

Tears suddenly stung her eyes. She said, softly: 'I'm sorry, Taylor. I know you two were good friends . . .'

'The best. We're best friends.'

'He was in the hospital. And something happened. We tried to help him, but there was – there was nothing –'

'He's dead. Isn't he?'

His direct question was a plea for an honest answer. She admitted, quietly: 'Yes. I'm afraid so.'

He dropped his face against his knees, and the words spilled out between sobs. 'Scotty never did anything wrong! He was such a wuss. That's what J.D. always called him, the dumb wuss. I never stood up for him. I should've said something, but I never did . . .'

'Taylor. Taylor, I need to ask you another question.'

'. . . I was afraid to.'

'You and Scotty were together a lot. Where did you two spend your time?'

He didn't answer; he just kept rocking on the bed.

'I really need to know this, Taylor. Where did you two hang out?'

He took in a shaky breath. 'With – with the other kids.'

'Where?'

'I don't know! All over.'

'In the woods? At someone's house?'

He stopped rocking, and for a moment she thought he hadn't heard the last question. Then he raised his head and looked at her. 'The lake.'

Locust Lake. It was the center of all activity in Tranquility, the place for picnics and swim races, for boaters and fishermen. Without it, there would be no summer visitors, no flow of money. The town itself would not exist.

It all has something to do with the lake, she thought suddenly. Water and rainfall. Floods and bacteria.

The night the water glowed.

'Taylor,' she said, 'did you and Scotty both swim in the lake?'

He nodded. 'Every day.'

15

The town meeting was scheduled for seven-thirty, and by seven-fifteen, every seat in the high school cafeteria was filled. People were crowding into the aisles, lining up along the walls, and spilling out the rear doors into the cold wind. From where Claire was standing, off to the side, she had a good view of the speakers' table at the front. There Lincoln, Fern Cornwallis, and the chairman of the Town Board of Selectmen, Glen Ryder, were seated. The five members of the board were clustered in the front row.

Claire recognized many of the faces in the audience. Most of them were other parents, whom she'd met at high school functions. She also saw a number of her colleagues from Knox Hospital. The dozen teenagers in attendance had chosen to stand at the rear of the cafeteria, and were tightly clustered together as though to ward off attack by their elders.

Glen Ryder banged his gavel, but the crowd was

too large, too agitated, to hear him. The frustrated Ryder had to climb onto a chair and yell: 'This meeting will come to order *now*!'

The cafeteria at last fell silent, and Ryder continued. 'I know there aren't enough seats for everyone in here. I know there are people outside who are upset about having to stand in eight-degree weather. But the fire chief says we've already exceeded this room's occupancy limit. We just can't allow anyone else to enter, unless someone else exits first.'

'Seems to me some of those kids in the back could leave and make room for adults,' a man grumbled.

One of the teenagers retorted: 'We've got a right to be here too!'

'You kids're the reason we're here in the first place!'

'If you're going to talk about us, then we want to hear what you're saying!'

Half a dozen people started to speak at once.

'No one's being kicked out of here!' yelled Ryder. 'It's a public meeting, Ben, and we can't exclude people. Now let's get on with it.' Ryder looked at Lincoln. 'Chief Kelly, why don't you bring us up to date with the problems in town.'

Lincoln rose to his feet. The last few days had drained him, both physically and emotionally, and it showed in the drooping slope of his shoulders. 'It hasn't been a good month,' he said. A typical Lincoln Kelly understatement. 'What everyone seems to focus on are the murders. The shooting at the high school on November second, and then the Braxtons on November fifteenth. That's two murders in two weeks. What scares me even more is, I don't think we've seen the worst of it yet. Last night, my officers responded to eight different calls involving juveniles assaulting others. I've never seen this before. I've been a cop in this town for twenty-two years. I've seen minor crime waves come and go. But what I'm seeing now – kids trying to hurt each other, *kill* each other – trying to kill the people they love . . .' He shook his head and sat down without another word.

'Miss Cornwallis?' said Ryder.

The high school principal rose to her feet. Fern Cornwallis was a handsome woman, and she had taken pains to look her best tonight. Her blond hair was swept into a gleaming French twist, and she was one of the few women in the room who'd bothered to apply makeup. But that touch of bright lipstick only emphasized the anxious pallor of her face.

'I want to echo everything Chief Kelly just said. What's happening in this town – the anger, the violence – I've never seen it before, either. And it's not just a problem in the school. It's also a problem in your homes. I know these children! I've watched them grow up. I've seen them around town, in the school hallways. Or in my office, as the occasion warranted. And the ones who are getting into fights now, none of them are

291

kids I would have labeled troublemakers. None of them gave any hint, in past years, of being violent. But suddenly I find I don't know these children anymore. I don't recognize them.' She paused and swallowed hard. 'I'm afraid of them,' she said quietly.

'So whose fault is it?' yelled Ben Doucette.

'We're not saying it's anyone's fault,' Fern said. 'We're just trying to understand why this is happening. Between our school and the middle school, we've brought in five new guidance counselors on an emergency basis. The high school has a district psychologist, Dr Lieberman, working intensively with our staff. Trying to come up with a plan of action.'

Ben stood up. A sour-faced bachelor in his fifties, he had lost an arm in Vietnam, and he was always clutching the stump with his good hand, as though to emphasize his sacrifice. 'I can tell you what the problem is,' he said. 'It's the same problem we've got all over this country. No goddamn discipline. When I was thirteen, you think I'd have dared to pick up a knife, threaten my mother? My old man woulda whapped me up the side of the head.'

'What are you suggesting, Mr Doucette?' said Fern. 'That we spank fourteen-year-olds?'

'Why not?'

'Try it!' yelled one of the teenage boys, and he was joined by the other kids in a chorus of jeers: *'Try it, try it, try it!'*

The meeting was out of control. Lincoln stood

up, raising his hand in a plea for order. It was a measure of the respect the town held for him that the crowd finally quieted down to hear him speak.

'It's time to talk about realistic solutions,' he said.

Jack Reid stood up. 'Can't talk about solutions till we talk about why it's happening in the first place. I hear from my boys that it's the new kids in school, the ones who moved here from other cities, who're causing most of the problems. Starting up gangs, maybe bringing in drugs.'

Lincoln's response was lost in a sudden crescendo of voices. Claire could see the frustration in his face, the deepening flush of anger.

'This is not a problem from away,' said Lincoln. 'This crisis is local. It's *our* problem, and *our* kids getting into trouble.'

'But who got them started?' said Reid. 'Who got 'em going? Some folks just don't belong here!'

Glen Ryder's gavel banged again and again, to no avail. Jack Reid had pushed a hot button with this crowd, and now everyone was yelling at once.

A woman's voice cut through the bedlam. 'What about the rumors of a centuries-old Satanic cult?' said Damaris Horne, rising to her feet. It was hard to miss that wild mane of blond hair. Also hard to miss were the interested glances men cast her way. 'We've all heard about those old bones they dug up by the lake. I understand it was a mass murder. Maybe even a ritual slaying.'

'That was over a hundred years ago,' said Lincoln. 'It's completely unrelated.'

'Maybe not. New England has a long history of Satanic cults.'

Lincoln was fast losing control of his temper. 'The only cult around here,' he shot back, 'is the one you made up for your trashy tabloid!'

'Then perhaps you'll explain all the disturbing rumors I've been hearing,' said Damaris, keeping her cool. 'For instance, the number *six-six-six* painted on the side of the high school.'

Lincoln aimed a startled glance at Fern. Claire realized at once what that look meant. Clearly they were both surprised by the reporter's knowledge of a real event.

'There was a barn found splashed with blood last month,' said Damaris. 'What about that?'

'That was a can of red paint. Not blood.'

'And those lights flickering at night up on Beech Hill. Which, I've been told, is nothing but forest reserve.'

'Now wait a minute,' interjected Lois Cuthbert, one of the town selectmen. 'That I can explain. It's that biologist fella, Dr Tutwiler, collecting salamanders at night. I almost ran over him in the dark a few weeks ago, when he came hiking back down.'

'All right,' conceded Damaris. 'Forget the lights up on Beech Hill. But I still say there's a lot of strange and unexplained things happening in this town. If anyone here wants to talk to me about it later, I'm ready to listen.' Damaris sat down again.

'I agree with her,' said a tremulous voice. The woman stood at the back of the room, a small, white-faced figure clutching at her coat. 'There's something wrong in this town. I've felt it for a long time. You can deny it all you want, Chief Kelly, but what we have here is *evil*. I'm not saying it's Satan. I don't know what it is. But I know I can't live here anymore. I've put my house up for sale, and I'm leaving next week. Before something happens to *my* family.' She turned and walked out of the hushed room.

The high-pitched beeping of Claire's pocket pager cut through the silence. She glanced down and saw it was the hospital trying to reach her. She pushed her way through the crowd and stepped outside to make the call on her cell phone.

After the overheated cafeteria, the wind felt piercingly cold, and she huddled, shivering, against the building, waiting for an answer.

'Laboratory, Clive speaking.'

'This is Dr Elliot. You paged me.'

'I wasn't sure if you still wanted us to call you on these results, since this patient's deceased. But I've got some reports back on Scotty Braxton.'

'Yes, I want to hear all the results.'

'First, I have a final report here from Anson Biologicals on the boy's comprehensive drug and tox screen. None were detected.'

'There's nothing about the peak on his chromatogram?'

'Not on this report.'

'This has to be a mistake. There must be something in his drug screen.'

295

'That's all it says here: "None detected." We've also got the final culture result on the boy's nasal discharge. It's a pretty long list of organisms, since you wanted everything identified. Mostly the usual colonizers. *Staph epidermidis*, alpha *strep*. Bugs we don't normally bother to report.'

'Is there anything unusual growing out?'

'Yes. *Vibrio fischeri*.'

She scribbled the name down on a scrap of paper. 'I've never heard of that organism.'

'Neither had we. It's never turned up in a culture here. It has to be a contaminant.'

'But I collected the specimen straight from the patient's nasal mucosa.'

'Well, I doubt this contamination came from our lab. This bacteria isn't something you'd find floating around in a hospital.'

'What is *Vibrio fischeri*? Where does it normally grow?'

'I checked with the microbiologist in Bangor, where they did the cultures. She says this species is usually a colonizer of invertebrates like squid or marine worms. It forms a symbiotic relationship. The host invertebrate provides a safe environment.'

'And what does the *Vibrio* do in exchange?'

'It provides the power for the host's light organ.'

It took a few seconds for the significance of that fact to sink in. She asked, sharply: 'Are you saying this bacteria is bioluminescent?'

'Yeah. The squid collects it in a translucent sac. It

uses the bacteria's glow to attract other squid. Sort of like a neon sign for sex.'

'I've got to go,' she cut in. 'I'll talk to you later.' She disconnected and hurried back into the school cafeteria.

Glen Ryder was trying to quiet down the audience again, his gavel thumping ineffectually against a chorus of competing voices. He looked startled as Claire pushed her way to the speakers' table.

'I have to make an announcement,' she said. 'I have a health alert for the town.'

'It's not exactly relevant to this meeting, Dr Elliot.'

'I believe it is relevant. Please let me speak.'

He nodded and resumed banging the gavel with new urgency. 'Dr Elliot has an announcement!'

Claire moved front and center, acutely aware that everyone's gaze was on her. She took a deep breath and began. 'These attacks are scaring us all, causing us to point fingers at our neighbors, at the school. At people from away. But I believe there's a medical explanation. I've just spoken to the hospital lab, and I have a clue to what's going on.' She held up the scrap of paper with the organism's name. 'It's a bacteria called *Vibrio fischeri*. It was growing in Scotty Braxton's nasal mucus. What we're seeing now – this aggressive behavior in our children – may be a symptom of infection. *Vibrio fischeri* could cause a case of meningitis we can't detect with our usual tests. It could also cause what doctors call a "neighborhood reaction" – an infection of the sinuses, extending into the brain –'

'Wait a minute,' said Adam DelRay, rising to his feet. 'I've been practicing medicine here for ten years. I've never come across an infection of this – what is it?'

'*Vibrio fischeri*. It's not normally seen in humans. But the lab's identified it as an organism infecting my patient.'

'And where did your patient pick up this bug?'

'I believe it was the lake. Scotty Braxton and Taylor Darnell both swam in that lake almost every day last summer. So did a lot of other kids in this town. If that lake has a high bacterial count of *Vibrio*, that could explain how they're getting infected.'

'I went swimming last summer,' said a woman. 'A lot of adults did. Why would only the kids get infected?'

'It may have to do with what part of the lake you swim in. I also know there's a similar infectious pattern for amoebic meningitis. That's a brain infection caused by amoebas growing in fresh water. Children and teenagers are most often infected. When they swim in contaminated water, the amoeba enters their nasal mucosa. From there it reaches the brain by passing through a porous barrier called the cribriform plate. Adults don't get infected, because their cribriform plates are sealed over, protecting their brains. Children don't have that protection.'

'So how do you treat this? With antibiotics or something?'

'That would be my guess.'

Adam DelRay let out an incredulous laugh. 'Are you suggesting we dispense antibiotics to every irritable kid in town? You have no proof anyone's infected!'

'I do have a positive culture.'

'*One* positive culture. And it's not from the spinal fluid, so how can you call this meningitis?' He looked at the audience. 'I can assure this town there is no epidemic. Last month, the Two Hills Pediatric Group got a lab grant to survey blood counts and hormone levels in kids. They've been drawing blood on all their teenage patients in the area. Any infection would have shown up in their blood counts.'

'What grant are you talking about?' asked Claire.

'From Anson Biologicals. To confirm baseline normals. They haven't reported anything unusual.' He shook his head. 'This infection theory of yours is the most crackpot thing I've heard yet, and it comes without a shred of evidence. You don't even know if *Vibrio* is growing in the lake.'

'I know it is,' said Claire. 'I've seen it.'

'You *saw* a bacteria? What, do you have microscopic vision?'

'*Vibrio fischeri* is bioluminescent. It glows. I've seen bioluminescence in Locust Lake.'

'Where are the cultures to back it up? Have you collected water samples?'

'I saw it just before the lake froze over. It's probably too cold now to grow out viable cultures. Which means we won't have confirmation until we do water sampling in the spring. These cultures take time to grow. It could be weeks or months after that before we get an answer.' She paused, reluctant to make her next suggestion. 'Until we rule out the lake as the source of this bacteria,' she said, 'I recommend we keep our children from swimming in it.'

The uproar was expected and immediate.

'Are you crazy? We can't let an announcement like that get out!'

'What about the tourists? You'll scare off the tourists!'

'How the hell are we s'posed to make a living?'

Glen Ryder was on his feet, banging at the table. 'Order! I will have *order*!' His face florid, he turned to confront Claire. 'Dr Elliot, this isn't the time or place to suggest such drastic action. It needs to be discussed by the Board of Selectmen.'

'This is a public health issue,' said Claire. 'It's a decision for the health department. Not politicians.'

'There's no need to involve the state!'

'It's irresponsible not to.'

Lois Cuthbert shot to her feet. 'I'll tell you what's irresponsible! It's getting up there, without any evidence, with all these reporters in the room, and claiming there's some deadly bacteria in our lake. You're going to destroy this town.'

300

'If there's a health risk, we have no other choice.'

Lois turned to Adam DelRay. 'What's your opinion, Dr DelRay? Is there a health risk?'

DelRay gave a derisive laugh. 'The only risk that I can see is that we'll be made laughingstocks if we take this seriously. Bacteria that glow in the dark? Do they sing and dance too?'

Claire flushed as laughter burst out all around her. 'I know what I saw,' she insisted.

'Right, Dr Elliot! Psychedelic bacteria.'

Lincoln's voice suddenly rang through the laughter. 'I saw it too.'

Everyone fell silent as he rose to his feet. Startled, Claire turned to look at him and he gave her a wry nod, a gesture that said: We might as well hang together.

'I was there that night, with Dr Elliot,' he said. 'We both saw the glow on the lake. I can't tell you what it was. It only lasted for a few minutes, and then it vanished. But there *was* a glow.'

'I've lived on that lake all my life,' said Lois Cuthbert. 'I've never seen any glow.'

'Me neither!'

'—or me!'

'Hey, Chief, you and the doc sniffing the same thing?'

New laughter erupted, and this time it was directed at both of them. The outrage had turned to ridicule, but Lincoln didn't back down; he bore the insults with calm equanimity.

'It may be an episodic occurrence,' said Claire.

'Something that doesn't happen every year. It could be related to weather conditions. Spring flooding or a particularly hot summer – we had both this year. The very same conditions that occurred fifty-two years ago.' She paused, and her challenging gaze swept the audience. 'I know there are people in this room who remember what happened fifty-two years ago.'

The crowd went silent.

The reporter from the *Portland Press Herald* asked, loudly: 'What happened fifty-two years ago?'

Abruptly Glen Ryder shot to his feet. 'The board will take it under advisement. Thank you, Dr Elliot.'

'This should be addressed now,' said Claire. 'The health department should be called in to test the water –'

'We will discuss it at our next board meeting,' Ryder repeated firmly. 'That's *all*, Dr Elliot.'

Cheeks burning, she walked away from the speakers' table.

The meeting continued, loud and rancorous, as suggestions were tossed out. There was no further mention of her theory; they had unanimously dismissed it as not worth further discussion. Someone suggested a nine P.M. curfew – all kids off the streets. The teens protested, 'Civil rights!' 'What about our civil rights?'

'You kids have no civil rights!' shot back Lois. 'Not until you learn responsibility!'

It went downhill from there.

At ten P.M., with everyone hoarse from shouting, Glen Ryder finally adjourned the meeting.

Claire remained standing at the side of the room, watching as the crowd exited. No one looked at her as they filed past. I've ceased to exist in this town, she thought wretchedly, except as an object of scorn. She wanted to thank Lincoln for supporting her, but she saw that he was under siege, surrounded by the Board of Selectmen, who were plying him with questions and complaints.

'Dr Elliot!' called out Damaris Horne. 'What happened fifty-two years ago?'

Claire fled toward the exit, Damaris and the other reporters trailing after her as she kept repeating, 'No comment. No comment.' She was relieved when no one pursued her out the door.

Outside, the chill wind seemed to slice right through her coat. Her car was parked some distance from the school. Thrusting her hands in her pockets, she began to walk as quickly as she dared along the icy road, squinting against the intermittent glare of headlights as other cars pulled away. By the time she reached her vehicle, she already had the keys out, and was about to unlock the door when she realized something was not right.

She took a step back and stared in shock at the pools of flaccid rubber that had been her tires. All four of them had been slashed. In fury, in frustration, she slammed her hand down on the car. Once, twice.

Across the road, a man walking back to his own car turned and looked at her in surprise. It was Mitchell Groome.

'Something wrong, Dr Elliot?' he called out.

'Look at my tires!'

He paused to let a car drive past, then crossed the road to join her. 'Jesus,' he murmured. 'Someone doesn't like you.'

'They slashed *all* of them!'

'I'd help you change them. But I don't suppose you'd have four spare tires in the trunk.'

She did not appreciate his weak attempt at humor. She turned her back on him and stared down at the ruined tires. Her exposed face stung from the wind, and the chill of the frozen ground seemed to seep through the soles of her boots. It was too late to call Joe Bartlett's garage; he wouldn't be able to get four new tires till morning, anyway. She was stranded, furious, and growing colder by the minute.

She turned to Groome. 'Could you give me a ride home?'

It was a deal with the devil, and she knew it. A journalist must ask questions, and barely ten seconds into the drive, he asked the one she'd expected:

'So what did happen in this town fifty-two years ago?'

She averted her eyes. 'I'm really not in the mood for this.'

'I'm sure you're not, but it's going to come out eventually. Damaris Horne will track it down, one way or the other.'

'That woman has no sense of ethics.'

'But she does have an inside source.'

Claire looked at him. 'Are you talking about the police department?'

'You already know about it?'

'Not the name of the officer. Which one is it?'

'Tell me what happened in 1946.'

She faced forward again. 'It's in the local newspaper archives. You can look it up for yourself.'

He drove for a moment in silence. 'It's happened to this town before, hasn't it?' he said. 'The killings.'

'Yes.'

'And you believe there's a biological reason for it?'

'It has something to do with that lake. It's some sort of natural phenomenon. A bacteria, or an algae.'

'What about my theory? That this is another Flanders, Iowa?'

'It's not drug abuse, Mitchell. I thought we'd turned up something in both boys' blood – an anabolic steroid of some kind. But the final tox screens on both of them came back negative. And Taylor denies any drug abuse.'

'Kids do lie.'

'Blood tests don't.'

They pulled into her driveway, and he turned to look at her. 'You've picked an uphill fight, Dr Elliot. Maybe you didn't sense the depth of anger in that room, but I certainly did.'

'Not only did I sense it, I have four slashed tires to prove it.' She stepped out. 'Thank you for the ride. Now you owe *me* something.'

'Do I?'

'The name of the cop who's been talking to Damaris Horne.'

He gave an apologetic shrug. 'I don't know his name. All I can tell you is that I've seen them together in, shall we say, close contact. Dark hair, medium build. Works the night shift.'

She nodded grimly. 'I'll figure it out.'

Lincoln climbed the stairs to the handsome Victorian, each step bringing him closer to exhaustion. It was well past midnight. He had spent the last few hours at an emergency meeting of the Board of Selectmen, held at Glen Ryder's house, where Lincoln had been told in no uncertain terms that his job was in jeopardy. The board had hired him, and they could fire him. He was an employee of the Town of Tranquility, and therefore a guardian of its welfare. How could he support Dr Elliot's suggestion to close down the lake?

I was just stating my honest opinion, he'd told them.

But in this case, honesty was clearly not the best policy.

What had followed was a mind-numbing litany of financial statistics, provided by the town treasurer. How much money came in every summer from tourists. How many jobs were created as a result. How many local businesses existed only to service the visitor trade.

Where Lincoln's salary came from.

The town lived and died by Locust Lake, and there would be no calls to close it, no health alerts, not even a whisper of public debate.

He'd left the meeting uncertain whether he still had a job, uncertain whether he even wanted the job. He'd climbed into his cruiser, had been halfway home, when he'd received the message from Dispatch that someone else wanted to speak to him tonight.

He rang the bell. As he waited for the door to open, he glanced up the street and saw that every house was dark, all the curtains drawn against this black and frigid night.

The door swung open, and Judge Iris Keating said: 'Thank you for coming, Lincoln.'

He stepped into the house. It felt airless, suffocating. 'You said it was urgent.'

'You've already met with the board?'

'A little while ago.'

'And they won't consider closing the lake. Will they?'

He gave her a resigned smile. 'Was there any doubt?'

'I know this town too well. I know how people

307

think, and what they're afraid of. How far they'll go to protect their own.'

'Then you know what I'm dealing with.'

She gestured toward the library. 'Let's sit down, Lincoln. I have something to tell you.'

A fire was dying behind the grate, only a few listless flames puffing up from the mound of cinders. Still, the room felt overwarm, and as Lincoln sank deeply into an overstuffed chair, he wondered if he could summon the energy to stay awake. To rise to his feet again and walk back out into the cold. Iris sat across from him, her face illuminated only by the fire's glow. The dim light was kind to her features, deepening her eyes, smoothing the wrinkles of sixty-six years into velvety shadow. Only her hands, thin and gnarled by arthritis, betrayed her age.

'I should have said something at the meeting tonight, but I didn't have the courage,' she confessed.

'Courage to say what?'

'When Claire Elliot spoke about the lake – about the night she saw the water glow – I should have added my voice to hers.'

Lincoln sat forward, the meaning of her words at last piercing his fatigue. 'You've seen it too.'

'Yes.'

'When?'

She looked down at her hands, grasping the armrests. 'It was in late summer. I was fourteen years old, and we had a house by the Boulders.

It's gone, now. Torn down years ago.' Her gaze shifted to the fire and remained there, focused on the sputtering flames. She leaned back, her hair like a halo of silver against the dark fabric of the chair. 'I remember that night, it was raining hard. I woke up, and I heard thunder. I went to the window, and there was something in the water. A light. A glow. It was there for only a few minutes, and then . . .' She paused. 'By the time I woke my parents, it was gone, and the water was dark again.' She shook her head. 'Of course they didn't believe me.'

'Did you ever see the glow again?'

'Once. A few weeks later, also during a rainstorm. Just the briefest shimmer, and then nothing.'

'The night Claire and I saw it, it was raining hard, too.'

Her gaze lifted to Lincoln's. 'All these years, I thought it was lightning. Or a trick of the eyes. But then tonight, for the first time, I learned I'm not the only one who's seen it.'

'Why didn't you say something? The town would have listened to *you*.'

'And people would ask all sorts of questions. When I saw it, which year it was.'

'Which year was it, Judge Keating?'

She looked away, but he saw the flash of tears in her eyes. 'Nineteen forty-six,' she whispered. 'It was the summer of '46.'

The year Iris Keating's parents had died at the hands of her fifteen-year-old brother. The year Iris, too, had killed, but in self-defense. She had pushed her own brother through the turret window, had watched him fall to his death.

'You understand now why I didn't speak,' she said.

'You could have made a difference.'

'No one wants to hear about it. I don't want to talk about it.'

'It was so long ago. Fifty-two years –'

'Fifty-two years is *nothing*! Look at how they still treat Warren Emerson. I'm just as guilty of it. When we were children, he and I were so close. I used to think that someday, we would . . .' She suddenly stopped. Her gaze settled on the fire, by now little more than glowing ashes. 'All these years, I've avoided him. Pretended he didn't exist. And now I hear it may not have been his fault at all, but merely a sickness. An infection of the brain. And it's too late to make it up to him.'

'It's not too late. Warren had surgery last week, and he's fine now. You could visit him.'

'I don't know what I'd say after all these years. I don't know that he'd want to see me.'

'Let Warren make that decision.'

She thought it over, her eyes glistening in the dying light of the embers. Then she rose stiffly from the chair. 'I believe the fire's gone out,' she said. And she turned and left the room.

There was a car parked in Lincoln's driveway.

He pulled up behind it and groaned. Though he

had not been home all day, the lights were on in his living room, and he knew what awaited him inside the house. Not again, he thought. Not tonight.

He trudged up the steps to his porch and found the front door was unlocked. When had Doreen stolen his new key?

He found her asleep on the couch. The sour stench of liquor permeated the room. If he woke her now, there would be another drunken scene, crying and shouting, neighbors awakened. Better to let her sleep it off, and deal with it in the morning when she was sober and he wasn't reeling from exhaustion. He stood looking down at her, regarding, with a sense of sad bewilderment, the woman he'd married. Her red hair was matted, shot through with gray. Her mouth hung open. Her sleep was a noisy rhythm of whistles and grunts. And yet he did not feel disgust when he looked at her. Rather he felt pity, and disbelief that he had ever been in love with her.

And a sense of stifling and never-ending responsibility for her welfare.

She would need a blanket. He turned toward the hall closet and heard the telephone ring. Quickly he answered it, afraid that it would wake Doreen and ignite the scene he dreaded.

It was Pete Sparks on the line. 'I'm sorry to call you so late,' he said, 'but Dr Elliot insisted. She was going to call you herself if I didn't.'

'Is this about the slashed tires? Mark already called me about it.'

'No, it's something else.'

'What happened?'

'I'm at her medical building. Someone's smashed all the windows.'

16

Glass was everywhere, bright shards littering the carpet, the magazine table, the waiting room couch. Through the broken windows, now open to the night air, wisps of snow slithered in and settled like fine lace on the furniture.

Stunned and silent, Claire moved through the waiting room to the business office. The window above Vera's desk had been smashed as well, and slivers of glass and broken icicles sparkled on the computer keyboard. Wind had blown loose papers and snow into drifts throughout the room, a blizzard of white that would soon melt to soggy heaps on the carpet.

She heard Lincoln's boots crunch across the glass. 'Plywood's on the way, Claire. There's more snow predicted, so they'll get those windows boarded up tonight.'

She just kept staring down at the snow on her carpet. 'It's because of what I said at the meeting tonight. Isn't it?'

'This isn't the only building that's been vandalized. There've been several this week.'

'But this is the second time for me in one night. First my tires. Now this. Don't you dare tell me this is a coincidence.'

Officer Pete Sparks came into the room. 'Not having much luck with the neighbors, Lincoln. They called in when they heard the breaking glass, but they didn't see who did it. It's like that incident down at Bartlett's garage last week. Smash and run.'

'But Joe Bartlett had only one broken window,' she said. 'They've smashed all of mine. This is going to shut me down for weeks.'

Sparks tried to be reassuring. 'It should only take a few days to get those windows replaced.'

'What about my computer? The ruined carpet? The snow's gotten into everything. The data will have to be replaced, and all my billing records reconstructed. I don't know if it's worth it. I don't know if I even *want* to start over again.'

She turned and walked out of the building.

She was huddled in her truck when Lincoln and Sparks emerged a short time later. They exchanged a few words, then Lincoln crossed the street to her pickup truck and slid into the seat beside her.

For a moment neither of them spoke. She kept her gaze focused straight ahead, and her vision blurred, the twirling lights of Sparks's cruiser softening to a pulsating haze. Quickly, angrily, she wiped her hand across her eyes. 'I'd say the

314

message came through loud and clear. This town doesn't want me here.'

'Not the whole town, Claire. One vandal. One person –'

'Who probably speaks for a lot of other people. I might as well pack up and leave tonight. Before they decide to burn down my house.'

He said nothing.

'That's what you're thinking, isn't it?' she said, and she finally looked at him. 'That I've lost any chance of making it here.'

'You made it hard on yourself tonight. When you talk about shutting down the lake, it threatens a lot of people.'

'I shouldn't have said anything.'

'No, you had to say it, Claire. You did the right thing, and I'm not the only one who thinks so.'

'No one's come up to shake my hand.'

'Take my word for it. There are others who have concerns about the lake.'

'But they're not going to close it down, are they? They can't afford to. So they shut me up instead, by doing this. By trying to drive me out of town.' She looked at her building. 'It's going to work, too.'

'You've been here less than a year. It takes time –'

'How long does it take to be accepted in this town? Five years, ten? A lifetime?' Reaching down, she turned on the ignition, and felt the initial blast of cold air from the heater.

'Your office can be repaired.'

'Yes, buildings are easy to fix.'

'It can all be replaced. The windows, the computer.'

'And what about my patients? I don't think I have any left after tonight.'

'You don't know that. You haven't given Tranquility a chance.'

'Haven't I?' She straightened and looked at him in fury. 'I've given it nine months of my life! Every minute, I worry about my practice, about why my appointment book is still half empty. Why someone hates me enough to send anonymous letters to my patients. There are people here who want me to fail, and they're doing their best to drive me out of town. It's taken me this long to realize it's never going to get better. Tranquility doesn't want me, Lincoln. They want another Dr Pomeroy, or maybe Marcus Welby. But not me.'

'It takes time, Claire. You're from away, and people need to get used to you, to feel confident you're not going to abandon them. That's where Adam DelRay has the advantage. He's a local boy, and everyone assumes he'll stay. The last doctor who came here from another state left after eighteen months. Couldn't take the winters. The doctor before him stayed less than a year. The town doesn't think you'll last, either. They're holding back, waiting to see if you make it through the winter. Or if you'll give up and leave town like the other two did.'

'It's not winter that's driving me away. I can take

the darkness and the cold. What I can't take is the feeling I don't belong. That I'll never belong.' She released a deep breath, and her anger suddenly dissolved, leaving only a feeling of weariness. 'I don't know why I thought this would work. Noah didn't want to move here, but I forced him. And now I see what a stupid thing it was to do . . .'

'Why *did* you come, Claire?' He'd asked the question so softly it was almost lost in the whisper of air from the heater.

It was a question he had never asked her, an elementary piece of information about herself she had never shared. *Why I came to Tranquility.* Now as he waited for her answer, the silence stretched between them, magnifying her reluctance to confide in him.

He sensed her discomfort and shifted his gaze to the street, granting her some measure of privacy. When he spoke again, it was almost as if the words weren't directed at her, that he was merely sharing his thoughts with no one in particular.

'The people who move here, from other places,' he said, 'most times it seems to me they're running away from something. A job they hate, an ex-husband. An ex-wife. Some tragedy that's shaken their lives.'

She sagged sideways and felt the icy window against her cheek. How does he know? she wondered. How much has he guessed?

'They come here, these people from away, and they think they've found paradise. Maybe they're on summer vacation. Maybe they're just driving through, and the name of the town catches their fancy. Tranquility. It sounds safe, a place to run to, a place to hide. They stop at the local realty office and look at the photos on the wall. All the farmhouses for sale, the cottages on the lake.'

It was a picture of a white farmhouse with daffodils nodding in the front yard and a maple tree just beginning to show its spring blush. I'd never had a house with a maple tree. I'd never lived in a town where I could look up at the sky at night and see stars, instead of the glare of city lights.

'They wonder what it'd be like, to live in a small town,' said Lincoln. 'A place where no one locks their doors, and neighbors welcome you with casseroles. A place that's more fantasy than reality, because the small town they imagine doesn't exist. And the problems they're trying to leave behind just follow them to their next home. And the next.'

Noah told me he didn't want to come. He told me he'd hate me if I forced him to leave Baltimore, to leave behind all his friends. But you can't let a fourteen-year-old boy run your life. I'm the parent. I'm in charge. I knew what was good for him, good for both of us.

I thought I did.

'For a while, maybe, it seems to work out,' he said. 'A new house, a new town – it keeps your mind off the things you were running away from. Everyone hopes for a new beginning, a chance to make things right. And they think, what better

318

time and place to start a new life than a summer by the lake?'

'He stole a car,' she said.

He didn't respond. She wondered what she'd see in his eyes if she were to turn and look at him now. Surely not surprise; somehow he had already known or guessed that her coming to Tranquility had been an act of desperation.

'It wasn't the only crime he committed, of course. After he was arrested, I learned about all the other things he'd done. The shoplifting. The graffiti. The break-ins at the neighborhood grocery store. They did it together, Noah and his friends. Three boys who just got bored and decided to add a little excitement to their lives. To their parents' lives.' She leaned back, her gaze focused on the empty street. Snow was beginning to fall, and as the flakes slithered onto the windshield they melted and slid down like tears on the glass. 'The worst part about it was I didn't know. That's how little he told me, how completely out of touch I was with my own son.

'When the police called me that night, and told me there'd been an accident – that Noah had been in a stolen car – I told them it was a mistake. My son wouldn't do something like that. My son was spending the night at a friend's house. But he wasn't. He was sitting in the emergency room with a scalp laceration. And his friend – one of the boys – was in a coma. I guess I should be grateful for the fact that my son never forgets to buckle his seat belt. Even in the act of stealing a car.' She shook her head and gave an ironic sigh. 'The other parents were as stunned as I was. They couldn't believe their boys would do such a thing. They thought Noah talked them into it. Noah was the bad influence. What could you expect from a boy who has no father?

'It made no difference to them that my son was the youngest of the three. They blamed it on his lack of a father. And the fact I was too busy working as a doctor, taking care of other peoples' families, to pay attention to my own.'

Outside the snow was falling more thickly now, blanketing the windshield, cutting off her view of the street.

'The worst part about it was, I agreed with them. I had to be doing something wrong, failing him in some way. And all I could think of was, how could I set things right again?'

'Packing up and leaving home is a pretty drastic measure.'

'I was looking for a miracle. A magic solution. We'd gotten to the point where we hated each other. I couldn't control where he went or what he did. Worst of all, I couldn't choose his friends. I could see where it was leading. Another stolen car, another arrest. Another round of useless family counseling . . .' She took a deep breath. The windshield was covered by snow now, and she felt buried away, entombed with this man beside her.

'And then,' she said, 'we visited Tranquility.'

'When?'

'It was a weekend in fall. A little over a year ago. Most of the tourists were gone, and the weather was still nice. Indian summer. Noah and I rented a cottage on the lake. Every morning, when I woke up, I'd hear the loons. And nothing else. Just the loons, and silence. That's what I loved most about that weekend, the feeling of complete peace. For once we didn't argue. We actually enjoyed being together. That's when I knew I wanted to leave Baltimore . . .' She shook her head. 'I guess you had me pegged right, Lincoln. I'm like every other outsider who moves to this town, who's running away from another life, another set of problems. I wasn't sure where I was going. I only knew I couldn't stay where I was.'

'And now?'

'I can't stay here either,' she said brokenly.

'It's too soon to make that decision, Claire. You haven't been here long enough to build up the practice.'

'I've had nine months. All summer and fall, I sat in that office waiting for the flood of patients. Almost all I got were tourists. Summer people coming in for a sprained ankle or an upset stomach. When summer was over, they all went home. And I suddenly realized how few of my patients actually lived in this town. I thought I could hang on, that people would learn to trust me. It might've happened in another year or two. But after tonight, there's no chance of it. I said what I had to say at that meeting and the town didn't like it. Now my best option is to pack up and leave. And hope it's not too late to go back to Baltimore.'

'You're giving up so easily?'

It was a statement designed to provoke. Angry, she turned to look at him. 'So easily? And when does it get hard?'

'It's not the whole town attacking you. It's a few disturbed individuals. You have more support than you realize.'

'Where is it? Why didn't anyone else stand up for me at the meeting? You were the only one.'

'Some of them are confused. Or they're afraid to speak up.'

'No wonder. They could get their tires slashed as well,' she said sarcastically.

'It's a very small town, Claire. People here think they know each other, but when you get right down to it, we really don't. We keep our secrets to ourselves. We stake out our private territory and we don't let others cross the line. Speaking up at a town meeting is opening ourselves to the public. Most choose to say nothing at all, even though they may agree with you.'

'All that silent support won't help me earn a living.'

'No, it won't.'

'There's no guarantee any patients will walk into my office now.'

'It'd be a gamble, yes.'

'So why should I? Give me one reason why I should stay in this town?'

'Because I don't want you to leave.'

This was not the answer she had expected. She stared at him, straining to read his expression in the gloom.

'This town needs someone like you,' he said. 'Someone who comes in and stirs things up a little. Who makes us ask ourselves questions we've never had the nerve to ask. It would be a loss if you left us, Claire. It would be a loss to us all.'

'So you're speaking on behalf of the town?'

'Yes.' He paused. And added softly, 'And for myself as well.'

'I'm not sure what that means.'

'I'm not sure what it means, either. I don't even know why I'm saying it. It doesn't do either of us any good.' Abruptly he grasped the door handle and was about to open it when she reached out and touched his arm. At once he fell still, his hand clutching the door, his body poised to step into the cold.

'I used to think you didn't like me,' she said.

He looked at her in surprise. 'I gave you that impression?'

'It wasn't anything you said.'

'What was it, then?'

'You never talked about anything personal. As if you didn't want me to know things about you. It didn't bother me. I realized that's just how it is up here. People keep to themselves, the way you did. But after a while, after we'd known each other, and that invisible wall still seemed to stand between us, I thought: Maybe it's not just the fact I'm an outsider. Maybe it's me. Something he doesn't like about *me*.'

'It is because of you, Claire.'

She paused. 'I see.'

'I knew what would happen if I didn't keep that wall up between us.' His shoulders sagged, as though under the weight of his unhappiness. 'A person gets used to anything, even misery, if it goes on long enough. I've been married to Doreen so long, I guess I accepted it as the way things are supposed to be. I made a bad choice, I took on a responsibility, and I've done the best I could.'

'One mistake shouldn't ruin your life.'

'When there's someone else who'll be hurt, it's not easy to be selfish, to think only of yourself. It's almost easier to do nothing and just let things slide. Add on another layer of numbness.'

A gust swept the windshield, leaving streaks of melting snow on the glass. Fresh snow swirled down, whitening over that fleeting glimpse of the night.

'If it seems I didn't warm up to you, Claire,' he said, 'it's only because I was trying so hard not to.'

He reached, once again, to open the door.

Once again, she stopped him with a touch, her hand lingering on his arm.

He turned to face her. This time their gazes held, neither one flinching away, neither one retreating.

He cupped her face in his hand and kissed her. Before he could pull away, before he had time to regret the impulse, she leaned toward him, welcoming his kiss with one of her own.

His lips, the taste of his mouth, were new and unfamiliar to her. The kiss of a stranger. A man whose longing for her, so long concealed, now burned like a fever. She too had caught the sickness, felt the same heat flush her face, her whole body, as he pulled her against him. He said her name once, twice, a murmur of wonder that she was the one in his arms.

The glare of headlights suddenly penetrated the snow-covered windshield. They pulled apart and sat in guilty silence, listening to the sound of footsteps approaching the truck. Someone rapped on the passenger side. Snowflakes slithered in as Lincoln rolled down the window.

Officer Mark Dolan stared into the truck. His gaze took in both Lincoln and Claire, and all he said was, 'Oh.' One syllable, an ocean's worth of meaning.

'I, uh, I saw the doc's engine running and wondered if everything was okay,' Dolan explained. 'You know, carbon monoxide poisoning and all . . .'

'Everything's fine,' said Lincoln.

'Yeah. All right.' Dolan backed away from the window. ''Night, Lincoln.'

'Good night.'

After Dolan had walked away, Claire and Lincoln sat without speaking for a moment. Then Lincoln said, 'It'll be all over town tomorrow.'

'I'm sure it will be. I'm sorry.'

'I'm not.' As he stepped out of her truck, he gave a reckless laugh. 'Truth is, Claire, I don't give a damn. Everything that's gone wrong in my life has been public knowledge in this town. Now, for once, something's gone right for me, and it might as well be public knowledge as well.'

She turned on the windshield wipers. Through the clearing glass she watched him wave good-night, then walk away to his car. Officer Dolan was still parked nearby, and Lincoln stopped to speak to him.

As she drove away, she suddenly remembered what Mitchell Groome had told her earlier that evening about Damaris Horne's inside source.

Dark-haired, medium build. Works the night shift.

Mark Dolan, she thought.

The next morning Lincoln drove south, to Orono. He had not slept well, had lain awake for hours mulling over the night's events. The town meeting. His conversation with Iris Keating. The damage to Claire's office. And Claire herself.

Most of all, he'd thought about Claire.

At seven he'd awakened unrefreshed, and gone downstairs. It was a cold slap of reality to find Doreen still asleep on his living room couch. She lay with one arm dangling off the side, her red hair dull and greasy, her mouth half open. He stood for a moment, looking down at her, pondering how to convince her to leave with a minimum of yelling and crying on her part, but he was too weary to deal with the problem at that moment. Worrying about Doreen had already drained so much energy from his life. Just the sight of her seemed to drag down on his limbs, making them hang heavy, as though Doreen and the force of gravity were intimately connected.

'I'm sorry, Honey,' he said softly. 'But I'm going on with my life.'

He made one phone call, then he left Doreen sleeping on the couch and walked out of the house. As he drove away, he felt the first layers of depression peel away like a worn outer skin. The roads were plowed, the pavement sanded; he pressed the accelerator, and as he picked up speed he felt he was shedding more and more layers, that if he just drove far enough, fast enough, the real Lincoln, the man he used to be, would finally emerge, scrubbed and clean and reborn. He sped past fields where the snow, so freshly fallen, puffed up in clouds of white powder with the slightest gust of wind. *Keep driving, don't stop, don't look back*. He had a destination in mind, and a purpose to this journey, but for now, what he experienced was the joyful rush of escape.

When he reached the University of Maine campus an hour later, he felt renewed and refreshed, as though he had enjoyed a long night's sleep in a comfortable bed. He parked his car and walked onto the campus, and the cold air, the crystalline morning, invigorated him.

Lucy Overlock was in her office in the physical anthropology department. With her six-foot frame clad in her usual attire of blue jeans and flannel shirt, she looked more like a lumberjack than a college professor.

She greeted him with a calloused hand and a no-nonsense nod and sat down behind her desk. Even seated, she was an imposing woman of Amazonian proportions. 'You said on the phone you had questions about the Locust Lake remains.'

'I want to know about the Gow family. How they died. Who killed them.'

She raised an eyebrow. 'It's about a hundred years too late to arrest anyone for that crime.'

'I'm bothered by the circumstances of their deaths. Did you ever locate any news articles about the murders?'

'Vince did – my grad student. He's using the Gow case for his doctoral thesis. A reconstruction of an old murder, based on the remains. It took him weeks to track down an account. Not every old newspaper, you see, has been archived. Your particular area was so sparsely populated at that time, there wasn't much news coverage.'

'So how did the Gow family die?'

She shook her head. 'I'm afraid it's the same old story. Unfortunately, family violence is not a modern phenomenon.'

'The father did it?'

'No. It was their seventeen-year-old son. His body was found weeks later, hanging from a tree. Apparently a suicide.'

'What about motive? Was the boy disturbed?'

Lucy leaned back, her tanned face catching the light from the window. Years of work in the outdoors had taken their toll on her complexion, and the wintry light illuminated every freckle, every deepening crease. 'We don't know. The family apparently lived in relative isolation. According to the deed maps for that period, the Gows' property encompassed the whole south shore of the lake. There may not have been any neighbors around who'd know the boy very well.'

'Then the family was wealthy?'

'I wouldn't say wealthy, but they'd be considered land rich. Vince said the property came into the Gow family in the late 1700s, and stayed with them until this . . . event. It was later sold off piece by piece. Developed.'

'Is Vince that scruffy kid with the ponytail?'

She laughed. 'All my students are scruffy. It's almost a prerequisite for graduation.'

'And where can I find Vince right now?'

'At nine o'clock, he should be in his office. The museum basement. I'll call and let him know you're coming.'

Lincoln had been here before. The broad wooden table was covered with pottery shards this time, not human remains, and the basement windows were blotted over by drifted snow. The lack of natural light, and the damp stone steps, made Lincoln feel he had descended into some vast underground cavern. He walked into the maze of storage shelves, past towering stacks of artifact boxes, their labels feathered by mold. 'Human mandible (male)' was all he could make out on one label. A wooden box, he thought, is a sadly anonymous resting place for what had once been a man's jaw. He moved deeper into the maze, his throat already scratchy from the dust and mildew and a faintly smoky odor that grew stronger as he progressed through the shadows, toward the far end of the basement. Marijuana.

'Mr Brentano?' he called out.

'I'm back here, Chief Kelly,' a voice answered. 'Take a left at the stuffed owl.'

Lincoln walked a few more paces and came to a great horned owl mounted in a glass case. He turned left.

Vince Brentano's 'office' was little more than a desk and a filing cabinet crammed in between artifact shelves. Though there was no ashtray in sight, the aroma of pot hung heavy in the air, and the young man, clearly uneasy in the presence of a cop, had assumed a defensive posture, barricaded behind his desk, arms braced in front of him. Looking the boy straight in the eye, Lincoln held out his hand in greeting.

After a hesitation, Vince shook it. They both

understood the meaning of that gesture: a treaty between them was now in force.

'Sit down,' offered Vince. 'You can set that box on the floor, but watch the chair – it wobbles a little. Everything in here wobbles. As you can see, I got the deluxe office.'

Lincoln removed the box from the chair and set it down. The contents gave an ominous clatter.

'Bones,' said Vince.

'Human?'

'Lowland gorilla. I use them for comparison teaching. I hand them to the undergrads and ask them for a diagnosis, but I don't tell them the bones aren't human. You should hear some of the crazy answers I get. Everything from acromegaly to syphilis.'

'That's a trick question.'

'Hey, all of life is a trick question.' Vince sat back, thoughtfully regarding Lincoln. 'I take it this visit is a trick question, too. The police don't usually waste their time on century-old murders.'

'The Gow family interests me for other reasons.'

'Which are?'

'I believe their deaths may be related to our current problems in Tranquility.'

Vince looked puzzled. 'Are you referring to the recent murders?'

'They were committed by otherwise normal kids. Teenagers who lost control and killed. We've got child psychologists psychoanalyzing every kid in town, but they can't explain it. So I got to thinking about what happened to the Gows. The parallels.'

'You mean the part about teenage killers?' Vince shrugged. 'The underdog will only take so much abuse. When authority clamps down too hard, young people rebel. It's happened again and again.'

'This isn't rebellion. It's kids going berserk, killing friends and family.' He paused. 'The same thing happened fifty-two years ago.'

'What did?'

'Nineteen forty-six, in Tranquility. Seven murders committed during the month of November.'

'*Seven?*' Vince's eyes widened behind the wire-rim glasses. 'In a town of how many people?'

'In 1946, there were seven hundred living in Tranquility. Now we're facing the same crisis, all over again.'

Vince gave a startled laugh. 'Man, you've obviously got some major sociological issues in your town, Chief. But don't blame it on the kids. Look to the adults. When children grow up with violence, they learn that violence is how they solve problems. Dad worships the almighty gun, goes out and blasts a deer to smithereens for sport. Junior gets the message: Killing is fun.'

'That's too pat an explanation.'

'Our society glorifies violence! And then we put guns in the hands of children. Ask any sociologist.'

'I don't think the sociologists can explain this.'

'Okay. What's your explanation, Chief Kelly?'

'Rainfall.'

There was a long silence. 'Excuse me?'

'In 1946, and again this year, we've had identical weather patterns. It started off in April, with heavy rains. The local bridge was washed out, livestock were drowned –'

Vince rolled his eyes heavenward. 'A flood of *Biblical* proportions?'

'Look, I'm not a religious man –'

'I'm not a believer, either, Chief Kelly. I'm a scientist.'

'Then you're always looking for patterns in nature, right? Correlations. Well, here's the pattern I'm seeing, both this year and in 1946. In April and May, our town has record rainfall. The Locust River floods, and there's major damage to homes along the riverbank. Then the rains stop, and in July and August, there's no rain at all. In fact, it's unusually hot, with temperatures high enough to make it into the record books, both those years.' He took a breath, slowly released it. 'Finally, in November,' he said, 'it starts to happen.'

'What does?'

'The killing.'

Vince said nothing, his expression shuttered.

'I know it sounds crazy,' said Lincoln.

'You have no idea how crazy it sounds.'

'But the correlation's there. Dr Elliot thinks it could be a natural phenomenon. A new bacteria or algae in the lake, causing personality changes. I read about a similar thing happening, in rivers down south. A microorganism's killing fish by the millions. It makes a toxin that affects humans as well. It damages their concentration, sometimes causes rage attacks.'

'You must mean the dinoflagellate, *Pfiesteria*.'

'Yes. It could parallel what's happening here. That's why I want to know about the Gows. Specifically, whether there were heavy rains the year they died. Government flood data doesn't go back that far. I need historical news accounts.'

Vince finally understood. 'You want to see my newspaper clippings.'

'It might have the information I'm looking for.'

'A flood.' Vince sat back, frowning, as though a memory had just floated to the surface. 'This is weird. I do seem to recall something about a flood . . .' He swiveled around to the filing cabinet, yanked open the drawer, and shuffled through folders. 'Where did I see that? Where, where . . .' He pulled out a file labeled: 'November, 1887, *Two Hills Herald*.' It contained a stack of photocopied news articles.

'The rain would have happened in the springtime,' said Lincoln. 'You wouldn't see it in the November clippings –'

'No, this had something to do with the Gow case. I remember jotting it down.' He flipped through the photocopies, then paused, staring at a wrinkled page. 'Okay, here's the article, dated November twenty-third. Headline: SEVENTEEN-YEAR-OLD SLAUGHTERS OWN FAMILY. FIVE DEAD. Goes on to mention the victims, Mr and Mrs Theodore Gow, their children, Jennie and Joseph, and Mrs Gow's mother, Althea Frick.' He set the page aside. 'I remember now. It was in the obituaries.'

'What was?'

Vince flipped to another photocopied page. 'The one for Mrs Gow's mother. "Althea Frick, age sixty-two, slain early last week, was buried November thirtieth at a combined graveside service for the Theodore Gow family. Born in Two Hills, she was a daughter of Petras and Maria Gosse, and was a devoted wife and mother of two. She was married for forty-one years to Donat Frick, who drowned this past spring . . ."' Vince's voice suddenly faded, and he looked up with startled eyes at Lincoln. '". . . in the Locust River flood."'

They stared at each other, both of them stunned by this confirmation. At Vince's feet, a space heater hummed on, its element glowing bright orange. But nothing could penetrate the chill Lincoln felt at that moment. He wondered if he would ever feel warm again.

'A few weeks ago,' said Lincoln, 'you mentioned the Penobscot Indians. You said they refused to settle anywhere near Locust Lake.'

'Yes. It was taboo, as was the lower half of Beech Hill, where the Meegawki Stream runs. They considered it an unhealthy place.'

'Do you know why it was considered unhealthy?'

'No.'

Lincoln thought it over for a moment. 'The

name *Meegawki* – I assume that's from a Penobscot word?'

'Yes. It's a bastardization of *Sankade'lak Migah'ke*, their name for the area. *Sankade'lak*, loosely translated, is their word for stream.'

'And what does the other word mean?'

'Let me look it up again.' Vince swiveled around and took down from the shelf a battered copy of *The Penobscot Language*. Quickly he flipped to the appropriate page. 'Okay. I'm right about *Sankade'lak*. It's the Penobscot word for "river" or "stream."'

'And the other?'

'*Migah'ke* means "to fight" or . . .' Vince paused. He looked up at Lincoln. '"To slaughter."'

They stared at each other.

'That would explain the taboo,' said Lincoln softly.

Vince swallowed. 'Yes. It's the Stream of Slaughter.'

17

'Fat ass,' whispered J.D. Reid from the trombone section. 'Barry's got a fat ass!'

Noah glanced up from his music and sneaked a peek at his stand partner, Barry Knowlton. The poor shlump was tightly gripping his saxophone, trying hard to concentrate on staying with the beat, but his face had turned red, and he was sweating again, which was what Barry did whenever he got stressed. Barry Knowlton sweated in gym. He sweated while conjugating verbs in French class. He sweated whenever a girl just *spoke* to him. First he'd blush, then little droplets would bead up on his forehead and temples, and before you knew it, Barry would be dripping like an ice cream cone in a heat wave.

'Man, that ass is so fat, you could launch it into space and we'd have ourselves another *moon*.'

A drop of sweat slid down Barry's face and plopped onto his sax. He was gripping the instrument so hard his fingers looked like bare bone.

Noah turned and said, 'Lay off him, J.D.'

'Ooh. Now skinny ass is jealous of all the attention. I got some view back here. Fat ass and skinny ass, side by side.'

'I said, lay off!'

The rest of the band had suddenly stopped playing, and Noah's *lay off* seemed to shout out across the abrupt silence.

'Noah, what is going on back there?'

Noah turned to see Mr Sanborn frowning at him. Mr Sanborn was a cool guy, one of Noah's favorite teachers, in fact, but the man was blind when it came to seeing what was happening in his own classroom.

'Noah's trying to pick a fight, sir,' said J.D.

'*What?* He's the one trying to pick a fight!' protested Noah.

'I don't *think* so,' jeered J.D.

'He won't let up! He keeps making stupid comments!'

Wearily Mr Sanborn crossed his arms. 'What comments, if I may ask?'

'He said – he said—' Noah stopped and looked at Barry, who was tensed up like a bomb about to explode. 'Insults.'

To everyone's shock, Barry suddenly kicked the stand over and it clanged to the floor, scattering sheets of music everywhere. 'He called me a fat ass! That's what he called me!'

'Hey, it's not an insult if it's true, is it?' said J.D.

Laughter erupted in the band room.

'Stop it!' yelled Barry. 'Stop laughing at me!'

'Barry, please settle down.'

Barry turned on Mr Sanborn. 'You never do anything! No one does! You let him screw around with my head, and no one gives a shit!'

'Barry, you have to calm down. Please go into the hall and cool off.'

Barry slammed his saxophone down on the chair. 'Thanks for *nothing*, Mr Sanborn,' he said, and walked out of the room.

'Ooh. Full moon receding,' whispered J.D.

Noah finally snapped. 'Shut up!' he yelled. 'You just shut up!'

'Noah!' said Mr Sanborn, whacking his baton against the stand.

'It's his fault, not Barry's! J.D. never lets up! None of the kids do!' He looked around at his classmates. 'All of you, you're always screwing around with Barry's head!'

Mr Sanborn's baton was now whipping the stand furiously.

'You're all jerks!'

J.D. laughed. 'Look who's talkin'.'

Noah shot to his feet, every muscle tensed to lunge at J.D. *I'm gonna kill him!*

A hand grabbed Noah by the shoulder. 'That's enough!' shouted Mr Sanborn, hauling Noah backwards. 'Noah, I'll deal with J.D.! You go cool off in the hallway.'

Noah shook him away. The rage that had peaked

so dangerously was still pumping through his body, but he managed to wrestle it under control. He shot a last look at J.D., a look that said: *Cross me again and you're toast*, and he walked out.

He found Barry standing by the lockers, sweating and sniffling as he struggled with his combination. In frustration, Barry punched the locker, then turned and sagged back against it, his weight threatening to buckle the metal. 'I'm going to kill him,' he said.

'You and me both,' said Noah.

'I mean it.' Barry looked at him, and Noah suddenly realized, *he does mean it*.

The bell rang, signaling the end of the period. A flood of kids spilled out of the classrooms, eddying into the halls. Noah just stood there, staring as Barry walked away, a sweating blimp swallowed up in the crowd. He didn't notice Amelia until she was standing right beside him. Touching his arm.

He gave a startled jerk and looked at her.

'I heard about you and J.D.,' she said.

'Then I guess you heard I'm the one who got kicked out of class.'

'J.D.'s a jerk. No one's ever stood up to him before.'

'Yeah, well I'm sorry I did.' He spun his combination and opened the locker. The door swung open with a bang. 'Not worth opening my big mouth.'

'It is worth it. I wish everyone was brave enough.'

Her head drooped, the golden hair sliding across her cheek. She turned away.

'Amelia?'

She looked at him. So many times before, he had sneaked furtive glances at her, just for the pleasure of looking at her face. So many times, he had fantasized about what it would be like to touch that face, that hair. To kiss her. He'd had opportunities, but had never mustered the courage to actually *do* it. Now she was gazing at him with such quiet intensity, he could not stop himself. His locker door hung open, concealing them from the hallway. He reached out, took her hand, and gently tugged her toward him.

She came willingly, her eyes wide, her cheeks flushing as she leaned close. Their lips brushed so softly, it was almost as if it didn't happen. They looked at each other, a wordless confirmation that it had not been long enough. That they were both willing to try again.

They came together in another kiss. Firmer, deeper, drawing courage from each other's lips. He put his arm around her, and she was as soft as he'd imagined, like sweet-smelling, lustrous silk. Now she had her arm around him as well, her hand clinging to the back of his neck, claiming him.

The locker door slammed wide open, and suddenly there was someone else standing there.

'What a *touching* scene,' sneered J.D.

Amelia jumped back, staring at her stepbrother.

'You cheap little tease,' said J.D., and he gave her a shove.

Amelia shoved right back. 'Don't you touch me!'

'Oh. You'd rather have Noah Elliot feel you up?'

'That's it!' said Noah. He advanced on J.D., his hand already closed in a fist. Then he froze. Mr Sanborn had just walked out of the band room and was standing in the hall, eyeing them both.

'Outside,' said J.D. softly, eyes glittering. 'The parking lot. *Now.*'

Fern Cornwallis dashed out of the building and ran through ankle-deep snow toward the faculty parking lot. By the time she reached the brawling boys, her brand new leather pumps were soaked through and her toes were numb. She was in no mood to be reasonable. She shoved her way into the circle of spectators and grabbed one of the boys by his jacket. *It's Noah Elliot again*, she thought furiously as she hauled him away from J.D. Reid. J.D. snorted like a mad bull and rammed his shoulder into Noah's chest, sending both Noah and Fern sprawling.

Fern landed flat on her back on the pavement, grinding sand and dirt into her wool suit. She scrambled to her feet, snagging her nylons in the process. Uncontrollable rage pulsing through her, she charged right back into the fight, this time grabbing hold of J.D.'s collar. She yanked him back so hard his face turned purple and he made choking sounds, but he continued to flail his arms, fists waving in Noah's general direction.

Two teachers dashed to Fern's aid, each one grabbing an arm, and they dragged J.D. backwards across the pavement.

'You stay away from my sister, Elliot!'

'I never touched your sister!' Noah yelled back.

'That's not what I saw!'

'Then you're blind *and* stupid!'

'I see you two together again, I kick both your asses!'

'Stop it! Both of you!' screamed Amelia, pushing forward and planting herself between the two boys. 'You're such a loser, J.D.!'

'Better a loser than the school slut.'

Amelia's face flushed bright red. 'Shut up.'

'Slut,' J.D. spat out. 'Slut, *slut*.'

Noah broke free and rammed his fist into J.D.'s mouth. The loud *thunk* of bone on flesh was as startling as gunshot in the crisp air.

Blood splattered on the snow.

'Some sort of action has to be taken,' said Mrs Lubec, the sophomore history teacher. 'We can't keep putting out small fires, Fern, while the whole forest burns down around us.'

Fern huddled in a borrowed sweatsuit and gulped her cup of tea. She knew everyone sitting around the conference table was watching her and waiting for some sort of decision, but they could

343

damn well wait a little longer. She had to get warm first, had to get the feeling back in her frostbitten bare feet, which were now swaddled in a towel under the table. The sweatsuit smelled like perspiration and stale perfume. It smelled like its owner, chubby Miss Boodles, the gym teacher, and it was stretched and saggy around the hips. Fern suppressed a shudder and focused on the five people sitting around the conference table. In two hours, she was scheduled to meet with the district superintendent of schools, and she had to present him with a new plan of action. For that, she needed guidance from her staff.

In the room with her now was the vice principal, two teachers, the school guidance counselor, and the district psychologist, Dr Lieberman. Lieberman was the only man in the room, and he'd assumed that superior attitude that men often adopt when they're the lone rooster among hens.

The freshmen English teacher said, 'I think it's time to clamp down harder. Be draconian. If it takes armed guards in the hallways and permanent expulsion of troublemakers, then that's what we do.'

'That's not the approach I would take,' said Dr Lieberman, adding with a noted lack of humility, 'in my humble opinion.'

'We've tried intensive counseling,' said Fern. 'We've tried conflict resolution classes. We've tried suspension, detention, and pleading. We've even taken desserts off the menu to cut down on their

344

sugar. These kids are out of control, and I don't know whose fault it is. I do know that my staff is wrung out, and I'm ready to call in the cavalry.' She glanced at the vice principal. 'Where's Chief Kelly? Isn't he joining us?'

'I left a message with the dispatcher. Chief Kelly's been delayed this morning.'

'Must be those late-night vehicle inspections,' Mrs Lubec wisecracked.

Fern looked at her. 'What?'

'I heard it over at Monaghan's. The Dinosaurs were all talking about it.'

'What did they say?' Fern's question came out more sharply than she'd intended. She fought to regain her composure, to keep the flush from rising to her cheeks.

'Oh, Chief Kelly and that Dr Elliot were really steaming up the car windows last night. I mean, it's not like the poor man doesn't deserve a break, after all these years . . .' Mrs Lubec's voice trailed off as she saw Fern's thunderstruck face.

'Look, can we get back to the problem at hand?' cut in Lieberman.

'Yes. By all means,' whispered Fern. *It's only gossip. Lincoln defends the woman in public, and the next thing you know, the town thinks they're sleeping together.* Just a few months ago, Fern herself had been the rumored woman in his life. More false gossip, based on the long hours they'd worked together on the student DARE project. She forced the subject of Claire Elliot out of her mind, and focused her irritation on Lieberman, who was trying to wrest control of her meeting.

'Brute authority doesn't work well with this age group,' he was saying. 'We're talking about a stage of development where authority is precisely what they rebel against. Clamping down on these kids – asserting your power – doesn't give them the right message.'

'I'm beyond caring what message I give these kids,' said Fern. 'My responsibility is to keep them from killing each other.'

'Then threaten them with the loss of something that matters to them. Sports, class trips. What about that dance you had on the schedule? That's a pretty major social event for them, isn't it?'

'We've canceled the harvest dance twice already,' said Fern. 'The first time because of Mrs Horatio, the second time because of all these fights.'

'But don't you see, it's something positive you can hold out to them. A carrot for good behavior. I wouldn't cancel it. What other incentives do they have?'

'How about the threat of death?' muttered the English teacher.

'Positive reinforcement,' said Lieberman. 'That's the mantra we have to keep in mind. Positive. Positive.'

'The dance could be a disaster,' said Fern. 'Two hundred kids in a crowded gym. All it takes is one fistfight, and we'd end up with a screaming mob.'

'Then you weed out the troublemakers ahead of time. That's what I mean by positive reinforcement. Any kid steps one inch out of line, they don't get to go.' He paused. 'Those two boys today – the ones who got in the fight.'

'Noah Elliot and J.D. Reid.'

'Start off by making examples of them.'

'I've suspended them for the rest of the week,' said Fern. 'Their parents are coming to pick them up now.'

'If I were you, I'd make it clear to the whole school that those boys won't be allowed into the dance, and neither will any other troublemakers. Turn them into poster boys for what *not* to do.'

In the prolonged silence, everyone looked to Fern for a decision. She was tired of being the one in charge, the one who got blamed when things went wrong. Now here was this Ph.D. Lieberman, telling her exactly what to do, and she almost welcomed the chance to defer to his judgment. To pass the responsibility to someone else.

'All right. The dance is back on the schedule,' she said.

There was a knock on the door. Fern's pulse quickened as Lincoln Kelly stepped into the room. He was out of uniform today, dressed in jeans and his old hunting jacket, and he brought with him the scent of winter, the sparkle of snowflakes on his hair. He looked tired, but fatigue only emphasized his appeal. It made her think, as she had so many times before: *You need a good woman to take care of you.*

'Sorry I'm late,' he said. 'I got back into town a few minutes ago.'

'We're just finishing up the meeting,' said Fern. 'But you and I need to talk, if you have the time right now.' She stood up, and instantly felt embarrassed when she saw him glance in surprise at her shabby attire. 'I had to break up another fight, and ended up getting shoved to the ground,' she explained. She tugged on the sweatshirt. 'Emergency change of clothes. Not exactly my most flattering color.'

'You weren't hurt, were you?'

'No. Although it is painful to ruin a good pair of Italian shoes.'

He smiled, an affirmation that despite her bedraggled appearance, she could still project both charm and wit, and that this man appreciated it.

'I'll wait for you in the other office,' he said, and stepped out again.

She could not just walk out of the room and join him. First she had to make the necessary graceful exit. By the time she'd successfully disengaged herself, it was five minutes later, and Lincoln was no longer alone in the outer office.

Claire Elliot was with him.

The two of them didn't seem to notice Fern as she came out of the conference room; their attention was focused so completely on each other.

They didn't touch, but Fern saw, in Lincoln's face, a vibrant intensity she'd never seen before. It was as if he'd suddenly awakened after a long hibernation to rejoin the living.

The pain she felt at that instant was almost physical. She took a step toward them, but found she had nothing to say. *What is it he sees in you that he never saw in me?* she wondered, looking at Claire. All these years she had watched Lincoln's marriage deteriorate, had thought that in the end, time would be her ally. Doreen would fade from the picture and Fern would step into the void. Instead here was this outsider, such an ordinary-looking woman in her snow boots and brown turtleneck, moving straight to the head of the line. *You don't fit in here*, thought Fern spitefully as Claire turned to face her. *You've never fit in.*

'Mary Delahanty called me,' said Claire. 'I understand Noah was in another fight.'

'Your son's been suspended,' said Fern, pulling no punches. If anything, she felt the urge to inflict damage on this woman, and she was glad to see Claire flinch.

'What happened?'

'He got into a fight over a girl. Apparently Noah's been playing fast and easy with his hands, and the girl's brother stepped in to protect his sister.'

'I have trouble believing this. My son's never mentioned any girl –'

'It's not easy for kids to communicate these days, when parents are so busy with their jobs.' Fern had wanted to hurt Claire Elliot, and it was obvious she had, because a guilty flush appeared on Claire's cheeks. Fern had known exactly what target to aim for, a parent's sorest point, where self-blame and overwhelming responsibility have already left them vulnerable.

'Fern,' said Lincoln. She heard reproval in his voice. Turning to look at him, she felt suddenly, deeply, ashamed. She'd lost control, had unleashed her anger, showing off her worst side, while Claire played the role of the innocent party.

In a subdued voice, she said, 'Your son's waiting in the detention room. You can take him home now.'

'When can he return to school?'

'I haven't decided. I'll meet with his teachers and consider their recommendations. The punishment has to be severe enough to make him think twice before he causes trouble again.' She gave Claire a knowing look. 'He's been in trouble before, hasn't he?'

'There was just that skateboarding incident –'

'No, I mean before. In Baltimore.'

Claire stared at her in shock. So it was true, thought Fern with satisfaction. The boy has always been a problem.

'My son,' said Claire with quiet defiance, 'is not a troublemaker.'

'Yet he does have a juvenile record.'

'How do you know that?'

'I received some newspaper clippings, taken from a Baltimore paper.'

'Who sent them?'

'I don't know. That's not relevant.'

'It's very relevant! Someone's trying to ruin my reputation, drive me out of town. Now they're going after my *son*.'

'But the clippings are true, aren't they? He did steal a car.'

'It happened right after his father died. Do you have any idea what it's like for a twelve-year-old boy to watch his father waste away? How completely it can break a child's heart? Noah has never recovered. Yes, he's still angry. He's still grieving. But I know him, and I'm telling you, *my son is not bad*.'

Fern held back a retort. There was no point arguing with an enraged mother. It was obvious to her that Dr Elliot was blind, unable to see beyond her love.

Lincoln asked, 'Who was the other boy?'

'Does that matter?' said Fern. 'Noah has to face the consequences of his own behavior.'

'You implied the other boy started the fight.'

'Yes, to protect his sister.'

'Have you spoken with the girl? Confirmed that she needed defending?'

'I don't need to confirm anything. I saw two boys fighting. I ran out to stop it, and I was shoved to the ground. What happened out there was ugly.

351

Brutal. I can't believe you're sympathizing with a boy who attacked me –'

'Attacked?'

'There was physical contact. I fell.'

'Do you wish to press charges?'

She opened her mouth to say yes, then stopped herself at the last instant. Pressing charges meant testifying in court. And what would she say under oath? She'd seen the rage in Noah's face, knew that he'd wanted to strike her. The fact he hadn't actually raised a hand against her was only a technicality; what mattered was his intent, the violence in his eyes. But had anyone else seen it?

'No, I don't wish to press charges,' she said. And added, magnanimously, 'I'll give him another chance.'

'I'm sure Noah will thank you for it, Fern,' he said.

And she thought miserably: *It's not the boy's approval I want. It's yours.*

'Do you want to talk about it?' Claire asked.

Noah's response was to draw away like an amoeba, shrinking to his side of the car.

'We have to talk about it sometime, Hon.'

'What's the point?'

'The point is, you've been suspended. We don't know when, or even if, you can go back to school.'

'So I don't go back, so what? I wasn't learning

anything anyway.' He turned and stared out the window, shutting her off.

She drove a mile without speaking, her gaze fixed on the road, but not really seeing it. She saw, instead, a vision of her son as a five-year-old child curled up, mute, on the couch, too upset to tell her about the teasing he'd endured in school that day. He has never been a communicator, she thought. He has always wrapped himself in silence, and now the silence has grown deeper, more impenetrable.

She said, 'I've been thinking about what we should do, Noah. I need you to tell me what you want: Whether you think I'm doing the right thing. You know my practice isn't going well. And now, with those broken windows, and the damage to the carpets, it'll be weeks before I can see patients again. If they even want to see me . . .' She sighed. 'All I was trying to do was find a place where you'd fit in, where we'd both fit in. And now it seems like I've made a mess of things.' She pulled into their driveway and turned off the engine. They sat without speaking for a moment. She turned to look at him. 'You don't have to tell me right away. But we need to talk about it soon. We need to decide.'

'Decide what?'

'Whether we should move back to Baltimore.'

'What?' His chin snapped up, his gaze focused at last on hers. 'You mean, *leave?*'

'It's what you've been saying fo months, that

you want to go back to the city. I called Grandma Elliot this morning. She said you could move back early and stay with her. I'd join you after I get our things packed, and put the house up for sale.'

'You're doing the same thing again. Making decisions about *my* life.'

'No, I'm asking you to help me choose.'

'You're not asking. You've already decided.'

'That's not true. I've made that mistake once already, and I'm not going to repeat it.'

'You want to leave, don't you? All these months, I've wanted to go back to Baltimore, and you didn't listen to me. Now *you* decide it's time, and suddenly you ask, *What do you want, Noah?*'

'I'm asking because it does matter to me! What you want has always mattered.'

'What if I said I want to stay? What if I told you I've got a friend I really care about, and she's *here*?'

'All you've talked about for the past nine months is how much you hate this place.'

'And you didn't care then.'

'What do you want? What can I do to make you happy? Is there anything that'll make you happy?'

'You're yelling at me.'

'I try so hard, and nothing ever satisfies you!'

'Stop yelling at me!'

'You think I like being your mother these days? You think you'd be happier with a different mother?'

He slammed his fist on the dashboard, punching it again and again as he roared: '*Stop – yelling – at – me!*'

She stared, shocked by the violence of his rage. And by the bright drop of blood that suddenly trickled from his nostril. It fell, spattering the front of his jacket.

'You're bleeding –'

Automatically he touched his upper lip and gazed down at the blood on his fingers. Another drop slid from his nostril and landed on his jacket in a bright splash of red.

He shoved open the door and ran into the house.

She followed him inside, and found he'd locked himself in the bathroom. 'Noah, let me in.'

'Leave me alone.'

'I want to stop the bleeding.'

'It's already stopped.'

'Can I take a look? Are you all right?'

'Jesus Christ,' he yelled, and she heard something crash to the floor and shatter. 'Can't you just *go away*?'

She stared at the closed door, silently demanding it swing open, knowing that it wouldn't. There were already too many closed doors between them, and this was just another one she couldn't hope to break through.

The telephone rang. As she hurried to the kitchen to answer it, she thought wearily: *In how many directions can I be pulled at once?*

Over the phone, a familiar voice blurted out in panic: 'Doc, you gotta come out here! She needs to be looked at!'

'Elwyn?' said Claire. 'Is this Elwyn Clyde?'

'Yes, ma'am. I'm over at Rachel's. She don't wanna go to the hospital, so's I thought I better call you.'

'What happened?'

'I don't know, exactly. But you better come here quick, 'cause she's bleeding all over the kitchen.'

18

Dusk had fallen when Claire arrived at Rachel Sorkin's house. She found Elwyn Clyde standing outside on the porch, watching his dogs run around in the front yard. 'Bad business,' he muttered darkly as Claire came up the steps.

'How is she?'

'Oh, she's wicked ornery. Gone and ordered me outside when all's I'm trying to do is help, y'know. Just wanta help, but she says, "You go outside Elwyn, you're smelling up my kitchen."' He looked down, his homely face drooping. 'She was good to me, what with my foot and all. I was just looking to return the favor.'

'You already have,' said Claire, and patted his shoulder. It felt like a bundle of twigs through the ratty coat. 'I'll go in and have a look at her.'

Claire stepped into the kitchen. At once her gaze shot to the far wall. *Blood* was her automatic reaction upon seeing the bright splashes. Then she saw the words, spray-painted in red across the cabinet doors:

SATAN'S WHORE

'I knew it was coming,' said Rachel softly. She was sitting at the kitchen table, clutching a plastic bag of ice to her head. Blood had dried on her cheek and matted the strands of her black hair. Broken glass littered the floor around her feet. 'It was just a matter of time.'

Claire pulled up a chair next to Rachel. 'Let me see your head.'

'People are so unbelievably ignorant. All it takes is one idiot to get them started, and it turns into a . . .' She gave a choked laugh. 'Witch hunt.'

Gently Claire lifted the ice pack from Rachel's scalp. Though the laceration wasn't deep, it had bled profusely and would require at least half a dozen stitches. 'Is this from the flying glass?'

Rachel nodded, then winced as though that simple motion had set off new stabs of pain. 'I didn't see the rock coming. I was so angry about the paint, about the mess they'd left in here. I didn't realize they were right outside, watching me walk into the house. I was standing there, looking at the cabinets, when the rock came through.' She gestured toward the broken window, now boarded over. 'Elwyn put up the boards.'

'How did he happen to come by?'

'Oh, that crazy Elwyn's always tramping through my yard with those dogs of his. He saw the broken window and came in to see if I was all right.'

'That was good of him. You could have a worse neighbor.'

Rachel answered with a grudging, 'I suppose. His heart's in the right place.'

Claire opened her medical bag and took out the suture set. She began dabbing Betadine on Rachel's wound. 'Did you lose consciousness?'

'I don't remember.'

'You're not sure?'

'I guess I was a little stunned. I found myself sitting on the floor, but I don't recall how I got there.'

'You should be under observation tonight. If there's any bleeding inside your skull –'

'I can't go to the hospital. I don't have insurance.'

'You can't be home alone. I can arrange a direct admission.'

'But I don't have the money, Dr Elliot. I can't pay for the hospital.'

Claire regarded her patient for a moment, wondering how hard she should push the issue. 'All right. But if you stay home, someone will have to be with you tonight.'

'There's no one.'

'A friend? A neighbor?'

'I can't think of anyone.'

They heard a loud knock. 'Hey!' yelled Elwyn through the closed door. 'Can I come in and use the bathroom?'

'Are you absolutely sure about that?' Claire

asked with a meaningful glance in Elwyn's direction.

Rachel closed her eyes and sighed.

A police car had just pulled up in the darkness when Claire came back out onto Rachel's porch. She and Elwyn watched as the officer stepped out of the cruiser and crossed the front yard toward them. He came into the light, and she recognized Mark Dolan. She was surprised to see him, because he normally worked the late night shift. She had never liked Dolan, and she wasn't kindly disposed to him today, either, when she remembered what Mitchell Groome had told her.

'Had some trouble here?' he asked.

'Called ya over an hour ago,' Elwyn said crossly.

'Yeah, well, we're up to our eyeballs in calls. Vandalism takes a lower priority. So what happened? Someone went and broke a window?'

'This is more than just vandalism,' said Claire. 'This is a hate crime. They threw a rock in the window, and Rachel Sorkin was hit in the head. She could have been seriously hurt.'

'How is that a hate crime?'

'They attacked her for her religious beliefs.'

'What religion?'

Elwyn blurted out, 'She's a witch, you goddamn imbecile! Everyone knows that!'

Dolan's smile was condescending. 'Elwyn, that's not very nice of you to call her that.'

'Nothing wrong with calling her a witch, if that's

what she is! If it's okay with her, hell, it's okay with me. I figure, better a witch than a vegetarian. I don't hold that against her, neither.'

'I wouldn't exactly call her beliefs a religion.'

'Don't matter what you call it. Just 'cause a woman wantsta believe some airy-fairy stuff don't mean people can throw rocks at her!'

'This *is* a hate crime,' insisted Claire. 'Don't pass it off as simple vandalism.'

Dolan's smile had thinned to a sneer. 'This will get the attention it deserves,' he said. And he walked up the porch steps and into the house.

Claire and Elwyn stood together for a moment in silence.

'She deserves better,' he said. 'She's a good woman, and she deserves better 'n this town has dealt her.'

Claire looked at him. 'And you're a good man, Elwyn. Thank you for staying with her tonight.'

'Yeah, well, it's turned into somethin' of a major operation now, hasn't it?' he muttered as he headed down the steps. 'I'll just take these dogs on home first, seein' as how they make her all tetchy like. Might as well get that other fool business over with, too. Since I did promise her.'

'What business?'

'Bath,' he grunted, and tramped off into the woods, the dogs trotting at his heels.

It was late at night, and Noah was asleep, when Lincoln finally called her.

'I've picked up the phone a dozen times to talk to you,' he said, 'but something always came up. We're pulling double shifts here, just to keep up with the calls.'

'Did you hear about the attack on Rachel Sorkin?'

'Mark mentioned it in passing.'

'Did he also mention he was a total jerk?'

'What did he do?'

'It's what he didn't do. He didn't take the attack seriously. He passed it off as simple vandalism.'

'He told me it was just a broken window.'

'The vandals spray-painted a message in her kitchen. It said, "Satan's Whore."'

There was a silence. When he spoke again, she heard barely controlled anger in his voice. 'These devil rumors have gone too goddamn far. I'm going to have it out with that Damaris Horne, before she starts writing about Penobscot Indian curses.'

'You haven't told her about your conversation with Vince, have you?'

'Hell, no. I've been trying to avoid her.'

'If you do talk to her, you might ask her about her good buddy, Officer Dolan.'

'Does that mean what I think it means?'

'I heard it from one of the reporters, Mitchell Groome. He saw them together.'

'I've already asked Mark whether he's been talking to her. He absolutely denies it. I can't take action against him without proof.'

'Do you trust his word?'

A pause. 'I honestly don't know, Claire,' he

sighed. 'Lately I've been learning things about my neighbors, about my friends, I never knew before. Things I didn't want to know.' The anger faded from his voice. 'I'm not calling to talk about Mark Dolan.'

'Why are you calling?'

'To talk about what happened last night. Between you and me.'

She closed her eyes, bracing herself to hear words of regret. Part of her wanted to be cut off, cut free. It meant she could leave this town without looking back, without struggling for the right decision.

But another part of her, the largest part, wanted *him*.

'Have you thought about what I said?' he asked. 'About whether you'll stay?'

'Are you still asking me to?'

'Yes.'

He said it without hesitation. He was not cutting her free, and she felt both joy and apprehension.

'I don't know, Lincoln. I keep thinking of all the reasons I should leave this town.'

'What about all the reasons you should stay?'

'Besides you, what other reasons are there?'

'We can talk about it. I can come over now.'

She wanted him to come, but was afraid of what would happen if he did. Afraid that she'd make a premature decision, that just his presence alone would prove to be the most convincing argument of all for her to stay in Tranquility. So many things were driving her away. Just to look out her window, to see the impenetrable darkness of a November night and to know that that night is cold enough to kill . . .

'I can be there in ten minutes.'

She swallowed. Nodded to the empty room. 'All right.'

The instant she hung up, a sense of panic seized her. Was she presentable? Was her hair combed, was the house tidy? She recognized these scattering thoughts for what they were, the feminine longing to impress one's lover, and she was startled to be experiencing it at this late stage of her life. Middle age, she thought with a rueful smile, does not automatically confer dignity.

She deliberately avoided even a glance at her mirror, and went downstairs to the front parlor, where she forced herself to occupy the next moments building a fire in the hearth. If Lincoln insisted on paying a visit at this late hour, he'd have to be satisfied with what he found. A woman with soot on her hands and the smell of wood smoke in her hair. The real Claire Elliot, beleaguered and unglamorous. Let him see me this way, she thought rebelliously, and let's see if he still wants me.

She lay down wood and kindling, then struck a match and touched the flame to the crumpled newspapers. The fire was well set and would burn without further attention, but she remained by the hearth, watching with primitive satisfaction as the kindling caught, and then the logs. The wood was fully seasoned and would burn hot and swift. She was like this wood, left dry and untouched for too long. She scarcely remembered what it was like to burn at all.

She heard him ring the doorbell. Instantly she was a bundle of nerves. She clapped her sooty hands, then rubbed them against her hips and succeeded only in transferring the soot to her slacks.

Let him see the real Claire. Let him decide if this is what he wants.

She went to the front hall, paused to regain her composure, and opened the door. 'Come in,' she said.

'Hello, Claire,' he answered, equally at a loss for words. They just looked at each other for a second, then broke eye contact, gazes drifting off to safer territory. He stepped inside, and she saw that his jacket was dusted with fine snow, that the darkness outside swirled with a powdery whiteness, like mist.

She closed the door. 'I've got a fire going in the other room. Can I hang up your jacket?'

He took it off and as she slipped it onto a hanger, she felt the heat of his body in the lining. So many times before, they had met, had spoken, yet this was the first time her awareness of him extended to all her senses, to the warmth of his body lingering in the jacket, to his scent of wood smoke and melting snow. To the certainty of knowing, even with her back turned, that at that moment, his gaze was on her.

She led the way into the parlor.

By now the fire was fully ablaze, throwing its bright circle of light against the gloom. Claire took a seat on the couch and turned off the lamp burning beside her. The fire gave off light enough; it was in shadow she sought refuge. Lincoln sat down beside her, a comfortable space apart, a statement of neutrality that did not distinguish between friend, lover, or mere acquaintance.

'How is Noah doing?' he finally asked, neutrality maintained even in conversation.

'He went to bed angry. In some ways, he wants to be a victim, he wants to feel like the world's against him. There's nothing I can do to change his mind.' She sighed and dropped her head against her hand. 'For nine months he's made me the villain for forcing him to move here. This afternoon, when I told him I was thinking of moving back to Baltimore, he blew up. Said I wasn't thinking of his needs, what he wanted. No matter what I do, I can't win. I can't please him.'

'Then all you can do is please yourself.'

'It feels selfish.'

'Does it?'

'It feels as if I'm not being the best mother I could be.'

'I see you trying so hard, Claire. As hard as any parent could.' He paused, and sighed as well. 'And now I suppose I'm throwing another complication into your life, at a time when you least need it. But Claire, there is no other time for me. I had to say it before you made a decision. Before you left Tranquility.' He added softly: 'Before it's too late for me to say anything at all.'

At last she looked at him. He was sitting with his gaze downcast, his head tilted wearily against his hand.

'Not that I blame you for wanting to leave,' he said. 'This town is slow to warm up to strangers, slow to trust them. There are a few who are just plain mean. But for the most part, they're like people everywhere else. Some of them are unbelievably generous. The best folks you could ever hope to find . . .' His voice faded to silence, as though he'd run out of things to say.

A moment passed between them.

'Are you speaking on behalf of the whole town again, Lincoln? Or yourself?'

He shook his head. 'It's not coming out right. I came to say something, and here I am, beating around the bush. I think about you a lot, Claire. The fact is, I think about you all the time. I'm not sure what to make of this, because it's a new experience for me. Walking around with my head in the clouds.'

She smiled. For so long she had thought of him as the stoic Yankee, plain-spoken and practical. A man whose boots were planted too firmly on earth to ever lose his head to the clouds.

He rose to his feet and stood, unsure of himself,

by the fire. 'That's all I came to tell you. I know there are complications. Doreen, mainly. And I know I don't have any experience being a father. But I have all the patience in the world when it comes to things I really care about.' He cleared his throat. 'I'll let myself out.'

He had already gone to the closet door and was reaching for his jacket when she caught up to him in the front hall. She put her hand on his shoulder, and he turned to look at her. His jacket slipped from the hanger and fell, unnoticed, to the floor.

'Come back and sit with me.' That whispered request, the smile on her lips, was all the invitation he needed. He touched her face, caressed her cheek. She had forgotten what it felt like, the touch of a man's hand against her flesh. It awakened a longing that was deep and unexpected and so powerful that she gave a sigh and closed her eyes. Gave another sigh as he kissed her, as their bodies folded into each other.

They kissed all the way to the front parlor and were still kissing as they sank onto the couch. In the hearth a log tipped over, and a shower of sparks and flames leapt up with startling brilliance. *Seasoned wood makes the hottest fire*. The heat of their own fire was consuming her now, reducing to ashes any resistance. They lay on the couch, bodies pressed together, hands exploring, discovering. She pulled his shirt loose and slid her hand across the breadth of his back. His skin there felt startlingly cool, as if all the heat he possessed was radiating toward her, in the kisses he pressed to her face, her throat. She unbuttoned his shirt, inhaling his scent. Those all-too-brief whiffs she'd had of him over the weeks had somehow been branded into her memory, and now the smell of him was both familiar and intoxicating.

'If we're going to stop,' he murmured, 'we'd better stop now.'

'I don't want to stop.'

'I'm not ready – I mean, I didn't come prepared –'

'It's all right. It's all right,' she heard herself saying, without knowing or caring if it *was* all right, so hungry was she for the touch of him.

'Noah,' he said. 'What if Noah wakes up . . .'

At that she opened her eyes and found herself looking directly into his. It was a view of him she'd never seen before, his face lit by the fire's glow, his gaze stark with need.

'Upstairs,' she said. 'My bedroom.'

Slowly he smiled. 'Is there a lock on the door?'

They made love three times that night. The first was a mindless collision of bodies, limbs tangled together, then the shuddering explosion deep within. The second time was the slower coupling of lovers, gazes locked, the touch and scent of each other now familiar.

The third time they made love, it was to say good-bye.

They'd awakened in the hours before dawn, and knowingly reached for each other in the darkness.

They spoke no words, their bodies joining of their own accord, two halves gliding together into one whole. When, in silence, he emptied himself into her, it was as though he was spilling tears of both joy and sorrow. The joy of having found her. The sorrow of what they would now have to face. Doreen's wrath. Noah's resistance. A town that might never accept her.

He did not want Noah to find them in bed together when morning came; neither he nor Claire was ready to deal with the repercussions. It was still dark when Lincoln got dressed and left the house.

From her bedroom window she watched his truck drive away. She heard the loud crackle of ice under his wheels and knew that the night had turned even colder, that this morning, to merely draw in a breath would be painful. For a long time, even after the taillights had vanished, she remained at the window, staring out through moonlit-silvered icicles. Already she felt his absence. And she felt something else, both unexpected and troubling: a mother's guilt that she was selfishly pursuing her own needs, her own passions.

She walked down the hall to Noah's door. There was silence within; knowing how deeply he slept, she felt certain he'd heard nothing of what had gone on in her bedroom last night. She stepped inside and crossed the darkness to kneel beside his bed.

When he was still a child, Claire had often lingered over her sleeping son, stroking his hair, inhaling the scent of warm linen and soap. He allowed so little contact between them now; she had almost forgotten what it was like to touch him and not have him automatically pull away. *If only I could have you back again*. She leaned over and kissed him on the eyebrow. He gave a moan and rolled over, turning his back to her. Even in his sleep, she thought, he pulls away from me.

She was about to rise to her feet when she suddenly froze, her gaze fixed on his pillow. On the streak of phosphorescent green where Noah's face had rested against the linen.

In disbelief she touched the streak and felt moistness there, like the warm leavings of tears. She stared at the tips of her fingers.

They glimmered with spectral light in the darkness.

19

'I need to know what's growing in that lake, Max. And I need to know *today*.'

Max gestured her into his cottage and shut the door against the bitter wind. 'How is Noah this morning?'

'I examined him from head to toe, and he seems perfectly healthy except for a stuffed-up nose. I left him in bed with juice and decongestants.'

'And the phosphorescence? Did you culture it?'

'Yes. I sent the swab off right away.' She took off her coat. Max had finally been able to get a fire going in the woodstove, and the cottage felt stiflingly hot. She almost preferred the bone-chilling wind outside. In here, surrounded by Max's clutter, the air hazy with smoke, she thought she might suffocate.

'I've just made coffee,' he said. 'Have a seat – if you can find an empty chair.'

She took one glance around the claustrophobic room and followed him, instead, into the kitchen.

'So tell me about those water culture results. The ones you took before the lake froze.'

'The report came back this morning.'

'Why didn't you call me right away?'

'Because there was nothing much to report.' He shuffled through a stack of papers on the kitchen counter, and handed her a computer printout. 'There. The final ID from the lab.'

She glanced down the long list of microorganisms. 'I don't recognize most of these,' she said.

'That's because they're not pathogens – they don't cause disease in humans. What's on that list are just the typical bacteria and algae you'd find in any northern freshwater pond. The coliform count is borderline high, which may indicate that someone's septic system is leaking from the shoreline, or into one of the feeder streams. But overall, it's an unremarkable bacterial spectrum.'

'No phosphorescent *Vibrio?*'

'No. If *Vibrio* was ever in that lake, then it didn't survive very long, which makes it an unlikely source of disease. Most likely the *Vibrio* isn't a pathogen, but an incidental bacteria. Harmless, like all the other bacteria we carry around in our bodies.'

She sighed. 'That's what the state health department told me.'

'You called them?'

'First thing this morning. I was in such a panic about Noah.'

He handed her a cup of coffee. She took one

sip, then set it down, wondering if Max had used bottled water to brew it, or if he had unthinkingly drawn the water from the tap.

From the lake.

Her gaze drifted out the window, to the unbroken expanse of white that was Locust Lake. In so many ways, that wide body of water defined the everyday course of their lives. In summer they swam and bathed in its water, pulled struggling fish from its depths. In winter they glided over its surface on skates, insulated their homes against the merciless winds that howled across its ice. Without the lake, the Town of Tranquility would not exist, and this would be only another valley in a dark expanse of forest.

Her beeper went off. On the digital readout was a number she didn't recognize, with a Bangor exchange.

She made the call from Max's phone, and a nurse from Eastern Maine Medical Center answered.

'Dr Rothstein asked us to call you, Dr Elliot. It's about that craniotomy patient you referred here last week, Mr Emerson.'

'How's Warren been doing since his surgery?'

'Well, the psychiatrist and the social worker have seen him several times, but nothing seems to be helping. That's why we're calling you. We thought, since he's your patient, you might know how to handle this situation.'

'What situation?'

'Mr Emerson refuses all his medications. Even

374

worse, he's stopped eating. All he'll take now is water.'

'Does he give a reason?'

'Yes. He says it's his time to die.'

Warren Emerson seemed to have shrunken since the last time she'd seen him, as though life itself was slowly leaking from him like air from a balloon. He sat in a chair by the window, his gaze focused on the parking lot below, where snow-covered cars were lined up like soft bread loaves. He did not turn to look at her when she walked into the room, but just kept staring out the window, a tired man bathed in the light of a gray day. She wondered if he realized she was there.

Then he said, 'It doesn't do any good, you know. So you might as well leave me alone. When your time comes, it comes.'

'But it isn't your time yet, Mr Emerson,' said Claire.

At last he turned, and if he was surprised to see her, he didn't show it. She had the feeling he was beyond surprise. Beyond pleasure or pain. He watched with bland indifference as she crossed toward him.

'Your operation was a success,' she said. 'They took out the brain mass, and the chances are, it's benign. You have every hope of a complete recovery. A normal life.'

Her words seemed to have no effect on him. He

simply turned back to the window. 'A man like me can't have a normal life.'

'But we can control the seizures. We might even be able to stop them from ever –'

'They're all afraid of me.'

That statement, spoken with such resignation, explained everything. This was the malady for which there was no cure, from which he could never recover. She could offer no surgery that would resect the fear and revulsion his neighbors felt toward him.

'I see it in their eyes,' he said. 'I see it whenever I pass them on the street, or brush against them in the grocery store. It's like they've been burned by acid. No one will touch me. No one has touched me in thirty years. Only doctors and nurses. People who have no choice. I'm poison, you see. I'm dangerous. They all stay away, because they know I'm the town monster.'

'No, Mr Emerson. You're not a monster. You blame yourself for what happened all those years ago, but I don't believe it was your fault. It was a sickness. You had no control over your actions.'

He didn't look at her, and she wondered if he had even heard her.

'Mr Emerson?'

He was still gazing out the window. 'It's kind of you to visit,' he murmured. 'But there's no need to lie to me, Dr Elliot. I know what I did.' He drew in a deep breath and slowly released it, and with that sigh he seemed to shrink even smaller.

'I'm so tired. Every night I go to sleep expecting not to wake up again. Hoping not to. And every morning, when I open my eyes, I'm disappointed. People think it's such a struggle to stay alive. But you know, that's the easy part. The hard part is the dying.'

There was nothing she could say. She looked down at the untouched meal tray by the window. A chicken breast in congealed gravy, a mound of rice, kernels glistening like tiny pearls. And bread, the staff of life. A life Warren Emerson no longer wished to experience or to suffer. I cannot make you want to go on living, she thought. I can force feed liquid nourishment, inject it into a tube that threads up your nostril and into your stomach, but I cannot breathe joy into your lungs.

'Dr Elliot?'

Turning, Claire saw a nurse standing in the doorway.

'Dr Clevenger from Pathology is on the phone, trying to reach you. He's on line three.'

Claire left Warren Emerson's room and picked up the extension in the nurses' station. 'This is Claire Elliot.'

'I'm glad I caught you,' said Clevenger. 'Dr Rothstein told me you'd be driving over this afternoon, and I thought you might want to come down to Pathology and take a look at these slides. Rothstein's on his way down now.'

'Which slides?'

'From your craniotomy patient's brain mass. It

377

took a week to fully fix the tissue. I just got the slides back today.'

'Is it a meningioma?'

'Not even close.'

'Then what is it?'

She heard the undertone of excitement in his voice. 'This you've got to see to believe.'

Fern Cornwallis looked up at the banner hanging from the gym rafters and she sighed.

KNOX HIGH SCHOOL – YOUR THE BEST!!!

How ironic that the students had gone to such effort to prepare the banner, had crawled up dizzyingly tall ladders to hang it on those rafters, but had neglected to double-check the grammar. It reflected badly on the school, on the teachers, and on Fern herself, but it was too much trouble to pull it down now and correct it. No one would notice it once the lights were turned down, the music was thudding, and the air turned to a steamy vapor of teen hormones.

'There's snow predicted tonight,' Lincoln said. 'Are you sure you don't want to cancel this event?'

Speaking of hormones. Fern turned and her stomach fluttered as it always did when she looked at him. It was a wonder he couldn't see the longing in her eyes. Men are so blind.

'We've postponed this dance twice already,' she

said. 'The kids need some sort of reward, just for getting through this awful month.'

'They're saying four to six inches, the worst of it coming around midnight.'

'The dance will be over by then. They'll all be home.'

Lincoln nodded, but he was obviously uneasy as he looked around at the gym, decorated with blue and white crepe streamers and silver balloons. The chilly colors of winter. A half dozen girls – why was it always the girls who did the work? – were setting up the refreshment table, lugging out the punch bowl, the trays of cookies, the paper plates and napkins. In the far corner, a shaggy student was adjusting the sound equipment, setting off ear-splitting squeals from the amplifier.

'Please keep it down!' yelled Fern, pressing her hand to her head. 'These kids are going to make me deaf.'

'It may be a blessing, considering the music they play.'

'Yeah, urban rap in the woods. Maybe they can mosh into a pile of leaves.'

'Do you know how many will show up tonight?'

'The first dance of the year? I expect a full house. Four grades, minus the thirty-eight troublemakers who've been suspended.'

'It's that many already?'

'I'm taking a proactive stance here, Lincoln. One false move and they're out of here for a week. Not even allowed on the school grounds.'

'That will make my job easier. I'm bringing in both Dolan and Pete Sparks for patrol shift tonight, so you'll have at least two of us here to keep an eye on things.'

The loud crash of a tray made them both turn, and they saw broken cookies scatter across the floor. A blond girl stared down in disbelief at the mess. She spun around and focused on a black-haired girl standing nearby. 'You tripped me.'

'No, I didn't.'

'You've been bumping into me all afternoon!'

'Look, Donna, don't blame me if you can't walk without falling over your own feet!'

'That's it!' said Fern. 'Clean up that mess or you're both suspended!'

Two angry faces stared at her. Almost simultaneously, they said, 'But Miss Cornwallis, she –'

'You heard me.'

The girls exchanged poisonous glances, and Donna stormed out of the gym.

'This is what it's come to,' Fern sighed. 'This is what I'm dealing with.' She looked up, at the high gym windows. At the fading daylight.

The first flakes of snow had begun to fall.

Nightfall was the time of day she dreaded most, for it was with the coming of darkness that all Doreen Kelly's fears seemed to rush forth like demons from their tightly lidded prisons. In the light of day, she could still feel flutterings of hope, and though it was thin as gossamer, she could plot out fantasy scenarios in which she was young again, charming again, and so irresistible she would surely lure Lincoln back home to her, as she had a dozen times before. Staying sober was the key. Oh, she had tried to hold the course! Again and again, she'd managed to convince Lincoln that this time she was dry for good. But then she'd get that familiar thirst, like an itch in her throat that needed scratching, and finally there'd be one little slip of the old willpower, the sweet taste of coffee brandy on the tongue, and she'd be spiraling downward, helpless to pull out of the descent. In the end, what hurt most wasn't the sense of failure or the loss of dignity. It was seeing the look of resignation in Lincoln's eyes.

Come back to me. I'm still your wife and you promised to love and cherish me. Come back just one more time.

Outside, the gray light of afternoon faded, and with it faded the hopes she'd nursed all day. The hopes that, in her more lucid moments, she knew were false. With nightfall came lucidity.

And despair.

She sat down at her kitchen table and poured the first drink. As soon as the coffee brandy hit her stomach, she could feel its heat racing through her veins, bringing with it the welcome flood of numbness. She poured another, felt the numbness spread to her lips, her face. Her fears.

By the fourth drink, she was no longer in pain, no longer in despair. Rather, she was feeling more sure of herself with every sip. Liquid confidence.

She'd made him fall in love with her once before; she could do it again. She still had her figure – a good one. He was a man, wasn't he? He could be coaxed. All it took was to catch him at a moment of weakness.

She stumbled to her feet and pulled on her coat.

Outside, it was starting to snow, soft and lacy flakes drifting down from a black sky. Snow was her friend; what better decoration for her hair than a few glittery snowflakes? She would step into his house with her hair long and loose, her cheeks prettily flushed from the cold. He would invite her in – he'd have to invite her in – and perhaps a spark of lust would leap between them. Yes, yes, that's how she saw it happening, with snowflakes in her hair.

But his house was too far to walk to. It was time to pick up a car.

She headed up the street to Cobb and Morong's. It was an hour before closing, and the evening rush was on to pick up that extra carton of milk, that emergency bag of sugar, on the way home. As Doreen had expected, there were several cars parked along the sidewalk in front of the general store, some of them with their engines running, the heaters blowing. There is nothing so disheartening on a cold night than to walk out and climb into your car, only to find your engine doesn't start.

Doreen walked along the street, eyeing the cars,

deciding which one to choose. Not the pickup – it wasn't a lady's vehicle, nor the VW, because she had more important things on her mind than wrestling with a stick shift.

The green sedan. That was just the car for her.

She glanced at the general store, saw that no one was coming out the door, and quickly slid into the sedan. The seat was nice and warm, the heater's breath toasty against her knees. She put it in gear, hit the gas, and jolted up and off the curb. Something in the trunk gave a loud thump.

She drove off just as a voice on the street yelled: 'Hey! Hey, come back with my car!'

It took her a few blocks of weaving back and forth to figure out how to turn on the headlights, another block to get the windshield wipers going. At last her view cleared, and she could actually see the road ahead. She accelerated, the sedan fishtailing on the newly fallen snow. She could hear things rolling around in the trunk, the sound of glass clinking together as she swerved around corners. She drove to Lincoln's house and skidded to a stop in his driveway.

The house was dark.

She climbed out of the car, stumbled onto the porch, and banged on the front door. 'Lincoln! Lincoln, I gotta talk to you! You're still my husband!' She banged again and again, but no lights came on, and the door was locked. He'd taken away her key, the bastard, and she couldn't get in.

She went back to the car and sat there for a long time with the engine running, the heater blowing. Snow continued to fall, just a dusting of it, fluttering soundlessly on the windshield. Saturday night was not Lincoln's usual shift, so where was he? She thought of all the places he might be spending the evening, and the possibilities gnawed at her with cruel teeth. She wasn't stupid; she knew that Fern Cornwallis had always had her predatory eye on Lincoln. There must be other women as well, dozens of women who'd find a cop in uniform irresistible. Agitation mounting, Doreen began to rock back and forth, moaning, in her seat. *Come home, come home. Come back to me.*

Even the heater wasn't enough to ward off the chill seeping into her bones, into her soul. She longed for the warmth of brandy, for the welcome flush of alcohol in her veins. Then she remembered the clink of glass in the trunk. Please let it be something worth drinking. Something stronger than soda pop.

She staggered out of the car, went around to the rear, and opened the trunk. It took her a moment to focus her eyes, and even when she did, she wondered if she was hallucinating. *So beautiful, so green. Like jars of emeralds glowing in the darkness.* She started to reach down for one, then turned at the sound of a car engine.

Approaching headlights blinded her. Dazed, she put up her hand to shield her eyes.

A silhouette stepped out of the car.

*   *   *

Dr Francis Clevenger was a man in miniature, small-boned, sparrow-faced, his lab coat drooping like a parent's oversize raincoat on his frail shoulders. That, and his absolutely beardless face, made him seem far younger than he was. He looked more like a pale adolescent than a board-certified pathologist. With quick grace he rose from his chair to greet Claire and Warren Emerson's neurosurgeon, Dr Rothstein.

'These slides are *so* cool,' Clevenger said. 'It was the last thing I expected to see. Go on, take a look!' He pointed to the dual-headed teaching microscope.

Claire and Rothstein sat on opposite sides of the scope and leaned into the eyepieces.

'So what do you see?' asked Clevenger, practically dancing beside them in anticipation.

'A mixture of cells,' said Rothstein. 'Astrocytes, I'd guess. Plus what looks to me like an interweaving of scar tissue.'

'That's a start. Dr Elliot, you see anything worth noting?'

Claire focused her eyepiece and gazed at the field of tissue. She was able to identify most of the cells, based on what she remembered from medical school histology classes years before. She recognized starshaped astrocytes, and the presence of macrophages – the cleanup crew, whose function is to tidy up after infection. She also saw what Rothstein had noticed: there were swirls of granulation tissue or scarring, possibly the aftermath of acute inflammation.

Reaching for the slide position knob, she shifted the field, scanning new cells. An unfamiliar pattern appeared under her gaze, a swirl of fibrous matter several cells thick, forming a microscopic rind of tissue. 'I see encapsulation here,' she said. 'A layer of scar tissue. Is this a cyst, maybe? Some sort of infectious process that his immune system managed to wall off and encase?'

'You're getting warm. Remember the CT scan?'

'Yes. It looked like he had a discrete brain mass, with calcifications.'

'An MRI was done here after transfer,' said Rothstein. 'It showed essentially the same thing. A discrete lesion, encapsulated, with calcifications.'

'Right,' said Clevenger. 'And what Dr Elliot has just identified is the cyst wall. Scar tissue formed by the body's immune system, surrounding and closing off the infection.'

'Infection by what organism?' asked Rothstein, raising his head to look at Clevenger.

'Well, that's the mystery here, isn't it?'

Slowly Claire moved the slide, shifting the field again. What appeared through her eyepiece was so startling her gaze froze in amazement. 'What on earth is *this*?' she said.

Clevenger made a sound of almost childish delight. 'You found it!'

'Yes, but I don't know what it is.'

Rothstein pressed his face back to the eyepiece. 'My god. I don't know what it is, either.'

'Describe it for us, Dr Elliot,' said Clevenger.

Claire was silent for a moment as she shifted the position knob and slowly scanned the field. What she saw was a strangely twisted architecture, partially calcified. 'It's some sort of degraded tissue. I don't know if this is all artifact or what – it's as if some organism collapsed into an accordion shape, and then became petrified.'

'Good. Good!' said Clevenger. 'I like that description – petrified. Like a fossil.'

'Yes, but of what?'

'Back off, look at the larger picture.'

She reduced magnification, trying to get an over-all view. The shape took more complete form, became a spiral that had folded upon itself. The realization of what she was looking at made her straighten in shock and stare at Clevenger. 'It's some sort of parasite,' she said.

'Yeah! And isn't it cool?'

'What on earth was a parasite doing in my patient's brain?' said Rothstein.

'It's probably been there for years. Invaded the gray matter, caused a temporary encephalitis. The immune system launched an inflammatory response. You get an influx of white blood cells, eosinophils, everything the host can muster to fight back. Eventually the host wins, and his body walls off the critter, encases it in granulation tissue, forming a sort of cyst. The parasite dies. Parts of it become calcified – petrified, if you will. Years later, that's what you have left.' He nodded at the microscope. 'A dead parasite, trapped in an envelope of scar tissue. It's probably the reason behind his seizures. The mass effect of that little pocket of dead worm and scar.'

'What parasite are we talking about?' asked Claire. 'The only one I can think of that invades the brain is cysticercus.'

'Exactly. I can't conclusively identify this species – it's too far degraded. But this is almost certainly the disease cysticercosis, caused by the larva of *Taenia solium*. The pork tapeworm.'

Rothstein looked disbelieving. 'I thought *Taenia solium* was only found in underdeveloped countries.'

'For the most part it is. You'll find it in Mexico, South America, sometimes in Africa and Asia. That's why I was so excited when I saw that slide. To find a case of cysticercosis here, in northern Maine, is unbelievable. It's definitely worth an article in *The New England Journal of Medicine*. What we need to figure out is when and where he got exposed to pork tapeworm eggs.'

'There's nothing in his history about foreign travel,' said Claire. 'He told me he's lived all his life in this state.'

'Which would make it a truly unusual case. I'll run antibody tests to confirm this is the right diagnosis. If it is *Taenia solium*, he'll have a positive ELISA test on his serum and CSF. Is there any history of an initial inflammatory response? Symptoms that might tell us when he was first infected?'

'What symptoms, specifically?' asked Rothstein.

'It could be a clinical picture as dramatic as full-blown meningitis or encephalitis. Or new onset epilepsy.'

'His first seizures occurred sometime before age eighteen.'

'That's one clue.'

'What other symptoms might show up?'

'Subtler signs, possibly. It can mimic brain tumors, cause a variety of psychiatric disorders.'

The back of Claire's neck was suddenly tingling. 'Violent behavior?' she asked.

'Possibly,' said Clevenger. 'I didn't see that specifically mentioned in my references. But it could be a sign of acute illness.'

'When Warren Emerson was fourteen years old,' said Claire, 'he murdered both his parents.'

The men stared at her. 'I didn't know that,' said Rothstein. 'You never mentioned it.'

'It wasn't relevant to his medical condition. At least, I didn't think so.' She looked down at the microscope, the image of the parasite still vivid in her mind. *An initial infection of parasitic eggs, followed by symptoms of encephalitis. Irritability. Even violence.*

'It's been a long time since medical school,' she said. 'I don't remember much about *Taenia solium*. What's the life cycle of this organism?'

'*Taenia solium* is a cestode,' said Clevenger. 'A tapeworm that usually lives in the intestinal tract of its host. People get it by eating undercooked

389

pork that's been infected with the larvae. The larva has sucking caps that hook on to the wall of the human small intestine, which is where it sets up housekeeping, absorbing food. The worms can live there for decades without causing symptoms, and grow as long as three meters – over nine feet long! Sometimes the worms will be passed or expelled. You can imagine what it'd be like to wake up one morning and find one of those critters lying in the sheets with you.'

Rothstein and Claire exchanged slightly nauseated glances. 'Sweet dreams,' muttered Rothstein.

'So how does the larva reach the brain?' asked Claire.

'It happens during a different part of the worm's life cycle. After the worm matures to adulthood in the human intestine, it begins to produce eggs. When those eggs are passed, they contaminate soil and food sources. People ingest them, the eggs hatch and penetrate the intestinal wall, and are then carried through the bloodstream to any number of organs, including the brain. There, after a few months, they develop into larvae. But it's a dead end, because they can't grow in that confined space, without nutrients. So they just sit there until they die, forming little cystlike pockets in the brain. The cause of this patient's seizures.'

'You said these eggs contaminate the soil,' said Claire. 'How long can the eggs stay alive outside of a host?'

'A number of weeks.'

'What about in water? Could they stay alive in a lake, for instance?'

'It's not mentioned in any of my reference books, but I suppose it's possible.'

'Would the *Taenia solium* ELISA test be a screen for infection? Because we should order it on another patient. A boy at the Maine Youth Center.'

'You think there's *another* case in this state?'

'Maybe a number of other cases in Tranquility. It would explain why so many of our children are suddenly showing violent behavior.'

'An epidemic of cysticercosis in Maine?' Rothstein looked skeptical.

Claire's excitement was rising. 'Both the boys I admitted had the same abnormality in their white blood cell count: a high percentage of eosinophils. At the time, I thought it was because of asthma or allergies. Now I realize it was caused by something else.'

'A parasitic infection,' said Rothstein. 'That raises the eosinophil count.'

'Exactly. And Warren Emerson could be the source of the infection. If he's been harboring a nine-foot tapeworm in his intestines, then he's been shedding parasitic eggs for years. A leak in his septic tank would contaminate the soil and groundwater. The eggs would find their way into the lake, exposing anyone who swims there. Anyone who accidentally takes in a gulp of water.'

'That's a lot of *ifs*,' said Clevenger. 'It's a house of cards you're building.'

'Even the time frame makes sense! The kids would have been infected during the summer, when they swam in the lake. You said the eggs take several months to develop into larvae. Now it's fall, and the symptoms are just starting to show up. A November syndrome.' She paused, suddenly frowning. 'The only thing I can't explain is their negative CT scans.'

'Maybe it was too early in the infection,' said Clevenger. 'During the acute symptoms, the larvae may still be too small to detect. And there wouldn't be any cyst formation yet.'

'Well, there's a simple screen for the parasite,' added Rothstein. 'The ELISA test.'

Claire nodded. 'If anyone shows antibodies to *Taenia solium*, then this theory is more than just a house of cards.'

'We can start by testing Warren Emerson,' said Rothstein. 'And that boy at the Youth Center. If they both come back negative, that kills your theory right there. But if they're positive . . .'

Clevenger, ever the scientist, eagerly rubbed his hands at the possibility. 'Then we'll get out the needles and tourniquets, folks,' he said. 'Because there are a whole lot of arms we have to poke.'

20

J.D. was jeering at her through her bedroom door, calling her a slut, a cheap lay, a whore. Amelia sat on the bed with her hands clapped over her ears, trying to shut out her stepbrother's voice, knowing that if she yelled back at him, it would only make things worse. J.D. was mad at everyone these days, looking to pick a fight with whoever was in reach.

Yesterday, the day he'd been sent home from school, she'd made the mistake of calling him a bastard. He'd slapped her so hard her ears had rung for hours. She'd run sobbing to her mother, but of course there'd been no support from Grace. 'You know how he is,' Grace had said in her I've-got-troubles-of-my-own voice. 'Just stay away from him.'

All day, Amelia had kept her distance by locking herself in her room and trying to concentrate on her homework, but now it was impossible to think. Earlier that day she'd heard J.D. raise hell downstairs, shoving Eddie around, yelling at Mom, even yelling at Jack. Maybe one of these days Jack and J.D. would kill each other. Like father, like son. She wouldn't mourn either one of them.

But now J.D. stood out in the hall, insulting her through the door. 'You like tiny weenies? That why you doing it with that loser, Noah Elliot? I'll show you a big dick! I'll show you how it's done! Or do you want Noah's little weenie?' He laughed, and began chanting, 'Little weenie! Little weenie!' until even Jack had had enough and he yelled up the stairs, 'Shut up, J.D.! I'm trying to watch TV!'

At which point J.D. went tearing downstairs to pick a fight with Jack. Amelia could hear them in the living room, their voices crescendoing to shouts. One big happy family. Now things were being knocked onto the floor. She heard furniture thudding, glass breaking. Jesus, how much worse could it get? Her mother was part of the chaos now, sobbing about her precious broken lamp. Amelia looked down at the school books spread open on her bed, at the list of assignments she'd hoped to complete by Monday, and knew she couldn't possibly finish them. I should have gone to the dance instead, she thought. If I can't do my homework, I might as well have some fun tonight.

Except the dance wouldn't be any fun either, since Noah Elliot wasn't there.

She heard another lamp smash to the floor, then her mother wailing: 'Why don't you do something,

Jack? Why don't you ever do anything?' There was a loud slap, and then Grace was sobbing.

In disgust, Amelia stuffed her books in her backpack, grabbed her jacket, and stalked out of her room. They didn't even hear her come down the stairs. She caught a glimpse of the living room, the floor littered with broken glass, J.D. red-faced and huffing like an angry bull as he faced his father and stepmother.

Amelia slipped out the front door and into a snowy night.

She began to walk down Toddy Point Road, not caring at first where she was going, just wanting to get away from *them*. By the time she'd passed the boat ramp, the cold was starting to penetrate her clothes, and melting snow dripped down her face. She had to go *somewhere*; walking aimlessly on a night like this was stupid and dangerous. But there was only one place she really wanted to go, one home where she knew she'd be welcomed.

Just the thought made her heart lift. She walked faster.

Since when did schoolgirls go out in public wearing fancy underwear? wondered Lincoln as he watched the students gather on the dance floor. He remembered the school dances of his own youth, the girls in their shiny hair and pastel dresses and satin miniskirts. Tonight the girls looked like a gathering of tarted-up vampires in their black lace and spaghetti straps. A few of them had painted their lips black too, and with their white winter faces, they reminded Lincoln of corpses wandering around the murky gym. As for the boys, well, they were just as likely to be wearing earrings as the girls were.

Pete Sparks, standing beside him, said, 'You'd think they'd catch pneumonia in those getups. Can't believe their mothers let 'em out looking like that.'

'I bet their mothers have no idea,' said Lincoln. He had seen many of the girls arrive modestly dressed, only to duck into the bathroom and emerge stripped down to the skimpiest of outfits.

Loud music suddenly blasted from the speakers in a driving beat. After only a few minutes of that racket, Lincoln was desperate to escape.

He stepped through the double doors of the gym, into the relative peace of a cold night.

The snowfall was gentle, just a fluttering of silver past the street-lamp. Standing beneath the building's overhang, he turned up his jacket collar and gratefully inhaled air that was sharp and clean.

Behind him, the door opened and shut, and he heard Fern say, 'Too much for you too?'

'I had to take a breather.'

She came to stand beside him. She was wearing her coat, which meant she'd come out with the intention of staying for a while.

'Does it ever feel like it's all just too much responsibility, Lincoln? Like you're ready to call it quits and just walk away?'

He gave a rueful laugh. 'At least twice a day.'

'Yet you're still here.'

He looked at her. 'So are you.'

'Not because I want to be. It's because I don't see any alternatives.' She looked up at the falling snow, and said softly, 'Doreen doesn't deserve you. She never did.'

'It's not a matter of people deserving good luck or bad, Fern.'

'Still, you should've had better. All these years, I've watched how miserable she's made you, and I kept thinking how unfair it was. How selfish she was. Life doesn't have to be unfair. We can choose happiness.' She paused, marshaling the nerve for what she had to say. He knew what it was; he'd always known, and had always avoided hearing the words spoken aloud, because he knew the aftermath would be humiliating for her, and painful for him. 'It's not too late for us,' she said.

He released a regretful sigh. 'Fern –'

'We could pick up where we left off. Before Doreen.'

He shook his head. 'We can't.'

'Why not?'

He heard the neediness in her voice, the desperation, and he had to force himself to meet her gaze. 'There's someone else I care about.'

She took a step back, retreating into the shadows, but not before he'd seen the tears in her eyes. 'I suppose I already knew that.'

'I'm sorry.'

'No. No, there's no reason to be sorry.' She shook her head and laughed. 'It's just the story of my life.'

He watched her turn back to the building. She paused to square her shoulders, regain her pride. *Why couldn't Fern have been the one*? he thought. Had he fallen in love with her, had they married, it might have been a reasonably happy union. She was attractive enough, intelligent enough. Yet something between them had always been missing. The magic.

In sorrow he watched her cross to the gym door and pull it open. At that instant, the sounds of shouting and running feet suddenly spilled out the open doorway.

'What's going on now?' said Fern, and she ran into the building with Lincoln right behind her.

Inside, they found mass confusion. The punch bowl had tipped over, and a pool of strawberry-colored liquid was spreading across the gym floor. The music was still pounding away, but half the students had retreated against one wall, where they milled together in alarm. Others were clustered in a circle near the sound system. Lincoln couldn't see what was happening at their center, but he heard a loudspeaker thud to the floor, and heard Pete Sparks and the chaperones all shouting: 'Break it up! Back off, back off!'

As Lincoln pushed into the circle, another amplifier tipped over and splashed into the river of punch. There was a deafening squeal and the crowd clapped their hands to their ears, backing away as electrical sparks shot up.

In the next instant, the music died. So did the gym lights.

The darkness lasted only a few seconds, but in that brief pause before the emergency lamp came on, panic seized the crowd. Lincoln felt screaming kids slam into him in their rush to reach the exits. He couldn't see who was coming at him, could only hear the sound of stampeding. He felt someone go down near his feet, and he blindly reached down and hauled a girl back up by her dress.

The emergency lamp at last flared on, one inadequate spotlight in the far corner of the gym. It was just enough light to see the shadowy chaos of running figures, kids stumbling back to their feet.

Then Lincoln focused on a scene that chilled him to the marrow. Pete Sparks had fallen to his knees and seemed too dazed to notice the overweight boy standing beside him. The boy reached down and removed the weapon from Pete's holster.

Lincoln was too far away to disarm the boy with a tackle. He managed to take only two steps forward, then froze as the boy turned to face him, rage glowing in his eyes. Lincoln recognized him. It was Barry Knowlton.

'Put it down, son,' said Lincoln quietly. 'Just put the gun down on the floor.'

'No. No, I'm tired of being kicked around!'

'We can talk about it. But first you have to put it down.'

'Like anyone ever bothers to talk to me!' Barry turned, his gaze circling wildly around the gym. 'You girls, you never bother. You just laugh at me! All the time, that's all I hear, the laughing.' His focus shot to another part of the room. 'Or you, stud! What'd you call me? Fat ass? Say it now! Go ahead, say it now!'

'Put the gun down,' Lincoln repeated, slowly reaching for his own weapon. It was the last resort; he didn't want to shoot the boy. He had to talk him down. Negotiate. Anything to keep the bullets from flying. Footsteps scurried in the shadows and he caught a glimpse of Fern's blond hair as she rushed a group of students out the door. But there were still dozens of people trapped against the far wall, unable to flee.

He took another step forward. Instantly the boy turned to face him.

'You've made your point, Barry,' said Lincoln. 'Let's go in the other room and talk, okay?'

'He called me fat ass.' Anguish had crept into the boy's voice. The desolation of the outsider.

'We'll talk, just the two of us,' said Lincoln.

'No.' The boy turned toward the trapped students, cowering against the wall. 'It's my turn to call the shots.'

Claire drove with her radio turned off, the silence interrupted only by the sweep of her windshield wipers as they cleared away the dusting of snow. She had spent the hour's drive from Bangor deep in thought, and by the time she reached the Tranquility town line, she had pieced it all together. Her theory centered on Warren Emerson.

Emerson's farmhouse was located on the lower slopes of Beech Hill, only a mile upstream from the lake. It was remote enough that it required its own septic system, which drained into a leach field. If a parasite had matured in his intestines, he would have been a continuing source of parasitic eggs. All it took was a leak in his aging septic tank, a year of heavy flooding, and those eggs could have been washed into the nearby Meegawki Stream.

Into the lake.

An elegantly logical explanation, she thought. It's not an epidemic of madness. Nor is it a centuries-old curse on this town. It's a microorganism, a parasitic larva lodging itself in the human brain, wreaking havoc as it grows. All they needed to confirm the diagnosis was a positive ELISA blood test. One more day, and they'd be certain.

A siren alerted her to an approaching police car. She looked up at the lights flashing in her rearview mirror, and saw a cruiser from Two Hills. It barreled past her and raced toward Tranquility. A moment later, a second cruiser screamed by, going in the same direction, followed by an ambulance.

Up ahead, she saw that the flashing lights had turned onto the road toward the high school.

She followed them.

It was a replay of the frightening scene from a month before, emergency vehicles parked at crazy angles outside the gym, clusters of teenagers standing in the road, crying and hugging each other. But this time snow was fluttering from the night sky, and the vehicles' flashing lights were muted, as though seen through white gauze.

Claire grabbed her medical bag and hurried toward the building. She was stopped half a block from the gym by Officer Mark Dolan, decked out in body armor. The look he gave her confirmed what she'd long suspected: their dislike for each other was mutual.

'Everyone has to stay back,' he said. 'We've got a hostage situation.'

'Has anyone been hurt?'

'Not yet, and we want to keep it that way.'

'Where's Lincoln?'

'He's trying to talk the kid down. Now you have to move back, Dr Elliot. Away from the building.'

Claire retreated to where the crowd had gathered. She watched Dolan turn and confer with the police chief from Two Hills. The men in uniform were in charge here, and she was merely another annoying civilian.

'Lincoln's all alone,' said Fern. 'And these goddamn heroes aren't doing anything to help him.'

Claire turned and saw that Fern's blond hair was in disarray, the loose strands crusted with snow. 'I left him in there,' said Fern softly. 'I didn't have a choice. I had to get the kids out . . .'

'Who else is inside?'

'At least a few dozen other kids.' She stared at

the building, melting snow dripping down her cheeks. 'Lincoln has a gun. Why doesn't he just use it?'

Claire looked back at the gym, the situation inside that building now vividly clear to her. An unstable boy. A room with dozens of hostages. Lincoln would not act rashly, nor would he shoot a boy in cold blood, if he could avoid it. The fact that there had been no gunfire yet meant there was still hope of avoiding bloodshed.

She glanced at the policemen gathered behind their parked cruisers, and she saw their agitation, heard the excitement in their voices. These were small-town cops, facing a big-city crisis, and they were champing at the bit to take action, any action.

Mark Dolan signaled to two officers, who were already in position on either side of the gym doors. With his chief trapped inside, Dolan had assumed authority, and he was letting his testosterone take command.

Claire ran through the snow to the cruisers. Dolan and the Two Hills police chief stared at her in surprise as she dropped to a crouch beside them.

'You're supposed to stay back!' said Dolan.

'Don't tell me you're going to send armed men in there!'

'The boy has a gun.'

'You're going to get people killed, Dolan!'

'They'll get killed if we *don't* do something,' said the Two Hills chief. He signaled to three cops crouched behind the next car.

Claire watched in alarm as the officers scrambled toward the building and took position by the doors.

'Don't do this,' she said to Dolan. 'You don't know the situation in there –'

'And you do?'

'There's been no gunfire. Give Lincoln a chance to negotiate.'

'Lincoln's not in charge, Dr Elliot. Now get out of my face or I'll have you arrested!'

She stared straight ahead at the gym doors. The snow was falling faster now, obscuring her view of the building, and through that gauzy curtain of white, the cops looked like ghostly figures floating toward the entrance.

One of them reached for the door.

Lincoln and the boy were at a stalemate. They faced each other across the shadowy gym, the distant beam from the emergency lamp slashing the darkness between them. The boy was still holding the gun, but so far all he'd done was wave it around in the air, eliciting terrified shrieks from the students huddled near the wall. He had not yet aimed at anyone, not even at Lincoln, who had his hand on his weapon, and was prepared to draw it. Two girls were standing just behind the boy, making any shot risky. Lincoln was relying on his instincts now, and they told him this boy could still be talked down, that even as the boy raged on, there was some part of him

404

struggling for control, needing only a calm voice to guide him.

Slowly, Lincoln lowered his hand from his holster. He was facing the boy with his arms at his sides now, a position of neutrality. Trust. 'I don't want to hurt you, son. And I don't think you want to hurt anyone. You're above that. You're better than that.'

The boy wavered. He started to kneel, to place the gun on the floor, then he changed his mind and straightened again. He turned to look at the classmates who cowered in the shadows. 'I'm not like you. I'm not like *any* of you.'

'Then prove it, son,' said Lincoln. 'Put the weapon down.'

The boy turned to look at him. At that moment, the flames of his anger seemed to flicker, grow dim. He was drifting between rage and reason, and in Lincoln's gaze he desperately sought anchor.

Lincoln moved toward him and held out his hand. 'I'll take it now,' he said quietly.

The boy nodded. Gazing steadily into Lincoln's eyes, he reached out to surrender the weapon.

The door crashed open, followed by the rapid-fire staccato of running footsteps. Lincoln saw a confusing blur of movement as men burst into the room from every direction. Shrieking students ran for cover. And caught in the knifelike beam of the emergency lamp stood a dazed Barry Knowlton, his arm still extended, the weapon gripped in his hand. In that split-second, Lincoln saw with sickening clarity what was about to happen. He saw the boy, still clutching the gun, as he turned toward the cops. He saw the men, pumped on adrenaline, weapons raised.

Lincoln screamed, '*Hold your fire!*'

His voice was lost in the deafening blast.

The thunder of gunfire momentarily paralyzed the crowd in the street. Then everyone reacted at once, the bystanders hysterical and screaming, the cops rushing toward the building.

A teacher ran out of the gym and shouted: 'We need an ambulance!'

Claire had to fight a stream of terrified kids pushing out the door as she struggled into the building. At first all she saw was a confusing jumble of silhouettes, men padded with body armor, paper streamers drifting, ghostlike, in the shadows above. The darkness smelled of sweat and fear.

And blood. She almost stepped in a pool of it as she forced her way into the gathering of cops. At their center was Lincoln, crouched on the floor, cradling a limp boy in his arms.

'Who gave the order?' he demanded, his voice hoarse with fury.

'Officer Dolan thought –'

'Mark?' Lincoln looked at Dolan.

'It was a joint decision,' said Dolan. 'Chief Orbison and I – we knew the boy was armed –'

'He was about to surrender!'

'We didn't know!'

'Get out of here,' said Lincoln. 'Go on, get *out* of here!'

Dolan turned and shoved Claire aside as he walked out the door.

She knelt down beside Lincoln. 'The ambulance is right outside.'

'It's too late,' he said.

'Let me see if I can help him!'

'There's nothing you can do.' He looked at her, his eyes glistening with tears.

She reached down for the boy's wrist and felt no pulse. Then Lincoln opened his arms and she saw the boy's head. What was left of it.

21

That night he needed her. After Barry Knowlton's body had been removed, after the ordeal of meeting the shattered parents, Lincoln had found himself trapped in the bright glare of reporters' flashbulbs. Twice he'd broken down and cried in front of the TV cameras. He was not ashamed of his tears, nor was he stinting in his angry condemnation of how the crisis had been resolved. He knew he was laying the groundwork for a wrongful death suit against his own employer, the Town of Tranquility. He didn't care. All he knew was that a boy had been shot down like a deer in November, and someone should have to pay.

Driving through a galaxy of falling snow, he realized he could not bear the thought of going home, of spending this night, like so many other nights, alone.

He drove instead to Claire's house.

Stumbling from his car through the calf-deep snow, he felt like some wretched pilgrim struggling toward sanctuary. He climbed to her porch and knocked again and again on the door, and when there was no response, he was suddenly gripped by despair at the thought she was not home, that this house was empty. That he faced the rest of the night without her.

Then above, a light came on, its warm halo filtering down through the falling snow. A moment later the door opened and she stood before him.

He stepped inside. Neither one of them said a word. She simply opened her arms to him, accepted him. He was dusted with snow, and it melted against her heat, trickling in cold rivulets to soak the flannel of her gown. She just kept holding him, even as melted snow puddled on the floor around her bare feet.

'I waited for you,' she said.

'I couldn't stand the thought of going home.'

'Then stay here. Stay with me.'

Upstairs they shed their clothes and slid between sheets still warm from her sleeping body. He had not come to make love, had come seeking only comfort. She gave him both, granting him the welcome exhaustion that eased him into sleep.

He awakened to a view through the window of a sky so sharply blue it hurt his eyes. Claire lay curled up asleep beside him, her hair an unruly tangle of curls on the pillow. He could see strands of gray mingled among the brown, and that first silvering of age in her hair was so unexpectedly touching that he found himself blinking back tears.

Half a lifetime of not knowing you, he thought. Half a lifetime wasted, until now.

He kissed her softly on the head, but she didn't awaken.

He got dressed while gazing out the window, at a world transformed by the night's storm. A fluffy mantle of snow had buried his car, turning it into an indistinct mound of white. The snow-covered branches of trees drooped under their heavy cloaks, and where once there'd been the front lawn, now there seemed to be a bright field of diamonds, glittering in the sunlight.

A pickup truck came up the road and turned onto Claire's property. It had a winter plow mounted in front, and Lincoln assumed at first that this was someone Claire had hired to clear her driveway. Then the driver stepped out, and Lincoln saw the Tranquility police department uniform. It was Floyd Spear.

Floyd waded over to the mound that was Lincoln's vehicle and brushed away the snow from the license plate. Then he looked up, questioningly, at the house. *Now the whole town will know where I spent the night.*

Lincoln went downstairs and opened the front door just as Floyd raised his gloved hand to knock. 'Morning,' said Lincoln.

'Uh . . . morning.'

'You looking for me?'

'Yeah, I – I drove over to your house, but you weren't home.'

'My pager's been on.'

'I know. But I – well, I didn't want to break the news over the phone.'

'What news?'

Floyd looked down at his own boots, crusted with snow. 'It's bad news, Lincoln. I'm real sorry. It's about Doreen.'

Lincoln said nothing. And strangely enough, he felt nothing, as if the cold air he was breathing in had somehow numbed his heart, and his brain as well. Floyd's voice seemed to be speaking to him from across a great distance, the words fading in and out of hearing.

'. . . found her body over on Slocum Road. Don't know how she got all the way out there. We think it must've happened early last night, 'round the same time as that trouble over at the school. But it's up to the ME to determine.'

Lincoln could barely force words from his throat. 'How . . . how did it happen?'

Floyd hesitated, his gaze rising, then dropping again to his boots. 'It looks like a hit-and-run to me. The state police are heading out to the scene.'

By Floyd's prolonged silence, Lincoln understood there was still more that hadn't been said. When Floyd looked up at last, his next words came out with painful reluctance. 'Last night, around nine, the dispatcher got a call about a drunken driver, weaving all over Slocum Road. Same vicinity where we found Doreen. That call came in

411

while we were all over at the high school, so no one managed to follow up on it –'

'Did the witness get a license number?'

Floyd nodded. And added miserably: 'The vehicle was registered to Dr Elliot.'

Lincoln felt the blood drain from his face. *Claire's car?*

'According to the registration, it's a brown Chevy pickup.'

'But she wasn't driving the pickup! I saw her last night at the school. She was driving that old Subaru sedan.'

'All I'm saying, Lincoln, is that the witness gave Dr Elliot's license number. So maybe – maybe I should take a look at the pickup?'

Lincoln stepped outside in his shirtsleeves, but scarcely felt the cold as he waded across to the barn. He reached elbow deep into the snow, found the handle, and raised the door.

Inside, both of Claire's vehicles were parked side by side, the pickup on the right. The first thing Lincoln noticed was the snowmelt puddled beneath both vehicles. Both of them had been driven sometime in the last day or two, recently enough so that the puddles had not yet evaporated.

His numbness was quickly giving way to a nauseating sense of dread. He circled around to the front of the pickup truck. At his first glimpse of the blood smeared across the fender, the world seemed to drop away from under his feet, to collapse beneath him.

Without a word, he turned and walked out of the barn.

Halting in calf-deep snow, he looked up at the house where Claire and her son now slept. He could think of no way to avoid the ordeal to come, no way to spare her from the pain he himself would now have to inflict. He had no choice in the matter. Surely she would understand. Perhaps some day she would even forgive him.

But today – today she would hate him.

'You know you're gonna have to step away from this,' said Floyd, softly. 'Hell, you're gonna have to stay *miles* away. Doreen was your wife. And you just spent the night with . . .' His voice faded. 'It's a state police case, Lincoln. They'll be wanting to talk to you. To both of you.'

Lincoln took a deep breath and welcomed the punishing sharpness of cold air in his lungs. Welcomed the physical pain. 'Then you get them on the radio,' he said. And he started, reluctantly, toward the house. 'I have to talk to Noah.'

She didn't understand how this could have happened. She had awakened to a parallel universe where people she knew, people she loved, were behaving in ways she did not recognize. There was Noah slouched in the kitchen chair, his whole body so electric with rage the air around him seemed to hum. There was Lincoln, grim and distant as he asked another question, and another. Neither one of them looked at her; clearly they both preferred she be out of the room, but they hadn't asked her to leave. She would not leave in any event; she saw the direction Lincoln's questions were taking, and she understood the dangerous nature of this drama now being played out in her kitchen.

'I need you to be honest with me, son,' said Lincoln. 'I'm not trying to play tricks on you. I'm not trying to trap you. I just have to know where you drove the truck last night, and what happened.'

'Who says I drove it anywhere?'

'The pickup has obviously been out of the barn. There's snowmelt under it.'

'My mom –'

'Your mom was driving the Subaru last night, Noah. She confirms it.'

Noah's gaze shot to Claire, and she saw the accusation in his eyes. *You're on his side.*

'Who gives a shit if I did take it out for a drive?' said Noah. 'I brought it back in one piece, didn't I?'

'Yes, you did.'

'So I drove without a license. Send me to the electric chair.'

'Where did you drive the truck, Noah?'

'Around.'

'Where?'

'Just around, okay?'

'Why are you asking him these questions?' said Claire. 'What are you trying to get him to say?'

Lincoln didn't answer; his attention remained

414

fixed on her son. That's how far he's pulled away from me, she thought. That's how little I know this man. Welcome to the morning after, the hard light of regret.

'This isn't about a simple joyride, is it?' said Claire.

At last Lincoln looked at her. 'There was a hit-and-run accident last night. Your pickup truck may have been involved.'

'How do you know that?'

'A witness saw your truck driving erratically and called it in. It was on the same road where the body was found.'

She sat back in her chair, as though someone had shoved her. *A body. Someone has been killed.*

'Where did you take the pickup last night, Noah?' Lincoln asked.

Suddenly Noah looked terrified. 'The lake,' he said, almost too softly to be heard.

'Where else?'

'Just the lake. Toddy Point Road. I parked for a while, on the boat ramp. Then it started to snow too hard, and we didn't want to get stuck there, so I – I drove home. I was already here when mom got back.'

'We? You said *we* didn't want to get stuck.'

Noah looked confused. 'I meant *me*.'

'Who was in the truck with you?'

'Nobody.'

'The truth, Noah. Who was with you when you hit Doreen?'

'Who?'

'Doreen Kelly.'

Lincoln's wife? Claire stood up so abruptly her chair toppled backwards. 'Stop it. Stop the questions!'

'They found her body this morning, Noah,' Lincoln continued, as though Claire hadn't spoken at all, and his quiet monotone barely disguised his pain. 'She was lying at the side of Slocum Road. Not far from where the witness saw you driving last night. You could have stopped to help her. You could have called someone, anyone. She didn't deserve to die that way, Noah. Not all alone, in the cold.' Claire heard more than pain in his voice; she heard guilt. His marriage may have been over, but Lincoln had never lost his sense of responsibility toward Doreen. With her death, he had taken on the new burden of self-blame.

'Noah wouldn't leave her there,' said Claire. 'I know he wouldn't.'

'You may think you know him.'

'Lincoln, I understand you're hurting. I understand you're in shock. But now you're lashing out, trying to assign blame to the nearest target.'

Lincoln looked at Noah. 'You've been in trouble before, haven't you? You've stolen cars.'

Noah's hands clenched into fists. 'You know?'

'Yes, I do. Officer Spear called your juvenile intake officer down in Baltimore.'

'So why are you bothering with the questions? You've already decided I'm guilty!'

'I want to hear your side.'

'I told you my side!'

'You say you drove around the lake. You also drove out to Slocum Road, didn't you? Did you realize you'd hit her? Did you ever think to get out and just take a goddamn *look*?'

'Stop it,' said Claire.

'I have to know!'

'I won't have a cop interrogating my son without legal counsel!'

'I'm not asking this as a cop.'

'You *are* a cop! And there'll be no more questions!' She stood behind her son, her hands on Noah's shoulders as she gazed straight at Lincoln. 'He has nothing more to say to you.'

'He'll have to come up with answers eventually, Claire. The state police will be asking him all these questions and more.'

'Noah won't be talking to them either. Not without an attorney.'

'Claire,' he said, anguish spilling into his voice. 'She was my wife. I need to know.'

'Are you placing my son under arrest?'

'It's not my decision –'

Claire's hands tightened on Noah's shoulders. 'If you're not arresting him, and you have no search warrant, then I want you to leave my house. I want you and Officer Spear off my property.'

'There's physical evidence. If Noah would just come clean with me and admit –'

'What physical evidence?'

417

'Blood. On your pickup truck.'

She stared at him, the shock like a vise crushing her chest.

'Your truck was driven recently. The blood on the front fender –'

'You had no right,' she said. 'You had no search warrant.'

'I didn't need one.'

The meaning of his words was instantly clear to her. *He was my guest last night. I gave him implied permission to be here. To search my property. I allowed him in my house as a lover, and he's turned against me.*

She said, 'I want you to leave.'

'Claire, please –'

'Get out of my house!'

Slowly Lincoln rose to his feet. There was no anger in his expression, just profound sadness. 'They'll be coming to talk to him,' he said. 'I suggest you call an attorney soon. I don't know how likely it is you'll find one on a Sunday morning . . .' He looked down at the table, then back up at her. 'I'm sorry. If there was any way I could change things – any way I could make this turn out right . . .'

'I have my son to think of,' she said. 'Right now he has to be my only concern.'

Lincoln turned to Noah. 'If you did anything wrong, it will come out. And you'll be punished. I won't have any sympathy for you, not one bit. I'm just sorry it's going to break your mother's heart.'

*   *   *

418

The men were not leaving. Claire stood in the front parlor, gazing out the window at Lincoln and Floyd, who lingered at the end of her driveway. They are not going to leave us unguarded, she thought. They're afraid Noah will slip away.

Lincoln turned to look at the house, and Claire stepped back from the window, not wanting him to see her, not allowing even the briefest eye contact. There could be nothing between them now. Doreen's death had changed everything.

She went back into the kitchen where Noah sat, and sank into the chair across from him. 'Tell me what happened, Noah. Tell me everything.'

'I did tell you.'

'You took the pickup out last night. Why?'

He shrugged.

'Have you done this before?'

'No.'

'The truth, Noah.'

His gaze shot up, dark with anger. 'You're calling me a liar. Just like he did.'

'I'm trying to get a straight answer out of you.'

'I gave you a straight answer, and you don't believe me! Okay, fine, believe what you want. I take the truck out every night for a joyride. Rack up thousands of miles – haven't you noticed? But why would you? You're never home for me anyway!'

Claire was stunned by the rage in his voice. Is that really how he sees me? she wondered. The mother who's never here, never home for her only

419

child? She swallowed the hurt, forcing herself to focus on the events of last night.

'All right, I'll accept your word that it was the only time you took out the truck. You still haven't told me why you did.'

Noah's gaze dropped to the table, a clear indication he was being evasive. 'I felt like it.'

'You drove to the boat ramp and just parked there?'

'Yeah.'

'Did you see Doreen Kelly?'

'I don't even know what she looks like!'

'Did you see anyone?'

A pause. 'I didn't see any lady named Doreen. Stupid name.'

'She was not just a name. She was a person, and she's dead. If you know anything at all –'

'I don't.'

'Lincoln seems to think you do.'

Again that angry gaze slanted up at her. 'And you believe *him*, don't you?' He shoved the chair back and stood up.

'Sit down.'

'You don't want me around. You want Mr Cop instead.' She saw the flash of tears in his eyes as he turned for the kitchen door.

'Where are you going?'

'What difference does it make?' He walked out, slamming the door behind him.

She stepped outside and saw that he was already stumbling away into the woods. He had no jacket, only those tattered jeans and a long-sleeved cotton shirt, but he didn't seem to care about the cold. His anger and hurt were driving him recklessly forward through the snow.

'Noah!' she yelled.

Now he had reached the lake's edge and he veered left, following its curve, crossing into the woods of the neighboring property.

'Noah!' She plunged into the snow after him. He was already far ahead and with each angry stride he increased the distance between them. *He's not coming back.* She began to run, shouting his name.

Now two figures, off to her left, caught her eye. Lincoln and Floyd had heard her voice and were in pursuit as well. They had nearly caught up when Noah glanced back and saw them.

He began to run, toward the lake.

Claire cried out: 'Don't hurt him!'

Floyd grabbed him just as they both reached the edge of the ice and he hauled him backwards. They both tumbled into deep snow. Noah scrambled back to his feet first and he flew at Floyd, fists swinging, his rage out of control. He thrashed, howling, as Lincoln grabbed him from behind and wrestled him to the ground.

Floyd scrambled back to his feet and drew his weapon.

'No!' screamed Claire, and terror sent her churning through the snow. She reached her son just as Lincoln cuffed the boy's hands behind his back.

'Don't fight them, Noah!' she pleaded. 'Stop fighting!'

Noah twisted around to look at her, his face so contorted by fury she didn't recognize him. *Who is this boy?* she thought in horror. *I don't know him.*

'*Let – me – go!*' he shrieked. A bright drop of blood slid from his nostril and splattered onto the snow.

She stared down in shock at the splash of red, then looked at her son, heaving like an exhausted beast, his breath steaming the air. A fine line of blood glistened on his upper lip.

New voices called out to them from a distance. Claire turned, and saw men crossing toward them. As they came closer, she recognized the uniforms.

State police.

22

The noise was driving her crazy. Amelia Reid leaned on her desk and clutched her head, wishing she could block out all the sounds assaulting her from different parts of the house. From the room next door came the thump of J.D.'s god-awful music, pounding like a demon's heartbeat against her wall. And from the living room downstairs came the shout of the TV, its volume turned up to the max. She could deal with the music, because it was just noise, an irritant that chewed away at the farthest margins of her concentration. The TV, though, insinuated itself right into her mind because it was the voices of people talking, their words distracting her from the book she was trying to read.

In frustration, she slammed it shut and went downstairs. She found Jack in his usual position for the evening, slumped in the plaid BarcaLounger, a beer in his hand. His Royal Highness, farting in his throne. What awful desperation had driven her mother to marry him? Amelia could not imagine ever choosing such an option, could not even bear to contemplate a future with such a man under her roof, belching at her table, discarding his filthy socks like droppings on the living room floor.

And at night, to lie in bed with him, to feel his hands on her flesh . . .

An involuntary sound of disgust escaped her throat, drawing Jack's attention from the evening news. He looked at her, and his blank expression changed to one of interest, maybe even speculation. She knew the reason for it, and almost felt the need to cross her arms over her chest.

'Can you turn it down?' she said. 'I can't study.'

'So shut your door.'

'I did shut my door. The TV's too loud.'

'It's my house, y'know. You're lucky I let you live here. I work hard all day. I deserve to relax in my own home.'

'I can't concentrate. I can't do my homework.'

Jack let out a half-belch, half-laugh. 'A girl like you doesn't need to blow a circuit in her brain. You don't even need a brain.'

'What's that supposed to mean?'

'Find a rich man, toss that pretty hair of yours, you got a meal ticket for the rest of your life.'

She bit back an angry retort. Jack was baiting her. She could see that smirk on his lips, the thin mustache tilting up at one corner. He liked to get her angry, enjoyed seeing her upset. He couldn't get her attention any other way, and

Amelia knew he was titillated by any flash of emotion she displayed, even if it was rage.

With a shrug, she focused instead on the TV. Icy withdrawal was the way to deal with Jack. Show no anger, no feelings at all, and it drove him crazy. It showed him exactly what he was: irrelevant. Inconsequential. Staring at the screen, she felt herself regain a measure of control over him. To hell with him. He couldn't get to her, or at her, because she wouldn't let him.

It took a few seconds for her brain to register the images on the screen. She saw a brown pickup being towed by a police truck, saw the blurred figure of a boy, face covered, as he was escorted into the Tranquility police station. When she finally understood what she was looking at, she forgot about Jack entirely.

'. . . the fourteen-year-old boy is currently being held for questioning. The body of forty-three-year-old Doreen Kelly was found this morning on a remote stretch of Slocum Road, east of Tranquility. According to an anonymous eyewitness report, the suspect's truck was seen weaving erratically on that same stretch of road around nine P.M. last night, and unspecified physical evidence has led police to take the youth into custody. The victim, wife of Tranquility Police Chief Lincoln Kelly, had a long and troubling history of alcoholism, according to several town residents . . .'

A new face appeared onscreen, a woman Amelia recognized as a cashier from Cobb and Morong's.

'Doreen was sort of the local tragic figure around here. She'd never, ever harm a soul, and I just can't believe someone would do this. Only a monster would leave her out there to die.'

Now the TV showed a stretcher bearing a shrouded body being loaded into an ambulance.

'In a community already rocked by the tragedy of last night's high school violence, this latest death is just one more blow to a town ironically named Tranquility . . .'

Amelia said, 'What are they talking about? What happened?'

Jack's colorless eyes showed an ugly flicker of amusement. 'Heard about it in town today,' he said. 'That doctor's kid is dead meat.'

Noah? Surely he's not talking about Noah.

'Ran over the police chief's wife last night, over on Slocum Road. That's what some witness says.'

'Who's saying that?'

Jack's expression of amusement had spread to the rest of his face, tugging his lips into an ugly smile. 'Well, that's the question, isn't it? Just who did see it?' He raised his eyebrows in mock surprise. 'Oh! I almost forgot. That's the boy you're all sweet on, isn't it? The one you think is something special. Well, I guess you're right.' He looked back at the TV and laughed. 'He's gonna be *real* special in prison.'

'Fuck you,' said Amelia, and she ran out of the room and up the stairs.

'Hey! Hey, you come back here and apologize!'

426

yelled Jack. 'You show me a little goddamn *respect*!'

Ignoring the demands he was hurling after her, she headed straight into her mother's bedroom and shut the door. *If he'll just leave me alone for five minutes. If he'll let me make this one call . . .*

She picked up the telephone and called Noah Elliot's house.

To her dismay, it rang four times and then an answering machine picked up with a recording of his mother's voice.

'This is Dr Elliot. I'm unable to answer the phone, so please leave a message. If this is an emergency, you can page me through the Knox Hospital operator, and I'll return your call as soon as I can.'

At the beep, Amelia blurted out: 'Dr Elliot, this is Amelia Reid. Noah didn't run over that woman! He couldn't have, because he was with –'

The bedroom door flew open. 'What the hell are you doing in my room, you little bitch?' Jack roared.

Amelia slammed the phone down and turned to face him.

'You apologize,' said Jack.

'For what?'

'For cussing at me, goddamn it.'

'You mean for saying *fuck you*?'

His slap made her head whip sideways. She raised a hand to her stinging cheek, then she focused her gaze back on his. She stared at him for a moment, and something deep inside her, some core of molten steel, at last seemed to solidify. When he reached up to slap her again, she didn't even flinch. She just looked at him, her eyes telling him that one more blow on his part would make him very, very sorry.

Slowly he lowered his hand, the blow never struck. He didn't try to stop her as she walked out and went to her own room. He was still standing there, motionless, as she swung the door shut behind her.

Claire and Max Tutwiler stood in front of Lincoln's desk, refusing to leave. They had walked into the police station together, and now Max had his briefcase open, and as Lincoln watched in bewilderment, Max unrolled a topographical map and spread it across the desk.

'What's this supposed to show me?' Lincoln asked.

'It's the explanation for my son's illness. For what's happening in this town,' said Claire urgently. 'Noah needs to be hospitalized. You *have* to release him.'

Reluctantly Lincoln looked up at her. Only twelve hours ago, they had been lovers. Now it was apparent he could barely bring himself to meet her gaze.

'He didn't look ill to me, Claire. In fact, he almost outran us this morning.'

'The sickness is in his brain. It's a parasite called *Taenia solium*, and during the initial infection, it can

428

cause personality changes. If Noah's infected, he needs to be treated. *Taenia solium* cysts cause brain swelling and symptoms of meningitis. That's what I've been seeing in him these past few days. The irritability, the rage. If I don't get him to a hospital, if he's developed a cyst and it ruptures . . .' She stopped, struggling to hold back tears. 'Please,' she whispered. 'I don't want to lose my son.'

'What it means,' said Max, 'is that he's not responsible for his actions. Neither are the other children.'

'But how did the kids get this parasite?' asked Lincoln.

'From Warren Emerson,' said Claire. 'A pathologist at Eastern Maine Medical Center is almost certain his brain lesion was caused by *Taenia solium*, the pork tapeworm. Emerson's probably been infected for years. Which means he's also been a carrier of the disease.'

'And this is how the kids got it from Emerson,' said Max. He smoothed out the topographical map, which he'd spread across Lincoln's desk. 'Claire came up with this theory. This shows the lower Meegawki Stream. The elevations, the flood pattern, even the subterranean sections of its flow.'

'What is this supposed to tell me?'

'Look here.' Max placed his finger on the map. 'It's the approximate location of Warren Emerson's farm, about a mile upstream from the lake. Elevation two hundred feet. The Meegawki Stream runs right past his property, close to the leach field for his septic system. It's probably a very old septic system.' Max looked up at Lincoln. 'Do you understand the significance of his farm's location?'

'Contamination of the stream?'

'Exactly. This past spring, you had record rainfall, and the stream would have flooded right up to Emerson's leach field. It could have washed parasitic eggs into the stream and carried it away. To the lake.'

'How would these eggs get into the leach field?'

'From Warren Emerson himself,' said Claire. 'He was probably infected years ago, when he ate undercooked pork containing the tapeworm larvae. The larvae grow and live in human intestines, sometimes for decades. They produce eggs.'

'If Emerson's harbored a tapeworm in his digestive tract,' said Max, 'then he's been passing parasitic eggs into his septic system. A leak in the tank, a heavy flood, could wash them into the feeder stream. And eventually, into the lake. They'd be at their highest concentration right here, where the Meegawki Stream empties in.' Max pointed to the Boulders. 'Precisely the spot where your local teenagers like to swim. Am I right?'

Lincoln suddenly looked up, his attention drawn to a commotion elsewhere in the building. They all turned as the door flew open and a panicked-looking Floyd Spear stuck his head in.

'The boy's having seizures! We're calling the ambulance now.'

Claire shot one terrified glance at Lincoln and ran out of the office. One of the state policemen tried to stop her, but Lincoln snapped, 'She's a doctor! Let her through!' Claire pushed into the hallway leading to the three-cell jail.

The door to the first cell was open. Inside, two policemen were crouched down. All she could see of her son was his legs, jerking in electric spasms. Then she noticed the blood on the floor, near his head, and saw that half his face was smeared with it.

'What did you do to him?' she cried.

'Nothing! We found him like this. He must've hit his head on the floor –'

'Get back. Get out of my way!'

The cops moved aside and Claire dropped to her knees beside Noah. The panic almost paralyzed her. She had to force herself to think, to shove aside the terrifying fact that this was her son, her only child, and that he might be dying before her eyes. *A grand mal seizure. Breathing's erratic.* She heard the gurgle of fluid in his throat, and his chest was seized by violent spasms as he struggled to suck air into his starved lungs.

Get him off his back. Don't let him aspirate!

She grabbed his shoulder. Another pair of hands came to her aid. Glancing sideways, she saw Lincoln kneeling beside her. Together they log-rolled Noah onto his side. He was still convulsing, still battering his head against the floor.

'I need padding to protect his head!' she yelled.

Max, who'd also pushed into the cell, yanked a blanket from the cot and tossed it to her. Gently she raised Noah's head and slid the blanket underneath. Many times before, when he was a child, she would find him asleep on the couch and would slide a pillow under his hair. This was not the head of a sleeping boy; with each new spasm, his neck turned rigid, the muscles taut and corded. And the blood – where was the blood coming from?

Again, she heard the gurgle and saw his chest heave as a fresh stream of red trickled out his nostril. So he hadn't cut himself; it was the nosebleed again. Was it blood she heard gurgling in his throat? She turned his face downward, hoping to clear any blood from his mouth, but only a trickle spilled out, mixed with saliva. The seizures were fading now, his limbs no longer jerking with such violence, but the sound of choking intensified.

Heimlich maneuver. Before he suffocates.

She left him lying on his side, placed one hand on his upper abdomen, and braced her other hand against his back. She gave a forceful thrust against his belly, aiming it toward the rib cage.

Air wheezed out of his throat. It wasn't a complete obstruction, she thought with relief. His lungs were still getting air.

She repeated the maneuver. Again, she positioned the heel of her hand against his belly and gave a firm thrust. She heard air rush out of his lungs, heard the wheeze clear as the reason for the obstruction was suddenly expelled from his throat and spilled partway out one nostril. When she saw what it was, she jerked back with a gasp of horror.

'Jesus Christ!' yelled the state cop. 'What the fuck is *that*?'

The worm was moving, lashing back and forth in a pink froth of blood and mucus. Now more of it slithered out, twisting into glistening loops as it frantically worked itself free. Claire was so shocked she could only stare as it wriggled out of her son's nose and slid to the floor. There it coiled up on itself, one end rising like a cobra as though to test the air.

In the next instant it whipped away and vanished under the nearby cot.

'Where is it? Get it!' yelled Claire.

Max was already scrambling on hands and knees, trying to peer under the cot. 'I don't see it –'

'We need it identified!'

'There, I see it,' said Lincoln, who'd dropped to his knees beside Max. 'It's still moving –'

The cut-off wail of an ambulance drew Claire's attention. She glanced toward the sound of approaching voices and the metallic rattle of a rolling stretcher. Noah was breathing easier now, his chest rising and falling without spasms, his pulse rapid but steady.

The EMTs pushed into the cell. Claire moved aside as they went to work, establishing an intravenous line, administering oxygen.

'Claire,' said Lincoln. 'You'd better take a look at this.'

She moved to his side and knelt down, peering into the narrow space beneath the cot. The cell was poorly lit, and it was hard to see much detail in the shadow of that sagging mattress. Where the light just slanted under the edge, she made out a few dust balls and a crumpled tissue. Beyond that, in the farthest recess, a bright green line was moving, forming hallucinogenic curlicues in the darkness.

'It's glowing, Claire,' said Lincoln. 'That's what we saw. That night, on the lake.'

'Bioluminescence,' said Max. 'Some worms have the capability.'

Claire heard a restraint buckle snap into place. Turning, she saw that the EMTs had already strapped Noah on the stretcher and were man-euvering him through the cell door.

'He seems stable,' said the EMT. 'We're taking him to Knox ER.'

'I'll be driving right behind you,' she said, then glanced at Max. 'I need that specimen.'

'You go on ahead with Noah,' said Max. 'I'll bring the worm to the pathology department.'

She nodded, and followed her son out of the building.

Claire stood in the X-ray department, frowning at the films clipped to the viewing box. 'What do you think?' she said.

'This CT scan looks normal,' said Dr Chapman, the radiologist. 'All the cuts appear symmetrical. I see no masses, no cysts. No evidence of bleeding into the brain.' He glanced up as Dr Thayer, the neurologist whom Claire had asked to be Noah's physician, walked into the room. 'We're just looking at the CT scan now. No abnormalities that I can see.'

Thayer slipped on his glasses and surveyed the films. 'I agree,' he said. 'What about you, Claire?'

Claire trusted both these men, but this was her son they were discussing, and she could not completely relinquish control. They understood this, and were careful to share with her the results of every blood test and X-ray. They were now sharing their bewilderment as well. She could see it in Chapman's face as he focused once again on the films. The light box cast back twin reflections of the X-rays on his glasses, obscuring his eyes, but his frown told her he did not have an answer.

'I see nothing here to explain the seizures,' he said.

'And nothing to contraindicate a spinal tap,' said Thayer. 'Given the clinical picture, I'd say a tap is definitely called for.'

'I don't understand. I was almost certain of the diagnosis,' said Claire. 'You don't see any indication of cysticercosis?'

'No,' said Chapman. 'No larval cysts. As I said, the brain looks normal.'

'So are the blood tests,' said Thayer. 'All except a slightly elevated white count, and that could be due to stress.'

'His differential wasn't normal,' Claire pointed

out. 'He has a high eosinophil count, which would go along with a parasitic infection. The other boys had high eosinophil counts as well. At the time I didn't pay attention to it. Now I think I missed the vital clue.' She looked at the CT scan. 'I *saw* that parasite with my own eyes. I saw it come out of my son's nostril. All we need is species identification.'

'It may have nothing to do with his seizures, Claire. That parasite could be an unrelated illness. Most likely it's just a common *Ascaris* infection. Those can turn up anywhere in the world. I saw a kid in Mexico cough up one of those worms and expel it from his nostril. *Ascaris* wouldn't cause neurologic symptoms.'

'But *Taenia solium* would.'

'Have they identified Warren Emerson's parasite?' asked Chapman. 'Is it *Taenia solium*?'

'His ELISA test should be done by tomorrow. If he has antibodies to *Taenia*, we'll know that's the parasite we're dealing with.'

Thayer, still looking at the X-ray, shook his head. 'This CT scan shows no evidence of larval cysts. True, it may be too early a stage to visualize yet. But in the meantime, we have to rule out other possibilities. Encephalitis. Meningitis.' He reached up and flicked off the light box. 'It's time to do a spinal tap.'

An X-ray clerk stuck her head in the room. 'Dr Thayer, Pathology's on the line for you.'

Thayer picked up the wall phone. A moment

later he hung up, and turned to Claire. 'Well, we have an answer on that worm. The one that your son expelled.'

'They've identified it?'

'They transmitted photos and microscopic sections online to Bangor. A parasitologist at Eastern Maine Medical Center just confirmed the ID. It's not *Taenia*.'

'Is it *Ascaris*, then?'

'No, it's from the Annelida phylum.' He shook his head in bewilderment. 'This has to be a mistake. Obviously they've misidentified it.'

Claire frowned in puzzlement. 'I'm not familiar with Annelida. What is it?'

'It's just a common earthworm.'

23

Claire sat in the darkness of Noah's hospital room, listening to her son rock side to side on the bed. Since the spinal tap earlier that evening, he had continued to fight against his restraints, and had dislodged two IVs. Thayer had finally relented to the nurses' requests and allowed them to administer a sedative. Even with sedation, even with the lights turned off, he didn't sleep, but continued rocking back and forth, uttering curses. It exhausted her just to hear his ceaseless struggle.

A little after midnight, Lincoln came into the room. She saw the door swing open, the light spill in from the hall, and recognized his silhouette as he hesitated in the doorway. He came in and sat down in the chair across from her.

'I spoke to the nurse,' he said. 'She says everything is stable.'

Stable. Claire shook her head at the word. *Unchanging* was all it meant, a state of constancy, good or bad. *Despair* could be thought of as a stable condition.

'He seems quieter,' said Lincoln.

'They've pumped him full of sedatives. They had to, after the spinal tap.'

'Have the results come back?'

'No meningitis. No encephalitis. Nothing in the CSF to explain what's happened to him. And now the parasite theory is dead as well.' She leaned back, her body heavy with fatigue, and gave a bewildered laugh. 'No one can explain it to me. How he managed to inhale an earthworm. It doesn't make sense, Lincoln. Earthworms don't glow. They don't use humans as hosts. There has to be some kind of mistake . . .'

'You need to go home and sleep,' he said.

'No, I need answers. I need my son. I need him back the way he was before his father died, before all this trouble, when he still loved me.'

'He does love you, Claire.'

'I don't know that anymore. I haven't felt it in so long. Not since we moved to this place.' She kept staring at Noah, remembering all the times in his childhood when she had watched him sleep. When her love for him had felt almost like obsession. Even desperation. 'You don't know what he was like, before,' she said. 'You've only seen him at his worst. His ugliest. A suspect in a crime. You can't imagine how warm and loving he was as a small child. He was my very best friend . . .' She brought her hand up and wiped her eyes, grateful

439

for the darkness. 'I'm just waiting for that boy to come back to me.'

Lincoln rose and went to her. 'I know you think of him as your best friend, Claire,' he said. 'But he's not your only friend.'

She allowed him to put his arms around her, to kiss her on the forehead, but even as he did she thought: *I can no longer trust you or depend on you.*

I have no one now, but myself. And my son.

He seemed to sense the barrier she had erected against him and slowly he released her. In silence he left the room.

She stayed all night at Noah's bedside, dozing in the chair, waking up every so often when a nurse came in to check his vital signs.

When she opened her eyes to a startlingly bright dawn, she found her thoughts had somehow crystallized. Noah was at last sleeping quietly. Though she too had managed to sleep, her brain had not shut down. It had, in fact, been working all night, trying to explain the puzzle of the earthworm, and how it could have found its way into her son's body. Now, as she stood at the window and gazed at the snow, she wondered how she'd missed an answer so obvious.

From the nurses' station, she called EMMC and asked to speak to Dr Clevenger in Pathology.

'I tried calling you last night,' he said. 'Left a message on your home phone.'

'Was it about Warren Emerson's ELISA test? Because that's why I'm calling you.'

'Yes, we got the results. I hate to disappoint you, but it's negative for *Taenia solium*.'

She paused. 'I see.'

'You don't sound too surprised. I am.'

'Could the test be wrong?'

'That's possible, but it's unlikely. Just to be certain, we also ran an ELISA test for that boy, Taylor Darnell.'

'And it was negative, too.'

'Oh, so you already knew that.'

'No, I didn't. It was a guess.'

'Well, that house of cards we were talking about the other day, it just collapsed. Neither patient has antibodies to the pork tapeworm. I can't explain why those kids are going berserk. I know it's not from cysticercosis. I can't explain how Mr Emerson got that cyst in his brain, either.'

'But you do think it was a larva of some kind?'

'Either that or a hell of a weird artifact from staining.'

'Could it be a different parasite – not *Taenia*?'

'What kind of parasite?'

'One that invades its host via the nasal passages. It could coil up inside one of the sinuses and hide there indefinitely. Until it's expelled or it dies. Any biological toxins it released would be absorbed right through the sinus membranes, into the host's bloodstream.'

'Wouldn't you see it on CT scan?'

'No. You'd miss it on CT, because it would look completely innocuous. Like nothing more than a mucoid cyst.' Like Scotty Braxton's CT scan.

'If it was coiled up in a sinus, how would it get into Warren Emerson's brain?'

'Think about the anatomy. There's only a thin layer of bone separating the brain from the frontal sinus. The parasite could have eroded through.'

'You know, it's a marvelous theory. But there's no parasite that fits that clinical picture. Nothing I can find in the textbooks.'

'What about something that's not in the text-books?'

'You mean an entirely new parasite?' Clevenger laughed. 'I wish! It'd be like hitting the scientific jackpot. I'd get my name immortalized for discovering it. *Taenia clevengeria*. It's got a nice ring, doesn't it? But all I've got is a degraded and unidentifiable larva on microscopic. And no living specimen for show and tell.'

Just an earthworm.

On the drive back to Tranquility, she realized she was still missing a number of pieces to the puzzle. Max Tutwiler would have to supply them. She would give him the opportunity to explain in private; he had been her friend, and she owed him the benefit of the doubt. She'd been married to a scientist, and she knew the fever that sometimes consumes them, that intense rush of excitement when they scent the first whiff of a discovery. Yes, she understood *why* Max might hoard the specimen, might keep it a secret until he could confirm it was a new species. What she could not understand, and could never forgive, was the fact he had concealed information from her, and from Noah's physicians. Information that might have been vital to her son's health.

She was growing angrier by the mile.

Talk to him first, she reminded herself. *You could be wrong. This could have nothing to do with Max.*

By the time she reached the Tranquility town line, she was too agitated to put off the meeting any longer. She wanted to have it out with him now.

She drove directly to Max's cottage.

His car wasn't there. She parked in his driveway and was crossing to the porch when she noticed, off to her right, footprints tracking away from the building. She followed them a short distance into the woods, where they halted at a churned up section of snow mixed with dirt. She squatted down, and with her gloved hand dug into the disturbed snow. About six inches deep, she reached a layer of loose soil and dead leaves. She picked up a handful of dirt and saw something glistening, moving in her palm. An earthworm. She buried it and retraced her steps out of the woods.

On the porch, she glanced around for a shovel, knowing one had to be there. She spotted it, along with a pickaxe, leaning against the woodpile, frozen soil still caked to the blade.

The door was unlocked; she stepped into the cottage and saw at once why Max hadn't bothered to secure the place. It had been cleaned out of almost all his belongings. What remained – the furniture, the cookware – had probably come with the rental. She walked through the bedrooms, the kitchen, and found only a few of his things left: a box of books, a basket of dirty clothes, and some food in the refrigerator. And tacked to the wall, his topographical map of the Meegawki Stream. He'll be coming back for these things, she thought. And I'll be waiting for him.

Her gaze fell to the box of books. To the corporate mailing label still affixed to the cardboard flap: ANSON BIOLOGICALS.

It was the name of the reference lab that had analyzed Scotty's and Taylor's blood, and had returned negative reports on both their drug screens. False negatives? she wondered, and if so, what were they trying to hide? It was the same lab that had recently paid a grant to the Two Hills Pediatric Group, to collect blood samples from the area's teenagers. What was Anson's interest in the children of Tranquility?

She took out her cell phone and called Anthony at the Knox Hospital lab. 'What do you know about Anson Biologicals?' she asked him. 'How did it end up with the contract for our hospital?'

'Well, it was a funny thing. We used to send all our GC-MS and radioimmunoassay tests to BloodTek, in Portland. Then about two months ago, we suddenly switched to Anson.'

'Who made the decision?'

'Our chief of pathology. The change made sense,

since Anson's charges are discounted. The hospital couldn't resist. We're probably saving tens of thousands of bucks.'

'Could you find out more about them? I need to know as soon as possible. You can reach me on beeper.'

'What do you want to know, exactly?'

'Everything. Whether they're more than just a diagnostic lab. And what other ties they have to Tranquility.'

'I'll see what I can find out.'

She hung up. Even with the electric heat turned on, the room felt cold. She built a fire in the woodstove and made breakfast out of Max's meager food supplies. Coffee and buttered toast and a slightly shriveled apple. By the time she'd finished eating, so much warmth was radiating from the woodstove, she was starting to feel drowsy from the heat. She called the hospital again to check on Noah's condition, then she sat down by the window to wait.

He couldn't avoid her forever.

It seemed like only moments later when she startled awake in the chair, her neck hurting from uncomfortable slumber. It was three o'clock, and the morning sunlight had shifted to the slanting rays of afternoon.

She rose and massaged her neck as she wandered restlessly around the cottage. Into the bedroom, back to the kitchen. Where was he? Surely he'd come back for his dirty laundry.

She stopped in the living room and her gaze rose to the topographical map, tacked on the wall. She moved closer to it, suddenly focusing on Beech Hill, elevation 980 feet. What was it Lois Cuthbert had said at the town meeting? It had to do with the lights people had seen flickering up on the hill, and the rumors that satanic cults were gathering in the woods at night.

Lois had explained the lights. *It's just that biologist fella, Dr Tutwiler, collecting salamanders at night. I almost ran over him in the dark a few weeks ago, when he came hiking back down.*

Claire had only an hour of daylight left; she would need it to find what she was looking for. She already knew where to start.

She left the cottage and got back in her car.

The snow would make her search easy. She turned onto the road leading up Beech Hill. As she neared Emerson's property, she slowed down and observed that the driveway to his house was unplowed. It had snowed since her last visit to feed the cat, and there were no new tire tracks. She drove on, past his property. There were no other homes beyond his on the hill, and the road became a dirt track. Decades before, this had been a logging road; it was now used only by hunters or hikers on their way to the panoramic lookout at the top. The town plows had not cleared the recent snowfall, and the road was barely navigable in her Subaru. Another vehicle had been up this road before her; she saw the tire tracks.

A few hundred yards past the Emerson property, the tracks veered off the road and ended abruptly at a stand of pine trees. There was no vehicle parked there now; whoever had been here had since departed. But he had left behind ankle-deep footprints in the snow.

She climbed out of her car to study the prints. They'd been made by large boots – a man's size. They led into the woods and back out again in several round trips.

She'd often heard that snow on the ground is a hunter's best friend. She was a hunter now, following a clear trail of broken snow through the forest. She wasn't afraid of getting lost. She had a penlight in case darkness fell, her cell phone was in her pocket, and she had the footprints to lead her back to the car. Off to the right, she heard water, and realized the streambed was nearby. The footprints ran parallel to the stream, climbing slightly toward a massive tumble of boulders.

She halted and looked up in wonder. Melting snow had dripped down and flash-frozen again into a rippling blue sculpture of waterfalls. Standing at the base of that ancient landslide, she puzzled over the abrupt disappearance of the footprints. Had Max scaled those boulders? Wind had polished the ice to a hard glaze. It would be a treacherously difficult climb.

The sound of the stream again drew her attention. She looked down, where the running water had dissolved the snow, and saw the faint mark of a heel in the mud. If he had waded into the stream, why did his footprints not reappear on the opposite bank?

She took a step into the stream and felt icy water seep through the lacing holes into her boots. She took another step, and the water was at her boot tops and already soaking into her trouser cuffs. Only then did she see the opening in the rocks.

The cleft was partly shielded by a bush that would be lush with foliage in summer. To reach the opening, she had to wade calf-deep into the stream. She pulled herself up onto a lip of rock, then squeezed under the low entrance into the wider chamber beyond.

It was just large enough for her to raise her head. Though scarcely any light shone through the small opening behind her, she found she could make out vague details of her surroundings. She heard the steady drip of moisture and saw trickles of water glistening on the walls. Sunlight must be filtering in some other way. Was there another opening up ahead? Beyond the shadowy outline of an archway, faint light seemed to glimmer. Another chamber.

She squeezed under the arch, and almost immediately tumbled off the ledge and began to roll, down and down, until she landed hard on wet stone. Pain rang like a bell in her skull. She lay stunned for a moment, waiting for her head to clear, for the lights to stop flashing in her eyes. Something fluttered overhead and whooshed away with a beat of frantic wings. *Bats*.

Slowly the throbbing in her head faded to a dull ache, but the lights were still flashing in streaks of psychedelic green. Symptoms of a retinal detachment, she thought in alarm. Impending blindness.

Slowly she rose to her feet, reaching out to the cave wall to steady herself. Instead of touching stone, her hand met something slimy and yielding. She screamed and jerked away, and more beating wings fluttered out of the cave.

It moved. The wall moved.

What she'd felt on the wall was cold, not the fur of a wriggling bat. She could still feel the wetness on her fingers. Shuddering, she started to wipe her hand on her trousers when she noticed the glow. It clung to her skin, outlining the shape of her hand in the darkness. In amazement, she looked up at the cave ceiling, and she saw a multitude of lights, like soft green stars in the night sky. Except these stars moved, swaying back and forth in gentle waves.

She stepped forward, splashing through puddles, to stand in the center of the chamber, and had to close her eyes for a moment; the swaying of those stars above her head made the ground seem to rock beneath her feet.

The source, she thought in wonderment. Max has found the source of the parasite, the cave that has probably harbored this species for millennia. Heat generated by organic decay, by the warm-blooded bodies of hundreds of bats, would keep this world constant, even as the seasons cycled on the surface above.

She took out her penlight and aimed the beam at a cluster of green stars on the wall. In that circle of light, the stars were extinguished, and what she saw in their place was a clump of worms, like a many-tentacled medusa, waving gently from the dripping stone. She turned off the light. In the restored blackness, the stars reappeared, rejoining that vast galaxy of green.

Bioluminescence. The worms used *Vibrio fischeri* bacteria as their source of light. Whenever this cave flooded, worm larvae and *Vibrio* together would be washed into the stream. Into Locust Lake. *We are just the accidental hosts*, she thought. A summer's swim, an unlucky inhalation of water, and a larva would find its way through the nasal passages into a human host. There, lodged in one of the sinuses, the larva would grow, releasing a hormone as it matured and died. That would account for the chromatographic peak in Taylor Darnell's and Scotty Braxton's blood: a hormone secreted by this parasite.

Tutwiler, and perhaps Anson, knew about that hormone, and about these worms, yet they didn't tell her. They had put her and her son through hell.

In fury, she reached down, grasped a rock, and hurled it at the green stars. It bounced off the cave ceiling, clattered across the ground, and landed with a strangely metallic clang. A fresh flurry of bats whooshed out of the chamber.

She stood immobilized for a moment, trying to process what she'd just heard. Moving cautiously through the gloom, she stepped toward the far end of the chamber, where she'd heard the rock clang. There were not as many worms here, and in the absence of their glow, the darkness seemed to thicken and almost solidify as she progressed.

Once again she turned on her penlight and shone it at the ground. Something reflected back at her. She bent down for a closer look and saw it was a camp stove coffee cup.

Next to it was the toe of a man's boot.

She jerked back, gasping. The beam of light zigzagged wildly as she brought it up in panic to shine on Max Tutwiler's sightless eyes. He'd slumped to the ground with his back propped up against the cave wall. His legs were sprawled out in front of him. Froth had spilled from his mouth and dribbled onto the front of his jacket. There it joined the blacker stain of blood, which had poured from the bullet wound torn into his throat.

She stumbled backwards, turned, and splashed to her knees in the puddled water.

Run. Run.

In an instant she was back on her feet and scrambling in panic up the sloping passage to the next chamber. Bats flapped past her head. She wriggled under the archway and rolled into the entrance chamber. The sound of her own gasping echoed back at her from the walls. On hands and knees, she scuttled like a frantic insect toward the opening.

The cleft grew brighter, closer.

Then her head emerged into daylight. She took in a desperate breath of air, and looked up, just as the blow came crashing down on her skull.

24

'We haven't seen Dr Elliot all day, Chief Kelly,' said the nurse. 'And frankly, we're starting to get a little concerned.'

'When did you last speak to her?'

'According to the day shift, she called around noon or so to check on Noah's condition. But there's been no word from her since, and we've been paging her for hours. We called her house, but all we get is her answering machine. We really think she should be here. The boy's been asking for her.'

Something was wrong, thought Lincoln as he walked up the hall to Noah's room. Claire would not let so much time pass without a visit, or at least a call, to her son. He'd driven by her house earlier that evening, and her car was not there, so he'd assumed she was at the hospital.

But she had not been here all day.

He nodded to the state cop guarding the door, and walked into Noah's room.

The bedside lamp was on, and caught in its brightness, the boy's face looked pale, exhausted. At the sound of the door closing, he looked up at Lincoln, and disappointment at once clouded his eyes. The rage is gone, thought Lincoln, and the difference was startling. Thirty-six hours ago, Noah had been beyond reason, possessed by such strength and fury it had taken two men to wrestle him to the ground. Now he looked like nothing more than a tired boy. A frightened boy.

His question was barely a whisper. 'Where is my mom?'

'I don't know where she is, son.'

'Call her. Please, can you call her?'

'We're trying to reach her.'

The boy blinked, and looked up at the ceiling. 'I want to tell her I'm sorry. I want to tell her . . .' He blinked again, then turned away, his voice almost muffled against the pillow. 'I want to tell her the truth.'

'About what?'

'About what happened. That night . . .'

Lincoln remained silent. This confession could not be forced; it had to spill out of its own accord.

'I took the truck because I had to drive a friend home. She walked all the way to see me, and we were gonna wait for my mom to drive her back. But then it got late, and Mom didn't get home. And it started to snow really hard . . .'

'So you drove the girl home yourself?'

'It was only two miles. It's not like I haven't driven before.'

'And what happened, Noah? On that drive?'

'Nothing. It was just a quick trip both ways. I swear it.'

'Did you drive to Slocum Road?'

'No, sir. I stayed on Toddy Point Road the whole way. I dropped her off at the end of her driveway, so her dad wouldn't see me. And then I came straight home.'

'What time was this?'

'I don't know. Ten o'clock, I guess.'

An hour after the anonymous witness had seen Claire's pickup weaving on Slocum Road.

'This doesn't fit the facts, son. It doesn't explain the blood on the fender.'

'I don't know how the blood got there.'

'You're not telling the whole truth.'

'I am telling the truth!' The boy turned to him, his frustration building toward rage. But this time his anger was somehow different. This time it was rooted in reason.

'If you are telling the truth,' said Lincoln, 'then the girl will support your story. Who is she?'

Noah averted his gaze and stared once again at the ceiling. 'I can't tell you.'

'Why not?'

'Her father will *kill* her. That's why not.'

'She could clear this up with one statement.'

'She's scared of him. I can't get her in trouble.'

'You're the one who's in trouble, Noah.'

'I have to talk to her first. I have to give her the chance to –'

'To what? Get her story to line up with yours?'

They regarded each other in silence, Lincoln waiting for an answer, the boy refusing to yield the information.

Through the closed door, Lincoln barely heard the page announced over the hospital address system:

'Dr Elliot, extension seven-one-three-three. Dr Elliot . . .'

Lincoln left Noah's room and went to the nurses' station to pick up the phone. He dialed 7133.

It was answered by Anthony, in the laboratory. 'Dr Elliot?'

'This is Chief Kelly. How long have you been paging Dr Elliot?'

'All afternoon. I tried her beeper, but she must have it turned off. No one answers at her house, so I thought I'd try paging her on the overhead. Just in case she's in the building.'

'If she does call you, could you tell her I'm trying to reach her too?'

'Sure thing. I'm kind of surprised she hasn't called me back.'

Lincoln paused. 'What do you mean, called you back? Did you talk to her earlier?'

'Yes, sir. She asked me to track down some information.'

'When was this?'

'She called about noon today. She seemed pretty anxious to get the answer. I thought she'd get back to me by now.'

'What information did she want?'

'About a company called Anson Biologicals.'

'What's that?'

'It turns out it's just the R and D branch of Sloan-Routhier. You know, the big pharmaceutical firm. But I have no idea why she wanted to know about it.'

'Do you know where she was when she called you?'

'Chief Kelly, I haven't got a clue.'

Lincoln hung up. No one had spoken to Claire since noon – nine hours ago.

He walked out to the hospital parking lot. It had been a clear day, with no snowfall, and all the cars were lightly glazed with frost. Driving slowly in his cruiser, he searched the parking lot row by row for Claire's Subaru. Her car was not there.

She left the hospital, then what? Where would she go?

He started back toward Tranquility, his apprehension mounting. Though the road was clear, the pavement free of ice, he took the drive slowly, scanning the snowy shoulders for any sign that a car might have slid off. He stopped at Claire's house only long enough to confirm that she was not there.

By now his apprehension was turning to dread.

From his house, he made another flurry of phone calls, to the hospital, to Max Tutwiler's cottage, to the police dispatcher. Claire was nowhere to be found.

He sat in his living room, staring at the telephone, the sense of dread growing, gnawing at him. To whom would she go? She no longer trusted *him*, and that was what hurt him most of all. He dropped his head in his hands, struggling to make sense of her disappearance.

She'd been distraught about Noah. She would do anything for her son.

Noah. This had something to do with Noah.

He reached for the phone again and called Fern Cornwallis.

She had barely picked up when he asked, 'Who was the girl Noah Elliot was fighting over?'

'Lincoln? What time is it?'

'Just the name, Fern. I need to know the girl's name.'

Fern gave a weary sigh. 'It was Amelia Reid.'

'Is that Jack Reid's girl?'

'Yes. He's her stepfather.'

There was blood on the snow.

As Lincoln turned into the front yard of the Reid farmhouse, the beams of his headlights swept across an ominously dark blot in the otherwise pristine expanse of white. He braked to a stop, his gaze fixed on the stained snow, fear suddenly coiling like a serpent in his stomach. Jack Reid's truck was parked in the driveway, but the house was dark. Was the family asleep?

Slowly he stepped out of the cruiser and aimed the beam of his flashlight at the ground. At first he saw only the one bright splash of red, a bleeding Rorschach butterfly. Then he saw the other splashes, a series of them, leading around the side of the house, accompanied by footprints, both human and canine. He stared at the footprints and suddenly thought: Where were the dogs? Jack Reid owned two of them, a pair of troublesome pit bulls who had the nasty habit of ripping apart any neighborhood cats they came across. Were these bloodstains left by some unfortunate creature who'd wandered into the wrong yard?

He knelt down for a closer look and saw that, mingled with the broken snow, was a clump of dark fur, bloodied flesh still attached. Just a dead animal – a cat, or a raccoon, he thought, his tension easing, but not entirely fading. Those pit bulls could still be loose somewhere in the yard, could even now be watching him.

The sensation of being observed was suddenly so strong he quickly straightened and swung his flashlight in a wide arc, cutting a circle through the darkness. As the beam swept past the trunk of the maple tree, he spotted the second clump of fur, this one larger, the animal recognizable. He moved toward it, and his fear was suddenly back full force, tension screaming along every nerve. The steel collar studs reflected back at him, as did the gleam of white teeth protruding from the open and lifeless jaw. *One of the pit bulls. Half of it, anyway.* It had been wearing a collar which was still fastened to the chain. The animal had been unable to escape, unable to avoid slaughter.

He didn't recall drawing his weapon; he knew only that it was suddenly in his hand, and that the fear was so thick it seemed to coat his throat. He swept the beam of his flashlight in a wider circle around the yard, and found the other half of the dog, and its intestines, lying in a bundle by the porch steps. He crossed to the bloody heap and forced himself to press a bare finger to the offal. The tissue was cold, but not yet frozen. Less than an hour old. Whatever had ripped apart this animal could still be lurking nearby.

The muffled explosion of breaking glass made him wheel around, his heart slamming against his chest. The sound had come from inside the house. He glanced up at the dark windows. There were five people living in there, one of them a fourteen-year-old girl. What had happened to them?

He climbed the porch steps to the front door. It was unlocked – another disturbing detail. He gave the knob a twist and nudged the door open. A quick sweep of his flashlight revealed a threadbare carpet and several pairs of shoes cluttering the front hall. Nothing alarming. He reached up and flicked the light switch. No lights. Had the power been shut off?

For a moment he hesitated near the front door, debating the wisdom of announcing his presence. He knew Jack Reid owned a shotgun, and the man would not hesitate to use it if he thought a prowler was in his house. Lincoln drew a breath, preparing to call out: 'Police!' when his gaze froze on something that instantly killed his voice.

There was a bloody handprint on the wall.

The gun suddenly felt slick in his hand. He moved toward the print. A closer look revealed it was indeed blood, and that there was more of it smeared along the wall, leading toward the kitchen.

Five people live in this house. Where are they?

Stepping into the kitchen, he found the first member of the family. Jack Reid lay sprawled on the floor, his throat cut ear to ear. The arterial spray of his blood had splattered all four walls of the room. He was still clutching his shotgun.

Something clattered, rolled across the floor. At once, Lincoln's weapon was up, his pulse roaring in his ears. The noise had come from below. From the cellar.

His lungs were like bellows, air rushing in and out in quick breaths. He eased toward the cellar door, paused for a one-two-three count, his heart accelerating, his sweating fingers clamped like a vise around his weapon. He took a breath, and with a burst of force, kicked the door.

It flew open, slamming into the opposite wall.

A set of steps dropped away into blackness.

Someone was down there. The darkness seemed charged with an alien energy. He could almost smell the other presence, lurking at the bottom of those stairs. He aimed his flashlight downward, the beam quickly sweeping the cellar. He caught only the flash of movement, a shadow slipping toward cover under the stairs.

'Police!' yelled Lincoln. 'Come out where I can see you!' He kept the beam steady, his weapon aimed at the bottom of the stairs. 'Come on, come on. Do it *now*!'

Slowly the darkness congealed into a solid shape. A single arm, materializing in the beam's circle. Then a face inched into view, peering out with terrified eyes from beneath the stairs. A boy.

'My mom,' whimpered Eddie Reid. 'Please, help me get my mom out of here.'

Now a woman's voice whispered from beneath the stairs. 'Help us. God in heaven, help us!'

Lincoln descended the stairs and shone his light directly at the woman. Grace Reid stared back at him, her face white as a corpse, her expression almost catatonic with terror.

'No light,' she pleaded. 'Turn off the lights or he'll find us!' She backed away. Behind her, the circuit breaker box hung open. She had flipped off the switches, cutting all power to the house.

Eddie tugged his mother toward the stairs. 'Mom, it's okay now. We gotta get out of here. Please, please *move*.'

Grace shook her head in almost violent protest.

'No, he's waiting for us.' She pulled away, refusing to budge. 'J.D.'s up there.'

Again Eddie grabbed his mother's arm and dragged her toward the steps. 'Now, Mom!'

'Wait,' cut in Lincoln. 'What about Amelia? Mrs Reid, where's Amelia?'

Grace looked at him with wide eyes. 'Amelia?' she murmured, as though she'd suddenly remembered her own daughter. 'In her room.'

'Let's get your mom out of the house,' Lincoln said to Eddie. 'My cruiser's parked right outside.'

'But what about –'

'I'll find your sister. First, I'll get you both into the car and I'll radio for help. Now let's go. Stay right behind me.' He turned and started slowly up the stairs. He could hear Grace and Eddie following behind him, Grace's breath coming out in frantic whimpers, Eddie murmuring words of encouragement.

J.D. They were both terrified of J.D.

Lincoln reached the top of the stairs. There was no way around it; he'd have to lead them through the blood-splattered kitchen, right past Jack Reid's body. If Grace was going to collapse in hysterics, it would be here.

Thank god for Eddie. The boy draped his arm around his stepmother, hugging her face against his chest. 'Go, Chief Kelly,' he whispered urgently. 'Please, just get us out of here.'

Lincoln led them through the kitchen, into the hallway. There he halted, every nerve suddenly giving off panic alarms. By the beam of his flashlight, he saw that the front door hung open. *Did I close it when I came in the house?*

He whispered, 'Wait here,' and he inched toward the front door. Glancing outside, he saw moonlit-silvered snow. The cruiser was parked about thirty feet away. Everything lay still, as silent as air trapped in a bell jar.

Something is wrong. We are being watched. We are being stalked.

He turned to Eddie and Grace and whispered: 'Run to the car. *Now!*'

But Grace didn't run. Instead she backed away, and as she stumbled past a moonlit window, Lincoln saw her face was gazing upward. Toward the stairs.

He pivoted, just as the shadow came hurtling down at him. He was slammed backwards so hard the breath whooshed from his lungs. Pain sliced across his cheek. He staggered sideways, just as the knife blade came down again, stabbing deep into the wall near his head. His weapon had fallen, knocked from his grasp by that first tackle. Now he scrabbled frantically on the floor, trying to locate the gun in the dark.

He heard the squeak of the knife being pried free from the wood, and spun around to see the shadow rushing at him. He brought his left arm up just as the knife came stabbing down. The blade struck bone, and he heard his own gasp of pain like a distant, foreign sound.

Somehow he grasped the boy's wrist in his right hand and twisted the knife free. It thudded to the floor. The boy wrenched away, stumbling backwards.

Lincoln dropped down and grabbed the knife. His sense of triumph lasted only for an instant.

The boy had risen to his feet as well, his silhouette framed by the window. He was holding Lincoln's gun. He swung it around, aiming the barrel straight at Lincoln.

The explosion was so loud it shattered the window. Glass blew out in a hail of shards, raining down onto the porch.

No pain. Why was he feeling no pain?

Frozen in bewilderment, Lincoln watched as J.D. Reid, backlit by moonlight through the broken window, slowly crumpled to the floor. A footstep creaked behind him, then he heard Eddie's tremulous voice ask:

'Did I kill him?'

'We need light,' said Lincoln.

He heard Eddie stumble through the darkness into the kitchen and down the cellar steps. Seconds later, he flipped the circuit breakers, and all the lights came on.

One look at the body told Lincoln J.D. was dead.

Eddie came back out of the kitchen, still holding Jack Reid's shotgun. He slowed, halted beside his stepmother. They were both unable to pry their gazes from the dead boy, unable to utter a

465

sound, as the terrible vision of J.D. Reid, collapsed in a pool of blood, burned its way forever into their brains.

'Amelia,' said Lincoln, and he glanced up the stairs, toward the second floor. 'Which bedroom is hers?'

Eddie looked at him with dazed eyes. 'The second one. On the right . . .'

Lincoln ran up the stairs. At his first glimpse of Amelia's bedroom door, he knew the worst had already happened. The door had been hacked open, and splinters of wood littered the hallway. The girl must have tried to lock J.D. out, but a few swings of an ax had shattered the wood. Dreading the scene he knew lay within, he stepped into the girl's room.

He saw the ax, embedded in a chair, almost cleaving it in two. He saw the shattered mirror, the ripped dresses, the closet door hanging askew on a broken hinge. Then he stared at the girl's bed.

It was empty.

Mitchell Groome was behind the wheel of Claire Elliot's Subaru as he drove slowly down Beech Hill. He had waited until midnight, an hour when no witnesses would be awake, but unfortunately the sky was clear, and the light of the full moon reflected with alarming brilliance off the snow. It made him feel exposed and vulnerable. Full moon or not, he had to finish this tonight. Too much had already gone wrong, and he had been forced to take far more drastic measures than he'd planned.

His job had started off as a simple assignment, to keep an eye on Dr Tutwiler's work, and, posing as a journalist asking questions, to quietly and discreetly assess the natural course of parasitic infection in the youth of Tranquility. His job had suddenly become complicated by Claire Elliot, whose suspicions had veered dangerously close to the truth. Then Doreen Kelly had added an even worse complication.

He would definitely have some explaining to do when he returned to Boston.

He felt certain he could come up with a reasonable explanation for Max Tutwiler's disappearance. He could hardly tell his superiors at Anson Biologicals what had actually happened: that Max had wanted to quit after he'd learned how Doreen Kelly really died. *I was hired to find the worms for you, Max had protested. Anson told me this was nothing more than a biological treasure hunt. No one said anything about murder, and for what? To keep this species a corporate secret?*

What Max refused to understand was that the development of a new drug was like prospecting for gold. Secrecy was paramount. You cannot let the competition know you are closing in on a fresh vein of treasure.

The treasure, in this case, was a hormone produced by a unique invertebrate, a hormone whose defining effect was the enhancement of aggression.

A minute dose was all it took to hone the fighting edge of a soldier in battle. It was a killing potion with obvious military applications.

Only two months ago, Anson Biologicals and its parent company, Sloan-Routhier Pharmaceuticals, had learned of the worms' existence when the teenage sons of a Virginia couple were admitted to the psychiatric wing of a military hospital. One of the boys had expelled a worm – a bioluminescent species that none of the military pathologists could identify.

The family had spent the month of July in a lakeside cottage in Maine.

Groome turned onto Toddy Point Road. In the seat beside him, Claire groaned and moved her head. He hoped, for her sake, that she didn't fully regain consciousness, because the end that awaited her was not a merciful one. It was another unpleasant necessity. The death of a woman as pitiful as Doreen Kelly had raised few eyebrows in town. But a local doctor couldn't simply vanish without questions being asked. It was important for the authorities to find her body, and to conclude her death was accidental.

The road was only gentle rises and dips now, a lonely drive at this hour of night. Groome's headlights skimmed across deserted blacktop crusted with ice and road sand, the beams illuminating an arc just wide enough to see the trees pressing in on both sides. A black tunnel, the only opening a swath of stars overhead.

He approached another curve, where the black-top veered sharply left, and braked to a stop at the top of the boat ramp.

Claire groaned again as he dragged her from the passenger seat and positioned her behind the steering wheel. He buckled her seat belt. Then, with the engine still running, he put the car in gear, released the hand brake, and let the door swing shut.

The car began to roll forward, down the gentle grade of the boat ramp.

Groome stood on the roadside, watching as the car reached the lake and continued rolling. There was snow on the ice, and the tires slowly churned through it, the headlights jittery on the barren expanse. Ten yards. Twenty. How far before it reached thin ice? It was only the first week of December; the lake would not yet be frozen thick enough to support the weight of a car.

Thirty yards. That's when Groome heard the *crack*, sharp as gunfire. The front of the car dipped down, its headlights suddenly swallowed up by snow and fracturing ice. Another *crack*, and the car tilted crazily forward, the red glow of its taillights pointing toward the sky. Now the ice beneath the rear wheels snapped, disintegrated, and the car splashed through. The headlights died, the circuits shorted out.

The end was played out in the glow of moon-light, in a landscape silvered by the luminous whiteness of snow, the car bobbing for a moment, engine flooding, the water dragging it down, claiming it as its own. Now the sound of splashing, the liquid turmoil as the car slipped deeper and began to turn over, rotated by the buoyancy of the tires. It sank upside down, its roof settling into the mud, and he imagined the swirl of dark sediment, blacking out the watery moonlight filtering from above.

Tomorrow, thought Groome, someone will spot the break in the ice and will put two and two together. Poor tired Dr Elliot, driving home in the dark, missed the curve in the road and veered onto the boat ramp instead. A tragedy.

He heard the distant wail of a police siren and he turned, his pulse suddenly racing. Only when the siren passed and then faded did he allow himself to breathe easier. The police had been called elsewhere; no one had witnessed his crime.

He turned and began to walk at a brisk pace up the road, toward the blackness of Beech Hill. It was a three-mile hike back to the cave, and he still had work to do.

25

She felt the darkness lurch around her, felt the shocking embrace of icy water as it engulfed her body, and she jolted awake into a reality far more horrifying than any nightmare could be.

She was trapped in blackness, in a coffinlike space, and was so disoriented she had no sense of up or down. All she knew was that water was creeping up around her in a numbing flood, lapping at her waist, now her chest. She flailed out in panic, instinctively craning her neck to keep her head above it, but found her body was strapped in. She tore at the restraints but could not free herself. The water was licking at her neck, now. Her breathing turned to frantic gasps and half-sobs of panic.

Then it all turned upside down.

She had time for one deep breath before she felt herself rolling sideways, before the water rushed over her head, flooding into her nostrils.

The darkness that swallowed her was total, a

world of liquid blackness. She thrashed, trapped head-down underwater. Her lungs ached, straining to hold on to that final breath.

Again she clawed at the strap across her chest, but it would not loosen, would not release her. *Air. I need air!* Her pulse roared in her ears and streaks of light exploded in her brain, the warning flashes of oxygen depletion. Already she was losing strength in her limbs, her efforts reduced to tugging uselessly at the restraint. Through thickening layers of confusion, she realized she was grasping something hard in her hand, something she recognized by its contours. A seat belt buckle. She was in her car. Strapped in her car.

Thousands of times before she had unbuckled that belt and now her fingers automatically found the release button. The strap fell away from her chest.

She kicked, limbs thrashing, battering against the inside of the car. Blinded by water, disoriented in the darkness, she could not even tell which way was up. Her frantically clawing fingers brushed against the steering wheel, the dashboard.

I need AIR!

She felt her lungs rebel and begin to draw in a fatal breath of water when she suddenly twisted around, and her face popped through the surface, into an air pocket. She gasped in a breath, then another, and another. There were only a few inches of air, and even that was rapidly filling with water. A few more gasps, and there would be nothing left to breathe.

With the fresh inrush of oxygen, her brain was functioning again. She forced back the panic, forced herself to think. The car was upside down. She had to find the latch – had to get the door open.

She held her breath and plunged into the water. Quickly she located the door release and gave it a tug. She felt the latch pop free, but the door wouldn't swing open. The roof of the vehicle was sunk too deeply in mud, miring the door shut.

Out of breath!

She surfaced back in the air pocket and found it reduced to a bare six inches. As she gasped in the last of the oxygen, she desperately tried to reorient herself to an upside-down world. *The window. Roll open the window.*

Last breath, last chance.

She sank back underwater, feeling frantically for the window crank. By now her fingers were so deadened from the cold, she could barely feel the handle, even when she finally managed to grasp it. Each revolution seemed to take an eternity, but she could feel the glass slide open, the gap widen. By the time she had cranked it all the way open, her hunger for air was growing desperate. She wriggled her head and shoulders through the opening, and suddenly could go no farther.

Her jacket! It was snagged!

She thrashed, trying to squeeze all the way

through, but her body was trapped, half in, half out of the car. She reached for the zipper, loosened the jacket.

All at once she slithered free, and suddenly she was shooting toward the surface, toward the faint glow of light far above.

She burst through into the air, water splashing like a million diamonds in the moonlight, and grasped the nearest broken edge of ice. There she clung for a moment, shaking and wheezing in the frigid night. Already she'd lost feeling in her legs, and her hands were so numb she could barely grasp the ice.

She tried to pull herself out, managed to lift her shoulders a few inches, but immediately fell back into the water. There was nothing to hold on to, nothing to pull against, only slick ice covered with powdery snow. Scrabbling uselessly at the ice, she found no purchase.

Again she tried to lift herself out; again she slid back with a splash, sinking in over her head. She resurfaced, sputtering, coughing, her legs almost paralyzed.

She couldn't do it. She couldn't pull herself out.

Half a dozen times more she struggled to climb out, but her clothes were soaked, dragging her down, and she was shaking so hard she could not even hold on to the ice. A profound lethargy was taking hold of her limbs, turning them wooden. Dead. She felt herself go under again, the

474

blackness sucking her down, welcoming her into a cold sleep. All her energy was spent. Nothing was left.

She sank, drifting deeper, exhaustion claiming her body. Looking up, she saw with strange detachment the shimmer of moonlight above, and felt the darkness pull her down into its embrace. She no longer felt the cold; she felt only a weary sense of inevitability.

Noah.

In the shimmering circle of light above, she imagined she saw his face, as he was when he was a child. Calling to her, reaching for her with needy arms. The circle of light seemed to fracture into fragments of silver.

Noah. Think of Noah.

Though she had no strength left, she reached up toward that phantom hand. It dissolved like liquid in her grasp. *You are too far away. I can't reach you.*

She felt herself sliding downward again, dragged into the murk. Noah's arms receded, but his voice continued to call to her. She reached up to him again, and saw the circle of light grow brighter, a halo of silver just within reach. If I can touch it, she thought, I will reach heaven. I will reach my baby.

She struggled toward it, limbs thrashing against the pull of darkness, every muscle straining toward the light.

Her arm broke through the surface, shattering

it to ripples, her head bursting through for one gasp of air. She caught a glimpse of the moon, so beautiful and brilliant it hurt her eyes, and she felt herself sink for the last time, her arm still outstretched toward heaven.

A hand grasped hers. A real hand, its grip solid around her wrist. *Noah*, she thought. *I've found my son.*

Now the hand dragged her upward, out of the murk. She stared in wonder as the light blossomed brighter, and then her head surfaced and she saw the face staring down at her. Not Noah's face, but a girl's. A girl with long hair, bright as silver in the moonlight.

Mitchell Groome poured half a can of gasoline over Max Tutwiler's body. Not that destroying the corpse really mattered. This cave had lain untouched all these millennia; Max's remains would not be found anytime soon. Still, as long as he was destroying the worm colony, he might as well dispose of a dead body as well.

Wearing a mask against the fumes and a headlamp to light the dim cave, he took his time emptying the contents of the three gasoline cans. He had no reason to rush; the doctor's submerged vehicle would not be found until daylight, and even if it was found before then, no one would link Groome to her death. If anyone were to draw suspicion, it would be Max, whose sudden disappearance would only solidify those suspicions.

Groome didn't like being forced to improvise; he had not planned this move, had not planned to kill anyone. But then, he hadn't counted on Doreen Kelly stealing his car, either.

One murder sometimes necessitates another.

He finished splashing the walls and tossed the last empty container into the shallow pool of gasoline at the center of the cavern. It was right beneath the thickest colony of worms. Already they seemed to sense impending disaster, for they were wriggling frantically in the rising fumes. The bats had long since fled, abandoning their invertebrate companions to the flames. Groome took one last look around the cavern, assuring himself he'd forgotten no detail. The last box of specimens, as well as Max's scientific log books, were in the trunk of his car, parked at the trailhead. With the strike of a match, everything in this cave would go up in flames.

It would be instant extinction of the species, except for the surviving specimens now being nurtured in the labs at Anson Biologicals. The hormone these worms secreted was worth a fortune in Defense Department contracts, but only if it stayed out of the hands of Anson's competitors.

With the destruction of this cave, only Anson would possess the species. To the rest of the world, the reason for this epidemic of violence, and for all the epidemics that came before it, would remain a mystery.

He crawled up the passageway leading to the

exit, dribbling a fine line of accelerant as he backed toward the opening. Crouching in the entrance chamber, he lit a match and touched the flame to the ground. A line of fire licked all the way down the tunnel, and then there was a *whoosh* as the cavern below exploded in flames. Groome felt the inrush of air as oxygen was sucked in to feed the conflagration. He turned off his headlamp and watched the fire burn for a moment, imagining the worms turning black, their charred carcasses dropping from the ceiling. And he thought of Max's corpse, reduced to unidentifiable bone and ash.

He backed out of the cave, his feet dropping into the icy stream, and pulled the branches over the opening. Beyond these thick woods, the glow of the fire in the cavern would be invisible. He waded to the streambank and stumbled onto land. His eyes were still dazzled by the fire, and he had not yet readjusted to the darkness. He turned on his headlamp, to light his way back to the car.

Only then, as his beam flared on, did he see the policemen standing among the trees, weapons drawn.

Expecting him.

Warren Emerson opened his eyes and thought: At last I have died. But why am I in heaven? It was a discovery that greatly surprised him, because he had always assumed that if there was existence after death, he would find himself in some dark and terrible place. An afterlife that was merely an extension of his despairing existence on earth.

Here there were flowers. Vases and vases of them.

He saw blood-red roses. Orchid blossoms like white butterflies fluttering on stalks across the window. And lilies, their fragrance sweeter than any perfume he had ever inhaled. He stared in wonder, for he had never seen anything so beautiful.

Then he heard a chair creak beside his bed, and he turned to see a woman smiling at him. A woman he had not seen in years.

Her hair was more silver than black, and age had left its deep engraving in the lines on her face. But he saw none of this. Looking into her eyes, what he saw instead was a laughing girl of fourteen. The girl he had always loved.

'Hello, Warren,' whispered Iris Keating. She reached out to take his hand in hers.

'I'm alive,' he said.

She heard the question in his voice, and with a smile she nodded. 'Yes. You most certainly are alive.'

He looked down at her hand, grasping his. Remembered how their fingers once had entwined all those years ago, when they had both been young, and they had sat together by the lake. So many changes in our hands, he thought. Mine are now scarred and leathery; hers are knobby with arthritis. But here we are, holding hands again, and she is still my Iris.

Through his tears, he looked at her. And decided he was not ready to die after all.

Lincoln knew where he would find her, and there she was, sitting in a chair at her son's bedside. Sometime in the night, Claire had climbed out of her own hospital bed, had shuffled down the long hallway in her robe and slippers, and found her way to Noah's room. Now she sat hugging a blanket to her shoulders, looking very tired and pale in the afternoon sunlight. God help the soul who dares to come between a mother bear and her cub, thought Lincoln.

He sat down in the chair across from her, and their gazes met over Noah's sleeping figure. It hurt him to see that she was still wary, still untrusting of him, but he understood the reason for it. Only a day ago, he had threatened to take from her the one thing in the world she loved most. Now she was watching him with an expression that was both fierce and, at the same time, afraid.

'My son didn't do it,' she said. 'He told me, this morning. He swore it to me, and I know he's telling the truth.'

He nodded. 'I spoke to Amelia Reid. They were together that night until after ten. And then he drove her home.'

By which time, Doreen was already dead.

Claire released a breath, tension melting from her body. She sank back in the chair and placed her hand protectively on Noah's head. At the touch of her fingers stroking his hair, his eyes flickered open, and he focused on Claire. Neither mother nor son spoke; their quiet smiles conveyed everything that needed to be said.

I could have spared them both this ordeal, thought Lincoln. If only he had known the truth. If only Noah had come right out and confessed he'd spent the evening with Amelia. But he had been protecting the girl from her stepfather's wrath. Lincoln knew of Jack Reid's temper, and he understood why Amelia would be afraid of him.

Afraid or not, the girl had been ready to share the truth with Claire. Last night, just before J.D.'s rage had exploded in murder, Amelia had slipped out of her house and walked through the clear, cold night, toward Claire's house. Her route had taken her along Toddy Point Road.

Right past the boat ramp.

The girl's fortunate journey had saved Claire's life. And in the process, Amelia had saved her own.

Noah had once again fallen asleep.

Claire looked at Lincoln. 'Is Amelia's word going to be enough? Will anyone believe a fourteen-year-old girl?'

'I believe her.'

'Yesterday you said you had physical evidence. The blood –'

'We also found blood in the trunk of Mitchell Groome's car.'

She paused as the significance of that fact sank in. 'Doreen's?' she said softly.

He nodded. 'I think Groome meant to implicate you, not Noah, when he smeared the blood on your pickup. He didn't know which car you'd been driving that night.'

They were both quiet for a moment, and he wondered if this was how it would end between them, with silence on her part, and longing on his. There was so much he still had to tell her about Mitchell Groome. There'd been the items they'd found in Groome's trunk: the jars of specimens and Max's handwritten log books. Both Anson Biologicals and Sloan-Routhier had denied any connection to the two men, and now Groome, angered by that disavowal, was threatening to drag the pharmaceutical giant down with him. Lincoln had come to tell Claire all this and more, but instead he remained silent, his unhappiness weighing down on him so heavily it seemed a burden just to take a deep breath.

He said, hopefully, 'Claire?'

She raised her eyes to his, and this time she did not look away.

'I can't turn back the clock,' he said. 'I can't erase the hurt I caused you. I can only say that I'm sorry. I wish there was some way we could go back to . . .' He shook his head. 'The way we were.'

'I'm not sure what that means, Lincoln. The way we were.'

He thought about it. 'Well, for one thing,' he said, 'we were friends.'

'Yes, that's true,' she admitted.

'Good friends. Weren't we?'

A faint smile touched her lips. 'Good enough to sleep together, anyway.'

He felt himself flush. 'That's not what I'm talking about! It's not just the sleeping together. It's—' He gazed at her with painful honesty. 'It's knowing there's a *possibility* for us. A possibility that I'll be seeing you every morning when I wake up. I can wait, Claire. I can live with the uncertainty. It's not easy, but I can stand it, as long as there's a chance we'll be together. That's all I'm really asking for.'

Something sparkled in her eyes. Tears of forgiveness? he wondered. She reached out and stroked his face. It was the gentle caress of a lover. Even better than that, it was the touch of a friend.

'Anything's possible, Lincoln,' she said softly. And she smiled.

He was actually whistling when he walked out of the hospital. And why shouldn't he? The sky was blue, the sun was shining, and the ice-encrusted branches of willow trees clacked and glittered like hanging crystals. In two weeks would come the longest night of the year. Then the days would open up again, the earth cycling back toward light and warmth. Toward hope.

Anything's possible.

Lincoln Kelly was a patient man, and he could wait.